THE FIFTH SEASON

THE BROKEN EARTH: BOOK ONE

N. K. JEMISIN

www.orbitbooks.net

ORBIT

First published in the USA in 2015 by Orbit
First published in the UK in 2016 by Orbit

1 3 5 7 9 10 8 6 4 2

A CIP catalogue record for this book is available from the British Library.

ISBN 978-0-356-50819-1

Printed and bound in Great Britain by
Clays Ltd, St Ives plc

Papers used by Orbit are from well-managed forests and other responsible sources.

MIX
Paper from
responsible sources
FSC® C104740

Orbit
An imprint of
Little, Brown Book Group
Carmelite House
50 Victoria Embankment
London EC4Y 0DZ

An Hachette UK Company
www.hachette.co.uk

www.orbitbooks.net

THE FIFTH SEASON

This is what you must remember: the ending of one story is just the beginning of another. This has happened before, after all. People die. Old orders pass. New societies are born. When we say "the world has ended," it's usually a lie, because *the planet* is just fine.

But this is the way the world ends.

This is the way the world ends.

This is the way the world ends.

For the last time.

Praise for N. K. Jemisin

"One of the most celebrated new voices in epic fantasy"
Salon

"N. K. Jemisin, you can do no wrong"
Felicia Day

"[*The Fifth Season* is] an ambitious book, with a shifting point of view, and a protagonist whose full complexity doesn't become apparent till toward the end of the novel . . . Jemisin's work itself is part of a slow but definite change in sci-fi and fantasy"
Guardian

"[Jemisin is] truly one of the greats . . . This is one of the most powerful novels that we've read in ages, and it's an amazing journey"
io9

"A tale that is both intensely moving and scientifically complex . . . *The Fifth Season* is the most subtle, nuanced story you'll ever read about giant explosions on an alien world"
New York Times

"Refreshingly unique"
Slant Magazine

"The worldbuilding is daring, relentlessly imaginative and stunningly ambitious . . . If you're looking for bold, fresh, exciting new work in the epic fantasy genre, this is the book for you"
New York Journal of Books

"Brilliant . . . gorgeous writing and unexpected plot twists"
Washington Post

For all those who have to fight for the respect that everyone else is given without question

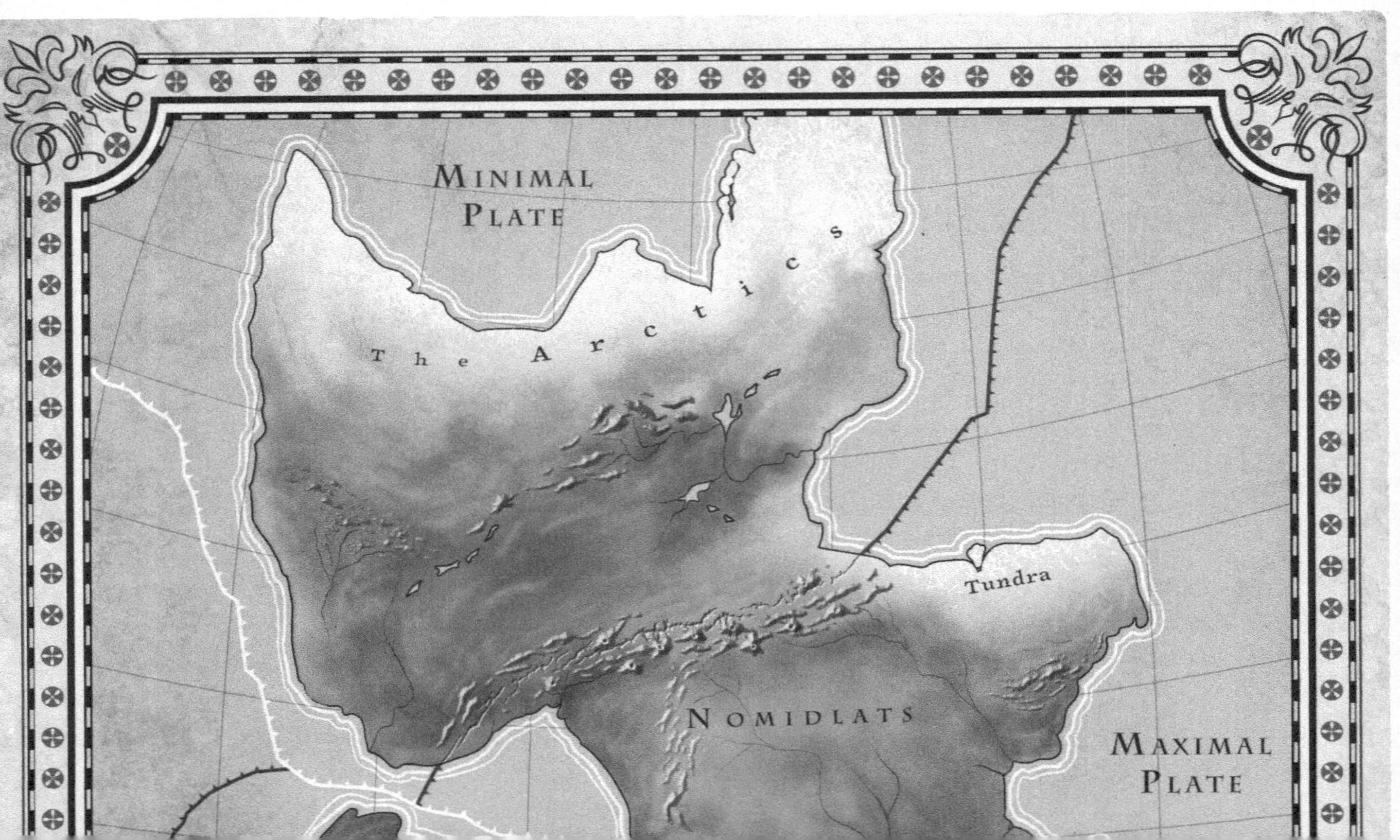
Minimal Plate
The Arctics
Tundra
Nomidlats
Maximal Plate

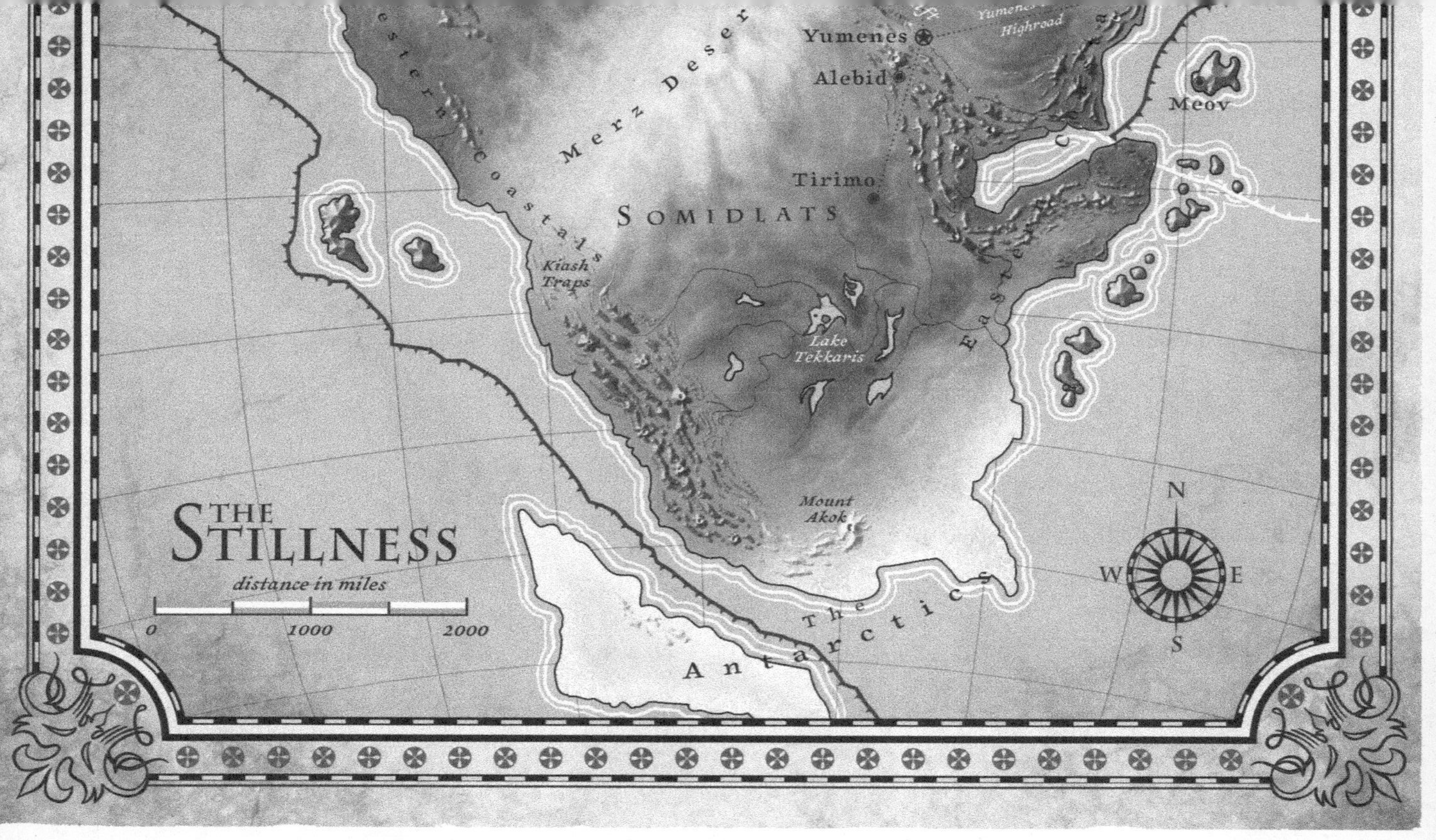
THE STILLNESS
distance in miles
0
1000
2000
Yumenes
Highroad
Alebid
Meov
Tirimo
Merz Deser
estern Coastals
SOMIDLATS
Kiash Traps
Lake Tekkaris
Mount Akok
The Arctics
Antar
Eas
N
S
E
W

PROLOGUE

you are here

Let's start with the end of the world, why don't we? Get it over with and move on to more interesting things.

First, a personal ending. There is a thing she will think over and over in the days to come, as she imagines how her son died and tries to make sense of something so innately senseless. She will cover Uche's broken little body with a blanket—except his face, because he is afraid of the dark—and she will sit beside it numb, and she will pay no attention to the world that is ending outside. The world has already ended within her, and neither ending is for the first time. She's old hat at this by now.

What she thinks then, and thereafter, is: *But he was free.*

And it is her bitter, weary self that answers this almost-question every time her bewildered, shocked self manages to produce it:

He wasn't. Not really. But now he will be.

* * *

But you need context. Let's try the ending again, writ continentally.

Here is a land.

It is ordinary, as lands go. Mountains and plateaus and canyons and river deltas, the usual. Ordinary, except for its size and its dynamism. It moves a lot, this land. Like an old man lying restlessly abed it heaves and sighs, puckers and farts, yawns and swallows. Naturally this land's people have named it *the Stillness.* It is a land of quiet and bitter irony.

The Stillness has had other names. It was once several other lands. It's one vast, unbroken continent at present, but at some point in the future it will be more than one again.

Very soon now, actually.

The end begins in a city: the oldest, largest, and most magnificent living city in the world. The city is called Yumenes, and once it was the heart of an empire. It is still the heart of many things, though the empire has wilted somewhat in the years since its first bloom, as empires do.

Yumenes is not unique because of its size. There are many large cities in this part of the world, chain-linked along the equator like a continental girdle. Elsewhere in the world villages rarely grow into towns, and towns rarely become cities, because all such polities are hard to keep alive when the earth keeps trying to eat them... but Yumenes has been stable for most of its twenty-seven centuries.

Yumenes is unique because here alone have human beings dared to build not for safety, not for comfort, not even for beauty, but for bravery. The city's walls are a masterwork of delicate mosaics and embossing detailing its people's long and brutal history. The clumping masses of its buildings are punctuated by great high towers like fingers of stone, hand-wrought lanterns powered by the modern marvel of hydroelectricity, delicately arching bridges woven of glass and audacity, and architectural structures called *balconies* that are so simple, yet so breathtakingly foolish, that no one has ever built them before in written history. (But much of history is unwritten. Remember this.) The streets are paved not with easy-to-replace cobbles, but with a smooth, unbroken, and miraculous substance the locals have dubbed *asphalt*. Even the shanties of Yumenes are daring, because they're just thin-walled shacks that would blow over in a bad windstorm, let alone a shake. Yet they stand, as they have stood, for generations.

At the core of the city are many tall buildings, so it is perhaps unsurprising that one of them is larger and more daring than all the rest combined: a massive structure whose base is a star pyramid of precision-carved obsidian brick. Pyramids are the most stable architectural form, and this one is pyramids times five because why not? And because this is Yumenes, a vast geodesic sphere whose faceted walls resemble translucent amber sits at the pyramid's apex, seeming to balance there lightly—though in truth, every part of the structure is channeled toward the sole purpose of supporting it. It *looks* precarious; that is all that matters.

The Black Star is where the leaders of the empire meet to do their leaderish things. The amber sphere is where they keep their emperor, carefully preserved and perfect. He wanders its golden halls in genteel despair, doing what he is told and dreading the day his masters decide that his daughter makes a better ornament.

None of these places or people matter, by the way. I simply point them out for context.

But here is a man who will matter a great deal.

You can imagine how he looks, for now. You may also imagine what he's thinking. This might be wrong, mere conjecture, but a certain amount of likelihood applies nevertheless. Based on his subsequent actions, there are only a few thoughts that could be in his mind in this moment.

He stands on a hill not far from the Black Star's obsidian walls. From here he can see most of the city, smell its smoke, get lost in its gabble. There's a group of young women walking along one of the asphalt paths below; the hill is in a park much beloved by the city's residents. (*Keep green land within the walls*, advises stonelore, but in most communities the land is fallow-planted with legumes and other soil-enriching crops. Only in Yumenes is greenland sculpted into prettiness.) The women laugh at something one of them has said, and the sound wafts up to the man on a passing breeze. He closes his eyes and savors the faint tremolo of their voices, the fainter reverberation of their footsteps like the wingbeats of butterflies against his sessapinae. He can't sess all seven million residents of the city, mind you; he's good, but not that good. Most of them, though, yes, they are there. *Here*. He breathes deeply and becomes a fixture of the earth. They tread upon the filaments of his nerves; their voices stir the fine hairs of his skin; their breaths ripple the air he draws into his lungs. They are on him. They are in him.

But he knows that he is not, and will never be, one of them.

"Did you know," he says, conversationally, "that the first stonelore was actually *written* in stone? So that it couldn't be changed to suit fashion or politics. So it wouldn't wear away."

"I know," says his companion.

"Hnh. Yes, you were probably there when it was first set down, I forget." He sighs, watching the women walk out of sight. "It's safe to love you. You won't fail me. You won't die. And I know the price up front."

His companion does not reply. He wasn't really expecting a response, though a part of him hoped. He has been so lonely.

But hope is irrelevant, as are so many other feelings that he knows will bring him only despair if he considers them again. He has considered this enough. The time for dithering is past.

"A commandment," the man says, spreading his arms, "is set in stone."

Imagine that his face aches from smiling. He's been smiling for hours: teeth clenched, lips drawn back, eyes crinkled so the crow's feet show. There is an art to smiling in a way that others will believe. It is always important to include the eyes; otherwise, people will know you hate them.

"Chiseled words are absolute."

He speaks to no one in particular, but beside the man stands a woman—of sorts. Her emulation of human gender is only superficial, a courtesy. Likewise the loose drapelike dress that she wears is not cloth. She has simply shaped a portion of her stiff substance to suit the preferences of the fragile, mortal creatures among whom she currently moves. From a distance the illusion would work to pass her off as a woman standing still, at least for a while. Up close, however, any hypothetical observer would notice that her skin is white porcelain; that is not a metaphor. As a sculpture, she would be beautiful, if too relentlessly realistic for local tastes. Most Yumenescenes prefer polite abstraction over vulgar actuality.

When she turns to the man—slowly; stone eaters are slow aboveground, except when they aren't—this movement pushes her beyond artful beauty into something altogether different. The man has grown used to it, but even so, he does not look at her. He does not want revulsion to spoil the moment.

"What will you do?" he asks her. "When it's done. Will your kind rise up through the rubble and take the world in our stead?"

"No," she says.

"Why not?"

"Few of us are interested in that. Anyway, you'll still be here."

The man understands that she means you in the plural. *Your kind. Humanity.* She often treats him as though he represents his whole species. He does the same to her. "You sound very certain."

She says nothing to this. Stone eaters rarely bother stating the obvious. He's glad, because her speech annoys him in any case; it does not shiver the air the way a human voice would. He doesn't know how that works. He doesn't *care* how it works, but he wants her silent now.

He wants *everything* silent.

"End," he says. "Please."

And then he reaches forth with all the fine control that the world has brainwashed and backstabbed and brutalized out of him, and all the sensitivity that his masters have bred into him through generations of rape and coercion and highly unnatural selection. His fingers spread and twitch as he feels several reverberating points on the map of his awareness: his fellow slaves. He cannot free them, not in the practical sense. He's tried before and failed. He can, however, make their suffering serve a cause greater than one city's hubris, and one empire's fear.

So he reaches deep and takes hold of the humming tapping bustling reverberating rippling vastness of the city, and the quieter bedrock beneath it, and the roiling churn of heat and pressure beneath that. Then he reaches wide, taking hold of the great sliding-puzzle piece of earthshell on which the continent sits.

Lastly, he reaches up. For power.

He takes all that, the strata and the magma and the people and the power, in his imaginary hands. Everything. He holds it. He is not alone. The earth is with him.

Then *he breaks it.*

* * *

Here is the Stillness, which is not still even on a good day.

Now it ripples, reverberates, in cataclysm. Now there is a line, roughly east–west and too straight, almost neat in its manifest unnaturalness, spanning the girth of the land's equator. The line's origin point is the city of Yumenes.

The line is deep and raw, a cut to the quick of the planet. Magma wells in its wake, fresh and glowing red. The earth is good at healing itself. This wound will scab over quickly in geologic terms, and then the cleansing ocean will follow its line to bisect the Stillness into two lands. Until this happens, however, the wound will fester with not only heat but gas and gritty, dark ash—enough to choke off the sky across most of the Stillness's face within a few weeks. Plants everywhere will die, and the animals that depend on them will starve, and the animals that eat those will starve. Winter will come early, and hard, and it will last a long, long time. It *will* end, of course, like every winter does, and then the world will return to its old self. Eventually.

Eventually.

The people of the Stillness live in a perpetual state of disaster preparedness. They've built walls and dug wells and put away food, and they can easily last five, ten, even twenty-five years in a world without sun.

Eventually meaning in this case *in a few thousand years*.

Look, the ash clouds are spreading already.

* * *

While we're doing things continentally, *planetarily*, we should consider the obelisks, which float above all this.

The obelisks had other names once, back when they were first built and deployed and used, but no one remembers those names or the great devices' purpose. Memories are fragile as slate in the Stillness. In fact, these days no one really pays much attention to the things at all, though they are huge and beautiful and a little terrifying: massive crystalline shards that hover amid the clouds, rotating slowly and drifting along incomprehensible flight paths, blurring now and again as if they are not quite real—though this may only be a trick of the light. (It isn't.) It's obvious that the obelisks are nothing natural.

It is equally obvious that they are irrelevant. Awesome, but purposeless: just another grave-marker of just another civilization successfully destroyed by Father Earth's tireless efforts. There are many other such cairns around the world: a thousand ruined cities, a million monuments to heroes or gods no one remembers, several dozen bridges to nowhere. Such things are not to be admired, goes the current wisdom in the Stillness. The people who built those old things were weak, and died as the weak inevitably must. More damning is that they *failed*. The ones who built the obelisks just failed harder than most.

But the obelisks exist, and they play a role in the world's end, and thus are worthy of note.

* * *

Back to the personal. Need to keep things grounded, ha ha.

The woman I mentioned, the one whose son is dead. She was not in Yumenes, thankfully, or this would be a very short tale. And you would not exist.

She's in a town called Tirimo. In the parlance of the Stillness a town is one form of *comm*, or community—but as comms go Tirimo is barely large enough to merit that name. Tirimo sits in a valley of the same name, at the foot of the Tirimas Mountains. The nearest body of water is an intermittent creek the locals call Little Tirika. In a language that no longer exists except in these lingering linguistic fragments, *eatiri* meant "quiet." Tirimo is far from the glittering, stable cities of the Equatorials, so people here build for the inevitability of shakes. There are no artful towers or cornices, just walls built out of wood and cheap brown local bricks, set upon foundations of hewn stone. No asphalted roads, just grassy slopes bisected by dirt paths; only some of those paths have been overlaid with wooden boards or cobblestones. It is a peaceful place, although the cataclysm that just occurred in Yumenes will soon send seismic ripples southward to flatten the entire region.

In this town is a house like any other. This house, which sits along one of these slopes, is little more than a hole dug into the earth that has been lined with clay and bricks to make it waterproof, then roofed over with cedar and cut sod. The sophisticated people of Yumenes laugh (laughed) at such primitive digs, when they deign (deigned) to speak of such things at all—but for the people of Tirimo, living in the earth is as sensible as it is simple. Keeps things cool in summer and warm in winter; resilient against shakes and storms alike.

The woman's name is Essun. She is forty-two years old. She's like most women of the midlats: tall when she stands, straight-backed and long-necked, with hips that easily bore two children and breasts that easily fed them, and broad, limber hands. Strong-looking, well-fleshed; such things are valued in the Stillness. Her hair hangs round her face in ropy fused locks, each perhaps as big around as her pinky finger, black fading to brown at the tips. Her skin is unpleasantly ocher-brown by some standards and unpleasantly olive-pale by others. Mongrel midlatters, Yumenescenes call (called) people like her—enough Sanzed in them to show, not enough to tell.

The boy was her son. His name was Uche; he was almost three years old. He was small for his age, big-eyed and button-nosed, precocious, with a sweet smile. He lacked for none of the traits that human children have used to win their parents' love since the species evolved toward something resembling reason. He was healthy and clever and he should still be alive.

This was the den of their home. It was cozy and quiet, a room where all the family could gather and talk or eat or play games or cuddle or tickle one another. She liked nursing Uche here. She thinks he was conceived here.

His father has beaten him to death here.

* * *

And now for the last bit of context: a day later, in the valley that surrounds Tirimo. By this time the first echoes of the cataclysm have already rippled past, although there will be aftershakes later.

At the northernmost end of this valley is devastation: shattered trees, tumbled rock faces, a hanging pall of dust that has not dissipated in the still, sulfur-tinged air. Where the initial shock wave hit, nothing remains standing: it was the sort of shake that jolts everything to pieces and rattles those pieces into pebbles. There are bodies, too: small animals that could not run away, deer and other large beasts that faltered in their escape and were crushed by rubble. A few of the latter are people who were unlucky enough to be traveling along the trade road on precisely the wrong day.

The scouts from Tirimo who came this way to survey the damage did not climb over the rubble; they just looked at it through longeyes from the remaining road. They marveled that the rest of the valley—the part around Tirimo proper, several miles in every direction forming a near-perfect circle—was unscathed. Well, really, they did not *marvel*, precisely. They looked at each other in grim unease, because everyone knows what such apparent fortune means. *Look for the center of the circle*, stonelore cautions. There's a rogga in Tirimo, somewhere.

A terrifying thought. But more terrifying are the signs coming out of the north, and the fact that Tirimo's headman ordered them to collect as many of the fresher animal carcasses as they could on the circuit back. Meat that has not gone bad can be dried, the furs and hides stripped and cured. Just in case.

The scouts eventually leave, their thoughts preoccupied by *just in case*. If they had not been so preoccupied, they might have noticed an object sitting near the foot of the newly sheared cliff, unobtrusively nestled between a listing gnarlfir and cracked boulders. The object would have been notable for its size and shape: a kidney-shaped oblong of mottled chalcedony, dark green-gray, markedly different from the paler sandstone tumbled around it. If they had gone to stand near it, they would have noticed that it was chest-high and nearly the length of a human body. If they had touched it, they might have been fascinated by the density of the object's surface. It's a heavy-looking thing, with an ironlike scent reminiscent of rust and blood. It would have surprised them by being warm to the touch.

Instead, no one is around when the object groans faintly and then splits, fissioning neatly along its long axis as if sawed. There is a loud scream-hiss of escaping heat and pressured gas as this happens, which sends any nearby surviving forest creatures skittering for cover. In a near-instantaneous flicker, light spills from the edges of the fissure, something like flame and something like liquid, leaving scorched glass on the ground around the object's base. Then the object grows still for a long while. Cooling.

Several days pass.

After a time, something pushes the object apart from within and crawls a few feet before collapsing. Another day passes.

Now that it has cooled and split, a crust of irregular crystals, some clouded white and some red as venous blood, line the object's inner surface. Thin pale liquid puddles near the bottom of each half's cavity, though most of the fluid the geode contained has soaked away into the ground underneath.

The body that the geode contained lies facedown amid the rocks, naked, his flesh dry but still heaving in apparent exhaustion. Gradually, however, he pushes himself upright. Every movement is deliberate and very, very slow. It takes a long time. Once he is upright, he stumbles—slowly—to the geode, and leans against its bulk to support himself. Thus braced, he bends—slowly—and reaches within it. With a sudden, sharp movement he breaks off the tip of a red crystal. It is a small piece, perhaps the size of a grape, jagged as broken glass.

The boy—for that is what he resembles—puts this in his mouth and chews. The noise of this is loud, too: a grind and rattle that echoes around the clearing. After a few moments of this, he swallows. Then he begins to shiver, violently. He wraps his arms around himself for a moment, uttering a soft groan as if it has suddenly occurred to him that he is naked and cold and this is a terrible thing.

With an effort, the boy regains control of himself. He reaches into the geode—moving faster now—and pulls loose more of the crystals. He sets them in a small pile atop the object as he breaks them loose. The thick, blunt crystal shafts crumble beneath his fingers as if made of sugar, though they are in fact much, much harder. But he is in fact not actually a child, so this is easy for him.

At last he stands, wavering and with his arms full of milky, bloody stone. The wind blows sharply for an instant, and his skin prickles in response. He twitches at this, fast and jerky as a clockwork puppet this time. Then he frowns down at himself.

As he concentrates, his movements grow smoother, more evenly paced. More *human*. As if to emphasize this, he nods to himself, perhaps in satisfaction.

The boy turns then, and begins walking toward Tirimo.

* * *

This is what you must remember: the ending of one story is just the beginning of another. This has happened before, after all. People die. Old orders pass. New societies are born. When we say "the world has ended," it's usually a lie, because *the planet* is just fine.

But this is the way the world ends.

This is the way the world ends.

This is the way the world ends.

For the last time.

1

you, at the end

You are she. She is you. You are Essun. Remember? The woman whose son is dead.

You're an orogene who's been living in the little nothing town of Tirimo for ten years. Only three people here know what you are, and two of them you gave birth to.

Well. One left who knows, now.

For the past ten years you've lived as ordinary a life as possible. You came to Tirimo from elsewhere; the townsfolk don't really care where or why. Since you were obviously well educated, you became a teacher at the local creche for children aged ten to thirteen. You're neither the best teacher nor the worst; the children forget you when they move on, but they learn. The butcher probably knows your name because she likes to flirt with you. The baker doesn't because you're quiet, and because like everyone else in town he just thinks of you as Jija's wife. Jija's a Tirimo man born and bred, a stoneknapper of the Resistant use-caste; everyone knows and likes him, so they like you peripherally.

He's the foreground of the painting that is your life together. You're the background. You like it that way.

You're the mother of two children, but now one of them is dead and the other is missing. Maybe she's dead, too. You discover all of this when you come home from work one day. House empty, too quiet, tiny little boy all bloody and bruised on the den floor.

And you . . . shut down. You don't mean to. It's just a bit much, isn't it? Too much. You've been through a lot, you're very strong, but there are limits to what even you can bear.

Two days pass before anyone comes for you.

You've spent them in the house with your dead son. You've risen, used the toilet, eaten something from the coldvault, drunk the last trickle of water from the tap. These things you could do without thinking, by rote. Afterward, you returned to Uche's side.

(You fetched him a blanket during one of these trips. Covered him up to his ruined chin. Habit. The steampipes have stopped rattling; it's cold in the house. He could catch something.)

Late the next day, someone knocks at the house's front door. You do not stir yourself to answer it. That would require you to wonder who is there and whether you should let them in. Thinking of these things would make you consider your son's corpse under the blanket, and why would you want to do that? You ignore the door knock.

Someone bangs at the window in the front room. Persistent. You ignore this, too.

Finally, someone breaks the glass on the house's back door. You hears footsteps in the hallway between Uche's room and that of Nassun, your daughter.

(Nassun, your daughter.)

The footsteps reach the den and stop. "Essun?"

You know this voice. Young, male. Familiar, and soothing in a familiar way. Lerna, Makenba's boy from down the road, who went away for a few years and came back a doctor. He's not a boy anymore, hasn't been for a while, so you remind yourself again to start thinking of him as a man.

Oops, thinking. Carefully, you stop.

He inhales, and your skin reverberates with his horror when he draws near enough to see Uche. Remarkably, he does not cry out. Nor does he touch you, though he moves to Uche's other side and peers at you intently. Trying to see what's going on inside you? *Nothing, nothing.* He then peels back the blanket for a good look at Uche's body. *Nothing, nothing.* He pulls the blanket up again, this time over your son's face.

"He doesn't like that," you say. It's your first time speaking in two days. Feels strange. "He's afraid of the dark."

After a moment's silence, Lerna pulls the sheet back down to just below Uche's eyes.

"Thank you," you say.

Lerna nods. "Have you slept?"

"No."

So Lerna comes around the body and takes your arm, drawing you up. He's gentle, but his hands are firm, and he does not give up when at first you don't move. Just exerts more pressure, inexorably, until you have to rise or fall over. He leaves you that much choice. You rise. Then with the same gentle firmness he guides you toward the front door. "You can rest at my place," he says.

You don't want to think, so you do not protest that you have your own perfectly good bed, thank you. Nor do you declare that you're fine and don't need his help, which isn't true. He walks you outside and down the block, keeping a grip on your elbow the whole time. A few others are gathered on the street outside. Some of them come near the two of you, saying things to which Lerna replies; you don't really hear any of it. Their voices are blurring noise that your mind doesn't bother to interpret. Lerna speaks to them in your stead, for which you would be grateful if you could bring yourself to care.

He gets you to his house, which smells of herbs and chemicals and books, and he tucks you into a long bed that has a fat gray cat on it. The cat moves out of the way enough to allow you to lie down, then tucks itself against your side once you're still. You would take comfort from this if the warmth and weight did not remind you a little of Uche, when he naps with you.

Napped with you. No, changing tense requires thought. *Naps.*

"Sleep," Lerna says, and it is easy to comply.

* * *

You sleep a long time. At one point you wake. Lerna has put food on a tray beside the bed: clear broth and sliced fruit and a cup of tea, all long gone to room temperature. You eat and drink, then go into the bathroom. The toilet does not flush. There's a bucket beside it, full of water, which Lerna must have put there for this purpose. You puzzle over this, then feel the imminence of thought and have to fight, fight, *fight* to stay in the soft warm silence of thoughtlessness. You pour some water down the toilet, put the lid back down, and go back to bed.

* * *

In the dream, you're in the room while Jija does it. He and Uche are as you saw them last: Jija laughing, holding Uche on one knee and playing "earthshake" while the boy giggles and clamps down with his thighs and waggles his arms for balance. Then Jija suddenly stops laughing, stands up—throwing Uche to the floor—and begins kicking him. You know this is not how it happened. You've seen the imprint of Jija's fist, a bruise with four parallel marks, on Uche's belly and face. In the dream Jija kicks, because dreams are not logical.

Uche keeps laughing and waggling his arms, like it's still a game, even as blood covers his face.

You wake screaming, which subsides into sobs that you cannot stop. Lerna comes in, tries to say something, tries to hold you, and finally makes you drink a strong, foul-tasting tea. You sleep again.

* * *

"Something happened up north," Lerna tells you.

You sit on the edge of the bed. He's in a chair across from you. You're drinking more nasty tea; your head hurts worse than a hangover. It's nighttime, but the room is dim. Lerna has lit only half the lanterns. For the first time you notice the strange smell in the air, not quite disguised by the lanternsmoke: sulfur, sharp and acrid. The smell has been there all day, growing gradually worse. It's strongest when Lerna's been outside.

"The road outside town has been clogged for two days with people coming from that direction." Lerna sighs and rubs his face. He's fifteen years younger than you, but he no longer looks it. He has natural gray hair like many Cebaki, but it's the new lines in his face that make him seem older—those, and the new shadows in his eyes. "There's been some kind of shake. A big one, a couple of days ago. We felt nothing here, but in Sume—" Sume is in the next valley over, a day's ride on horseback. "The whole town is . . ." He shakes his head.

You nod, but you know all this without being told, or at least you can guess. Two days ago, as you sat in your den staring at the ruin of your child, something came toward the town: a convulsion of the earth so powerful you have never sessed its like. The word *shake* is inadequate. Whatever-it-was would have collapsed the house on Uche, so you put something in its way—a breakwater of sorts, composed of your focused will and a bit of kinetic energy borrowed from the thing itself. Doing this required no thought; a newborn could do it, although perhaps not so neatly. The shake split and flowed around the valley, then moved on.

Lerna licks his lips. Looks up at you, then away. He's the other one, besides your children, who knows what you are. He's known for a while, but this is the first time he's been confronted by the actuality of it. You can't really think about that, either.

"Rask isn't letting anyone leave or come in." Rask is Rask Innovator Tirimo, the town's elected headman. "It's not a full-on lockdown, he says, not yet, but I was going to head over to Sume, see if I could help. Rask said no, and then he set the damn miners on the wall to supplement the Strongbacks while we send out scouts. Told them specifically to keep *me* within the gates." Lerna clenches his fists, his expression bitter. "There are people out there on the Imperial Road. A lot of them are sick, injured, and that rusty bastard won't let me *help*."

"First guard the gates," you whisper. It is a rasp. You screamed a lot after that dream of Jija.

"What?"

You sip more tea to soothe the soreness. "Stonelore."

Lerna stares at you. He knows the same passages; all children learn them, in creche. Everyone grows up on campfire tales of wise lorists and clever geomests warning skeptics when the signs begin to show, not being heeded, and saving people when the lore proves true.

"You think it's come to that, then," he says, heavily. "Fire-under-Earth, Essun, you can't be serious."

You are serious. It has come to that. But you know he will not believe you if you try to explain, so you just shake your head.

A painful, stagnating silence falls. After a long moment, delicately, Lerna says, "I brought Uche back here. He's in the infirmary, the, uh, in the coldcase. I'll see to, uh... arrangements."

You nod slowly.

He hesitates. "Was it Jija?"

You nod again.

"You, you saw him—"

"Came home from creche."

"Oh." Another awkward pause. "People said you'd missed a day, before the shake. They had to send the children home; couldn't find a substitute. No one knew if you were home sick, or what." Yes, well. You've probably been fired. Lerna takes a deep breath, lets it out. With that as forewarning, you're almost ready. "The shake didn't hit us, Essun. It passed around the town. Shivered over a few trees and crumbled a rock face up by the creek." The creek is at the northernmost end of the valley, where no one has noticed a big chalcedony geode steaming. "Everything in and around town is fine, though. In almost a perfect circle. Fine."

There was a time when you would have dissembled. You had reasons to hide then, a life to protect.

"I did it," you say.

Lerna's jaw flexes, but he nods. "I never told anyone." He hesitates. "That you were . . . uh, orogenic."

He's so polite and proper. You've heard all the uglier terms for what you are. He has, too, but he would never say them. Neither would Jija, whenever someone tossed off a careless *rogga* around him. *I don't want the children to hear that kind of language,* he always said—

It hits fast. You abruptly lean over and dry-heave. Lerna starts, jumping to grab something nearby—a bedpan, which you haven't needed. But nothing comes out of your stomach, and after a moment the heaves stop. You take a cautious breath, then another. Wordlessly, Lerna offers a glass of water. You start to wave it away, then change your mind and take it. Your mouth tastes of bile.

"It wasn't me," you say at last. He frowns in confusion and you realize he thinks you're still talking about the shake. "Jija. He didn't find out about me." You think. You shouldn't think. "I don't know how, what, but Uche—he's little, doesn't have much control yet. Uche must have done something, and Jija realized—"

That your children are like you. It is the first time you've framed this thought completely.

Lerna closes his eyes, letting out a long breath. "That's it, then."

That's not it. That should never have been enough to provoke a father to murder his own child. Nothing should have done that.

He licks his lips. "Do you want to see Uche?"

What for? You looked at him for two days. "No."

With a sigh, Lerna gets to his feet, still rubbing a hand over his hair. "Going to tell Rask?" you ask. But the look Lerna turns on you makes you feel boorish. He's angry. He's such a calm, thoughtful boy; you didn't think he could get angry.

"I'm not going to tell Rask anything," he snaps. "I haven't said anything in all this time and I'm not going to."

"Then what—"

"I'm going to go find Eran." Eran is the spokeswoman for the Resistant use-caste. Lerna was born a Strongback, but when he came back to Tirimo after becoming a doctor, the Resistants adopted him; the town had enough Strongbacks already, and the Innovators lost the shard-toss. Also, you've claimed to be a Resistant. "I'll let her know you're all right, have her pass that on to Rask. *You* are going to rest."

"When she asks you why Jija—"

Lerna shakes his head. "Everyone's guessed already, Essun. They can read maps. It's clear as diamond that the center of the circle was this neighborhood. Knowing what Jija did, it hasn't been hard for anyone to jump to conclusions as to *why*. The timing's all wrong, but nobody's thinking that far." While you stare at him, slowly understanding, Lerna's lip curls. "Half of them are appalled, but the rest are glad Jija did it. Because *of course* a three-year-old has the power to start shakes a thousand miles away in Yumenes!"

You shake your head, half startled by Lerna's anger and half unable to reconcile your bright, giggly boy with people who think he would—that he could—But then, Jija thought it.

You feel queasy again.

Lerna takes another deep breath. He's been doing this throughout your conversation; it's a habit of his that you've seen before. His way of calming himself. "Stay here and rest. I'll be back soon."

He leaves the room. You hear him doing purposeful-sounding things at the front of the house. After a few moments, he leaves to go to his meeting. You contemplate rest and decide against it. Instead you rise and go into Lerna's bathroom, where you wash your face and then stop when the hot water coming through the tap spits and abruptly turns brown-red and smelly, then slows to a trickle. Broken pipe somewhere.

Something happened up north, Lerna said.

Children are the undoing of us, someone said to you once, long ago.

"Nassun," you whisper to your reflection. In the mirror are the eyes your daughter has inherited from you, gray as slate and a little wistful. "He left Uche in the den. Where did he put you?"

No answer. You shut off the tap. Then you whisper to no one in particular, "I have to go now." Because you do. You need to find Jija, and anyway you know better than to linger. The townsfolk will be coming for you soon.

* * *

The shake that passes will echo. The wave that recedes will come back. The mountain that rumbles will roar.

—*Tablet One, "On Survival," verse five*

2

Damaya, in winters past

The straw is so warm that Damaya doesn't want to come out of it. Like a blanket, she thinks through the bleariness of half-sleep; like the quilt her great-grandmother once sewed for her out of patches of uniform cloth. Years ago and before she died, Muh Dear worked for the Brevard militia as a seamstress, and got to keep the scraps from any repairs that required new cloth. The blanket she made for Damaya was mottled and dark, navy and taupe and gray and green in rippling bands like columns of marching men, but it came from Muh Dear's hands, so Damaya never cared that it was ugly. It always smelled sweet and gray and a bit fusty, so it is easy now to imagine that the straw—which smells mildewy and like old manure yet with a hint of fungal fruitiness—is Muh's blanket. The actual blanket is back in Damaya's room, on the bed where she left it. The bed in which she will never sleep again.

She can hear voices outside the straw pile now: Mama and someone else talking as they draw closer. There's a rattle-creak as the barn door is unlocked, and then they come inside.

Another rattle as the door shuts behind them. Then Mother raises her voice and calls, "DamaDama?"

Damaya curls up tighter, clenching her teeth. She hates that stupid nickname. She hates the way Mother says it, all light and sweet, like it's actually a term of endearment and not a lie.

When Damaya doesn't respond, Mother says: "She can't have gotten out. My husband checked all the barn locks himself."

"Alas, her kind cannot be held with locks." This voice belongs to a man. Not her father or older brother, or the comm headman, or anyone she recognizes. This man's voice is deep, and he speaks with an accent like none she's ever heard: sharp and heavy, with long drawled *o*'s and *a*'s and crisp beginnings and ends to every word. Smart-sounding. He jingles faintly as he walks, so much so that she wonders whether he's wearing a big set of keys. Or perhaps he has a lot of money in his pockets? She's heard that people use metal money in some parts of the world.

The thought of keys and money makes Damaya curl in on herself, because of course she's also heard the other children in creche whisper of child-markets in faraway cities of beveled stone. Not all places in the world are as civilized as the Nomidlats. She laughed off the whispers then, but everything is different now.

"Here," says the man's voice, not far off now. "Fresh spoor, I think."

Mother makes a sound of disgust, and Damaya burns in shame as she realizes they've seen the corner she uses for a bathroom. It smells terrible there, even though she's been throwing straw down as a cover each time. "Squatting on the ground like an animal. I raised her better."

"Is there a toilet in here?" asks the child-buyer, in a tone of polite curiosity. "Did you give her a bucket?"

Silence from Mother, which stretches on, and belatedly Damaya realizes the man has *reprimanded* Mother with those quiet questions. It isn't the sort of reprimand Damaya is used to. The man hasn't raised his voice or called anyone names. Yet Mother stands still and shocked as surely as if he'd followed the words with a smack to the head.

A giggle bubbles up in her throat, and at once she crams her fist into her mouth to stop it from spilling out. They'll hear Damaya laugh at her mother's embarrassment, and then the child-buyer will know what a terrible child she really is. Is that such a bad thing? Maybe her parents will get less for her. That alone almost makes the giggles break free, because Damaya hates her parents, she *hates* them, and anything that will make them suffer makes her feel better.

Then she bites down on her hand, hard, and hates herself, because *of course* Mother and Father are selling Damaya if she can think such thoughts.

Footsteps nearby. "Cold in here," says the man.

"We would have kept her in the house if it was cold enough to freeze," says Mother, and Damaya almost giggles again at her sullen, defensive tone.

But the child-buyer ignores Mother. His footsteps come closer, and they're... strange. Damaya can sess footsteps. Most people can't; they sess big things, shakes and whatnot, but not anything so delicate as a footfall. (She has known this about herself all her life but only recently realized it was a warning.) It's harder to perceive when she's out of direct contact with the ground, everything conveyed through the wood of the barn's frame and the metal of the nails holding it together—but still, even from a story up, she knows what to expect. *Beat* beat, the step and then its reverberation into the depths, *beat* beat, *beat* beat. The child-buyer's steps, though, go nowhere and do not echo. She can only hear them, not sess them. That's never happened before.

And now he's coming up the ladder, to the loft where she huddles under the straw.

"Ah," he says, reaching the top. "It's warmer up here."

"DamaDama!" Mother sounds furious now. "Get down here!"

Damaya scrunches herself up tighter under the straw and says nothing. The child-buyer's footsteps pace closer.

"You needn't be afraid," he says in that rolling voice. Closer. She feels the reverberation of his voice through the wood and down to the ground and into the rock and back again. Closer. "I've come to help you, Damaya Strongback."

Another thing she hates, her use name. She doesn't have a strong back at all, and neither does Mother. All "Strongback" means is that her female ancestors were lucky enough to join a comm but too undistinguished to earn a more secure place within it. *Strongbacks get dumped same as commless when times get hard,* her brother Chaga told her once, to tease her. Then he'd laughed, like it was funny. Like it wasn't true. Of course, Chaga is a Resistant, like Father. All comms like to have them around no matter how hard the times, in case of sickness and famine and such.

The man's footsteps stop just beyond the straw pile. "You

needn't be afraid," he says again, more softly now. Mother is still down on the ground level and probably can't hear him. "I won't let your mother hurt you."

Damaya inhales.

She's not stupid. The man is a child-buyer, and child-buyers do terrible things. But because he has said these words, and because some part of Damaya is tired of being afraid and angry, she uncurls. She pushes her way through the soft warm pile and sits up, peering out at the man through coils of hair and dirty straw.

He is as strange-looking as he sounds, and not from anywhere near Palela. His skin is almost white, he's so paper-pale; he must smoke and curl up in strong sunlight. He has long flat hair, which together with the skin might mark him as an Arctic, though the color of it—a deep heavy black, like the soil near an old blow—doesn't fit. Eastern Coasters' hair is black like that, except fluffy and not flat, but people from the east have black skin to match. And he's big—taller, and with broader shoulders, than Father. But where Father's big shoulders join a big chest and a big belly, this man sort of *tapers*. Everything about the stranger seems lean and attenuated. Nothing about him makes racial sense.

But what strikes Damaya most are the child-buyer's eyes. They're *white*, or nearly so. She can see the whites of his eyes, and then a silvery-gray disc of color that she can barely distinguish from the white, even up close. The pupils of his eyes are wide in the barn's dimness, and startling amid the desert of colorlessness. She's heard of eyes like these, which are called *icewhite* in stories and stonelore. They're rare, and always an ill omen.

But then the child-buyer smiles at Damaya, and she doesn't

even think twice before she smiles back. She trusts him immediately. She knows she shouldn't, but she does.

"And here we are," he says, still speaking softly so that Mother won't hear. "DamaDama Strongback, I presume?"

"Just Damaya," she says, automatically.

He inclines his head gracefully, and extends a hand to her. "So noted. Will you join us, then, Damaya?"

Damaya doesn't move and he does not grab her. He just stays where he is, patient as stone, hand offering and not taking. Ten breaths pass. Twenty. Damaya knows she'll have to go with him, but she likes that he makes it *feel* like a choice. So at last, she takes his hand and lets him pull her up. He keeps her hand while she dusts off as much of the straw as she can, and then he tugs her closer, just a little. "One moment."

"Hnh?" But the child-buyer's other hand is already behind her head, pressing two fingers into the base of her skull so quickly and deftly that she doesn't startle. He shuts his eyes for a moment, shivers minutely, and then exhales, letting her go.

"Duty first," he says, cryptically. She touches the back of her head, confused and still feeling the lingering sensation of his fingers' pressure. "Now let's head downstairs."

"What did you do?"

"Just a little ritual, of sorts. Something that will make it easier to find you, should you ever become lost." She cannot imagine what this means. "Come, now; I need to tell your mother you'll be leaving with me."

So it really is true. Damaya bites her lip, and when the man turns to head back to the ladder, she follows a pace or two behind.

"Well, that's that," says the child-buyer as they reach Mother on the ground floor. (Mother sighs at the sight of her, perhaps in exasperation.) "If you could assemble a package for her—one or two changes of clothing, any travel food you can provide, a coat—we'll be on our way."

Mother draws up in surprise. "We gave away her coat."

"Gave it away? In winter?"

He speaks mildly, but Mother looks abruptly uncomfortable. "She's got a cousin who needed it. We don't all have wardrobes full of fancy clothes to spare. And—" Here Mother hesitates, glancing at Damaya. Damaya just looks away. She doesn't want to see if Mother looks sorry for giving away the coat. She especially doesn't want to see if Mother's *not* sorry.

"And you've heard that orogenes don't feel cold the way others do," says the man, with a weary sigh. "That's a myth. I assume you've seen your daughter take cold before."

"Oh, I." Mother looks flustered. "Yes. But I thought..."

That Damaya might have been faking it. That was what she'd said to Damaya that first day, after she got home from creche and while they were setting her up in the barn. Mother had raged, her face streaked with tears, while Father just sat there, silent and white-lipped. Damaya had hidden it from them, Mother said, hidden everything, pretended to be a child when she was really a monster, that was what monsters *did*, she had always known there was something *wrong* with Damaya, she'd always been such a little *liar*—

The man shakes his head. "Nevertheless, she will need some protection against the cold. It will grow warmer as we approach the Equatorials, but we'll be weeks on the road getting there."

Mother's jaw flexes. "So you're really taking her to Yumenes, then."

"Of course I—" The man stares at her. "Ah." He glances at Damaya. They both look at Damaya, their gazes like an itch. She squirms. "So even thinking I was coming to kill your daughter, you had the comm headman summon me."

Mother tenses. "Don't. It wasn't, I didn't—" At her sides, her hands flex. Then she bows her head, as if she is ashamed, which Damaya knows is a lie. Mother isn't ashamed of anything she's done. If she was, why would she do it?

"Ordinary people can't take care of...of children like her," says Mother, very softly. Her eyes dart to Damaya's, once, and away, fast. "She almost killed a boy at school. We've got another child, and neighbors, and..." Abruptly she squares her shoulders, lifting her chin. "And it's any citizen's duty, isn't it?"

"True, true, all of it. Your sacrifice will make the world better for all." The words are a stock phrase, praise. The tone is uniquely not. Damaya looks at the man again, confused now because child-buyers don't kill children. That would defeat the point. And what's this about the Equatorials? Those lands are far, far to the south.

The child-buyer glances at Damaya and somehow understands that she does not understand. His face softens, which should be impossible with those frightening eyes of his.

"To Yumenes," the man says to Mother, to Damaya. "Yes. She's young enough, so I'm taking her to the Fulcrum. There she will be trained to use her curse. Her sacrifice, too, will make the world better."

Damaya stares back at him, realizing just how wrong she's

been. Mother has not sold Damaya. She and Father have *given* Damaya away. And Mother does not hate her; actually, she *fears* Damaya. Is there a difference? Maybe. Damaya doesn't know how to feel in response to these revelations.

And the man, the man is not a child-buyer at all. He is—

"You're a Guardian?" she asks, even though by now, she knows. He smiles again. She did not think Guardians were like this. In her head they are tall, cold-faced, bristling with weapons and secret knowledge. He's tall, at least.

"I am," he says, and takes her hand. He likes to touch people a lot, she thinks. "I'm *your* Guardian."

Mother sighs. "I can give you a blanket for her."

"That will do, thank you." And then the man falls silent, waiting. After a few breaths of this, Mother realizes he's waiting for her to go fetch it. She nods jerkily, then leaves, her back stiff the whole way out of the barn. So then the man and Damaya are alone.

"Here," he says, reaching up to his shoulders. He's wearing something that must be a uniform: blocky shoulders and long, stiff lines of sleeve and pant leg, burgundy cloth that looks sturdy but scratchy. Like Muh's quilt. It has a short cape, more decorative than useful, but he pulls it off and wraps it around Damaya. It's long enough to be a dress on her, and warm from his body.

"Thank you," she says. "Who are you?"

"My name is Schaffa Guardian Warrant."

She's never heard of a place called Warrant, but it must exist, because what good is a comm name otherwise? "'Guardian' is a use name?"

"It is for Guardians." He drawls this, and her cheeks grow warm with embarrassment. "We aren't much use to any comm, after all, in the ordinary course of things."

Damaya frowns in confusion. "What, so they'll kick *you* out when a Season comes? But..." Guardians are many things, she knows from the stories: great warriors and hunters and sometimes—often—assassins. Comms need such people when hard times come.

Schaffa shrugs, moving away to sit on a bale of old hay. There's another bale behind Damaya, but she keeps standing, because she likes being on the same level with him. Even sitting he's taller, but at least not by so much.

"The orogenes of the Fulcrum serve the world," he says. "You will have no use name from here forth, because your usefulness lies in what you are, not merely some familial aptitude. From birth, an orogene child can stop a shake; even without training, you are orogene. Within a comm or without one, *you are orogene*. With training, however, and with the guidance of other skilled orogenes at the Fulcrum, you can be useful not merely to a single comm, but all the Stillness." He spreads his hands. "As a Guardian, via the orogenes in my care, I have taken on a similar purpose, with a similar breadth. Therefore it's fitting that I share my charges' possible fate."

Damaya is so curious, so full of questions, that she doesn't know which to ask first. "Do you have—" She stumbles over the concept, the words, the acceptance of herself. "Others, l-like me, I," and she runs out of words.

Schaffa laughs, as if he senses her eagerness and it pleases him. "I am Guardian to six right now," he says, inclining his head to let Damaya know that this is the right way to say it, to think it. "Including you."

"And you brought them all to Yumenes? You found them like this, like me—"

"Not exactly. Some were given into my care, born within the Fulcrum or inherited from other Guardians. Some I have found since being assigned to ride circuit in this part of the Nomidlats." He spreads his hands. "When your parents reported their orogenic child to Palela's headman, he telegraphed word to Brevard, which sent it to Geddo, which sent it to Yumenes—and they in turn telegraphed word to me." He sighs. "It's only luck that I checked in at the node station near Brevard the day after the message arrived. Otherwise I wouldn't have seen it for another two weeks."

Damaya knows Brevard, though Yumenes is only legend to her, and the rest of the places Schaffa has mentioned are just words in a creche textbook. Brevard is the town closest to Palela, and it's much bigger. It's where Father and Chaga go to sell farmshares at the beginning of every growing season. Then she registers his words. Two more weeks in this barn, freezing and pooping in a corner. She's glad he got the message in Brevard, too.

"You're very lucky," he says, perhaps reading her expression. His own has grown sober. "Not all parents do the right thing. Sometimes they don't keep their child isolated, as the Fulcrum and we Guardians recommend. Sometimes they do, but we get the message too late, and by the time a Guardian arrives a mob has carried the child off and beaten her to death. Don't think unkindly of your parents, Dama. You're alive and well, and that is no small thing."

Damaya squirms a little, unwilling to accept this. He sighs. "And sometimes," he continues, "the parents of an orogene will try to hide the child. To keep her, untrained and without a Guardian. That always goes badly."

This is the thing that's been in her mind for the past two weeks, ever since that day at school. If her parents loved her, they would not have locked her in the barn. They would not have called this man. Mother would not have said those terrible things.

"Why can't they—" she blurts, before she realizes he has said this on purpose. To see if *why can't they just hide me and keep me here* is something she's been thinking—and now he knows the truth. Damaya's hands clench on the cape where she's holding it closed around herself, but Schaffa merely nods.

"First because they have another child, and anyone caught harboring an unregistered orogene is ejected from their comm as a minimum punishment." Damaya knows this, though she resents the knowledge. Parents who cared about her would *risk*, wouldn't they? "Your parents could not have wanted to lose their home, their livelihood, and custody of both their children. They chose to keep something rather than lose everything. But the greatest danger lies in what you are, Dama. You can no more hide that than you can the fact that you are female, or your clever young mind." She blushes, unsure if this is praise. He smiles so she knows it is.

He continues: "Every time the earth moves, you will hear its call. In every moment of danger you will reach, instinctively, for the nearest source of warmth and movement. The ability to do this is, to you, as fists are to a strong man. When a threat is imminent, of course you'll do what you must to protect yourself. And when you do, people will die."

Damaya flinches. Schaffa smiles again, as kindly as always. And then Damaya thinks about that day.

It was after lunch, in the play-yard. She had eaten her bean roll while sitting by the pond with Limi and Shantare as she usually did while the other children played or threw food at each other. Some of the other kids were huddled in a corner of the yard, scratching in the dirt and muttering to each other; they had a geomestry test that afternoon. And then Zab had come over to the three of them, though he'd looked at Damaya in particular as he said, "Let me cheat off you."

Limi giggled. She thought Zab liked Damaya. Damaya didn't like *him*, though, because he was awful—always picking on Damaya, calling her names, poking her until she yelled at him to stop and got in trouble with their teacher for doing it. So she said to Zab, "I'm not getting in trouble for you."

He'd said: "You won't, if you do it right. Just move your paper over—"

"*No*," she'd said again. "I'm not going to do it right. I'm not going to do it *at all*. Go away." She'd turned back to Shantare, who had been talking before Zab interrupted.

Next thing Damaya knew, she was on the ground. Zab had shoved her off the rock using both hands. She tumbled head over heels literally, landing on her back. Later—she'd had two weeks in the barn to think about it—she would recall the look of shock on his face, as if he hadn't realized she would go over so easily. But at the time, all she had known was that she was on the ground. The *muddy* ground. Her whole back was cold and wet and foul, everything smelled of fermenting bog and crushed grass, it was in her *hair* and this was her best *uniform* and Mother was going to be *furious* and *she* was furious and so she'd grabbed the air and—

Damaya shivers. *People will die.* Schaffa nods as if he has heard this thought.

"You're firemountain-glass, Dama." He says this very softly. "You're a gift of the earth—but Father Earth hates us, never forget, and his gifts are neither free nor safe. If we pick you up, hone you to sharpness, treat you with the care and respect you deserve, then you become valuable. But if we just leave you lying about, you'll cut to the bone the first person who blunders across you. Or worse—you'll shatter, and hurt many."

Damaya remembers the look on Zab's face. The air had gone cold for only an instant, billowing around her like a burst balloon. That was enough to make a crust of ice on the grass beneath her, and to make the sweatdrops go solid on Zab's skin. They'd stopped and jerked and stared at each other.

She remembers his face. *You almost killed me*, she had seen there.

Schaffa, watching her closely, has never stopped smiling.

"It isn't your fault," he says. "Most of what they say about orogenes isn't true. There's nothing you did to be born like this, nothing your parents did. Don't be angry with them, or with yourself."

She begins to cry, because he's right. All of it, everything he says, it's right. She hates Mother for putting her in here, she's hated Father and Chaga for letting Mother do it, she hates herself for being born as she is and disappointing them all. And now Schaffa knows just how weak and terrible she is.

"Shh," he says, standing and coming over to her. He kneels and takes her hands; she starts crying harder. But Schaffa squeezes her hands sharply, enough to hurt, and she starts and draws breath and blinks at him through the blur. "You mustn't, little one. Your mother will return soon. Never cry where they can see you."

"Wh-what?"

He looks so sad—for Damaya?—as he reaches up and cups her cheek. "It isn't safe."

She has no idea what this means.

Regardless, she stops. Once she's wiped her cheeks, he thumbs away a tear that she's missed, then nods after a quick inspection. "Your mother will probably be able to tell, but that should do for everyone else."

The barn door creaks and Mother is back, this time with Father in tow. Father's jaw is tight, and he doesn't look at Damaya even though he hasn't seen her since Mother put her in the barn. Both of them focus on Schaffa, who stands and moves a little in front of Damaya, nodding thanks as he accepts the folded blanket and twine-wrapped parcel that Mother gives him.

"We've watered your horse," Father says, stiffly. "You want provender to carry?"

"No need," says Schaffa. "If we make good time, we should reach Brevard just after nightfall."

Father frowns. "A hard ride."

"Yes. But in Brevard, no one from this village will get the fine idea to come seek us out along the road, and make their farewells to Damaya in a ruder fashion."

It takes a moment for Damaya to understand, and then she realizes: People from Palela want to kill Damaya. But that's wrong, isn't it? They can't really, can they? She thinks of all the people she knows. The teachers from creche. The other children. The old ladies at the roadhouse who used to be friends with Muh before she died.

Father thinks this, too; she can see that in his face, and he frowns and opens his mouth to say what she's thinking: *They wouldn't do something like that.* But he stops before the words leave his mouth. He glances at Damaya, once and with his face full of anguish, before remembering to look away again.

"Here you are," Schaffa says to Damaya, holding out the blanket. It's Muh's. She stares at it, then looks at Mother, but Mother won't look back.

It isn't safe to cry. Even when she pulls off Schaffa's cloak and he wraps the blanket around her instead, familiar-fusty and scratchy and perfect, she keeps her face completely still. Schaffa's eyes flick to hers; he nods, just a little, in approval. Then he takes her hand and leads her toward the barn door.

Mother and Father follow, but they don't say anything. Damaya doesn't say anything. She does glance at the house once, catching a glimpse of someone through a gap in the curtains before the curtains flick shut. Chaga, her big brother, who taught her how to read and how to ride a donkey and how to skip rocks on a pond. He doesn't even wave goodbye . . . but this is not because he hates her. She sees that, now.

Schaffa lifts Damaya onto a horse bigger than any she's ever seen, a big glossy bay with a long neck, and then Schaffa's in the saddle behind her, tucking the blanket around her legs and shoes so she won't chafe or get chilblains, and then they are away.

"Don't look back," Schaffa advises. "It's easier that way." So she doesn't. Later, she will realize he was right about this, too.

Much later, though, she will wish that she had done it anyway.

* * *

[obscured] the icewhite eyes, the ashblow hair, the
filtering nose, the sharpened teeth, the salt-split tongue.

—Tablet Two, "The Incomplete Truth," verse eight

3

you're on your way

You're still trying to decide who to be. The self you've been lately doesn't make sense anymore; that woman died with Uche. She's not useful, unobtrusive as she is, quiet as she is, ordinary as she is. Not when such extraordinary things have happened.

But you still don't know where Nassun is buried, if Jija bothered to bury her. Until you've said farewell to your daughter, you have to remain the mother that she loved.

So you decide not to wait for death to come.

It *is* coming for you—perhaps not right now, but soon. Even though the big shake from the north missed Tirimo, everyone knows it *should* have hit. The sessapinae do not lie, or at least not with such jangling, nerve-racking, mind-screaming strength. Everyone from newborns to addled elders sessed that one coming. And by now, with refugees wandering down the road from less fortunate towns and villages—refugees who are all heading southward—the folk of Tirimo will have begun to hear stories. They will have noticed the sulfur on the wind.

They will have looked up at the increasingly strange sky, and seen the change there as an ill omen. (It is.) Perhaps the headman, Rask, has finally sent someone over to see about Sume, the town in the next valley over. Most Tirimos have family there; the two towns have been trading goods and people for generations. Comm comes before all else, of course, but as long as nobody's starving, kin and race can mean something, too. Rask can still afford to be generous, for now. Maybe.

And once the scouts return and report the devastation that you know they'll find in Sume—and the survivors that you know they *won't* find, or at least not in any great number—denial will no longer be possible. That will leave only fear. Frightened people look for scapegoats.

So you make yourself eat, this time carefully not thinking of other times and other meals with Jija and the kids. (Uncontrollable tears would be better than uncontrollable vomiting, but hey, you can't choose your grief.) Then, letting yourself quietly out through Lerna's garden door, you go back to your house. No one's around, outside. They must all be at Rask's waiting for news or duty assignments.

In the house, one of the storecaches hidden beneath the rugs holds the family's runny-sack. You sit on the floor in the room where Uche was beaten to death, and there you sort through the sack, taking out anything you won't need. The set of worn, comfortable travel-clothing for Nassun is too small; you and Jija put this pack together before Uche was born, and you've been neglectful in not refreshing it. A brick of dried fruit has molded over in fuzzy white; it might still be edible, but you're not desperate enough for that. (Yet.) The sack contains papers that prove you and Jija own your house, and other papers showing that you're current on your quartent taxes and were both registered Tirimo comm and Resistant use-caste members. You leave this, your whole financial and legal existence for the past ten years, in a little discarded pile with the moldy fruit.

The wad of money in a rubber wallet—paper, since there's so much of it—will be irrelevant once people realize how bad things are, but until then it's valuable. Good tinder once it's not. The obsidian skinning knife that Jija insisted upon, and which you're unlikely to ever use—you have better, natural weapons—you keep. Trade goods, or at least a visual warn-off. Jija's boots can also be traded, since they're in good condition. He'll never wear them again, because soon you will find him, and then you will end him.

You pause. Revise that thought to something that better befits the woman you've chosen to be. Better: You will find him and ask him why he did what he did. *How* he could do it. And you will ask him, most importantly, where your daughter is.

Repacking the runny-sack, you then put it inside one of the crates Jija used for deliveries. No one will think twice of seeing you carry it around town, because until a few days ago you did so often, to help out Jija's ceramics and tool-knapping business. Eventually it will occur to someone to wonder why you're filling delivery orders when the headman is probably on the brink of declaring Seasonal Law. But most people will not think of it *at first*, which is what matters.

As you leave, you pass the spot on the floor where Uche lay for days. Lerna took the body and left the blanket; the blood splatters are not visible. Still, you do not look in that direction.

Your house is one of several in this corner of town, nestled between the southern edge of the wall and the town greenland. You picked the house, back when you and Jija decided to buy it, because it's isolated on a narrow, tree-shrouded lane. It's a straight run across the green to the town center, which Jija always liked. That was something you and he always argued about: You didn't like being around other people more than necessary, while Jija was gregarious and restless, frustrated by silence—

The surge of absolute, grinding, head-pounding rage catches you by surprise. You have to stop in the doorway of your home, bracing your hand against the door frame and sucking in deep breaths so that you don't start screaming, or perhaps stabbing someone (yourself?) with that damn skinning knife. Or worse, making the temperature drop.

Okay. You were wrong. Nausea isn't so bad as a response to grief, comparatively speaking.

But you have no time for this, no *strength* for this, so you focus on other things. Any other things. The wood of the doorsill, beneath your hand. The air, which you notice more now that you're outside. The sulfur smell doesn't seem to be getting worse, at least for now, which is perhaps a good thing. You sess that there are no open earth vents nearby—which means this is coming from up north, where the wound is, that great suppurating rip from coast to coast that you *know* is there even though the travelers along the Imperial Road have only brought rumors of it so far. You hope the sulfur concentration doesn't get much worse, because if it does people will start to retch and suffocate, and the next time it rains the creek's fish will die and the soil will sour...

Yes. Better. After a moment you're able to walk away from the house at last, your veneer of calm back firmly in place.

Not many people are out and about. Rask must have finally declared an official lockdown. During lockdown the comm's gates are shut—and you guess by the people moving about near one of the wall watchtowers that Rask has taken the preemptive step of putting guards in place. That's not supposed to happen till a Season is declared; privately you curse Rask's caution. Hopefully he hasn't done anything else that will make it harder for you to slip away.

The market is shut down, at least for the time being, so that no one will hoard goods or fix prices. A curfew starts at dusk, and all businesses that aren't crucial for the protection or supply of the town are required to close. Everyone knows how things are supposed to go. Everyone has assigned duties, but many of these are tasks that can be done indoors: weaving storage baskets, drying and preserving all perishable food in the house, repurposing old clothing and tools. It's all Imperially efficient and lore-letter, following rules and procedures that are simultaneously meant to be practical and to keep a large group of anxious people busy. Just in case.

Still, as you walk the path around the green's edge—during lockdown no one walks on it, not because of any rule but because such times remind them that the green is *cropland to be* and not just a pretty patch of clover and wildflowers—you spy a few other Tirimo denizens out and about. Strongbacks, mostly. One group is building the paddock and shed that will segregate a corner of the green for livestock. It's hard work, building something, and the people doing it are too engrossed in the task to pay much heed to a lone woman carrying a crate. A few faces you vaguely recognize as you walk, people you've seen before at the market or via Jija's business. You catch a few glances from them, too, but these are fleeting. They know your face enough that you are Not Stranger. For now, they're too busy to remember that you may also be *rogga's mother.*

Or to wonder from which parent your dead rogga child might have inherited his curse.

In the town center there are more people about. Here you blend in, walking at the same pace as everyone else, nodding if nodded to, trying to think about nothing so that your face falls into bored, disengaged lines. It's busy around the headman's office, block captains and caste spokespeople coming in to report what lockdown duties have been completed before heading back out to organize more. Others mill about, clearly hoping for word on what's happened in Sume and elsewhere—but even here, no one cares about you. And why should they? The air stinks of broken earth and everything past a twenty-mile radius has been shattered by a shake greater than any living person has ever known. People have more important matters to concern them.

That can change quickly, though. You don't relax.

Rask's office is actually a small house nestled between the stilted grain-caches and the carriageworks. As you stand on tiptoe to see above the crowd, you're unsurprised to see Oyamar, Rask's second, standing on its porch and talking with two men and a woman who are wearing more mortar and mud than clothing. Shoring up the well, probably; that's one of the things stonelore advises in the event of a shake, and which Imperial lockdown procedure encourages, too. If Oyamar is here, then Rask is elsewhere either working or—knowing Rask—sleeping, after having worn himself out in the three days since the event. He won't be at home because people can find him too easily there. But because Lerna talks too much, you know where Rask hides when he doesn't want to be disturbed.

Tirimo's library is an embarrassment. The only reason they have one is that some previous headwoman's husband's grandfather raised a stink and wrote letters to the quartent governor until finally the governor funded a library to shut him up. Few people have used it since the old man died, but although there are always motions to shut it down at the all-comm meetings, those motions never get quite enough votes to proceed. So it lingers: a ratty old shack not much bigger than the den of your house, packed nearly full with shelves of books and scrolls. A thin child could walk between the shelves without contorting; you're neither thin nor a child, so you have to slip in sideways and sort of crabwalk. Bringing the crate is out of the question: You set it down just inside the door. But that doesn't matter, because there's no one here to peek inside it—except Rask, who's curled up on a tiny pallet at the back of the shack, where the shortest shelf leaves a space just wide enough for his body.

As you finally manage to push your way between the stacks, Rask starts out of a snore and blinks up at you, already beginning to scowl at whoever has disturbed him. Then he *thinks*, because he's a levelheaded fellow and that's why Tirimo elected him, and you see in his face the moment when you go from being Jija's wife to Uche's mother to *rogga*'s mother to, oh Earth, rogga, too.

That's good. Makes things easier.

"I'm not going to hurt anyone," you say quickly, before he can recoil or scream or whatever he has tensed to do. And to your own surprise, at these words Rask blinks and *thinks* again, and the panic recedes from his face. He sits up, leaning his back against a wooden wall, and regards you for a long, thoughtful moment.

"You didn't come here just to tell me that, I assume," he says.

You lick your lips and try to hunker down in a crouch. It's awkward because there's not much room. You have to brace your butt against a shelf, and your knees encroach more than you like on Rask's space. He half-smiles at your obvious discomfort, then his smile fades as he remembers what you are, and then he frowns to himself as if both reactions annoy him.

You say, "Do you know where Jija might have gone?"

Rask's face twitches. He's old enough to be your father, just, but he's the least paternal man you've ever met. You've always wanted to sit down somewhere and have a beer with him, even though that doesn't fit the ordinary, meek camouflage you've built around yourself. Most of the people in town think of him that way, despite the fact that as far as you know he doesn't drink. The look that comes into his face in this moment, however, makes you think for the first time that he would make a good father, if he ever had children.

"So that's it," he says. His voice is gravelly with sleep. "He kill the kid? That's what people think, but Lerna said he wasn't sure."

You nod. You couldn't say the word *yes* to Lerna, either.

Rask's eyes search your face. "And the kid was . . . ?"

You nod again, and Rask sighs. He does not, you note, ask whether *you* are anything.

"Nobody saw which way Jija went," he says, shifting to draw his knees up and rest one arm on them. "People have been talking about the—the killing—because it's easier than talking about—" He lifts and drops his hands in a helpless gesture. "Lots of gossip, I mean, and a lot of it's more mud than stone. Some people saw Jija load up your horse cart and go off with Nassun—"

Your thoughts stutter. "*With* Nassun?"

"Yeah, with her. Why—" Then Rask understands. "Oh, shit, she's one, too?"

You try not to start shaking. You do clench your fists in an effort to prevent this, and the earth far below you feels momentarily closer, the air immediately around you cooler, before you contain your desperation and joy and horror and fury.

"I didn't know she was alive," is all you say, after what feels like a very long moment.

"Oh." Rask blinks, and that compassionate look returns. "Well, yeah. She was when they left, anyway. Nobody knew anything was wrong, or thought anything of it. Most people figured it was just a father trying to teach his firstborn the business, or keep a bored child out of trouble, the usual. Then that shit up north happened, and everybody forgot about it till Lerna said he'd found you and . . . and your boy." He pauses here, jaw flexing once. "Never would've figured Jija for the type. He hit you?"

You shake your head. "Never." It might have been easier to bear, somehow, if Jija had been violent beforehand. Then you could have blamed yourself for poor judgment or complacency, and not just for the sin of reproducing.

Rask takes a deep, slow breath. "Shit. Just... shit." He shakes his head, rubs a hand over the gray fuzz of his hair. He's not a born-gray, like Lerna and others with ashblow hair; you remember when his hair was brown. "You going after him?" His gaze flickers away and back. It is not quite hope, but you understand what he is too tactful to say. *Please leave town as soon as possible.*

You nod, happy to oblige. "I need you to give me a gate pass."

"Done." He pauses. "You know you can't come back."

"I know." You make yourself smile. "I don't really want to."

"Don't blame you." He sighs, then shifts again, uncomfortable. "My... my sister..."

You didn't know Rask had a sister. Then you understand. "What happened to her?"

He shrugs. "The usual. We lived in Sume, then. Somebody realized what she was, told a bunch of other somebodies, and they came and took her in the night. I don't remember much about it. I was only six. My folks moved here with me after that." His mouth twitches, not really smiling. "S'why I never wanted kids, myself."

You smile, too. "I didn't, either." Jija had, though.

"Rusting Earth." He closes his eyes for a moment, then abruptly gets to his feet. You do, too, since otherwise your face will be entirely too close to his stained old trousers. "I'll walk you to the gate, if you're going now."

This surprises you. "I'm going now. But you don't have to." You're not sure this is a good idea, really. It might draw more attention than you want. But Rask shakes his head, his jaw set and grim.

"I do. Come on."

"Rask—"

He looks at you, and this time you are the one who winces. This isn't about you anymore. The mob that took his sister from him wouldn't have dared to do so if he'd been a man at the time.

Or maybe they'd have just killed him, too.

He carries the crate as you walk down Seven Seasons, the town's main street, all the way up to Main Gate. You're twitchy, trying to look confident and relaxed even though you feel anything but. It would not have been your choice to walk this route, through all these people. Rask draws all the attention at first, as people wave or call out to him or come over to ask him if there's any news . . . but then they notice you. People stop waving. They stop approaching and start—at a distance, in twos and threes—watching. And occasionally following. There's nothing to this except the usual small-town nosiness, at least on the surface. But you see these knots of people also *whispering*, and you feel them *staring*, and that sets all your nerves a-jangle in the worst way.

Rask hails the gate guards as you approach. A dozen or so Strongbacks who are probably miners and farmers under ordinary circumstances are there, just milling about in front of the gate with no real organization. Two are up in the crow's nests built atop the wall, where they can overlook the gate; two are standing near the gate's eyeholes at ground level. The rest are just there, looking bored or talking or joking with one another.

Rask probably chose them for their ability to intimidate, because all of them are Sanzed-big and look like they can handle themselves even without the glassknives and crossbows they carry.

The one who steps forward to greet Rask is actually the smallest of them—a man you know, though you don't remember his name. His children have been in your classes at the town creche. He remembers you, too, you see, when his eyes fix on you and narrow.

Rask stops and sets the crate down, opening it and handing you the runny-sack. "Karra," he says to the man you know. "Everything okay here?"

"Was till now," Karra says, not taking his eyes off you. The way he's looking at you makes your skin tighten. A couple of the other Strongbacks are watching, too, glancing from Karra to Rask and back, ready to follow someone's lead. One woman is openly glaring at you, but the rest seem content to glance at you and away in quick slashes.

"Good to hear," Rask says. You see him frown a little, perhaps as he reads the same signals you're picking up on. "Tell your people to open the gate for a minute, will you?"

Karra doesn't take his eyes off you. "Think that's a good idea, Rask?"

Rask scowls and steps sharply up to Karra, getting right in his face. He's not a big man, Rask—he's an Innovator, not a Strongback, not that it really matters anymore—and right now he doesn't need to be. "Yeah," Rask says, his voice so low and tight that Karra focuses on him at last with a stiffening of surprise. "I do. Open the gate, if you don't *mind*. If you're not too rusting *busy*."

You think of a line from stonelore, Structures, verse three. *The body fades. A leader who lasts relies on more.*

Karra's jaw flexes, but after a moment he nods. You try to look absorbed in shrugging on the runny-sack. The straps are loose. Jija was the last one to try it on.

Karra and the other gate-minders get moving, working on the system of pulleys that helps to winch the gate open. Most of Tirimo's wall is made of wood. It's not a wealthy comm with the resources to import good stone or hire the number of masons needed, although they're doing better than poorly managed comms, or newcomms that don't even have a wall yet. The gate, though, is stone, because a gate is the weakest point of every comm wall. They only need to open it a little for you, and after a few slow, grinding moments and calls from those hauling to those spotting for approaching intruders, they stop.

Rask turns to you, plainly uncomfortable. "Sorry about—about Jija," he says. Not about Uche, but maybe that's for the best. You need to keep your head clear. "About all of it, shit. Hope you find the bastard."

You only shake your head. Your throat is tight. Tirimo has been your home for ten years. You only started to think of it as such—home—around the time of Uche's birth, but that's more than you ever expected to do. You remember chasing Uche across the green after he first learned to run. You remember Jija helping Nassun build a kite and fly it, badly; the kite's remmants are still in a tree somewhere on the eastern side of town.

But it is not as hard to leave as you thought it would be. Not now, with your former neighbors' stares sliding over your skin like rancid oil.

"Thanks," you mutter, meaning for it to cover many things, because Rask didn't have to help you. He has damaged himself by doing so. The gate-minders respect him less now, and they'll talk. Soon everyone will know he's a rogga-lover, which is dangerous. Headmen can't afford that kind of weakness when a Season's coming on. But for the moment what matters most to you is this moment of public decency, which is a kindness and an honor you never expected to receive. You aren't sure how to react to it.

He nods, uncomfortable as well, and turns away as you start toward the gap in the gate. Perhaps he does not see Karra nod to another of the gate-minders; perhaps he does not see the latter woman quickly shoulder her weapon and orient it on you. Perhaps, you will think later, Rask would have stopped the woman, or somehow prevented everything to come, if he had seen.

You see her, though, mostly out of the periphery of your vision. Then everything happens too fast to think. And because you *don't* think, because you've been trying *not* to think and this means you're out of the habit, because thinking means you will remember that your family is *dead* and everything that meant happiness is now *a lie* and thinking of that will make you *break* and start screaming and screaming and screaming

and because once upon a time and in another life you learned to respond to sudden threats in a very particular way, you

reach for the air around you and *pull* and

brace your feet against the earth beneath you and *anchor* and *narrow* and

when the woman fires the crossbow, the bolt blurs toward

you. Just before the bolt hits, it bursts into a million glittering, frozen flecks.

(*Naughty, naughty,* chides a voice in your head. The voice of your conscience, deep and male. You forget this thought almost the instant it occurs. That voice is from another life.)

Life. You look at the woman who just tried to kill you.

"What the—Shit!" Karra stares at you, as if stunned by your failure to fall down dead. He crouches, hands balled into fists, nearly jumping up and down in his agitation. "Shoot her again! Kill her! Shoot, Earth damn it, before—"

"What the fuck are you doing?" Rask, finally noticing what's happening, turns back. It's too late.

Down below your feet and everyone else's, a shake begins.

It's hard to tell, at first. There is no warning jangle of sesuna, as there would be if the movement of the earth came *from* the earth. That's why people like these fear people like you, because you're beyond sense and preparation. You're a surprise, like a sudden toothache, like a heart attack. The vibration of what you're doing rises, fast, to become a rumble of tension that can be perceived with ears and feet and skin if not sessapinae, but by this point it's too late.

Karra frowns, looking at the ground beneath his feet. Crossbow Woman pauses in the middle of loading another bolt, eyes widening as she stares at the shivering string of her weapon.

You stand surrounded by swirling flecks of snow and disintegrated crossbow bolt. Around your feet, there is a two-foot circle of frost riming the packed earth. Your locks waft gently in the rising breeze.

"You can't." Rask whispers the words, his eyes widening at

the look on your face. (You don't know what you look like right now, but it must be bad.) He shakes his head as if denial will stop this, taking a step back and then another. "Essun."

"You killed him," you say to Rask. This is not a rational thing. You mean you-plural, even though you're speaking to you-specific. Rask didn't try to kill you, had nothing to do with Uche, but the attempt on your life has triggered something raw and furious and cold. *You cowards. You animals, who look at a child and see prey.* Jija's the one to blame for Uche, some part of you knows that—but Jija grew up here in Tirimo. The kind of hate that can make a man murder his own son? It came from everyone around you.

Rask inhales. "Essun—"

And then the valley floor splits open.

The initial jolt of this is violent enough to knock everyone standing to the ground and sway every house in Tirimo. Then those houses judder and rattle as the jolt smooths into a steady, ongoing vibration. Saider's Cart-Repair Shop is the first to collapse, the old wooden frame of the building sliding sideways off its foundation. There are screams from inside, and one woman manages to run out before the door frame crumples inward. On the eastern edge of town, closest to the mountain ridges that frame the valley, a rockslide begins. A portion of the eastern comm wall and three houses are buried beneath a sudden grinding slurry of mud and trees and rocks. Far below the ground, where no one but you can detect, the clay walls of the underground aquifer that supplies the village wells are breached. The aquifer begins to drain. They will not realize for weeks that you killed the town in this moment, but they will remember when the wells run dry.

Those who survive the next few moments will, anyhow. From your feet, the circle of frost and swirling snow begins to expand. Rapidly.

It catches Rask first. He tries to run as the edge of your torus rolls toward him, but he's simply too close. It catches him in mid-lunge, glazing his feet and solidifying his legs and eating its way up his spine until, in the span of a breath, he falls to the ground stone-stiff, his flesh turning as gray as his hair. The next to be consumed by the circle is Karra, who's still screaming for someone to kill you. The shout dies in his throat as he falls, flash-frozen, the last of his warm breath hissing out through clenched teeth and frosting the ground as you steal the heat from it.

You aren't just inflicting death on your fellow villagers, of course. A bird perched on a nearby fence falls over frozen, too. The grass crisps, the ground grows hard, and the air hisses and howls as moisture and density is snatched from its substance... but no one has ever mourned earthworms.

Fast. The air swirls briskly all down Seven Seasons now, making the trees rustle and anyone nearby cry out in alarm as they realize what's happening. The ground hasn't stopped moving. You sway with the ground, but because you know its rhythms, it is easy for you to shift your balance with it. You do this without thinking, because there is only room left in you for one thought.

These people killed Uche. Their hate, their fear, their unprovoked violence. They.

(He.)

Killed your son.

(Jija killed your son.)

People run out into the streets, screaming and wondering why there was no warning, and you kill any of them who are stupid or panicked enough to come near.

Jija. They are Jija. The whole rusting town is *Jija*.

Two things save the comm, however, or at least most of it. The first is that most of the buildings don't collapse. Tirimo might be too poor to build with stone, but most of its builders are ethical and well paid enough to use only techniques that stonelore recommends: the hanging frame, the center beam. Second, the fault line of the valley—which you're currently peeling apart with a thought—is actually a few miles to the west. Because of these things, most of Tirimo will survive this, at least until the wells die.

Because of these things. And because of the terrified, bouncing scream of a little boy as his father runs out of a madly swaying building.

You pivot toward the sound instantly, habitually, orienting on the source with a mother's ears. The man clutches the boy with both arms. He doesn't even have a runny-sack; the first and only thing he took the time to grab was his son. The boy looks nothing like Uche. But you stare as the child bounces and reaches back toward the house for something the man has left behind (favorite toy? the boy's mother?), and suddenly, finally, you *think*.

And then you stop.

Because, oh uncaring Earth. Look what you've done.

The shake stops. The air hisses again, this time as warmer, moister air rushes into the space around you. The ground and your skin grow instantly damp with condensation. The rumble of the valley fades, leaving only screams and the creak of falling wood and the shake-siren that has only belatedly, forlornly, begun to wail.

You close you eyes, aching and shaking and thinking, *No. I killed Uche. By being his mother.* There are tears on your face. And here you thought you couldn't cry.

But there's no one between you and the gate now. The gate-minders who could, have fled; besides Rask and Karra, several more were too slow to get away. You shoulder the runny-sack and head for the gate opening, scrubbing at your face with one hand. You're smiling, too, though, and it is a bitter, aching thing. You just can't help acknowledging the irony of the whole thing. Didn't want to wait for death to come for you. Right.

Stupid, stupid woman. Death was always here. Death is you.

* * *

Never forget what you are.

—*Tablet One, "On Survival," verse ten*

4

Syenite, cut and polished

*T*HIS IS SHIT, SYENITE THINKS, behind the shield of her pleasant smile.

She doesn't let the affront show on her face, however. Nor does she shift even minutely in the chair. Her hands—four fingers ringed respectively in plain bands of carnelian, white opal, gold, and onyx—rest on her knees. They're out of sight below the edge of the desk, from Feldspar's perspective. She could clench them with Feldspar none the wiser. She doesn't.

"Coral reefs *are* challenging, you realize." Feldspar, her own hands occupied with the big wooden cup of safe, smiles over its rim. She knows full well what's behind Syenite's smile. "Not like ordinary rock. Coral is porous, flexible. The fine control required to shatter it without triggering a tsunami is difficult to achieve."

And Syen could do it in her sleep. A two-ringer could do this. A grit could do it—though, admittedly, not without substantial collateral damage. She reaches for her own cup of safe, turning the wooden hemisphere in her fingers so that they will not shake, then taking a sip. "I appreciate that you have assigned me a mentor, senior."

"No, you don't." Feldspar smiles, too, and sips from her cup of safe, ringed pinky in the air while she does so. It's as if they're having a private contest, etiquette versus etiquette, best shit-eating grin take all. "If it's any consolation, no one will think less of you."

Because everyone knows what this is really about. That doesn't erase the insult, but it does give Syen a degree of comfort. At least her new "mentor" is a ten-ringer. That, too, is comforting, that they thought so much of her. She'll scrape whatever morsels of self-esteem she can out of this.

"He recently completed a circuit in the Somidlats," Feldspar says, gently. There's no actual gentleness to the conversation's subject matter, but Syen appreciates the older woman's effort. "Ordinarily we'd allow him more time to rest before setting him back on the road, but the quartent governor was insistent that we do something about Allia's harbor blockage as soon as possible. You're the one who'll do the work; he's just there to supervise. Getting there should take a month or so, if you don't make many detours and travel at an easy pace—and there's no hurry, given that the coral reef isn't exactly a sudden problem."

At this, Feldspar looks fleetingly, but truly, annoyed. The quartent governor of Allia, or possibly Allia's Leadership, must have been especially irritating. In the years since Feldspar became her assigned senior, Syen has never seen the old woman show any expression worse than a brittle smile. They both know the rules: Fulcrum orogenes—Imperial orogenes, blackjackets, the ones you probably shouldn't kill, whatever people want to call them—must be always polite and professional. Fulcrum orogenes must project confidence and expertise whenever they are in public. Fulcrum orogenes must never show anger because it makes the stills nervous. Except Feldspar would never be so improper as to use a slur like *the stills*—but that is why Feldspar is a senior and has been given supervisory responsibilities, while Syenite merely grinds her own edges alone. She'll have to demonstrate more professionalism if she wants Feldspar's job. That, and she'll apparently have to do a few other things.

"When do I meet him?" Syenite asks. She takes a sip of safe so this question will seem casual. Just a bit of conversation between old friends.

"Whenever you like." Feldspar shrugs. "He has quarters in the seniors' hall. We did send him a briefing and a request that he attend this meeting..." Again she looks mildly irritated. This whole situation must be terrible for her, just terrible. "...but it's possible he missed the message, since as I said he's been recovering from his circuit. Traveling the Likesh Mountains alone is difficult."

"Alone?"

"Five-ringers and above are no longer required to have a partner or Guardian when traveling outside the Fulcrum." Feldspar sips from her cup of safe, oblivious to Syenite's shock. "At that point we are judged stable enough in our mastery of orogeny to be granted a modicum of autonomy."

Five rings. She has four. It's bullshit that this has anything to do with orogenic mastery; if a Guardian has doubts about an orogene's willingness to follow the rules, that orogene doesn't make it to the first ring, let alone the fifth. But… "So it'll be just him and me."

"Yes. We've found that arrangement to be most effective in circumstances like this."

Of course.

Feldspar continues. "You'll find him in Shaped Prominence." That's the complex of buildings that houses most of the Fulcrum's complement of seniors. "Main tower, top floor. There are no set-aside quarters for the most senior orogenes because there are so few—he is our only ten-ringer, at present—but we could at least spare him a bit of extra space up there."

"Thank you," Syen says, turning her cup again. "I'll go see him after this."

Feldspar pauses for a long moment, her face going even more pleasantly unreadable than usual, and that is Syenite's warning. Then Feldspar says: "As a ten-ringer, he has the right to refuse any mission short of a declared emergency. You should know that."

Wait. Syen's fingers stop turning the cup, and her eyes flick up to meet those of the older woman. Is Feld saying what it sounds like she's saying? Can't be. Syen narrows her eyes, no longer bothering to conceal her suspicion. And yet. Feldspar has given her a way out. Why?

Feldspar smiles thinly. "I have six children."

Ah.

Nothing more to be said, then. Syen takes another sip, trying not to grimace at the chalky grit near the bottom of the cup. Safe is nutritious, but it's not a drink anyone enjoys. It's made from a plant milk that changes color in the presence of any contaminant, even spit. It's served to guests and at meetings because, well, it's safe. A polite gesture that says: *I'm not poisoning you. At least, not right now.*

After that Syen takes her leave of Feldspar, then heads out of Main, the administrative building. Main sits amid a cluster of smaller buildings at the edge of the sprawling, half-wild expanse that comprises the Ring Garden. The garden is acres wide, and runs in a broad strip around the Fulcrum for several miles. It's just that huge, the Fulcrum, a city in itself nestled within the greater body of Yumenes like . . . well. Syenite would've continued the thought with *like a child in a woman's belly*, but that comparison seems especially grotesque today.

She nods to her fellow juniors in passing as she recognizes them. Some of them are just standing or sitting around in knots and talking, while others lounge on patches of grass or flowers and read, or flirt, or sleep. Life for the ringed is easy, except during missions beyond the Fulcrum's walls, which are brief and infrequent. A handful of grits tromp through along the wending cobbled path, all in a neat line overseen by juniors who've volunteered as instructors, but grits aren't permitted to enjoy the garden yet; that is a privilege reserved only for those who've passed their first-ring test and been approved for initiation by the Guardians.

And as if the thought of Guardians summons them, Syen spies a few burgundy-uniformed figures standing in a knot near one of the Ring's many ponds. There's another Guardian on the other side of the pond, lounging in an alcove surrounded by rosebushes, appearing to listen politely while a young junior sings to a small seated audience nearby. Perhaps the Guardian *is* just listening politely; sometimes they do that. Sometimes they need to relax, too. Syen notes this Guardian's gaze lingering on one of the audience members in particular, however: a thin, white youth who doesn't seem to be paying much attention to the singer. He's looking at his hands, instead, which are folded in his lap. There's a bandage around two of his fingers, holding them together and straight.

Syen moves on.

She stops first at Curving Shield, one of many clusters of buildings that house the hundreds of junior orogenes. Her roommates aren't home to see her fetch a few necessary items from her chest, for which she is painfully grateful. They'll hear about her assignment soon enough through the rumor mill. Then she heads out again, eventually reaching Shaped Prominence. The tower is one of the older buildings of the Fulcrum complex, built low and wide of heavy white marble blocks and stolid angles atypical of the wilder, fanciful architecture of Yumenes. The big double doors open into a wide, graceful foyer, its walls and floor embossed with scenes from Sanzed history. She keeps her pace unhurried, nodding to the seniors she sees whether she recognizes them or not—she *does* want Feldspar's job, after all—and taking the wide stairways gradually, pausing now and again to appreciate the artfully arranged patterns of light and shadow cast by the narrow windows. She's not sure what makes the patterns so special, actually, but everyone says they're stunning works of art, so she needs to be seen appreciating.

On the topmost floor, where the plush hall-length rug is overlaid by a herringbone pattern of sunlight, she stops to catch her breath and appreciate something genuinely: silence. Solitude.

There's no one moving in this corridor, not even low-level juniors on cleaning or errand duty. She's heard the rumors and now she knows they're true: The ten-ringer has the whole floor to himself.

This, then, is the true reward for excellence: privacy. And choice. After closing her eyes for a moment in aching want, Syen heads down the hall until she reaches the only door with a mat in front of it.

In that moment, though, she hesitates. She knows nothing about this man. He's earned the highest rank that exists within their order, which means no one really cares what he does anymore so long as he keeps any embarrassing behaviors private. And he is a man who has been powerless most of his life, only lately granted autonomy and privilege over others. No one will demote him for anything so trivial as perversion or abuse. Not if his victim is just another orogene.

There's no point to this. *She* doesn't have a choice. With a sigh, Syenite knocks.

And because she isn't expecting *a person* so much as *a trial to be endured*, she's actually surprised when an annoyed voice snaps from within, "*What?*"

She's still wondering how to reply to that when footsteps slap against stone—briskly, annoyed even in their sound—and the door whisks open. The man who stands there glaring at her is wearing a rumpled robe, one side of his hair flattened, fabric lines painting a haphazard map over his cheek. He's younger than she expected. Not *young*; almost twice her age, at least forty. But she'd thought... well. She's met so many six- and seven-ringers in their sixth and seventh decades that she'd expected a ten-ringer to be ancient. And calmer, dignified, more self-possessed. Something. He's not even wearing his rings, though she can see a faint paler stripe on some of his fingers, in between his angry gesticulations.

"*What*, in the name of every two-minute earth jerk?" When Syen just stares at him, he lapses into another tongue—something she's never heard before, though the sound of it is vaguely Coaster, and distinctly pissed. Then he rubs a hand over his hair, and Syen almost laughs. His hair is dense, tight-curled stuff, the kind of hair that needs to be shaped if it's to look stylish, and what he's doing just messes it up more.

"I told Feldspar," he says, returning to perfectly fluent Sanzed and plainly struggling for patience, "and those other cackling meddlers on the senior advisory board to *leave me alone*. I just got off circuit, I haven't had two hours to myself in the last year that weren't shared with a horse or a stranger, and if you're here to give me more orders, I'm going to ice you where you stand."

She's pretty sure this is hyperbole. It's the kind of hyperbole he shouldn't use; Fulcrum orogenes just don't joke about certain things. It's one of the unspoken rules... but maybe a ten-ringer is beyond such things. "Not orders, exactly," she manages, and his face twists.

"Then I don't want to hear whatever you're here to tell me. *Go the rust away*." And he starts to close the door in her face.

She can't believe it at first. What kind of—Really? It is indignity on top of indignity; bad enough to have to do this in the first place, but to be disrespected in the process?

She jams a foot in the door's path before it can build up much momentum and leans in to say, "I'm Syenite."

It doesn't mean anything to him, she can see by his now-furious glare. He inhales to start shouting, she has no idea what but she doesn't want to hear it, and before he can she snaps, "I'm here to *fuck* you, Earth burn it. Is that worth disturbing your beauty rest?"

Part of her is appalled at her own language, and her own anger. The rest of her is satisfied, because that shuts him right the rust up.

He lets her in.

Now it's awkward. Syen sits at the small table in his suite—a *suite,* he's got a whole suite of furnished rooms *to himself*—and watches while he fidgets. He's sitting on one of the room's couches, pretty much perched on its edge. The *far* edge, she notes, as if he fears to sit too close to her.

"I didn't think it would start again this soon," he says, looking at his hands, which are laced together before him. "I mean, they always tell me there's a need, but that's...I didn't..." He sighs.

"Then this isn't the first time for you," Syenite says. He only earned the right to refuse with his tenth ring.

"No, no, but..." He takes a deep breath. "I didn't always know."

"Didn't know what?"

He grimaces. "With the first few women...I thought they were *interested*."

"You—" Then she gets it. The deniability is always there, of course; even Feldspar never came right out and said *Your assignment is to produce a child within a year with this man.* That lack of acknowledgment is supposed to make it easier, somehow. She's never seen the point: Why pretend the situation is anything other than what it is? But for him, she realizes, it wasn't pretending. Which astounds her because, come on. How naive can he be?

He glances at her and his expression grows pained. "Yes. I know."

She shakes her head. "I see." It doesn't matter. This isn't about his intelligence. She stands up and unbuckles the belt of her uniform.

He stares. "Just like that? I don't even know you."

"You don't need to."

"I don't *like* you."

The feeling is mutual, but Syen refrains from pointing out the obvious. "I finished menstruating a week ago. This is a good time. If you'd rather, you can just lie still and let me take care of things." She's not extraordinarily experienced, but it's not plate tectonics. She gets her uniform jacket off, then pulls something out of the pocket to show him: a bottle of lubricant, still mostly full. He looks dimly horrified. "In fact, it's probably better if you don't move. This will be awkward enough as it is."

He stands up, too, actually backing away. The look of agitation on his face is—well, it's not funny, not really. But Syenite cannot help feeling a modicum of relief at his reaction. No, not just relief. *He* is the weak one here, despite his ten rings. She's the one who has to carry a child she doesn't want, which might kill her and even if it doesn't will change her body forever, if not her life—but here and now, at least, she is the one with all the power. It makes this . . . well, not right. But better, somehow, that she's the one in control.

"We don't have to do this," he blurts. "I can refuse." He grimaces. "I know you can't, but I can. So—"

"Don't refuse," she says, scowling.

"What? Why not?"

"You said it: I have to do this. You don't. If not you, it will be someone else." Six children, Feldspar had. But Feldspar was never a particularly promising orogene. Syenite is. If Syen isn't careful, if she pisses off the wrong people, if she lets herself get labeled *difficult,* they will kill her career and assign her permanently to the Fulcrum, leaving her nothing to do but lie on her back and turn men's grunting and farting into babies. She'll be lucky to have only six if that's how things turn out.

He's staring as if he doesn't understand, even though she knows he does. She says, "I want this over with."

Then he surprises her. She's expecting more stammering and protests. Instead his hand clenches at his side. He looks away, a muscle working in his jaw. He still looks ridiculous in that robe with his hair askew, but the look on his face . . . he might as well have been ordered to submit himself to torture. She knows she's no looker, at least not by Equatorial standards. Too much midlatter mongrel in her. But then, he's obviously not well-bred, either: that hair, and skin so black it's almost blue, and he's small. Her height, that is, which is tall for either women or men—but he's lean, not at all broad or intimidating. If his ancestors include any Sanzeds, they're far back, and they gave him nothing of their physical superiority.

"Over with," he mutters. "Right." The muscle in his jaw is practically jumping up and down, he's grinding his teeth so hard. And—whoa. He's not looking at her, and suddenly she's glad. Because *that's hate*, in his face. She's seen it before in other orogenes—rust, she's felt it herself, when she has the luxury of solitude and unfettered honesty—but she's never let it *show* like that. Then he looks up at her, and she tries not to flinch.

"You weren't born here," he says, cold now. Belatedly she realizes it's a question.

"No." She doesn't like being the one on the receiving end of the questions. "Were you?"

"Oh, yes. I was bred to order." He smiles, and it's strange seeing a smile layered over all that hate. "Not even as haphazardly as our child will be. I'm the product of two of the Fulcrum's oldest and most promising lineages, or so I'm told. I had a Guardian practically from birth." He shoves his hands into the pockets of his rumpled robe. "You're a feral."

This comes out of nowhere. Syen actually spends a second wondering if this is some new way of saying rogga and then realizing what he really means. Oh, that is just the limit. "Look, I don't care how many rings you wear—"

"That's what *they* call you, I mean." He smiles again, and his bitterness so resonates with her own that she falls silent in confusion. "If you didn't know. Ferals—the ones from outside—often don't know, or care. But when an orogene is born from parents who weren't, from a family line that's never shown the curse before, that's how they think of you. A wild mutt to my domesticated purebred. An accident, to my plan." He shakes his head; it makes his voice shake. "What it actually means is that they couldn't *predict* you. You're the proof that they'll never understand orogeny; it's not science, it's something else. And they'll never control us, not really. Not completely."

Syen isn't sure what to say. She didn't know about the feral thing, about being different somehow—though now that she thinks about it, most of the other orogenes she knows were Fulcrum-bred. And yeah, she's noticed how they look at her. She just thought that was because they were Equatorials and she was from the Nomidlats, or because she got her first ring before they did. And yet, now that he's said this... is being feral a bad thing?

It must be. If the problem is that ferals are not predictable... well, orogenes have to prove themselves reliable. The Fulcrum has a reputation to maintain; that's part of this. So's the training, and the uniform, and the endless rules they must follow, but the breeding *is* part of it, too, or why is she here?

It's somewhat flattering to think that despite her feral status, they actually want something of her infused into their breeding lines. Then she wonders why a part of her is trying to find value in degradation.

She's so lost in thought that he surprises her when he makes a weary sound of capitulation.

"You're right," he says tersely, all business now because, well, there was really only one way this could end. And staying businesslike will allow both of them to maintain some semblance of dignity. "Sorry. You're... rusting Earth. Yeah. Let's just get this done."

So they go into his bedroom and he strips and lies down and tries for a while to work himself up to it, which doesn't go well. The hazard of having to do this with an older man, Syen decides—though really, it's probably more the fact that sex doesn't usually go well when you don't feel like having it. She keeps her expression neutral as she sits beside him and brushes his hands out of the way. He looks embarrassed, and she curses because if he gets self-conscious about it, this will take all day.

He comes around once she takes over, though, perhaps because he can shut his eyes and imagine that her hands belong to whoever he wants. So then she grits her teeth and straddles him and rides until her thighs ache and her breasts grow sore from bouncing. The lube only helps a little. He doesn't feel as good as a dildo or her fingers. Still, his fantasies must be sufficient, because after a while he makes a strained sort of whimper and then it's done.

She's pulling on her boots when he sighs and sits up and looks at her so bleakly that she feels vaguely ashamed of what she's done to him.

"What did you say your name was?" he asks.

"Syenite."

"That the name your parents gave you?" When she glares back at him, his lips twitch in something less than a smile. "Sorry. Just jealous."

"Jealous?"

"Fulcrum-bred, remember? I've only ever had the one name."

Oh.

He hesitates. This is apparently hard for him. "You, uh, you can call me—"

She cuts him off, because she knows his name already and anyway she doesn't intend to call him anything but *you*, which should be enough to distinguish him from their horses. "Feldspar says we're to leave for Allia tomorrow." She gets her second boot on and stands to kick the heel into place.

"Another mission? Already?" He sighs. "I should have known."

Yes, he should have. "You're mentoring me, and helping me clear some coral out of a harbor."

"Right." He knows it's a bullshit mission, too. There's only one reason they'd send him along for something like this. "They gave me a briefing dossier yesterday. Guess I'll finally read it. Meet at the stableyard at noon?"

"You're the ten-ringer."

He rubs his face with both hands. She feels a little bad, but only a little.

"Fine," he says, all business again. "Noon it is."

So she heads out, sore and annoyed that she smells faintly like him, and tired. Probably it's just stress that's wearing her out—the idea of a month on the road with a man she cannot stand, doing things she doesn't want to do, on behalf of people she increasingly despises.

But this is what it means to be *civilized*—doing what her betters say she should, for the ostensible good of all. And it's not like she gains no benefit from this: a year or so of discomfort, a baby she doesn't have to bother raising because it will be turned over to the lower creche as soon as it's born, and a high-profile mission completed under the mentorship of a powerful senior. With the experience and boost to her reputation, she'll be that much closer to her fifth ring. That means her own apartment; no more roommates. Better missions, longer leave, more say in her own life. That's worth it. *Earthfire yes,* it's worth it.

She tells herself this all the way back to her room. Then she packs to leave, tidies up so she'll come home to order and neatness, and takes a shower, methodically scrubbing every bit of flesh she can reach until her skin burns.

* * *

> "Tell them they can be great someday, like us. Tell them they belong among us, no matter how we treat them. Tell them they must earn the respect which everyone else receives by default. Tell them there is a standard for acceptance; that standard is simply perfection. Kill those who scoff at these contradictions, and tell the rest that the dead deserved annihilation for their weakness and doubt. Then they'll break themselves trying for what they'll never achieve."
>
> —*Erlsset, twenty-third emperor of the Sanzed Equatorial Affiliation, in the thirteenth year of the Season of Teeth. Comment recorded at a party, shortly before the founding of the Fulcrum.*

5

you're not alone

Night has fallen, and you sit in the lee of a hill in the dark.

You're so tired. Takes a lot out of a you, killing so many people. Worse because you didn't do nearly as much as you could have done, once you got all worked up. Orogeny is a strange equation. Take movement and warmth and life from your surroundings, amplify it by some indefinable process of concentration or catalysis or semi-predictable chance, push movement and warmth and death from the earth. Power in, power out. To keep the power in, though, to *not* turn the valley's aquifer into a geyser or shatter the ground into rubble, takes an effort that makes your teeth and the backs of your eyes ache. You walked a long time to try to burn off some of what you took in, but it still brims under your skin even as your body grows weary and your feet hurt. You are a weapon meant to move mountains. A mere walk can't take that out of you.

Still, you walked until darkness fell, and then you walked some more, and now you're here, huddled and alone at the edge of an old fallow field. You're afraid to start a fire, even though it's getting cool. Without a fire you can't see much, but also nothing can see you: a woman alone, with a full pack and only a knife to defend herself. (You're not helpless, but an attacker wouldn't know that till it was too late, and you'd rather not kill anyone else today.) In the distance you can see the dark arc of a highroad, rising above the plains like a taunt. Highroads usually have electric lanterns, courtesy of Sanze, but you're not surprised this one's dark: Even if the shake from the north hadn't occurred, Seasonal standard procedure is to shut down all nonessential hydro and geo. It's too far to be worth the detour, anyway.

You're wearing a jacket, and there's nothing to fear in the field but mice. Sleeping without a fire won't kill you. You can see relatively well anyway, despite the lack of fire or lanterns. Rippling bands of clouds, like hoed rows in the garden you once kept, have covered the sky above. They're easy to see because something to the north has underlit the clouds in bands of redglow and shadow. When you stare that way, there's an uneven line of mountains against the northern horizon, and the flicker of a distant bluish gray obelisk where its lower tip peeks through a knot of clouds, but these things tell you nothing. Closer by there's a flitter of what might be a colony of bats out feeding. Late for bats, but *all things change during a Season*, the stonelore warns. All living things do what they must to prepare, and survive.

The source of the glow is beyond the mountains, as if the setting sun went the wrong way and got stuck there. You know what's causing this glow. It must be an awesome thing to see up close, that great terrible rent spewing fire into the sky, except you don't ever *want* to see it.

And you won't, because you're heading south. Even if Jija hadn't started out going in that direction, he would surely have turned south after the shake from the north passed through. That's the only sane way to go.

Of course, a man who would beat his own child to death might not still fit the label of *sane*. And a woman who found that child and stopped thinking for three days . . . hmm, not you, either. Nothing to do but follow your crazy, though.

You've eaten something from your pack: cachebread smeared with salty akaba paste from the jar you stuffed into it a lifetime and a family ago. Akaba keeps well after it's opened, but not forever, and now that you've opened it you'll have to eat it for the next few meals until it's gone. That's okay because you like it. You've drunk water from the canteen that you filled a few miles back, at a roadhouse's well pump. There'd been people there, several dozen, some of them camping around the roadhouse and some of them just stopping there briefly. All of them had the look you're starting to identify as slow-building panic. Because everyone's finally begun to realize what the shake and the redglow and the clouded sky all mean, and to be outside of a community's gates at a time like this is—in the long run—a death sentence, except for a handful who are willing to become brutal enough or depraved enough to do what they must. Even those only have a chance at survival.

None of the people at the roadhouse wanted to believe they had that in them, you saw as you looked around, assessing faces and clothes and bodies and threats. None of them looked like survival fetishists or would-be warlords. What you saw at that roadhouse were ordinary people, some still caked in filth after digging themselves out of mudslides or collapsed buildings, some still bleeding from wounds haphazardly bandaged, or untreated entirely. Travelers, caught away from home; survivors, whose homes no longer existed. You saw an old man, still wearing a sleeping gown half ragged and dusty on one side, sitting with a youth clad in only a long shirt and smears of blood, both of them hollow-eyed with grief. You saw two women holding each other, rocking in an effort at comfort. You saw a man your own age with the look of a Strongback, who gazed steadily at his big, thick-fingered hands and perhaps wondered if he was hale enough, young enough, to earn a place somewhere.

These are the stories the stonelore prepared you for, tragic as they are. There is nothing in stonelore about husbands killing children.

You're leaning on an old post that someone jammed up against the hill, maybe the remnants of a fence that ended here, drifting off with your hands tucked into your jacket pockets and your knees drawn up. And then, slowly, you become aware that something has changed. There's no sound to alert you, other than the wind and the small prickles and rustles of the grass. No smell transcends the faint sulfur scent that you've already gotten used to. But there's something. Something else. Out there.

Some*one* else.

Your eyes snap open, and half your mind falls into the earth, ready to kill. The rest of your mind freezes—because a few feet away, sitting crosslegged on the grass and looking at you, is a little boy.

You don't realize what he is at first. It's dark. *He's* dark. You wonder if he's from an eastern Coastal comm. But his hair moves a little when the wind soughs again, and you can tell that some of it's straight as the grass around you. Westcoaster, then? The rest of it seems stuck down with... hair pomade or something. No. You're a mother. It's dirt. He's covered in dirt.

Bigger than Uche, not quite as big as Nassun, so maybe six or seven years old. You actually aren't sure he's a he; confirmation of that will come later. For now you make a judgment call. He sits in a hunched way that would look odd in an adult and is perfectly normal for a child who hasn't been told to sit up straight. You stare at him for a moment. He stares back at you. You can see the pale glisten of his eyes.

"Hello," he says. A boy's voice, high and bright. Good call.

"Hello," you say, at last. There are horror tales that start this way, with bands of feral commless children who turn out to be cannibals. Bit early for that sort of thing, though, the Season having just started. "Where did you come from?"

He shrugs. Unknowing, maybe uncaring. "What's your name? I'm Hoa."

It's a small, strange name, but the world is a big, strange place. Stranger, though, that he gives only one name. He's young enough that he might not have a comm name yet, but he had to have inherited his father's use-caste. "Just Hoa?"

"Mmm-hmm." He nods and twists aside and sets down some kind of parcel, patting it as if to make sure it's safe. "Can I sleep here?"

You look around, and sess around, and listen. Nothing moving but the grass, no one around but the boy. Doesn't explain how he approached you in total silence—but then, he's small, and you know from experience that small children can be very quiet if they want to be. Usually that means they're up to something, though. "Who else are you with, Hoa?"

"Nobody."

It's too dim for him to see your eyes narrow, but somehow he reacts to this anyway, leaning forward. "Really! It's just me. I saw some other people by the road, but I didn't like them. I hid from them." A pause. "I like you."

Lovely.

Sighing, you tuck your hands back into your pockets and draw yourself out of earth-readiness. The boy relaxes a little—that much you can see—and starts to lie down on the bare earth.

"Wait," you say, and reach for your pack. Then you toss him the bedroll. He catches it and looks confused for a few moments, then figures it out. Happily he rolls it out and then curls up on top of it, like a cat. You don't care enough to correct him.

Maybe he's lying. Maybe he is a threat. You'll make him leave in the morning because you don't need a child tagging along; he'll slow you down. And someone must be looking for him. Some mother, somewhere, whose child is not dead.

For tonight, however, you can manage to be human for a little while. So you lean back against the post, and close your eyes to sleep.

The ash begins to fall in the morning.

* * *

They are an arcane thing, you understand, an alchemical thing. Like orogeny, if orogeny could manipulate the infinitesimal structure of matter itself rather than mountains. Obviously they possess some sort of kinship with humanity, which they choose to acknowledge in the statue-like shape we most often see, but it follows that they can take other shapes. We would never know.

—Umbl Innovator Allia, "A Treatise on Sentient Non-Humans," Sixth University, 2323 Imperial/ Year Two Acid Season

6

Damaya, grinding to a halt

The first few days on the road with Schaffa are uneventful. Not boring. There are boring parts, like when the Imperial Road along which they ride passes through endless fields of kirga stalks or samishet, or when the fields give way to stretches of dim forest so quiet and close that Damaya hardly dares speak for fear of angering the trees. (In stories, trees are always angry.) But even this is a novelty, because Damaya has never gone beyond Palela's borders, not even to Brevard with Father and Chaga at market time. She tries not to look like a complete yokel, gawping at every strange thing they pass, but sometimes she cannot help it, even when she feels Schaffa chuckling against her back. She cannot bring herself to mind that he laughs at her.

Brevard is cramped and narrow and high in a way that she has never before experienced, so she hunches in the saddle as they ride into it, looking up at the looming buildings on either side of the street and wondering if they ever collapse in on passersby. No one else seems to notice that these buildings are ridiculously tall and crammed right up against each other, so it must have been done on purpose. There are dozens of people about even though the sun has set and, to her reckoning, everyone should be getting ready for bed.

Except no one is. They pass one building so bright with oil lanterns and raucous with laughter that she is overcome with curiosity enough to ask about it. "An inn, of sorts," Schaffa replies, and then he chuckles as though she's asked the question that's in her mind. "But we won't be staying at that one."

"It's really loud," she agrees, trying to sound knowledgeable.

"Hmm, yes, that, too. But the bigger problem is that it's not a good place to bring children." She waits, but he doesn't elaborate. "We're going to a place I've stayed at several times before. The food is decent, the beds are clean, and our belongings aren't likely to walk off before morning."

Thus do they pass Damaya's first night in an inn. She's shocked by all of it: eating in a room full of strangers, eating food that tastes different from what her parents or Chaga made, soaking in a big ceramic basin with a fire under it instead of an oiled half-barrel of cold water in the kitchen, sleeping in a bed bigger than hers and Chaga's put together. Schaffa's bed is bigger still, which is fitting because he's huge, but she gawps at it nevertheless as he drags it across the inn room's door. (This, at least, is familiar; Father did it sometimes when there were rumors of commless on the roads around town.) He apparently paid extra for the bigger bed. "I sleep like an earthshake," he says, smiling as if this is some sort of joke. "If the bed's too narrow, I'll roll right off."

She has no idea what he means until the middle of that

night, when she wakes to hear Schaffa groaning and thrashing in his sleep. If it's a nightmare, it's a terrible one, and for a while she wonders if she should get up and try to wake him. She hates nightmares. But Schaffa is a grown-up, and grown-ups need their sleep; that's what her father always said whenever she or Chaga did something that woke him up. Father was always angry about it, too, and she does not want Schaffa angry with her. He's the only person who cares about her in all the world. So she lies there, anxious and undecided, until he actually cries out something unintelligible, and it sounds like he's dying.

"Are you awake?" She says it really softly, because obviously he isn't—but the instant she speaks, he is.

"What is it?" He sounds hoarse.

"You were..." She isn't sure what to say. *Having a nightmare* sounds like something her mother would say to her. Does one say such things to big, strong grown-ups like Schaffa? "Making a noise," she finishes.

"Snoring?" He breathes a long weary sigh into the dark. "Sorry." Then he shifts, and is silent for the rest of the night.

In the morning Damaya forgets this happened, at least for a long while. They rise and eat some of the food that has been left at their door in a basket, and take the rest with them as they resume the trip toward Yumenes. In the just-after-dawn light Brevard is less frightening and strange, perhaps because now she can see piles of horse dung in the gutters and little boys carrying fishing poles and stablehands yawning as they heft crates or bales. There are young women carting buckets of water into the local bathhouse to be heated, and young men stripping to the waist to churn butter or pound rice in sheds behind the big buildings. All these things are familiar, and they help her see that Brevard is just a bigger version of a small town. Its people are no different from Muh Dear or Chaga—and to the people who live here, Brevard is probably as familiar and tedious as she found Palela.

They ride for half a day and stop for a rest, then ride for the rest of the day, until Brevard is far behind and there's nothing but rocky, ugly shatterland surrounding them for miles around. There's an active fault nearby, Schaffa explains, churning out new land over years and decades, which is why in places the ground seems sort of *pushed up* and bare. "These rocks didn't exist ten years ago," he says, gesturing toward a huge pile of crumbling gray-green stone that looks sharp-edged and somehow damp. "But then there was a bad shake—a niner. Or so I hear; I was on circuit in another quartent. Looking at this, though, I can believe it."

Damaya nods. Old Father Earth does feel closer, here, than in Palela—or, not *closer,* that's not really the word for it, but she doesn't know what words would work better. Easier to touch, maybe, if she were to do so. And, and . . . it feels . . . fragile, somehow, the land all around them. Like an eggshell laced with fine lines that can barely be seen, but which still spell imminent death for the chick inside.

Schaffa nudges her with his leg. "Don't."

Startled, Damaya does not think to lie. "I wasn't doing anything."

"You were listening to the earth. That's something."

How does Schaffa know? She hunches a little in the saddle, not sure whether she should apologize. Fidgeting, she settles her hands on the pommel of the saddle, which feels awkward because the saddle is huge like everything that belongs to Schaffa. (Except her.) But she needs to do *something* to distract herself from listening again. After a moment of this, Schaffa sighs.

"I suppose I can expect no better," he says, and the disappointment in his tone bothers her immediately. "It isn't your fault. Without training you're like...dry tinder, and right now we're traveling past a roaring fire that's kicking up sparks." He seems to think. "Would a story help?"

A story would be wonderful. She nods, trying not to seem too eager. "All right," Schaffa says. "Have you heard of Shemshena?"

"Who?"

He shakes his head. "Earthfires, these little midlatter comms. Didn't they teach you anything in that creche of yours? Nothing but lore and figuring, I imagine, and the latter only so you could time crop plantings and such."

"There's no time for more than that," Damaya says, feeling oddly compelled to defend Palela. "Kids in Equatorial comms probably don't need to help with the harvest—"

"I know, I know. But it's still a shame." He shifts, getting more comfortable in his saddle. "Very well; I'm no lorist, but I'll tell you of Shemshena. Long ago, during the Season of Teeth—that's, hmm, the third Season after Sanze's founding, maybe twelve hundred years ago?—an orogene named Misalem decided to try to kill the emperor. This was back when the emperor actually did things, mind, and long before the Fulcrum was established. Most orogenes had no proper training in those days; like you, they acted purely on emotion and instinct, on the rare occasions that they managed to survive childhood. Misalem had somehow managed to not only survive, but to train himself. He had superb control, perhaps to the fourth or fifth ring-level—"

"What?"

He nudges her leg again. "Rankings used by the Fulcrum. Stop interrupting." Damaya blushes and obeys.

"Superb control," Schaffa continues, "which Misalem promptly used to kill every living soul in several towns and cities, and even a few commless warrens. Thousands of people, in all."

Damaya inhales, horrified. It has never occurred to her that roggas—she stops herself. She. *She* is a rogga. All at once she does not like this word, which she has heard most of her life. It's a bad word she's not supposed to say, even though the grown-ups toss it around freely, and suddenly it seems uglier than it already did.

Orogenes, then. It is terrible to know that orogenes can kill so many, so easily. But then, she supposes that is why people hate them.

Her. That is why people hate *her.*

"Why did he do that?" she asks, forgetting that she should not interrupt.

"Why, indeed? Perhaps he was a bit mad." Schaffa leans down so that she can see his face, crossing his eyes and waggling his eyebrows. This is so hilarious and unexpected that Damaya giggles, and Schaffa gives her a conspiratorial smile. "Or perhaps Misalem was simply evil. Regardless, as he approached Yumenes he sent word ahead, threatening to shatter the entire city if its people did not send the Emperor out to meet him, and die.

The people were saddened when the Emperor announced that he would meet Misalem's terms—but they were relieved, too, because what else could they do? They had no idea how to fight an orogene with such power." He sighs. "But when the Emperor arrived, he was not alone: with him was a single woman. His bodyguard, Shemshena."

Damaya squirms a little, in excitement. "She must have been really good, if she was the Emperor's bodyguard."

"Oh, she was—a renowned fighter of the finest Sanzed lineages. Moreover, she was an Innovator in use-caste, and thus she had studied orogenes and understood something of how their power worked. So before Misalem's arrival, she had every citizen of Yumenes leave town. With them they took all the livestock, all the crops. They even cut down the trees and shrubs and burned them, burned their houses, then doused the fires to leave only cold wet ash. That is the nature of your power, you see: kinetic transferrence, sesunal catalysis. One does not move a mountain by will alone."

"What is—"

"No, no." Schaffa cuts her off gently. "There are many things I must teach you, little one, but that part you will learn at the Fulcrum. Let me finish." Reluctantly, Damaya subsides.

"I will say this much. Some of the strength you need, when you finally learn how to use your power properly, will come from within you." Schaffa touches the back of her head as he did that time in the barn, two fingers just above the line of her hair, and she jumps a little because there is a sort of spark when he does this, like static. "Most of it, however, must come from elsewhere. If the earth is already moving, or if the fire under the earth is at or near the surface, you may use that strength. You are *meant* to use that strength. When Father Earth stirs, he unleashes so much raw power that taking some of it does no harm to you or anyone else."

"The air doesn't turn cold?" Damaya tries, really tries, to restrain her curiosity, but the story is too good. And the idea of using orogeny in a safe way, a way that will cause no harm, is too intriguing. "No one dies?"

She feels him nod. "Not when you use earth-power, no. But of course, Father Earth never moves when one wishes. When there is no earth-power nearby, an orogene can still make the earth move, but only by taking the necessary heat and force and motion from the things around her. Anything that moves or has warmth—campfires, water, the air, even rocks. And, of course, living things. Shemshena could not take away the ground or the air, but she most certainly could, and did, take away everything else. When she and the Emperor met Misalem at the obsidian gates of Yumenes, they were the only living things in the city, and there was nothing left of the city but its walls."

Damaya inhales in awe, trying to imagine Palela empty and denuded of every shrub and backyard goat, and failing. "And everybody just... went? Because she said?"

"Well, because the emperor said, but yes. Yumenes was much smaller in those days, but it was still a vast undertaking. Yet it was either that or allow a monster to make hostages of them." Schaffa shrugs. "Misalem claimed he had no desire to rule in the Emperor's stead, but who could believe that? A man willing to threaten a city to get what he wants will stop at nothing."

That makes sense. "And he didn't know what Shemshena had done until he got to Yumenes?"

"No, he didn't know. The burning was done by the time he arrived; the people had traveled away in a different direction. So as Misalem faced the Emperor and Shemshena, he reached for the power to destroy the city—and found almost nothing. No power, no city to destroy. In that moment, while Misalem floundered and tried to use what little warmth he could drag from the soil and air, Shemshena flung a glassknife over and into the torus of his power. It didn't kill him, but it distracted him enough to break his orogeny, and Shemshena took care of the rest with her other knife. Thus was ended the Old Sanze Empire's—pardon; *the Sanzed Equatorial Affiliation's*—greatest threat."

Damaya shivers in delight. She has not heard such a good story in a long time. And it's true? Even better. Shyly she grins up at Schaffa. "I liked that story." He's good at telling them, too. His voice is so deep and velvety. She could see all of it in her head as he talked.

"I thought you might. That was the origin of the Guardians, you know. As the Fulcrum is an order of orogenes, we are the order that *watches* the Fulcrum. For we know, as Shemshena did, that despite all your terrible power, you are not invincible. You can be beaten."

He pats Damaya's hands on the saddle-pommel, and she doesn't squirm anymore, no longer liking the story quite as much. While he told it, she imagined herself as Shemshena, bravely facing a terrible foe and defeating him with cleverness and skill. With every *you* and *your* that Schaffa speaks, however, she begins to understand: He does not see her as a potential Shemshena.

"And so we Guardians train," he continues, perhaps not noticing that she has gone still. They are deep into the shatterland now; sheer, jagged rock faces, as high as the buildings in Brevard, frame the road on both sides for as far as the eye can see. Whoever built the road must have carved it, somehow, out of the earth itself. "We train," he says again, "as Shemshena did. We learn how orogenic power works, and we find ways to use this knowledge against you. We watch for those among your kind who might become the next Misalems, and we eliminate them. The rest we take care of." He leans over to smile at her again, but Damaya does not smile back this time. "I am your Guardian now, and it is my duty to make certain you remain helpful, never harmful."

When he straightens and falls silent, Damaya does not prompt him to tell another story, as she might have done. She doesn't like the one he just told, not anymore. And she is somehow, suddenly certain: He did not *intend* for her to like it.

The silence lingers as the shatterlands finally begin to subside, then become rolling green hillside. There's nothing out here: no farms, no pastures, no forests, no towns. There are hints that people once lived here: She sees a crumbling, moss-overgrown hump of something in the distance that might have been a fallen-over silo, if silos were the size of mountains. And other structures, too regular and jagged to be natural, too decayed and strange for her to recognize. Ruins, she realizes, of some city that must have died many, many Seasons ago, for there to be so little of it left now. And beyond the ruins, hazy against the cloud-drifted horizon, an obelisk the color of a thundercloud flickers as it slowly turns.

Sanze is the only nation that has ever survived a Fifth Season intact—not just once, but seven times. She learned this in creche. Seven ages in which the earth has broken somewhere and spewed ash or deadly gas into the sky, resulting in a lightless winter that lasted years or decades instead of months. Individual comms have often survived Seasons, if they were prepared. If they were lucky. Damaya knows the stonelore, which is taught to every child even in a little backwater like Palela. *First guard the gates.* Keep storecaches clean and dry. Obey the lore, make the hard choices, and maybe when the Season ends there will be people who remember how civilization should work.

But only once in known history has a whole nation, *many* comms all working together, survived. Thrived, even, over and over again, growing stronger and larger with each cataclysm. Because the people of Sanze are stronger and smarter than everyone else.

Gazing at that distant, winking obelisk, Damaya thinks, *Smarter even than the people who built that?*

They must be. Sanze is still here, and the obelisk is just another deadciv leftover.

"You're quiet now," says Schaffa after a while, patting her hands on the pommel to bring her out of her reverie. His hand is more than twice the size of hers, warm and comforting in its hugeness. "Still thinking about the story?"

She has been trying not to, but of course, she has. "A little."

"You don't like that Misalem is the villain of the tale. That you are like Misalem: a potential threat, without a Shemshena to control you." He says this matter-of-factly, not as a question.

Damaya squirms. How does he always seem to know what she's thinking? "I don't want to be a threat," she says in a small voice. Then, greatly daring, she adds, "But I don't want to be... controlled...either. I want to be—" She gropes for the words, then remembers something her brother once told her about what it meant to grow up. "*Responsible*. For myself."

"An admirable wish," Schaffa says. "But the plain fact of the matter, Damaya, is that you *cannot* control yourself. It isn't your nature. You are lightning, dangerous unless captured in wires. You're fire—a warm light on a cold dark night to be sure, but also a conflagration that can destroy everything in its path—"

"I won't destroy anybody! I'm not bad like that!" Suddenly it's too much. Damaya tries to turn to look at him, though this overbalances her and makes her slip on the saddle. Schaffa immediately pushes her back to face forward, with a firm gesture that says without words, *sit properly*. Damaya does so, gripping the pommel harder in her frustration. And then, because she is tired and angry and her butt hurts from three days on horseback, and because her whole life has gone *wrong* and it hits her all at once that she will never again be normal, she says more than she means to. "And anyway, I don't need you to control me. I can control myself!"

Schaffa reins the horse to a snorting halt.

Damaya tenses in dread. She's smarted off to him. Her mother always whopped her in the head when she did that back home. Will Schaffa whop her now? But Schaffa sounds as pleasant as usual as he says, "Can you really?"

"What?"

"Control yourself. It's an important question. The *most* important, really. Can you?"

In a small voice, Damaya says, "I . . . I don't . . ."

Schaffa puts a hand on hers, where they rest atop the saddle-pommel. Thinking that he means to swing down from the saddle, she starts to let go so he can get a grip. He squeezes her right hand to hold it in place, though he lets the left one go. "How did they discover you?"

She knows, without having to ask, what he means. "In creche," she says in a small voice. "At lunch. I was . . . A boy pushed me."

"Did it hurt? Were you afraid, or angry?"

She tries to remember. It feels so long ago, that day in the yard. "Angry." But that had not been all, had it? Zab was bigger than her. He was always *after* her. And it had hurt, just a little, when he'd pushed her. "Afraid."

"Yes. It is a thing of instinct, orogeny, born of the need to survive mortal threat. That's the danger. Fear of a bully, fear of a volcano; the power within you does not distinguish. It does not recognize *degree*."

As Schaffa speaks, his hand on hers has grown heavier, tighter.

"Your power acts to protect you in the same way no matter how powerful, or minor, the perceived threat. You should know, Damaya, how lucky you are: It's common for an orogene to discover themselves by killing a family member or friend. The people we love are the ones who hurt us the most, after all."

He's upset, she thinks at first. Maybe he's thinking of something terrible—whatever it is that makes him thrash and groan in the night. Did someone kill a family member or best friend of his? Is that why his hand presses down on hers so hard? "Sch-Schaffa," she says, suddenly afraid. She does not know why.

"Shhh," he says, and adjusts his fingers, aligning them carefully with her own. Then he bears down harder, so that the weight of his hand presses on the bones of her palm. He does this deliberately.

"Schaffa!" It hurts. He *knows* it hurts. But he does not stop.

"Now, now—calm down, little one. There, there." When Damaya whimpers and tries to pull away—it *hurts,* the steady grind of his hand, the unyielding cold metal of the pommel, her own bones where they crush her flesh—Schaffa sighs and folds his free arm around her waist. "Be still, and be brave. I'm going to break your hand now."

"Wha—"

Schaffa does something that causes his thighs to tighten with effort and his chest to bump her forward, but she barely notices these things. All her awareness has focused on her hand, and his hand, and the horrid wet *pop* and jostle of things that have never moved before, the pain of which is sharp and immediate and so powerful that she *screams.* She scrabbles at his hand with her free one, desperate and thoughtless, clawing. He yanks her free hand away and presses it against her thigh so that she claws only at herself.

And through the pain, she becomes suddenly aware of the cold, reassuring peace of the stone beneath the horse's feet.

The pressure eases. Schaffa lifts her broken hand, adjusting his grip so that she can see the damage. She keeps screaming, mostly from the sheer horror of seeing *her hand* bent in a way it should not be, the skin tenting and purpled in three places like another set of knuckles, the fingers already stiffening in spasm.

The stone beckons. Deep within it there is warmth and power that can make her forget pain. She almost reaches for that promise of relief. And then she hesitates.

Can you control yourself?

"You could kill me," Schaffa says into her ear, and despite everything she falls silent to hear him. "Reach for the fire within the earth, or suck the strength from everything around you. I sit within your torus." This has no meaning for her. "This is a bad place for orogeny, given that you have no training—one mistake and you'll shift the fault beneath us, and trigger quite the shake. That might kill you, too. But if you manage to survive, you'll be free. Find some comm somewhere and beg your way in, or join a pack of commless and get along as best you can. You can hide what you are, if you're clever. For a while. It never lasts, and it will be an illusion, but for a time you can feel normal. I know you want that more than anything."

Damaya barely hears it. The pain throbs throughout her hand, her arm, her teeth, obliterating any fine sensation. When he stops speaking she makes a sound and tries again to pull away. His fingers tighten warningly, and she stills at once.

"Very good," he says. "You've controlled yourself through pain. Most young orogenes can't do that without training. Now comes the real test." He adjusts his grip, big hand enveloping her smaller one. Damaya cringes, but this is gentle. For now. "Your hand is broken in at least three places, I would guess. If it's splinted, and if you take care, it can probably heal with no permanent damage. If I crush it, however—"

She cannot breathe. The fear has filled her lungs. She lets out the last of the air in her throat and manages to shape it round a word. "No!"

"*Never say no to me,*" he says. The words are hot against her skin. He has bent to murmur them into her ear. "Orogenes have no right to say no. I am your Guardian. I will break every bone in your hand, every bone in your *body*, if I deem it necessary to make the world safe from you."

He wouldn't crush her hand. Why? He wouldn't. While she trembles in silence, Schaffa brushes his thumb over the swollen knots that have begun to form on the back of her hand. There is something *contemplative* about this gesture, something *curious*. Damaya can't watch. She closes her eyes, feeling tears run freely from her lashes. She's queasy, cold. The sound of her own blood pounds in her ears.

"Wh-why?" Her voice is hitchy. It takes effort to draw breath. It seems impossible that this is happening, on a road in the middle of nowhere, on a sunny, quiet afternoon. She doesn't understand. Her family has shown her that love is a lie. It isn't stone-solid; instead it bends and crumbles away, weak as rusty metal. But she had thought that Schaffa *liked* her.

Schaffa keeps stroking her broken hand. "I love you," he says.

She flinches, and he soothes her with a soft shush in her ear, while his thumb keeps stroking the hand he's broken. "Never doubt that I do, little one. Poor creature locked in a barn, so afraid of herself that she hardly dares speak. And yet there is the fire of wit in you along with the fire of the earth, and I cannot help but admire both, however evil the latter might be." He shakes his head and sighs. "I hate doing this to you. I hate that it's necessary. But please understand: I have hurt you so that you will hurt no one else."

Her hand *hurts*. Her heart pounds and the pain throbs with it, BURN burn, BURN burn, BURN burn. It would feel so good to cool that pain, whispers the stone beneath her. That would mean killing Schaffa, however—the last person in the world who loves her.

Schaffa nods, as if to himself. "You need to know that I will never lie to you, Damaya. Look under your arm."

It takes an effort of ages for Damaya to open her eyes, and to then move her other arm aside. As she does, however, she sees that his free hand holds a long, beveled, black glass poniard. The sharp tip rests on the fabric of her shirt, just beneath her ribs. Aimed at her heart.

"It's one thing to resist a reflex. Another altogether to resist the conscious, deliberate desire to kill another person, for self-defense or any other reason." As if to suggest this desire, Schaffa taps the glassknife against her side. The tip is sharp enough to sting even through her clothing. "But it seems you can, as you said, control yourself."

And with that Schaffa pulls the knife from her side, twirls it expertly along his fingers, and slides it into his belt sheath without looking. Then he takes her broken hand in both of his. "Brace yourself."

She can't, because she doesn't understand what he means to do. The dichotomy between his gentle words and cruel actions has confused her too much. Then she screams again as Schaffa begins to methodically set each of her hand bones. This takes only seconds. It feels like much more.

When she flops against him, dazed and shaking and weak, Schaffa urges the horse forward again, this time at a brisk trot. Damaya is past pain now, barely noticing as Schaffa keeps her injured hand in his own, this time tucking it against her body to minimize accidental jostling. She does not wonder at this. She thinks of nothing, does nothing, says nothing. There is nothing left in her to say.

The green hills fall behind them, and the land grows flat again. She pays no attention, watching the sky and that distant smoky gray obelisk, which never seems to shift position even as the miles pass. Around it, the sky grows bluer and begins to darken into black, until even the obelisk becomes nothing more than a darker smudge against the emerging stars. At last, as the sun's light fades from the evening, Schaffa reins the horse just off the road and dismounts to make camp. He lifts Damaya off the horse and down, and she stands where he put her while he clears the ground and kicks small rocks into a circle to make a fire. There's no wood out here, but he pulls from his bags several chunks of something and uses them to start a fire. Coal, to judge by the stink, or dried peat. She doesn't really pay attention. She just stands there while he removes the saddle from the horse and tends the animal, and while he lays out the bedroll and puts a little pot into the flames. The aroma of cooking food soon rises over the fire's oily stink.

"I want to go home," Damaya blurts. She's still holding her hand against her chest.

Schaffa pauses in his dinner-making, then looks up at her. In the flickering light of the fire his icewhite eyes seem to dance. "You no longer have a home, Damaya. But you will, soon, in

Yumenes. You'll have teachers there, and friends. A whole new life." He smiles.

Her hand has mostly gone numb since he set the bones, but there is a lingering dull throb. She closes her eyes, wishing it would go away. All of it. The pain. Her hand. The world. The smell of something savory wafts past, but she has no appetite for it. "I don't want a new life."

Silence greets her for a moment, then Schaffa sighs and rises, coming over. She twitches back from him, but he kneels before her and puts his hands on her shoulders.

"Do you fear me?" he asks.

For a moment the desire to lie rises within her. It will not please him, she thinks, for her to speak the truth. But she hurts too much, and she is too numb right now, for fear or duplicity or the desire to please. So she speaks the truth: "Yes."

"Good. You should. I'm not sorry for the pain I've caused you, little one, because you needed to learn the lesson of that pain. What do you understand about me now?"

She shakes her head. Then she makes herself answer, because of course that is the point. "I have to do what you say or you'll hurt me."

"And?"

She closes her eyes tighter. In dreams, that makes the bad creatures go away.

"And," she adds, "you'll hurt me even when I do obey. If you think you should."

"Yes." She can actually hear his smile. He nudges a stray braid away from her cheek, letting the backs of his fingers brush her skin. "What I do is not random, Damaya. It's about control.

Give me no reason to doubt yours, and I will never hurt you again. Do you understand?"

She does not *want* to hear the words, but she does hear them, in spite of herself. And in spite of herself, some part of her relaxes just a little. She doesn't respond, though, so he says, "Look at me."

Damaya opens her eyes. Against the firelight, his head is a dark silhouette framed by darker hair. She turns away.

He takes hold of her face and pulls it back, firmly. "Do you understand?"

Of course it is a warning.

"I understand," she says.

Satisfied, he lets go of her. Then he pulls her over to the fire and gestures for her to sit on a rock he has rolled over, which she does. When he gives her a small metal dish full of lentil soup, she eats—awkwardly, since she isn't left-handed. She drinks from the canteen he hands her. It's difficult when she needs to pee; she stumbles over the uneven ground in the dark away from the fire, which makes her hand throb, but she manages. Since there's only one bedroll, she lies down beside him when he pats that spot. When he tells her to sleep, she closes her eyes again—but she does not fall asleep for a long while.

When she does, however, her dreams are full of jolting pain and heaving earth and a great hole of white light that tries to swallow her, and it seems only a moment later that Schaffa shakes her awake. It's still the middle of the night, though the stars have shifted. She does not remember, at first, that he has broken her hand; in that moment, she smiles at him without thinking. He blinks, then smiles back in genuine pleasure.

"You were making a noise," he says.

She licks her lips, not smiling anymore, because she has remembered, and because she doesn't want to tell him how much the nightmare frightened her. Or the waking.

"Was I snoring?" she asks. "My brother says I do that a lot."

He regards her for a moment in silence, his smile fading. She is beginning to dislike his little silences. That they are not simply pauses in the conversation or moments in which he gathers his thoughts; they are tests, though she isn't sure of what. He is always testing her.

"Snoring," he says at last. "Yes. Don't worry, though. I won't tease you about it like your brother did." And Schaffa smiles, as if this is supposed to be funny. The brother she no longer has. The nightmares that have consumed her life.

But he is the only person left whom she can love, so she nods and closes her eyes again, and relaxes beside him. "Good night, Schaffa."

"Good night, little one. May your dreams be ever still."

* * *

BOILING SEASON: 1842–1845 Imperial. A hot spot beneath Lake Tekkaris erupted, aerosolizing sufficient steam and particulate matter to trigger acidic rain and sky occlusion over the Somidlats, the Antarctics, and the eastern Coastal comms. The Equatorials and northern latitudes suffered no harm, however, thanks to prevailing winds and ocean currents, so historians dispute whether this qualifies as a "true" Season.

—*The Seasons of Sanze, textbook for year 12 creche*

7

you plus one is two

In the morning you rise and move on, and the boy comes with you. The two of you trudge south through hill country and falling ash.

The child is an immediate problem. He's filthy, for one. You couldn't see this the night before in the dark, but he's absolutely covered in dried and drying mud, stuck-on twigs, and Earth knows what else. Caught in a mudslide, probably; those happen a lot during shakes. If so, he's lucky to be alive—but still when he wakes up and stretches, you grimace at the smears and flakes of dirt he's left on your bedroll. It takes you twenty minutes to realize he's naked under all the mess.

When you question him about this—and everything else—he's cagey. He shouldn't be old enough to be effectively cagey, but he is. He doesn't know the name of the comm he's from or the people who birthed him, who apparently are "not very many" in number. He says he doesn't have any parents. He doesn't know his use name—which, you are certain, is a blatant lie. Even if his mother didn't know his father, he would've inherited her use-caste. He's young, and maybe orphaned, but not too young to know his place in the world. Children far younger than this boy understand things like that. Uche was only three and he knew that he was an Innovator like his father, and that this was why all his toys were tools and books and items that could be used for building things. And he knew, too, that there were things he could not discuss with anyone except his mother, and even then only when they were alone. Things about Father Earth and his whispers, *way-down-below things* as Uche had called them—

But you're not ready to think about that.

Instead you ponder the mystery of Hoa, because there's so very much to ponder. He's a squat little thing, you notice when he stands up; barely four feet tall. He acts maybe ten years old, so he's either small for his age or has a manner too old for his body. You think it's the latter, though you're not sure why you think this. You can't tell much else about him, except that he's probably lighter-skinned; the patches where he's shed mud are gray-dirty, not brown-dirty. So maybe he's from somewhere near the Antarctics, or the western continental coast, where people are pale.

And now he's here, thousands of miles away in the north-eastern Somidlats, alone and naked. Okay.

Well, maybe something happened to his family. Maybe they were comm-changers. Lots of people do that, pick up roots and spend months or years traveling cross-continent to beg their way into a comm where they'll stick out like pale flowers in a dun meadow...

Maybe.

Right.

Anyway.

Hoa also has icewhite eyes. Real, actual icewhite. Scared you a bit when you woke up in the morning and he looked at you: all that dark mud surrounding two points of glaring silvery-blue. He doesn't look quite human, but then people with icewhite eyes rarely do. You've heard that in Yumenes, among the Breeder use-caste, icewhite eyes are—were—especially desirable. Sanzeds liked that icewhite eyes were intimidating, and a little creepy. They are. But the eyes aren't what makes Hoa creepy.

He's inordinately cheerful, for one. When you rose the morning after he joined you, he was already awake, and playing with your tinderbox. There was nothing in the meadow with which to make a fire—only the meadowgrass, which would've burned up in seconds even if you could have found enough dry, and probably touched off a grassfire in the process—so you hadn't taken the box out of your pack the night before. But he had it, humming idly to himself as he twirled the flint in his fingers, and that meant he'd been digging in your pack. It didn't put you in the best of moods for the day. The image stuck in your mind, though, as you packed up: a child who'd obviously been through some disaster, sitting naked in the middle of a meadow, surrounded by falling ash—and yet, playing. Humming, even. And when he saw you awake and looking, he smiled.

This is why you've decided to keep him with you, even though you think he's lying about not knowing where he comes from. Because. Well. He *is* a child.

So when you've got your pack on, you look at him, and he

looks back at you. He's clutching to his chest that bundle you glimpsed the night before—a wad of rags tied around something, is all you can tell. It rattles a little when he squeezes it. You can tell that he's anxious; those eyes of his can't hide anything. His pupils are huge. He fidgets a little, shifting onto one foot and using the other to scratch the back of his calf.

"Come on," you say, and turn away to head back to the Imperial Road. You try not to notice his soft exhalation, and the way he trots to catch up to you after a moment.

When you step onto the road again, there are a few people moving along it in knots and trickles, nearly all of them going south. Their feet stir up the ash, which is light and powdery for now. Big flakes: no need for masks yet, for those who remembered to pack one. A man walks beside a rickety cart and half-spavined horse; the cart is full of belongings and old people, though the walking man is hardly younger. All of them stare at you as you step from behind the hill. A group of six women who have clearly banded together for safety whisper among themselves at the sight of you—and then one of them says loudly to another, "Rusting Earth, *look* at her, no!" Apparently you look dangerous. Or undesirable. Or both.

Or maybe it's Hoa's appearance that puts them off, so you turn to the boy. He stops when you do, looking worried again, and you feel abruptly ashamed for letting him walk around like this, even if you didn't ask to have some strange child tagging along.

You look around. There's a creek on the other side of the road. No telling how long before you reach another roadhouse; they're supposed to be stationed every twenty-five miles on an

Imperial Road, but the shake from the north might have damaged the next one. There are more trees around now—you're leaving the plains—but not enough to provide any real cover, and many of the trees are broken, anyway, after the shake from the north. The ashfall helps, a little; you can't see more than a mile off. What you can see, though, is that the plainsland around the road is beginning to give way to rougher territory. You know from maps and talk that below the Tirimas mountains there's an ancient, probably-sealed minor fault, a strip of young forest that's grown up since the last Season, and then in perhaps a hundred miles the plains become salt flats. Beyond that is desert, where comms become few and far between, and where they tend to be even more heavily defended than comms in more hospitable parts.

(Jija can't be going as far as the desert. That would be foolish; who would take him in there?)

There will be comms along the road between here and the salt plains, you're certain. If you can get the boy decent-looking, one of them will probably take him in.

"Come with me," you say to the boy, and veer off the road. He follows you down the gravel bed; you notice how sharp some of the rocks are and add good boots to the list of things you need to get for him. He doesn't cut his feet, thankfully—though he does slip on the gravel at one point, badly enough that he falls and rolls down the slope. You hurry over when he stops rolling, but he's already sitting up and looking disgruntled, because he's landed square in the mud at the edge of the creek. "Here," you say, offering him a hand up.

He looks at the hand, and for a moment you're surprised to

see something like unease on his face. "I'm okay," he says then, ignoring your hand and pushing himself to his feet. The mud squelches as he does it. Then he brushes past you to collect the rag bundle, which he lost hold of during the fall.

Fine, then. Ungrateful little brat.

"You want me to wash," he says, a question.

"How'd you guess?"

He doesn't seem to notice the sarcasm. Setting his bundle down on the gravel bank, he walks forward into the water until it rises to about his waist, then he squats to try to scrub himself. You remember and rummage in your pack until you find the slab of soap. He turns at your whistle and you toss it to him. You flinch when he misses the catch entirely, but he immediately dives under and resurfaces with it in his hands. Then you laugh, because he's staring at the soap like he's never seen such a thing.

"Rub it on your skin?" You pantomime doing it: sarcasm again. But he straightens and smiles a little as if that actually clarified something for him, and then he obeys.

"Do your hair, too," you say, rummaging in the pack again and shifting so you can keep an eye on the road. Some of the people passing by up there glance down at you, curiosity or disapproval in their gaze, but most don't bother looking. You like it that way.

Your other shirt is what you were looking for. It'll be like a dress on the boy, so you cut a short length off the spool of twine in your pack, which he can use to belt the shirt below his hips for modesty and to retain a little warmth around his torso. It won't do in the long term, of course. Lorists say that it doesn't take long for things to turn cold when a Season begins. You'll have to see if the next town you pass is willing to sell you clothes and additional supplies, if they haven't already implemented Seasonal Law.

Then the boy comes out of the water, and you stare.

Well. That's different.

Free of mud, his hair is ashblow-coarse, that perfect weatherproof texture the Sanzed value so much, already beginning to stiffen and pouf up as it dries. It will be long enough to keep his back warm, at least. But it is *white,* not the normal gray. And his skin is white, not just pale; not even Antarctic people are ever quite that colorless, not that you've seen. His eyebrows are white, above his icewhite eyes. White white white. He almost disappears amid the falling ash as he walks.

Albino? Maybe. There's also something off about his face. You wonder what you're seeing, and then you realize: There's nothing *Sanzed* about him, except the texture of his hair. There's a broadness to his cheekbones, an angularity to his jaw and eyes, that seems wholly alien to your eyes. His mouth is full-lipped but narrow, so much so that you think he might have trouble eating, though obviously that's not true or he wouldn't have survived to this age. His short stature is part of it, too. He's not just small but stocky, as if his people are built for a different kind of sturdiness than the ideal that Old Sanze has spent millennia cultivating. Maybe his race are all this white, then, whoever they are.

But none of this makes sense. Every race in the world these days is part Sanzed. They did rule the Stillness for centuries, after all, and they continue to do so in many ways. And they weren't always peaceful about it, so even the most insular races bear the Sanzed stamp whether their ancestors wanted the admixture or not. Everyone is measured by their standard deviations from the Sanzed mean. This boy's people, whoever they are, have clearly managed to remain outliers.

"What in fire-under-Earth are you?" you say, before it occurs to you that this might hurt his feelings. A few days of horror and you forget everything about taking care of children.

But the boy only looks surprised—and then he grins. "Fire-under-Earth? You're weird. Am I clean enough?"

You're so thrown by him calling *you* weird that only much later do you realize he avoided the question.

You shake your head to yourself, then hold out a hand for the soap, which he gives to you. "Yes. Here." And you hold up the shirt for him to slip his arms and head into. He does this a bit clumsily, as if he's not used to being dressed by someone else. Still, it's easier than getting Uche dressed; at least this boy doesn't wiggle—

You stop.

You go away for a bit.

When you return to yourself, the sky is brighter and Hoa has stretched out on the nearby low grass. At least an hour has passed. Maybe more.

You lick your lips and focus on him uncomfortably, waiting for him to say something about your . . . absence. He just perks up once he sees you're back, gets to his feet, and waits.

Okay, then. You and he might get along, after all.

After that you get back on the road. The boy walks well despite having no shoes; you watch him closely for signs of limping or weariness, and you stop more frequently than you would have on your own. He seems grateful for the chance to rest, but aside from that, he does all right. A real little trouper.

"You can't stay with me," you say, though, during one of your rest breaks. Might as well not let him get his hopes up. "I'll try to find you a comm; we'll be stopping at several along the way, if they'll open the gates to trade. But I have to move on, even if I find you a place. I'm looking for someone."

"Your daughter," the boy says, and you stiffen. A moment passes. The boy ignores your shock, humming and petting his little bundle of rags like it's a pet.

"How did you know that?" you whisper.

"She's very strong. I'm not sure it's her, of course." The boy looks back at you and smiles, oblivious to your stare. "There's a bunch of you in that direction. That always makes it hard."

There are a lot of things that probably should be in your mind right now. You only muster the wherewithal to speak one of them aloud. "*You know where my daughter is.*"

He hums again, noncommitally. You're sure he knows just how insane this all sounds. You're sure he's laughing, somewhere behind that innocent mask of a face.

"How?"

He shrugs. "I just know."

"*How?*" He's not an orogene. You'd know your own. Even if he was, orogenes can't *track each other like dogs*, homing in from a distance as if orogeny has a smell. Only Guardians can do anything like that, and then only if the rogga is ignorant or stupid enough to let them.

He looks up, and you try not to flinch. "I just *know*, all right?

It's something I can do." He looks away. "It's something I've always been able to do."

You wonder. But. Nassun.

You're willing to buy a lot of cockamamie things if any of them can help you find her.

"Okay," you say. Slowly, because this is crazy. *You're* crazy, but now you're aware that the boy probably is, too, and that means you need to be careful. But on the thin chance that he's *not* crazy, or that his crazy actually works the way he says it does...

"How...how far is she?"

"Many days' walking. She's going faster than you."

Because Jija took the cart and horse. "Nassun's still alive." You have to pause after this. Too much to feel, too much to contain. Rask told you Jija left Tirimo with her then, but you've been afraid to let yourself think of her as alive *now*. Even though a part of you doesn't want to believe that Jija could kill his own daughter, the rest of you not only believes it but *anticipates* it to some degree. An old habit, bracing yourself for pain to come.

The boy nods, watching you; his little face is oddly solemn now. There's really not much that's childlike about this child, you notice absently, belatedly.

But if he can find your daughter, he can be the Evil Earth incarnate and you won't give a damn.

So you rummage in the pack and find your canteen, the one with the good water; you refilled the other at the creek but need to boil it first. After you take a swig yourself, however, you hand it to him. When he's finished drinking, you give him a handful of raisins. He shakes his head and hands them back. "I'm not hungry."

"You haven't eaten."

"I don't eat much." He picks up his bundle. Maybe he's got supplies in there. Doesn't matter. You don't really care, anyway. He's not your kid. He just knows where your kid is.

You break camp and resume the journey south, this time with the boy walking beside you, subtly leading the way.

* * *

Listen, listen, listen well.

There was an age before the Seasons, when life and Earth, its father, thrived alike. (Life had a mother, too. Something terrible happened to Her.) Earth our father knew He would need clever life, so He used the Seasons to shape us out of animals: clever hands for making things and clever minds for solving problems and clever tongues for working together and clever sessapinae to warn us of danger. The people became what Father Earth needed, and then more than He needed. Then we turned on Him, and He has burned with hatred for us ever since.

Remember, remember, what I tell.

—*Lorist recitation, "The Making of the Three Peoples," part one*

8

Syenite on the highroad

It eventually becomes necessary for Syenite to ask her new mentor's name. Alabaster, he tells her—which she assumes someone gave him ironically. She needs to use his name fairly often because he keeps falling asleep in his saddle during the long days of riding, which leaves her to do all the work of paying attention to their route and watching out for potential hazards, as well as keeping herself entertained. He wakes readily when she speaks his name, which at first leads her to believe he's just faking it in order to avoid talking to her. When she says this, he looks annoyed and says, "Of course I'm really asleep. If you want anything useful out of me tonight, you'll *let* me sleep."

Which pisses her off, because it's not like *he's* the one who's got to have a baby for empire and Earth. It's also not like the sex takes any great effort on his part, brief and boring as it is.

But perhaps a week into their trip, she finally notices what he's doing during their daily rides and even at night, while they're lying tired and sticky in the sleeping bag they share. She can be forgiven for missing it, she thinks, because it's a constant thing, like a low murmur in a room full of chattering people—but he's quelling all the shakes in the area. *All* of them, not just the ones people can feel. All the tiny, infinitesimal flexes and adjustments of the earth, some of which are building momentum to greater movement and some of which are essentially random: Wherever she and Alabaster pass, those movements go still for a time. Seismic stillness is common in Yumenes, but should not exist out here in the hinterlands where node network coverage is thin.

Once Syenite figures this out, she is…confused. Because there's no point to quelling microshakes, and indeed, doing so might make things worse the next time a larger shake occurs. They were very careful to teach her this, back when she was a grit learning basic geomestry and seismology: The earth does not like to be restrained. Redirection, not cessation, is the orogene's goal.

She ponders this mystery for several days as they pass along the Yumenes–Allia Highroad, beneath a turning obelisk that glints like a mountain-sized tourmaline whenever it's solid enough to catch the sunlight. The highroad is the fastest route between the two quartent capitals, built as straight as possible in ways that only Old Sanze would dare: elevated along lengthy stone bridges and crossing vast canyons, and occasionally even tunneling through mountains too high to climb. This means the trip to the coast will take only a few weeks if they take it easy—half what it would take via lowroad travel.

But rusted reeking Earth, highroads are dull. Most people think they're deathtraps waiting to be sprung, despite the fact that they're usually safer than ordinary roads; all Imperial Roads were built by teams of the best geoneers and orogenes, deliberately placed only in locations deemed permanently stable. Some of them have survived multiple Seasons. So for days at a time Syenite and Alabaster encounter only hard-driving merchant caravanners, mailpost-riders, and the local quartent patrol—all of whom give Syenite and Alabaster the eye upon noticing their black Fulcrum uniforms, and do not deign to speak to them. There are few comms lining the route's turnoffs, and almost no shops at which to buy supplies, although there are regular platforms along the road itself with prepared areas and lean-tos for camping. Syen has spent every evening swatting bugs beside a fire, with nothing to do but glare at Alabaster. And have sex with him, but that only kills a few minutes.

This, though, is interesting. "What are you doing that for?" Syenite finally asks, three days after she first noticed him quelling microshakes. He's just done it again now, while they wait for dinner—cachebread heated with slabs of beef and soaked prunes, yum yum. He yawned as he did it, though of course it must have taken some effort. Orogeny always costs something.

"Doing what?" he asks as he shuts down a subsurface aftershock and pokes at the fire in apparent boredom. She wants to hit him.

"*That.*"

His eyebrows rise. "Ah. You *can* feel it."

"Of course I can feel it! You're doing it all the time!"

"Well, you didn't say anything before now."

"*Because I was trying to figure out what you were doing.*"

He looks perplexed. "Then maybe you should've asked."

She's going to kill him. Something of this must translate through the silence, because he grimaces and finally explains.

"I'm giving the node maintainers a break. Every microshake I settle eases the burden on them."

Syen knows of the node maintainers, of course. As the Imperial Roads link the former vassals of the old empire with Yumenes, so do the nodes connect far-flung quartents with the Fulcrum, to extend its protections as far as possible. All over the continent—at whatever points the senior orogenes have determined is best for manipulating nearby faults or hot spots—there is an outpost. Within that outpost is stationed a Fulcrum-trained orogene whose sole task is to keep the local area stable. In the Equatorials, the nodes' zones of protection overlap, so there's nary a twitch; this, and the Fulcrum's presence at its core, is why Yumenes can build as it does. Beyond the Equatorials, though, the zones are spaced to provide the greatest protection for the largest populations, and there are gaps in the net. It's just not worthwhile—at least, not according to the Fulcrum seniors—to put nodes near every little farming or mining comm in the hinterlands. People in those places fend for themselves as best they can.

Syen doesn't know any of the poor fools assigned to such tedious duty, but she's very, very glad no one has ever suggested it for her. It's the sort of thing they give to orogenes who'll never make it to fourth ring—the ones who have lots of raw power and little control. At least they can save lives, even if they're doomed to spend their own lives in relative isolation and obscurity.

"Maybe you should leave the micros to the node maintainers," Syenite suggests. The food is warm enough; she uses a stick to push it out of the fire. In spite of herself, her mouth is watering. It's been a long day. "Earth knows they probably need *something* to keep them from dying of boredom."

She's intent on the food at first, and doesn't notice his silence until she offers him his portion. Then she frowns, because that look is on his face again. That hatred. And this time at least a little of it is directed at her.

"You've never been to a node, I take it."

What the rust? "No. Why would I possibly go to one?"

"Because you should. All roggas should."

Syenite flinches, just a little, at his *rogga*. The Fulcrum gives demerits to anyone who says it, so she doesn't hear it much—just the odd muttered epithet from people riding past them, or grits trying to sound tough when the instructors aren't around. It's such an ugly word, harsh and guttural; the sound of it is like a slap to the ear. But Alabaster uses it the way other people use *orogene*.

He continues, still in the same cold tone: "And if you can feel what I'm doing, then you can do it, too."

This startles Syen more, and angers her more. "Why in Earthfires would I quell microshakes? Then I'll be—" And then she stops herself, because she was about to say *as tired and useless as you,* and that's just rude. But then it occurs to her that he *has* been tired and useless, maybe *because* he's been doing this.

If it's important enough that he's been wearing himself out to do it, then maybe it's wrong of her to refuse out of hand. Orogenes have to look out for each other, after all. She sighs. "All right. I guess I can help some poor fool who's stuck in the back end of beyond with nothing to do but keep the land steady." At least it will pass the time.

He relaxes, just a little, and she's surprised to see him smile. He hardly ever does that. But no, that muscle in his jaw is still going *twitch twitch twitch.* He's still upset about something. "There's a node station about two days' ride from the next highroad turnoff."

Syen waits for this statement to conclude, but he starts eating, making a little sound of pleasure that has more to do with him being hungry than with the food being especially delicious. Since she's hungry, too, Syenite tucks in—and then she frowns. "Wait. Are you planning to *go* to this station? Is that what you're saying?"

"*We* are going, yes." Alabaster looks up at her, a quick flash of command in his expression, and all of a sudden she hates him more than ever.

It's completely irrational, her reaction to him. Alabaster outranks her by six rings and would probably outrank her by more if the ring rankings went past ten; she's heard the rumors about his skill. If they ever fought, he could turn her torus inside out and flash-freeze her in a second. For that alone she should be nice to him; for the potential value of his favor, and her own goals for advancement within the Fulcrum's ranks, she should even try to *like* him.

But she's tried being polite with him, and flattering, and it doesn't work. He just pretends to misunderstand or insults her until she stops. She's offered all the little gestures of respect that seniors at the Fulcrum usually seem to expect from juniors, but these just piss him off. Which makes *her* angry—and strangely, this state of affairs seems to please him most.

So although she would never do this with another senior, she snaps, "Yes, *sir*," and lets the rest of the evening pass in resentful, reverberating silence.

They go to bed and she reaches for him, as usual, but this time he rolls over, putting his back to her. "We'll do it in the morning, if we still have to. Isn't it time for you to menstruate by now?"

Which makes Syenite feel like the world's biggest boor. That he hates the sex as much as she does isn't in question. But it's horrible that he's been *waiting for a break* and she hasn't been counting. She does so now, clumsily because she can't remember the exact day the last one started, and—he's right. She's late.

At her surprised silence he sighs, already halfway to sleep. "Doesn't mean anything yet if you're late. Traveling's hard on the body." He yawns. "In the morning, then."

In the morning they copulate. There are no better words she can use for the act—vulgarities don't fit because it's too dull, and euphemisms aren't necessary to downplay its intimacy because it's not intimate. It's perfunctory, an exercise, like the stretches she's learned to do before they start riding for the day. More energetic this time because he's rested first; she almost enjoys it, and he actually makes some noise when he comes. But that's it. When they're done he lies there watching while she gets up and does a quick basin bath beside the fire. She's so used to this that she starts when he speaks. "Why do you hate me?"

Syenite pauses, and considers lying for a moment. If this were the Fulcrum, she would lie. If he were any other senior, obsessed with propriety and making sure that Fulcrum orogenes comport themselves well at all times, she would lie. He's made it clear, however, that he prefers honesty, however indelicate. So she sighs. "I just do."

He rolls onto his back, looking up at the sky, and she thinks that's the end of the conversation until he says, "I think you hate me because... I'm someone you *can* hate. I'm here, I'm handy. But what you really hate is the world."

At this Syen tosses her washcloth into the bowl of water she's been using and glares at him. "*The world* doesn't say inane things like that."

"I'm not interested in mentoring a sycophant. I want you to be yourself with me. And when you are, you can barely speak a civil word to me, no matter how civil I am to *you*."

Hearing it put that way, she feels a little guilty. "What do you mean, then, that I hate the world?"

"You hate the way we live. The way the world makes us live. Either the Fulcrum owns us, or we have to hide and be hunted down like dogs if we're ever discovered. Or we become monsters and try to kill everything. Even within the Fulcrum we always have to think about how *they* want us to act. We can never just... be." He sighs, closing his eyes. "There should be a better way."

"There isn't."

"There must be. Sanze can't be the first empire that's managed to survive a few Seasons. We can see the evidence of other ways of life, other people who became mighty." He gestures away from the highroad, toward the landscape that spreads all around them. They're near the Great Eastern Forest; nothing but a carpet of trees rising and falling for as far as the eye can see. Except—

—except, just at the edge of the horizon, she spots something that looks like a skeletal metal hand, clawing its way out of the trees. Another ruin, and it must be truly massive if she can see it from here.

"We pass down the stonelore," Alabaster says, sitting up, "but we never try to remember anything about what's already been tried, what else might have worked."

"Because it *didn't* work. Those people died. We're still alive. Our way is right, theirs was wrong."

He throws her a look she interprets as *I can't be bothered to tell you how stupid you are,* although he probably doesn't mean it that way. He's right; she just doesn't like him. "I realize you only have the education the Fulcrum gave you, but think, will you? Survival doesn't mean *rightness.* I could kill you right now, but that wouldn't make me a better person for doing so."

Maybe not, but it wouldn't matter to *her.* And she resents his casual assumption of her weakness, even though he's completely right. "All right." She gets up and starts dressing, pulling her clothes on with quick jerks. "Tell me what other way there is, then."

He doesn't say anything for a moment. She turns to look at him finally, and he's looking uneasy. "Well..." He edges into the statement. "We could try letting orogenes run things."

She almost laughs. "That would last for about ten minutes before every Guardian in the Stillness shows up to lynch us, with half the continent in tow to watch and cheer."

"They kill us because they've got stonelore telling them at every turn that we're born evil—some kind of agents of Father Earth, monsters that barely qualify as human."

"Yes, but you can't change stonelore."

"Stonelore changes all the time, Syenite." He doesn't say her name often, either. It gets her attention. "Every civilization adds to it; parts that don't matter to the people of the time are forgotten. There's a reason Tablet Two is so damaged: someone, somewhere back in time, decided that it wasn't important or was wrong, and didn't bother to take care of it. Or maybe they even deliberately tried to obliterate it, which is why so many of the early copies are damaged in exactly the same way. The archeomests found some old tablets in one of the dead cities on Tapita Plateau—they'd written down their stonelore, too, ostensibly to pass it on to future generations. But what was on the tablets was different, *drastically* so, from the lore we learned in school. For all we know, the admonition against changing the lore is itself a recent addition."

She didn't know that. It makes her frown. It also makes her not want to believe him, or maybe that's just her dislike for him surfacing again. But . . . stonelore is as old as intelligence. It's all that's allowed humankind to survive through Fifth Season after Fifth Season, as they huddle together while the world turns dark and cold. The lorists tell stories of what happens when people—political leaders or philosophers or well-meaning meddlers of whatever type—try to change the lore. Disaster inevitably results.

So she doesn't believe it. "Where'd you hear about tablets on Tapita?"

"I've been taking assignments outside the Fulcrum for twenty years. I have friends out here."

Friends who talk to an orogene? About historical heresy? It sounds ridiculous. But then again . . . well. "Okay, so how do you change the lore in a way that—"

She's not paying attention to the ambient strata, because the argument has engrossed her more than she wants to admit. He, however, is apparently still quelling shakes even as they speak. Plus he's a ten-ringer, so it's fitting that he abruptly inhales and jerks to his feet as if pulled by strings, turning toward the western horizon. Syen frowns and follows his gaze. The forest on that side of the highroad is patchy from logging and bifurcated by two lowroads branching away through the trees. There's another deadciv ruin, a dome that's more tumbled stone than intact, in the far distance, and she can see three or four small walled comms dotting the treescape between here and there. But she doesn't know what he's reacting to—

—and then she sesses it. Evil Earth, it's a big one! An eighter or niner. No, *bigger.* There's a hot spot about two hundred miles away, beneath the outskirts of a small city called Mehi...but that can't be right. Mehi is at the edge of the Equatorials, which means it's well within the protective network of nodes. Why—

It doesn't matter why. Not when Syen can *see* this shake making all the land around the highroad shiver and all the trees twitch. Something has gone wrong, the network has failed, and the hot spot beneath Mehi is welling toward the surface. The proto-shakes, even from here, are powerful enough to make her mouth taste of bitter old metal and the beds of her fingernails to itch. Even the most sess-numb stills can feel these, a steady barrage of wavelets rattling their dishes and making old people gasp and clutch their heads while babies suddenly cry. If nothing stops this upwelling, the stills will feel a lot more when a volcano erupts right under their feet.

"What—" Syenite starts to turn to Alabaster, and then she stops in shock, because he is on his hands and knees growling at the ground.

An instant later she feels it, a shock wave of raw orogeny rippling *out* and *down* through the pillars of the Highroad and *into* the loose schist of the local ground. It's not actual force, just the strength of Alabaster's will and the power it fuels, but she cannot help watching on two levels as his power races—faster than she could ever go—toward that distant radiating churn.

And before Syen even realizes what's happening, Alabaster has *grabbed* her, in some way that she's never experienced before. She feels her own connection to the earth, her own orogenic awareness, suddenly co-opted and steered *by someone else,* and she does not like it one bit. But when she tries to reclaim control of her power it *burns,* like friction, and in the real world she yelps and falls to her knees and she has no idea what's happening. Alabaster has chained them together somehow, using her strength to amplify his own, and there's not a damned thing she can do about it.

And then they are together, diving into the earth in tandem, spiraling through the massive, boiling well of death that is the hot spot. It's huge—miles wide, bigger than a mountain. Alabaster does something, and something shoots away and Syenite cries out in sudden agony that stills almost at once. Redirected. He does it again and this time she realizes what he's doing: *cushioning* her from the heat and pressure and rage of the hot spot. It's not bothering him because he has become heat and pressure and rage as well, attuning himself to it as Syen has only ever done with small heat chambers in otherwise stable strata—but those were campfire sparks in comparison to this firestorm. There is nothing in her that can equal it. So he uses her power, but he also vents the force that she can't process, sending it elsewhere before it can overwhelm her awareness and . . . and . . . actually, she's not sure what would happen. The Fulcrum teaches orogenes not to push past their own limits; it does not speak of what happens to those who do.

And before Syenite can think through this, before she can muster the wherewithal to *help* him if she cannot *escape* him, Alabaster does something else. A sharp punch. Something has been pierced, somewhere. At once the upward pressure of the magma bubble begins to ebb. He pulls them back, out of the fire and into the still-shuddering earth, and she knows what to do here because these are just are shakes, not Father Earth's rage incarnate. Abruptly something changes and *his* strength is at *her* disposal. So much strength; Earth, he's a monster. But then it becomes easy, easy to smooth the ripples and seal the cracks and thicken the broken strata so that a new fault does not form here where the land has been stressed and weakened. She can sess lines of striation across the land's surface with a clarity that she has never known before. She smooths them, tightens the earth's skin around them with a surgical focus she has never previously been able to achieve. And as the hot spot settles into just another lurking menace and the danger passes, she comes back to herself to find Alabaster curled into a ball in front of her and a scorchlike pattern of frost all around them both which is already sublimating into vapor.

She's on her hands and knees, shaking. When she tries to move, it takes real effort not to fall onto her face. Her elbows keep trying to buckle. But she makes herself do it, crawl a foot or two to reach Alabaster, because he looks dead. She touches his arm and the muscle is hard through the uniform fabric, cramped and locked instead of limp; she thinks that's a good sign. Tugging him a little, she gets closer and sees that his eyes are open, wide, and staring—not with the blank emptiness of death but with an expression of pure surprise.

"It's just like Hessionite said," he whispers suddenly, and she jumps because she didn't think he was conscious.

Wonderful. She's on a highroad in the middle of nowhere, half dead after her orogeny has been used by someone else against her will, with no one to help her but the rustbrained and ridiculously powerful ass who did it in the first place. Trying to pull herself together after... after...

Actually, she has no idea what just happened. It makes no sense. Seismics don't just *happen* like that. Hot spots that have abided for aeons don't just suddenly explode. Something triggers them: a plate shift somewhere, a volcanic eruption somewhere else, a ten-ringer having a tantrum, something. And since it was so powerful an event, she should've sessed the trigger. Should've had some warning besides Alabaster's gasp.

And what the rust did Alabaster *do*? She can't wrap her head around it. Orogenes cannot work together. It's been proven; when two orogenes try to exert the same influence over the same seismic event, the one with the greater control and precision takes precedence. The weaker one can keep trying and will burn themselves out—or the stronger one can punch through their torus, icing them along with everything else. It's why the senior orogenes run the Fulcrum—they aren't just more experienced, they can kill anyone who crosses them, even though they're not supposed to. And it's why ten-ringers get choices: Nobody's going to *force* them to do anything. Except the Guardians, of course.

But what Alabaster did is unmistakable, if inexplicable.

Rust it all. Syenite shifts to sit before she flops over. The world spins unprettily and she props her arms on her updrawn knees and puts her head down for a while. They haven't gone anywhere today, and they won't be going anywhere, either. Syen doesn't have the strength to ride, and Alabaster looks like he might not make it off the bedroll. He never even got dressed; he's just curled up there bare-assed and shaking, completely useless.

So it's left to Syen to eventually get up and rummage through their packs, finding a couple of derminther mela—small melons with a hard shell that burrow underground during a Season, or so the geomests say—and rolling them into the remnants of their fire, which she's very glad they hadn't gotten around to smothering yet. They're out of kindling and fuel, but the coals should be enough to cook the mela so they'll have dinner in a few hours. She pulls a fodder bundle out of the pile for the horses to share, pours some water into a canvas bucket so they can drink, looks at the pile of their droppings and thinks about shoveling it off the highroad's edge so they don't have to smell it.

Then she crawls back to the bedroll, which is thankfully dry after its recent icing. There she flops down at Alabaster's back, and drifts. She doesn't sleep. The minute contortions of the land as the hot spot recedes keep jerking at her sessapinae, keeping her from relaxing completely. Still, just lying there is enough to restore her strength somewhat, and her mind goes quiet until the cooling air pulls her back to herself. Sunset.

She blinks, finding that she has somehow ended up spooned behind Alabaster. He's still in a ball, but this time his eyes are closed and body relaxed. When she sits up, he jerks a little and pushes himself up as well.

"We have to go to the node station," he blurts in a rusty voice, which really doesn't surprise her at all.

"No," she says, too tired to be annoyed, and finally giving up the effort of politeness for good. "I'm not riding a horse off the highroad in the dark while exhausted. We're out of dried peat, and running low on everything else; we need to go to a comm to buy more supplies. And if you try to order me to go to some node in the ass end of beyond instead, you'll need to bring me up on charges for disobedience." She's never disobeyed an order before, so she's a little fuzzy on the consequences. Really, she's too tired to care.

He groans and presses the heels of his hands to his forehead as if to push away a headache, or maybe drive it deeper. Then he curses in that language she heard him use before. She still doesn't recognize it, but she's even more certain that it's one of the Coaster creoles—which is odd, given that he says he was bred and raised at the Fulcrum. Then again, somebody had to raise him for those first few years before he got old enough to be dumped in the grit pool. She's heard that a lot of the eastern Coaster races are dark-skinned like him, too, so maybe they'll hear the language being spoken once they get to Allia.

"If you don't go with me, I'll go alone," he snaps, finally speaking in Sanze-mat. And then he gets up, fumbling around for his clothing and pulling it on, like he's serious. Syenite stares as he does this, because he's shaking so hard he can hardly stand up straight. If he gets on a horse in this condition, he'll just fall off.

"Hey," she says, and he continues his feverish preparations

as if he can't hear her. "*Hey*." He jerks and glares, and belatedly she realizes he *didn't* hear her. He's been listening to something entirely different all this time—the earth, his inner crazy, who knows. "You're going to kill yourself."

"I don't care."

"This is—" She gets up, goes over to him, grabs his arm just as he's reaching for the saddle. "This is stupid, you can't—"

"*Don't you tell me what I can't do*." His arm is wire in her hand as he leans in to snarl the words into her face. Syen almost jerks back…but up close she sees his bloodshot whites, the manic gleam, the blown look of his pupils. Something's *wrong* with him. "You're not a Guardian. You don't get to order me around."

"Have you lost your mind?" For the first time since she's met him, she's…uneasy. He used her orogeny so easily, and she has no idea how he did it. He's so skinny that she could probably beat him senseless with relative ease, but he'd just ice her after the first blow.

He isn't stupid. She has to make him see. "I will go with you," she says firmly, and he looks so grateful that she feels bad for her earlier uncomplimentary thoughts. "At *first light*, when we can take the switchback pass down to the lowroads without breaking our horses' legs and our own necks. All right?"

His face constricts with anguish. "That's too long—"

"We've already slept all day. And when you talked about this before, you said it was a two-day ride. If we lose the horses, how much longer will it take?"

That stops him. He blinks and groans and stumbles back, thankfully away from the saddle. Everything's red in the light of sunset. There's a rock formation in the distance behind him, a tall straight cylinder of a thing that Syenite can tell isn't natural at a glance; either it was pushed up by an orogene, or it's yet another ancient ruin, better camouflaged than most. With this as his backdrop, Alabaster stands gazing up at the sky as if he wants to start howling. His hands flex and relax, flex and relax.

"The node," he says, at last.

"Yes?" She stretches the word out, trying not to let him hear the *humoring the crazy man* note of her voice.

He hesitates, then takes a deep breath. Another, calming himself. "You know shakes and blows never just come out of nowhere like that. The trigger for this one, the shift that disrupted that hot spot's equilibrium, was the node."

"How can you—" Of course he can tell, he's a ten-ringer. Then she catches his meaning. "Wait, you're saying *the node maintainer* set that thing off?"

"That's exactly what I'm saying." He turns to her, his hands flexing into fists again. "Now do you see why I want to get there?"

She nods, blankly. She does. Because an orogene who spontaneously creates a supervolcano does not do so without generating a torus the size of a town. She cannot help but look out over the forest, in the direction of the node. She can't see anything from here, but somewhere out there, a Fulcrum orogene has killed everything in a several-mile radius.

And then there's the possibly more important question, which is: Why?

"All right," Alabaster blurts suddenly. "We need to leave first thing in the morning, and go as fast as we can. It's a two-day trip if we take it easy, but if we push the horses—" He speeds up his words when she opens her mouth, and rides over her objection like a man obsessed. "If we push them, if we leave before dawn, we can get there by nightfall."

It's probably the best she's going to get out of him. "Dawn, then." She scratches at her hair. Her scalp is gritty with road dust; she hasn't been able to wash in three days. They were supposed to pass over Adea Heights tomorrow, a mid-sized comm where she would've pressed to stay at an inn...but he's right. They have to get to that node. "We'll have to stop at the next stream or roadhouse, though. We're low on water for the horses."

He makes a sound of frustration at the needs of mortal flesh. But he says, "Fine."

Then he hunkers down by the coals, where he picks up one of the cooled mela and cracks it open, eating with his fingers and chewing methodically. She doubts he tastes it. Fuel. She joins him to eat the other mela, and the rest of the night passes in silence, if not restfulness.

The next day—or really, later in the night—they saddle up and start cautiously toward the switchback road that will take them off the highroad and down to the lands below. By the time they reach ground level the sun's up, so at that point Alabaster takes the lead and pushes his horse to a full canter, interspersed with walking jags to let them rest. Syen's impressed; she'd thought he would just kill the horses in the grip of whatever urgency possesses him. He's not stupid, at least. Or cruel.

So at this pace they make good time along the more heavily traveled and intersecting lowroads, where they bypass light carters and casual travelers and a few local militia units—all of whom quickly make way for them, as Syen and Alabaster come into view. It's almost ironic, she thinks: Any other time, their black uniforms would make others give them a wide berth because no one likes orogenes. Now, however, everyone must have felt what almost happened with the hot spot. They clear the way eagerly now, and there is gratitude and relief in their faces. The Fulcrum to the rescue. Syen wants to laugh at them all.

They stop for the night and sleep a handful of hours and start again before dawn, and still it's almost full dark by the time the node station appears, nestled between two low hills at the top of a winding road. The road's not much better than a dirtpacked wilderness trail with a bit of aged, cracking asphalt laid along it as a nod to civilization. The station itself is another nod. They've passed dozens of comms on the way here, each displaying a wild range of architecture—whatever's native to the region, whatever fads the wealthier comm members have tried to bring in, cheap imitations of Yumenescene styles. The station is pure Old Empire, though: great looming walls of deep red scoria brick around a complex comprising three small pyramids and a larger central one. The gates are some kind of steely metal, which makes Syen wince. No one puts metal gates on anything they actually want to keep secure. But then, there's nothing in the station except the orogene who lives here, and the staff that supports him or her. Nodes don't even have storecaches, relying instead on regular resupply caravans from nearby comms. Few would want to steal anything within its walls.

Syen's caught off guard when Alabaster abruptly reins his horse well before they reach the gates, squinting up at the station. "What?"

"No one's coming out," he says, almost to himself. "No one's moving beyond the gate. I can't hear anything coming from inside. Can you?"

She hears only silence. "How many people should be here? The node maintainer, a Guardian, and . . . ?"

"Node maintainers don't need Guardians. Usually there's a small troop of six to ten soldiers, Imperials, posted at the station to protect the maintainer. Cooks and the like to serve them. And there's always at least one doctor."

So many headscratchers in so few words. An orogene who doesn't need a Guardian? Node maintainers are below fourth ring; lowringers are never allowed outside the Fulcrum without Guardians, or at least a senior to supervise. The soldiers she understands; sometimes superstitious locals don't draw much distinction between Fulcrum-trained orogenes and any other kind. But why a doctor?

Doesn't matter. "They're probably all dead," she says—but even as she says this, her reasoning falters. The forest around them should be dead, too, for miles around, trees and animals and soil flash-frozen and thawed into slush. All the people traveling the road behind them should be dead. How else could the node maintainer have gotten enough power to disturb that hot spot? But everything seems fine from here, except the silence of the node station.

Abruptly Alabaster spurs his horse forward, and there's no time for more questions. They ride up the hill and toward the locked, closed gates that Syen can't see a way to open, if there's no one inside to do it for them. Then Alabaster hisses and leans forward and for an instant a blistering, narrow torus flickers into view—not around them, but around the gate. She's never seen anyone do that, throw their torus somewhere else, but apparently tenth-ringers can. Her horse utters a nervous little whicker at the sudden vortex of cold and snow before them, so she reins it to a halt, and it shies back a few extra steps. In the next moment something groans and there is a cracking sound beyond the gate. Alabaster lets the torus go as one of the big steel doors drifts open; he's already dismounting.

"Wait, give it time to warm up," Syen begins, but he ignores her and heads toward the gates, not even bothering to watch his step on the slippery frost-flecked asphalt.

Rusting Earthfires. So Syen dismounts and loops the horses' reins around a listing sapling. After the day's hard ride she'll have to let them cool down before she feeds or waters them, and she should rub them down at least—but something about this big, looming, silent building unnerves her. She's not sure what. So she leaves the horses saddled. Just in case. Then she follows Alabaster in.

It's quiet inside the compound, and dark. No electricity for this backwater, just oil lamps that have gone out. There's a big open-air courtyard just past the metal main gates, with scaffolds on the inner walls and nearby buildings to surround any visitors on all sides with convenient sniper positions. Same kind of oh-so-friendly entryway as any well-guarded comm, really, though on a much smaller scale. But there's no one *in* this courtyard, although Syen spies a table and chairs to one side where the people who usually stand guard must have been playing cards and eating snacks not so long ago. The whole compound is silent. The ground is scoria-paved, scuffed and uneven from the passage of many feet over many years, but she hears no feet moving on it now. There's a horse shed on one side of the courtyard, but its stalls are shut and still. Boots covered in dried mud line the wall nearest the gate; some have been tossed or piled there rather than positioned neatly. If Alabaster's right about Imperial soldiers being stationed here, they're clearly the sort who aren't much for inspection-readiness. Figures; being assigned to a place like this probably isn't a reward.

Syen shakes her head. And then she catches a whiff of animal musk from the horse shed, which makes her tense. She smells horses, but can't see them. Edging closer—her hands clench before she makes herself unclench them—she peers over the first stall's door, then glances into the other stalls for a full inventory.

Three dead horses, sprawled on their sides in the straw. Not bloating yet, probably because only the animals' limbs and heads are limp with death. The barrel of each corpse is crusted with ice and condensation, the flesh still mostly hard-frozen. Two days' thaw, she guesses.

There's a small scoria-bricked pyramid at the center of the compound, with its own stone inner gates—though these stand open for the time being. Syenite can't see where Alabaster's gone, but she guesses he's within the pyramid, since that's where the node maintainer will be.

She climbs up on a chair and uses a nearby bit of matchflint to light one of the oil lamps, then heads inside herself—moving faster now that she knows what she'll find. And yes, within the pyramid's dim corridors she sees the soldiers and staffers who once lived here: some sprawled in mid-run, some pressed against the walls, some lying with arms outstretched toward the center of the building. Some of them tried to flee what was coming, and some tried to get to its source to stop it. They all failed.

Then Syen finds the node chamber.

That's what it has to be. It's in the middle of the building, through an elegant archway decorated with paler rose marble and embossed tree-root designs. The chamber beyond is high and vaulted and dim, but empty—except at the room's center, where there's a big...thing. She would call it a chair, if it was made of anything but wires and straps. Not very comfortable-looking, except in that it seems to hold its occupant at an easy recline. The node maintainer is seated in it, anyway, so it must be—

Oh. *Oh.*

Oh bloody, burning Earth.

Alabaster's standing on the dais that holds the wire chair, looking down at the node maintainer's body. He doesn't look up as she comes near. His face is still. Not sad, or bleak. Just a mask.

"Even the least of us must serve the greater good," he says, with no irony in his voice.

The body in the node maintainer's chair is small, and naked. Thin, its limbs atrophied. Hairless. There are things—tubes and pipes and *things*, she has no words for them—going into the stick-arms, down the goggle-throat, across the narrow crotch. There's a flexible bag on the corpse's belly, *attached to* its belly somehow, and it's full of—ugh. The bag needs to be changed.

She focuses on all this, these little details, because it helps. Because there's a part of her that's gibbering, and the only way she can keep that part internal and silent is to concentrate on everything she's seeing. Ingenious, really, what they've done. She didn't know it was possible to keep a body alive like this: immobile, unwilling, indefinite. So she concentrates on figuring out how they've done it. The wire framework is a particular bit of genius; there's a crank and a handle nearby, so the whole aparatus can be flipped over to facilitate cleaning. The wire minimizes bed-sores, maybe. There's a stench of sickness in the air, but nearby is a whole shelf of bottled tinctures and pills; understandable, since it would take better antibiotics than ordinary comm-made penicillin to do something like this. Perhaps one of the tube things is for putting that medicine into the node maintainer. And this one is for pushing in food, and that one is for taking away urine, oh, and that cloth wrapping is for sopping up drool.

But she sees the bigger picture, too, in spite of her effort to concentrate on the minutiae. The node maintainer: a child, kept like this for what must have been months or years. A *child*, whose skin is almost as dark as Alabaster's, and whose features might be a perfect match for his if they weren't so skeletal.

"What." It's all she can say.

"Sometimes a rogga can't learn control." Now she understands that his use of the slur is deliberate. A dehumanizing word for someone who has been made into a thing. It helps. There's no inflection in Alabaster's voice, no emotion, but it's all there in his choice of words. "Sometimes the Guardians catch a feral who's too old to train, but young enough that killing's a waste. And sometimes they notice someone in the grit pool, one of the especially sensitive ones, who can't seem to master control. The Fulcrum tries to teach them for a while, but if the children don't develop at a pace the Guardians think is appropriate, Mother Sanze can always find another use for them."

"As—" Syen can't take her eyes off the body's, *the boy's*, face. His eyes are open, brown but clouded and gelid in death. She's distantly surprised she's not vomiting. "As *this*? Underfires, Alabaster, I *know* children who were taken off to the nodes. I didn't... this doesn't..."

Alabaster unstiffens. She hadn't realized how stiff he was holding himself until he bends enough to slide a hand under the boy's neck, lifting his oversize head and turning it a little. "You should see this."

She doesn't want to, but she looks anyway. There, across the back of the child's shaved head, is a long, vining, keloided scar, embellished with the dots of long-pulled stitches. It's just at the juncture of skull and spine.

"Rogga sessapinae are larger and more complex than those of normal people." When she's seen enough, Alabaster drops the child's head. It thumps back into its wire cradle with a solidity and carelessness that makes her jump. "It's a simple matter to apply a lesion here and there that severs the rogga's self-control completely, while still allowing its *instinctive* use. Assuming the rogga survives the operation."

Ingenious. Yes. A newborn orogene can stop an earthshake. It's an inborn thing, more certain even than a child's ability to suckle—and it's this ability that gets more orogene children killed than anything else. The best of their kind reveal themselves long before they're old enough to understand the danger.

But to reduce a child to nothing *but* that instinct, nothing *but* the ability to quell shakes...

She really should be vomiting.

"From there, it's easy." Alabaster sighs, as if he's giving an especially boring lecture at the Fulcrum. "Drug away the infections and so forth, keep him alive enough to function, and you've got the one thing even the Fulcrum can't provide: a reliable, harmless, completely beneficial source of orogeny." Just as Syenite can't understand why she's not sick, she's not sure why *he's* not screaming. "But I suppose someone made the mistake of letting this one wake up."

His eyes flick away, and Syenite follows Alabaster's gaze to the body of a man over by the far wall. This one's not dressed like one of the soldiers. He's wearing civilian clothes, nice ones.

"The doctor?" She's managed to adopt the detached, steady voice that Alabaster's using. It's easier.

"Maybe. Or some local citizen who paid for the privilege." Alabaster actually *shrugs*, gesturing toward a still-livid bruise on the boy's upper thigh. It's in the shape of a hand, finger marks clearly visible even against the dark skin. "I'm told there are many who enjoy this sort of thing. A helplessness fetish, basically. They like it more if the victim is aware of what they're doing."

"Oh, oh Earth, Alabaster, you can't mean—"

He rides over her words again, as if she hasn't spoken. "Problem is, the node maintainers feel terrible pain whenever they use orogeny. The lesions, see. Since they can't stop themselves from reacting to every shake in the vicinity, even the microshakes, it's considered humane to keep them constantly sedated. And all orogenes react, instinctively, to any perceived threat—"

Ah. That does it.

Syen stumbles away to the nearest wall and retches up the dried apricots and jerky she made herself swallow a-horseback on the way to the station. It's wrong. It's all so wrong. She thought—she didn't think—she didn't know—

Then as she wipes her mouth, she looks up and sees Alabaster watching.

"Like I said," he concludes, very softly. "Every rogga should see a node, at least once."

"I didn't know." She slurs the words around the back of her hand. The words don't make sense but she feels compelled to say them. "I didn't."

"You think that matters?" It's almost cruel, the emotionlessness of his voice and face.

"It matters to *me*!"

"You think *you* matter?" All at once he smiles. It's an ugly thing, cold as the vapor that curls off ice. "You think any of us matter beyond what we can do for them? Whether we obey or not." He jerks his head toward the body of the abused, murdered child. "You think he mattered, after what they did to him? The only reason they don't do this to all of us is because we're more versatile, more useful, if we control ourselves. But each of us is just another weapon, to them. Just a useful monster, just a bit of new blood to add to the breeding lines. Just another fucking *rogga*."

She has never heard so much hate put into one word before.

But standing here, with the ultimate proof of the world's hatred dead and cold and stinking between them, she can't even flinch this time. Because. If the Fulcrum can do this, or the Guardians or the Yumenescene Leadership or the geomests or whoever came up with this nightmare, then there's no point in dressing up what people like Syenite and Alabaster really are.

Not people at all. Not *orogenes*. Politeness is an insult in the face of what she's seen. *Rogga*: This is all they are.

After a moment, Alabaster turns and leaves the room.

* * *

They make camp in the open courtyard. The station's buildings hold all the comforts Syen's been craving: hot water, soft beds, food that isn't just cachebread and dried meat. Out here in the courtyard, though, the bodies aren't human.

Alabaster sits in silence, staring into the fire that Syenite's built. He's wrapped in a blanket, holding the cup of tea she's made; she did, at least, replenish their stores from those of the station. She hasn't seen him drink from the cup. It might've been nice, she thinks, if she could've given him something stronger to drink. Or not. She's not really sure what an orogene of his skill could do, drunk. They're not supposed to drink for that exact reason...but rust reason, right now. Rust everything.

"Children are the undoing of us," Alabaster says, his eyes full of the fire.

Syenite nods, though she doesn't understand it. He's talking. That has to be a good thing.

"I think I have twelve children." Alabaster pulls the blanket more closely about himself. "I'm not sure. They don't always tell me. I don't always see the mothers, after. But I'm guessing it's twelve. Don't know where most of them are."

He's been tossing out random facts like this all evening, when he talks at all. Syenite hasn't been able to bring herself to reply to most of the statements, so it hasn't been much of a conversation. This one, though, makes her speak, because she's been thinking about it. About how much the boy in the wire chair resembles Alabaster.

She begins, "Our child..."

He meets her eyes and smiles again. It's kindly this time, but she's not sure whether to believe that or the hatred beneath the smile's surface.

"Oh, this is only one possible fate." He nods at the station's looming red walls. "Our child could become another me burning through the ring ranks and setting new standards for orogeny, a Fulcrum legend. Or she could be mediocre and never do anything of note. Just another four- or five-ringer clearing coral-blocked harbors and making babies in her spare time."

He sounds so rusting *cheerful* that it's hard to pay attention to the words and not just his tone. The tone soothes, and some part of her craves soothing right now. But his words keep her on edge, stinging like sharp glass fragments amid smooth marbles.

"Or a still," she says. "Even two roggas—" It's hard to say the word, but harder to say *orogene,* because the more polite term now feels like a lie. "Even we can make a still."

"I hope not."

"You hope *not?*" That's the best fate she can imagine for their child.

Alabaster stretches out his hands to the fire to warm them. He's wearing his rings, she realizes suddenly. He hardly ever does, but sometime before they reached the station, even with fear for his child burning in his blood, he spared a thought for propriety and put them on. Some of them glitter in the firelight, while others are dull and dark; one on each finger, thumbs included. Six of Syenite's fingers itch, just a little, for their nakedness.

"Any child of two ringed Fulcrum orogenes," he says, "should be an orogene, too, yes. But it's not that exact a thing. It's not *science*, what we are. There's no logic to it." He smiles thinly. "To be safe, the Fulcrum will treat any children born to any rogga as potential roggas themselves, until proven otherwise."

"But once they've proven it, after that, they'll be... *people*." It is the only hope she can muster. "Maybe someone will adopt them into a good comm, send them to a real creche, let them earn a use name—"

He sighs. There's such weariness in it that Syen falls silent in confusion and dread.

"No comm would adopt our child," he says. The words are deliberate and slow. "The orogeny might skip a generation, maybe two or three, but it always comes back. Father Earth never forgets the debt we owe."

Syenite frowns. He's said things like this before, things that hark to the lorists' tales about orogenes—that they are a weapon not of the Fulcrum, but of the hateful, waiting planet beneath their feet. A planet that wants nothing more than to destroy the life infesting its once-pristine surface. There is something in the things Alabaster says that makes her think he *believes* those old tales, at least a little. Maybe he does. Maybe it gives him comfort to think their kind has some purpose, however terrible.

She has no patience for mysticism right now. "Nobody will adopt her, fine." She chooses *her* arbitrarily. "What, then? The Fulcrum doesn't keep stills."

Alabaster's eyes are like his rings, reflecting the fire in one moment, dull and dark the next. "No. She would become a Guardian."

Oh, rust. That explains so much.

At her silence, Alabaster looks up. "Now. Everything you've seen today. Unsee it."

"*What?*"

"That thing in the chair wasn't a child." There's no light in his eyes now. "It wasn't *my* child, or anyone else's. It was nothing. It was no one. We stabilized the hot spot and figured out what caused it to almost blow. We've checked here for survivors and found none, and that's what we'll telegraph to Yumenes. That's what we'll both say if we're questioned, when we get back."

"I, I don't know if I can . . ." The boy's slack-jawed, dead gaze. How horrible, to be trapped in an endless nightmare. To awaken to agony, and the leer of some grotesque parasite. She can feel nothing but pity for the boy, relief for his release.

"You will do exactly as I say." His voice is a whip, and she glares at him, instantly furious. "If you mourn, mourn the wasted resource. If anyone asks, you're glad he's dead. Feel it. Believe it. He almost killed more people than we can count, after all. And if anyone asks how you feel about it, say you understand that's why they do these things to us. You know it's for our own good. You know it's for everyone's."

"You rusting bastard, I *don't* know—"

He laughs, and she flinches, because the rage is back now, whiplash-quick. "Oh, don't push me right now, Syen. Please don't." He's still laughing. "I'll get a reprimand if I kill you."

It's a threat, at last. Well, then. Next time he sleeps. She'll have to cover his face while she stabs him. Even lethal knife wounds take a few seconds to kill; if he focuses his orogeny on her in that brief window, she's dead. He's less likely to target her accurately without eyes, though, or if he's distracted by suffocation—

But Alabaster is still laughing. Hard. That's when Syenite becomes aware of a hovering jitter in the ambient. A looming *almost* in the strata beneath her feet. She frowns, distracted and alerted and wondering if it's the hot spot again—and then, belatedly, she realizes that the sensation is not jittering, it's jerking in a rhythmic sort of way. In time with the harsh exhalations of Alabaster's laughter.

While she stares at him in chilled realization, he even slaps his knee with one hand. Still laughing, because what he *wants* to do is destroy everything in sight. And if his half-dead, half-grown son could touch off a supervolcano, there's really no telling what that boy's father could do if he set his mind to it. Or even by accident, if his control slips for a moment.

Syen's hands clench into fists on her knees. She sits there, nails pricking her palms, until he finally gets ahold of himself. It takes a while. Even when the laughter's done he puts his face into his hands and chuckles now and again, shoulders shaking. Maybe he's crying. She doesn't know. Doesn't really care, either.

Eventually he lifts his head and takes a deep breath, then another. "Sorry about that," he says at last. The laughter has stopped, but he's all cheer again. "Let's talk about something else, why don't we?"

"Where the rust is your Guardian?" She hasn't unclenched her hands. "You're mad as a bag of cats."

He *giggles*. "Oh, I made sure she was no threat years ago."

Syen nods. "You killed her."

"No. Do I look stupid?" Giggling to annoyance in half a breath. Syen is terrified of him and no longer ashamed to admit it. But he sees this, and something in his manner changes. He takes another deep breath, and slumps. "Shit. I... I'm sorry."

She says nothing. He smiles a little, sadly, like he doesn't expect her to. Then he gets up and goes to the sleeping bag. She watches while he lies down, his back to the fire; she watches him until his breathing slows. Only then does she relax.

Though she jumps, again, when he speaks very softly.

"You're right," he says. "I've been crazy for years. If you stay with me for long, you will be, too. If you see enough of this, and understand enough of what it all means." He lets out a long sigh. "If you kill me, you'll be doing the whole world a favor." After that he says nothing more.

Syen considers his last words for longer than she probably should.

Then she curls up to sleep as best she can on the hard courtyard stones, wrapped in a blanket and with a saddle as an especially torturous sort of pillow. The horses shift restlessly, the way they have been all evening; they can smell the death in the station. But eventually, they sleep, and Syenite does, too. She hopes Alabaster eventually does the same.

Back along the highroad they just traveled, the tourmaline obelisk drifts out of sight behind a mountain, implacable in its course.

* * *

Winter, Spring, Summer, Fall; Death is the fifth, and master of all.

—*Arctic proverb*

INTERLUDE

A break in the pattern. A snarl in the weft. There are things you should be noticing, here. Things that are missing, and conspicuous by their absence.

Notice, for example, that no one in the Stillness speaks of islands. This is not because islands do not exist or are uninhabited; quite the contrary. It is because islands tend to form near faults or atop hot spots, which means they are ephemeral things in the planetary scale, there with an eruption and gone with the next tsunami. But human beings, too, are ephemeral things in the planetary scale. The number of things that they do not notice are literally astronomical.

People in the Stillness do not speak of other continents, either, though it is plausible to suspect they might exist elsewhere. No one has traveled around the world to see that there aren't any; seafaring is dangerous enough with resupply in sight and tsunami waves that are only a hundred feet high rather than the legendary mountains of water said to ripple across the unfettered deep ocean. They simply take as given the bit of lore passed down from braver civilizations that says there's nothing else. Likewise, no one speaks of celestial objects, though the skies are as crowded and busy here as anywhere else in the universe. This is largely because so much of the people's attention is directed toward the ground, not the sky. They notice what's there: stars and the sun and the occasional comet or falling star. They do not notice what's missing.

But then, how can they? Who misses what they have never, ever even imagined? That would not be human nature. How fortunate, then, that there are more people in this world than just humankind.

9

Syenite among the enemy

They reach Allia a week later, beneath a bright blue midday sky that is completely clear except for a winking purple obelisk some ways off-coast.

Allia's big for a Coaster comm—nothing like Yumenes, of course, but respectably sized; a proper city. Most of its neighborhoods and shops and industrial districts are packed into the steep-sided bowl of a natural harbor formed from an old caldera that has collapsed on one side, with several days of outlying settlement in every direction. On the way in, Syenite and Alabaster stop at the first cluster of buildings and farmhouses they see, ask around, and—in between ignoring the glares elicited by their black uniforms—learn that several lodging-houses are nearby. They skip the first one they could've gone to, because a young man from one of the farmhouses decides to follow them for a few miles, reining his horse back to keep it out of what he probably thinks is their range. He's alone, and he says nothing, but one young man can easily become a gang of them, so they keep going in hopes his hatred won't outlast his boredom—and eventually he does turn his horse and head back the way they came.

The next lodging-house isn't as nice as the first, but it's not bad, either: a boxy old stucco building that's seen a few Seasons but is sturdy and well kept. Someone's planted rosebushes at every corner and let ivy grow up its walls, which will probably mean its collapse when the next Season comes, but that's not Syenite's problem to worry about. It costs them two Imperial mother-of-pearls for a shared room and stabling for two horses for the night: such a ridiculously obvious gouging that Syenite laughs at the proprietor before she catches herself. (The woman glares back at them.) Fortunately, the Fulcrum understands that orogenes in the field sometimes have to bribe citizens into decent behavior. Syenite and Alabaster have been generously provisioned, with a letter of credit that will allow them to draw additional currency if necessary. So they pay the proprietor's price, and the sight of all that nice white money makes their black uniforms acceptable for at least a little while.

Alabaster's horse has been limping since the push to the node station, so before they settle in they also see a drover and trade for an uninjured animal. What they get is a spirited little mare who gives Alabaster such a skeptical look that Syenite cannot help laughing again. It's a good day. And after a good night's rest in actual beds, they move on.

Allia's main gates are a massive affair, even more ostentatiously large and embellished than those of Yumenes. Metal, though, rather than proper stone, which makes them look like the garish imitation they are. Syen can't understand how the damn things are supposed to actually secure anything, despite the fact that they're fifty feet tall and made of solid plates of bolted chromium steel, with a bit of filigree for decoration. In a Season, the first acid rain will eat those bolts apart, and one good sixer will warp the precision plates out of alignment, making the great huge things impossible to close. Everything about the gates screams that this is a comm with lots of new money and not enough lorists talking to its Leadership caste.

The gate crew seems to consist of only a handful of Strongbacks, all of them wearing the pretty green uniforms of the comm's militia. Most are sitting around reading books, playing cards, or otherwise ignoring the gate's back-and-forth commerce; Syen fights not to curl her lip at such poor discipline. In Yumenes they would be armed, visibly standing guard, and at least making note of every inbound traveler. One of the Strongbacks does do a double take at the sight of their uniforms, but then waves them through with a lingering glance at Alabaster's many-ringed fingers. He doesn't even look at Syen's hands, which leaves her in a very foul mood by the time they finally traverse the town's labyrinthine cobbled streets and reach the governor's mansion.

Allia is the only large city in the entire quartent. Syen can't remember what the other three comms of the quartent are called, or what the nation was called before it became a nominal part of Sanze—some of the old nations reclaimed their names after Sanze loosened control, but the quartent system worked better, so it didn't really matter. She knows it's all farming and fishing country, as backwater as any other coastal region. Despite all this, the governor's mansion is impressively beautiful, with artful Yumenescene architectural details all over it like cornices and windows made of glass and, ah yes, a single decorative balcony overlooking a vast forecourt. Completely unnecessary ornamentation, in other words, which probably has to be repaired after every minor shake. And did they really have to paint the whole building bright yellow? It looks like some kind of giant rectangular fruit.

At the mansion gates they hand off their horses to a stablehand and kneel in the forecourt to have their hands soaped and washed by a household Resistant servant, which is a local tradition to reduce the chance of spreading disease to the comm's Leadership. After that, a very tall woman, almost as black-skinned as Alabaster and dressed in a white variation on the militia's uniform, comes to the court and gestures curtly for them to follow. She leads them through the mansion and into a small parlor, where she closes the door and moves to sit at the room's desk.

"It took you both long enough to get here," she says by way of greeting, looking at something on her desk as she gestures peremptorily for them to sit. They take the chairs on the other side of the desk, Alabaster crossing his legs and steepling his fingers with an unreadable expression on his face. "We expected you a week ago. Do you want to proceed to the harbor right way, or can you do it from here?"

Syenite opens her mouth to reply that she'd rather go to the harbor, since she's never shaken a coral ridge before and being closer will help her understand it better. Before she can speak, however, Alabaster says, "I'm sorry; who are you?"

Syenite's mouth snaps shut and she stares at him. He's smiling politely, but there's an edged quality to the smile that immediately puts Syenite on alert. The woman stares at him, too, practically radiating affront.

"My name is Asael Leadership Allia," she says, slowly, as if speaking to a child.

"Alabaster," he replies, touching his own chest and nodding. "My colleague is Syenite. But forgive me; I didn't want just your name. We were told the quartent governor was a man."

That's when Syenite understands, and decides to play along. She doesn't understand *why* he's decided to do this, but then there's no real way to understand anything he does. The woman doesn't get it; her jaw flexes visibly. "I am deputy governor."

Most quartents have a governor, a lieutenant governor, and a seneschal. Maybe a comm that's trying so hard to outdo the Equatorials needs extra layers of bureaucracy. "How many deputy governors are there?" Syenite asks, and Alabaster makes a "tut" sound.

"We must be polite, Syen," he says. He's still smiling, but he's furious; she can tell because he's flashing too many teeth. "We're only orogenes, after all. And this is a member of the Stillness's most esteemed use-caste. We are merely here to wield powers greater than she can comprehend in order to save her region's economy, while *she*—" He waggles a finger at the woman, not even trying to hide his sarcasm. "She is a pedantic minor bureaucrat. But I'm sure she's a *very important* pedantic minor bureaucrat."

The woman isn't pale enough for her skin to betray her, but that's all right: Her rock-stiff posture and flared nostrils are clue enough. She looks from Alabaster to Syenite, but then her gaze swings back to him, which Syen completely understands.

Nobody's more irritating than her mentor. She feels a sudden perverse pride.

"There are six deputy governors," she says at last, answering Syenite's question even as she glares shards at Alabaster's smiling face. "And the fact that I am a deputy governor should be irrelevant. The governor is a very busy man, and this is a minor matter. Therefore a *minor bureaucrat* should be more than sufficient to deal with it. Yes?"

"It is not a minor matter." Alabaster's not smiling anymore, although he's still relaxed, fingers tapping each other. He looks like he's considering getting angry, though Syen knows he's already there. "I can sess the coral obstruction from here. Your harbor's almost unusable; you've probably been losing heavier-hauling merchant vessels to other Coaster comms for a decade, if not longer. You've agreed to pay the Fulcrum such a vast sum—I know it's vast because you're getting me—that you'd better hope the cleared harbor restores all that lost trade, or you'll never pay off the debt before the next tsunami wipes you out. So we? The two of us?" He gestures briefly at Syen, then re-steeples his fingers. "We're your whole rusting future."

The woman is utterly still. Syenite cannot read her expression, but her body is stiff, and she's drawn back ever so slightly. In fear? Maybe. More likely in reaction to Alabaster's verbal darts, which have surely stricken tender flesh.

And he continues. "So the least you could do is first offer us some hospitality, and then introduce us to the man who made us travel several hundred miles to solve your little problem. That's courtesy, yes? That's how officials of note are generally treated. Wouldn't you agree?"

In spite of herself, Syen wants to cheer.

"Very well," the woman manages at last, with palpable brittleness. "I will convey your...request...to the governor." Then she smiles, her teeth a white flash of threat. "I'll be sure to convey your disappointment with our usual protocol regarding guests."

"If this is how you usually treat guests," Alabaster says, glancing around with that perfect arrogance only a lifelong Yumenescene can display to its fullest, "then I think you *should* convey our disappointment. Really, right to business like this? Not even a cup of safe to refresh us after our long journey?"

"I was told that you had stopped in the outlying districts for the night."

"Yes, and that took the edge off. The accommodations were also...less than optimal." Which is unfair, Syen thinks, since the lodging-house had been warm and its beds comfortable; the proprietor had been scrupulously courteous once she had money in hand. But there's no stopping him. "When was the last time you traveled fifteen hundred miles, Deputy Governor? I assure you, you'll need more than a day's rest to recover."

The woman's nostrils all but flare. Still, she's Leadership; her family must have trained her carefully in how to bend with blows. "My apologies. I did not think."

"No. You didn't." All at once Alabaster rises, and although he keeps the movement smooth and unthreatening, Asael flinches back as if he's about to come at her. Syen gets up, too—belatedly, since Alabaster caught her by surprise—but Asael doesn't even look at her. "We'll stay the night in that inn we passed on the way here," Alabaster says, ignoring the woman's obvious unease.

"About two streets over. The one with the stone kirkhusa in front? Can't recall the name."

"Season's End." The woman says it almost softly.

"Yes, that sounds right. Shall I have the bill sent here?"

Asael is breathing hard now, her hands clenched into fists atop the desk. Syen's surprised, because the inn's a perfectly reasonable request, if a bit pricey—ah, but that's the problem, isn't it? This deputy governor has no authorization to pay for their accommodations. If her superiors are annoyed enough about this, they'll take the cost out of her pay.

But Asael Leadership Allia does not drop her polite act and just start shouting at them, as Syen half-expects. "Of course," she says—even managing a smile, for which Syen almost admires her. "Please return tomorrow at this time, and I will further instruct you then."

So they leave, and head down the street to the very fancy inn that Alabaster has secured for them.

As they stand at the window of their room—sharing again, and they're taking care not to order particularly expensive food, so that no one can call their request for accommodation exhorbitant—Syenite examines Alabaster's profile, trying to understand why he still radiates fury like a furnace.

"Bravo," she says. "But was that necessary? I'd rather get the job done and start back as soon as possible."

Alabaster smiles, though the muscles of his jaw flex repeatedly. "I would've thought you'd like being treated like a human being for a change."

"I do. But what difference does it make? Even if you pull rank now, it won't change how they feel about us—"

"No, it won't. And I don't care how they feel. They don't have to rusting like us. What matters is what they *do*."

That's all well and good for him. Syenite sighs and pinches the bridge of her nose between thumb and forefinger, trying for patience. "They'll complain." And Syenite, since this is technically her assignment, will be the one censured for it.

"Let them." He turns away from the window then and heads toward the bathroom. "Call me when the food comes. I'm going to soak until I turn pruney."

Syenite wonders if there is any point in hating a crazy man. It's not like he'll notice, anyway.

Room service arrives, bringing a tray of modest but filling local food. Fish is cheap in most Coaster comms, so Syen has treated herself by ordering a temtyr fillet, which is an expensive delicacy back in Yumenes. They only serve it every once in a while in the Fulcrum eateries. Alabaster comes out of the bathroom in a towel, indeed looking pruney—which is when Syen finally notices how whipcord thin he has become in the past few weeks of traveling. He's muscle and bone, and all he's ordered to eat is a bowl of soup. Granted, it's a big bowl of hearty seafood stew, which someone has garnished with cream and a dollop of some kind of beet chutney, but he clearly needs more.

Syenite has a side dish of garlic yams and carmelized silvabees, in addition to her own meal, on a separate smaller plate. She deposits this on his tray.

Alabaster stares at it, then at her. After a moment his expression softens. "So that's it. You prefer a man with more meat on his bones."

He's joking; they both know she wouldn't enjoy sex with him even if she found him attractive. "Anyone would, yes."

He sighs, then obediently begins eating the yams. In between bites—he doesn't seem hungry, just grimly determined—he says, "I don't feel it anymore."

"What?"

He shrugs, which she thinks is less confusion and more his inability to articulate what he means. "Much of anything, really. Hunger. Pain. When I'm in the earth—" He grimaces. That's the real problem: not his inability to say it, but the fact that words are inadequate to the task. She nods to show that she's understood. Maybe someday someone will create a language for orogenes to use. Maybe such a language has existed, and been forgotten, in the past. "When I'm in the earth, the earth is all I can sess. I don't feel—*this*." He gestures around the room, at his body, at her. "And I spend so much time in the earth. Can't help it. When I come back, though, it's like . . . it's like some of the earth comes with me, and . . ." He trails off. But she thinks she understands. "Apparently this is just something that happens past the seventh or eighth ring. The Fulcrum has me on a strict dietary regimen, but I haven't been following it much."

Syen nods, because that's obvious. She puts her sweetweed bun on his plate, too, and he sighs again. Then he eats everything on his plate.

They go to bed. And later, in the middle of the night, Syenite dreams that she is falling upward through a shaft of wavering light that ripples and refracts around her like dirty water. At the top of the shaft, something shimmers *there* and *away* and back again, like it is not quite real, not quite there.

She starts awake, unsure of why she suddenly feels like *something is wrong*, but certain that she needs to do something about it. She sits up, rubbing her face blearily, and only as the remnants of the dream fade does she become aware of the hovering, looming sense of doom that fills the air around her.

In confusion she looks down at Alabaster—and finds him awake beside her, oddly stiff, his eyes wide and staring and his mouth open. He sounds like he's gargling, or trying to snore and failing pathetically. What the rust? He doesn't look at her, doesn't move, just keeps making that ridiculous noise.

And meanwhile his orogeny gathers, and gathers, and *gathers*, until the entire inside of her skull aches. She touches his arm, finds it clammy and stiff, and only belately understands that *he can't move.*

"'Baster?" She leans over him, looking into his eyes. They don't look back at her. Yet she can clearly sess something there, awake and reacting within him. His power flexes as his muscles seem to be unable, and with every gargling breath she feels it spiral higher, curl tighter, ready to snap at any moment. Burning, flaking *rust*. He can't move, and he's *panicking*.

"Alabaster!" Orogenes should never, ever panic. Ten-ringer orogenes especially. He can't answer her, of course; she says it mostly to let him know she's here, and she's helping, so hopefully he'll calm down. It's some kind of seizure, maybe. Syenite throws off the covers and rolls onto her knees and puts her fingers into his mouth, trying to pull his tongue down. She finds his mouth full of spit; he's drowning in his own damn drool. This prompts her to turn him roughly onto his side, tilting his head so the spit will run out, and they are both rewarded by the sound of his first clear breath. But it's shallow, that breath, and it takes him far too long to inhale it. He's struggling. Whatever it is that's got him, it's paralyzing his lungs along with everything else.

The room rocks, just a little, and throughout the inn Syenite hears voices rise in alarm. The cries end quickly, however, because nobody's really worried. There's no sess of impending shake. They're probably chalking it up to a strong wind gust against the building's side . . . for now.

"Shit shit shit—" Syenite crouches to get into his line of sight. "'Baster, you stupid cannibalson ruster—*rein it in*. I'm going to help you, but I can't do that if you kill us all!"

His face doesn't react, his breathing doesn't change, but that looming sense of doom diminishes almost at once. Better. Good. Now—"I have to go and find a doctor—"

The jolt that shakes the building is sharper this time; she hears dishes rattle and clink on their discarded food cart. So that's a no. "I can't help you! I don't know what this is! You're going to die if—"

His whole body jerks. She isn't sure whether that's something deliberate or some kind of convulsion. But she realizes it was a warning a moment later, when *that thing* happens again: his power, clamping on to hers like a vise. She grits her teeth and waits for him to use her to do whatever he needs to do . . . but nothing happens. He has her, and she can feel him doing *something*. Flailing, sort of. Searching, and finding nothing.

"What?" Syenite peers into his slack face. "What are you looking for?"

No response. But it's obviously something he can't find without moving on his own.

Which makes no sense. Orogenes don't need eyes to do what they do. *Infants in the crib* can do what they do. But, but—she tries to think. Before, when this happened on the highroad, he had first turned toward the source of distress. She pictures the scene in her mind, trying to understand what he did and how he did it. No, that's not right; the node station had been slightly to the northwest, and he'd stared dead west, at the horizon. Shaking her head at her own foolishness even as she does it, Syenite jumps up and hurries to the window, opening it and peering out. Nothing to see but the sloping streets and stuccoed buildings of the city, quiet at this late hour. The only activity is down the road, where she can glimpse the dock and the ocean beyond: People are loading a ship. The sky is patchy with clouds, nowhere near dawn. She feels like an idiot. And then—

Something clenches in her mind. From the bed behind her she hears Alabaster make a harsh sound, feels the tremor of his power. Something caught his attention. When? When she looked at the sky. Puzzled, she does it again.

There. *There.* She can almost feel his elation. And then his power folds around her, and she stops seeing with anything like eyes.

It's like the dream she had. She's falling, up, and this somehow makes sense. All around her, the place she's falling through, is color and faceted flickering, like water—except it's purple-pale instead of blue or clear, low-quality amethyst with a dollop of smoky quartz. She flails within it, sure for an instant that she's drowning, but this is something she perceives with sessapinae and not skin or lungs; she can't be flailing because it's not water and she's not really here. And she can't drown because, somehow, Alabaster has her.

Where she flails, he is purposeful. He drags her up, falling faster, searching for something, and she can almost hear the howl of it, feel the drag of forces like pressure and temperature gradually chilling and prickling her skin.

Something engages. Something else shunts open. It's beyond her, too complex to perceive in full. Something pours through somewhere, warms with friction. Someplace inside her smooths out, intensifies. *Burns.*

And then she is elsewhere, floating amid immense gelid things, and there is something on them, among them

a contaminant

That is not her thought.

And then it's all gone. She snaps back into herself, into the real world of sight and sound and hearing and taste and smell and sess—real sess, sess the way it's *supposed to* work, not whatever-the-rust Alabaster just did—and Alabaster is vomiting on the bed.

Revolted, Syen jerks away, then remembers that he's paralyzed; he shouldn't be able to move at all, let alone vomit. Nevertheless, he's doing it, having half-pushed himself up off the bed so that he can heave effectively. Obviously the paralysis has eased.

He doesn't throw up much, just a teaspoon or two of greasy-looking white-clear stuff. They ate hours ago; there shouldn't be anything in his upper digestive tract at all. But she remembers

a contaminant

and realizes belatedly what's come out of him. And further, she realizes *how* he's done it.

When he finally gets it all up, and spits a few times for emphasis or good measure, he flops back onto the bed on his back, breathing hard, or maybe just enjoying the sensation of being able to breathe at will.

Syenite whispers, "What in the rusted burning Earth did you just do?"

He laughs a little, opening his eyes to roll them toward her. She can tell it's another of those laughs he does when he really wants to express something other than humor. Misery this time, or maybe weary resignation. He's always bitter. How he shows it is just a matter of degree.

"F-focus," he says, between pants. "Control. Matter of degree."

It's the first lesson of orogeny. Any infant can move a mountain; that's instinct. Only a trained Fulcrum orogene can deliberately, specifically, move a boulder. And only a ten-ringer, apparently, can move the infinitesimal substances floating and darting in the interstices of his blood and nerves.

It should be impossible. She shouldn't believe that he's done this. But she helped him do it, so she can't do anything *but* believe the impossible.

Evil Earth.

Control. Syenite takes a deep breath to master her nerves. Then she gets up, fetches a glass of water, and brings it over. He's still weak; she has to help him sit up to sip from the glass. He spits out the first mouthful of that, too, onto the floor at her feet. She glares. Then she grabs pillows to prop under his back, helps him into a recline, and pulls the unstained part of the blanket over his legs and lap. That done, she moves to the chair across from the bed, which is big and more than plush enough to sleep in for the night. She's tired of dealing with his bodily fluids.

After Alabaster's caught his breath and regained a little of his strength—she is not uncharitable—she speaks very quietly. "Tell me what the rust you're doing."

He seems unsurprised by the question, and doesn't move from where he's slumped on the pillows, his head lolling back. "Surviving."

"On the highroad. Just now. *Explain* it."

"I don't know if . . . I can. Or if I should."

She keeps her temper. She's too scared not to. "What do you mean, if you should?"

He takes a long, slow, deep breath, clearly savoring it. "You don't have . . . control yet. Not enough. Without that . . . if you tried to do what I just did . . . you'd die. But if I tell you how I did it—" He takes a deep breath, lets it out. "You may not be able to stop yourself from trying."

Control over things too small to see. It sounds like a joke. It has to be a joke. "Nobody has that kind of control. Not even ten-ringers." She's heard the stories; they can do amazing things. Not impossible things.

" 'They are the gods in chains,' " Alabaster breathes, and she realizes he's falling asleep. Exhausted from fighting for his life—or maybe working miracles is just harder than it seems. " 'The tamers of the wild earth, themselves to be bridled and muzzled.' "

"What's that?" He's quoting something.

"Stonelore."

"Bullshit. That's not on any of the Three Tablets."

"Tablet Five."

He's so full of shit. And he's drifting off. Earth, she's going to kill him.

"Alabaster! Answer my rusting *question*." Silence. Earth damn it. "What is it you keep doing to me?"

He exhales, long and heavily, and she thinks he's out. But he says, "Parallel scaling. Pull a carriage with one animal and it goes only so far. Put two in a line, the one in front tires out first. Yoke them side by side, *synchronize* them, reduce the friction lost between their movements, and you get more than you would from both animals individually." He sighs again. "That's the theory, anyway."

"And you're what, the yoke?"

She's joking. But he nods.

A yoke. That's worse. He's been treating her like an *animal,* forcing her to work for him so he won't burn out. "How are you—" She rejects the word *how,* which assumes possibility where none should exist. "Orogenes can't work together. One torus subsumes another. The greater degree of control takes precedence." It's a lesson they both learned in the grit crucibles.

"Well, then." He's so close to sleep that the words are slurred. "Guess it didn't happen."

She's so furious that she's blind with it for an instant; the world goes white. Orogenes can't afford that kind of rage, so she releases it in words. "Don't give me that shit! I don't want you to ever do that to me again—" But how can she stop him? "Or I'll kill you, do you hear? You have no right!"

"Saved my life." It's almost a mumble, but she hears it, and it stabs her anger in the back. "Thanks."

Because really, can she blame a drowning man for grabbing anyone nearby to save himself?

Or to save thousands of people?

Or to save his son?

He's asleep now, sitting beside the little puddle of ick he threw up. Of course that's on her side of the bed. In disgust, Syen drags her legs up to curl into the plush chair and tries to get comfortable.

Only when she settles does it occur to her what's happened. The core of it, not just the part about Alabaster doing the impossible.

When she was a grit, she did kitchen duty sometimes, and every once in a while they would open a jar of fruit or vegetables that had gone bad. The funky ones, those that had cracked or come partially open, were so foul-smelling that the cooks would have to open windows and set some grits on fanning duty to get the stench out. But far worse, Syen had learned, were the jars that didn't crack. The stuff inside them looked fine; opened, it didn't smell bad. The only warning of danger was a little buckling of the metal lid.

"Kill you deader than swapthrisk bite," the head cook, a grizzled old Resistant, would say as he showed them the suspect jar so they could know what to watch for. "Pure poison. Your muscles lock up and stop working. You can't even breathe. And it's potent. I could kill everybody in the Fulcrum with this one jar." And he would laugh, as if that notion were funny.

Mixed into a bowl of stew, a few drops of that taint would be more than enough to kill one annoying middle-aged rogga.

Could it have been an accident? No reputable cook would use anything from a pucker-lidded jar, but maybe the Season's End Inn hires incompetents. Syenite had placed the order for the food herself, speaking with the child who'd come up to see if they needed anything. Had she specified whose order was whose? She tries to remember what she said. "*Fish and yams for me.*" So they would've been able to guess that the stew was for Alabaster.

Why not dose them both, then, if someone at the inn hates roggas enough to try to kill them? Easy enough to drop some toxic vegetable juice into all the food, not just Alabaster's. Maybe they have, and it just hasn't affected her yet? But she feels fine.

You're being paranoid, she tells herself.

But it's not her imagination that everyone hates her. She's a rogga, after all.

Frustrated, Syen shifts in the chair, wrapping her arms around her knees and trying to make herself sleep. It's a losing game. Her head's too full of questions, and her body's too used to hard ground barely padded by a bedroll. She ends up sitting up for the rest of the night, gazing out the window at a world that has begun to make less and less sense, and wondering what the rust she's supposed to do about it.

But in the morning when she leans out the window to inhale the dew-laden air in a futile attempt to shake herself to alertness, she happens to glance up. There, winking in the dawn light, is a great hovering shard of amethyst. Just an obelisk—one she vaguely remembers seeing the day before, as they were riding into Allia. They're always beautiful, but so are the lingering stars, and she hardly pays attention to either in the normal course of affairs.

She notices this one now, however. Because today, it's a lot closer than it was yesterday.

* * *

Set a flexible central beam at the heart of all structures.
Trust wood, trust stone, but metal rusts.

—Tablet Three, "Structures," verse one

10

you walk beside the beast

YOU THINK, MAYBE, YOU NEED to be someone else.

You're not sure who. Previous yous have been stronger and colder, or warmer and weaker; either set of qualities is better suited to getting you through the mess you're in. Right now you're cold and weak, and that helps no one.

You could become someone new, maybe. You've done that before; it's surprisingly easy. A new name, a new focus, then try on the sleeves and slacks of a new personality to find the perfect fit. A few days and you'll feel like you've never been anyone else.

But. Only one you is Nassun's mother. That's what's forestalled you so far, and ultimately it's the deciding factor. At the end of all this, when Jija is dead and it's finally safe to mourn your son... if she still lives, Nassun will need the mother she's known all her life.

So you must stay Essun, and Essun will have to make do with the broken bits of herself that Jija has left behind. You'll jigsaw them together however you can, caulk in the odd bits with willpower wherever they don't quite fit, ignore the occasional sounds of grinding and cracking. As long as nothing important breaks, right? You'll get by. You have no choice. Not as long as one of your children could be alive.

* * *

You wake to the sounds of battle.

You and the boy have camped at a roadhouse for the night, amid several hundred other people who clearly had the same idea. No one's actually sleeping *in* the roadhouse—which in this case is little more than a windowless stone-walled shack with a well pump inside—because by unspoken agreement it is neutral territory. And likewise none of the several dozen camps of people arrayed around the roadhouse have made much effort to interact, because by unspoken agreement they are all terrified enough to stab first and ask questions later. The world has changed too quickly and too thoroughly. Stonelore might have tried to prepare everyone for the particulars, but the all-encompassing horror of the Season is still a shock that no one can cope with easily. After all, just a week ago, everything was normal.

You and Hoa settled down and built a fire for the night in a nearby clearing amid the plainsgrass. You have no choice but to split a watch with the child, even though you fear he'll just fall asleep; with this many people around it's too dangerous to be careless. Thieves are the greatest potential problem, since you've got a full runny-sack and the two of you are just a woman and a boy traveling alone. Fire's a danger, too, with all these people who don't know the business end of a matchflint spending the night in a field of dying grass. But you're exhausted. It's only been a week since you were living your own cushy, predictable life, and it's going to take you a while to get back up to traveling condition. So you order the boy to wake you as soon as the peat block burns out. That should've given you four or five hours.

But it's *many* hours later, almost dawn, when people start screaming on the far side of the makeshift camp. Shouts rise on this side as people around you cry alarm, and you struggle out of the bedroll and to your feet. You're not sure who's screaming. You're not sure why. Doesn't matter. You just grab the runny-sack with one hand and the boy with the other, and turn to run.

He jerks away before you can do so, and grabs his little rag bundle. Then he takes your hand again, his icewhite eyes very wide in the dimness.

Then you—all of you, everyone nearby as well as you and the boy—are running, running, farther into the plains and away from the road because that's the direction the first screams came from, and because thieves or commless or militias or whoever is causing the trouble will probably use the road to leave when they've finished whatever they're doing. In the ashy predawn half-light all the people around you are merely half-real shadows running in parallel. For a time, the boy and the sack and the ground under your feet are the only parts of the world that exist.

A long while later your strength gives out, and you finally stagger to a halt.

"What was that?" Hoa asks. He doesn't sound out of breath at all. The resilience of children. Of course, you didn't run the whole way; you're too flabby and unfit for that. The bottom line was to keep moving, which you did do, walking when you couldn't muster the breath to run.

"I didn't see," you reply. It doesn't really matter what it was, anyway. You rub at a cramp in your side. Dehydration; you take out your canteen to drink. But when you do, you grimace at its near-empty slosh. Of course you didn't take the chance to fill it while you were at the roadhouse. You'd been planning to do that come morning.

"I didn't see, either," says the boy, turning back and craning his neck as if he ought to be able to. "Everything was quiet and then..." He shrugs.

You eye him. "You didn't fall asleep, did you?" You saw the fire before you fled. It was down to a smolder. He should've woken you hours ago.

"No."

You give him the look that has cowed two of your own and several dozen other people's children. He draws back from it, looking confused. "I *didn't*."

"Why didn't you wake me when the peat burned down?"

"You needed to sleep. I wasn't sleepy."

Damnation. That means he *will* be sleepy later. Earth eat hardheaded children.

"Does your side hurt?" Hoa steps closer, looking anxious. "Are you hurt?"

"Just a stitch. It'll go away eventually." You look around, though visibility in the ashfall is iffy past twenty feet or so. There's no sign that anyone else is nearby, and you can't hear any other sounds from the area around the roadhouse. There's no sound around you, in fact, but the very soft tipple of ash on the grass. Logically, the other people who were camped around the roadhouse can't be that far away—but you *feel* completely alone, aside from Hoa. "We're going to have to go back to the roadhouse."

"For your things?"

"Yes. And water." You squint in the direction of the roadhouse, useless as that is when the plain just fades into white-gray haze a short ways off. You can't be sure the next roadhouse will be usable. It might have been taken over by would-be warlords, or destroyed by panicked mobs; it might be malfunctioning.

"You could go back." You turn to the boy, who is sitting down on the grass—and to your surprise, he's got something in his mouth. He didn't have any food before . . . oh. He knots his rag bundle firmly shut and swallows before speaking again. "To the creek where you made me take a bath."

That's a possibility. The creek vanished underground again not far from where you used it; that's only a day's walk away. But it's a day's walk *back* the way you came, and . . .

And nothing. Going back to the stream is the safest option. Your reluctance to do this is stupid and wrong.

But Nassun is somewhere *ahead*.

"What is he doing to her?" you ask, softly. "He must know what she is, by now."

The boy only watches. If he worries about you, he doesn't let it show on his face.

Well, you're about to give him more reason for concern. "We'll go back to the roadhouse. It's been long enough. Thieves or bandits or whatever would've taken what they wanted by now and moved on."

Unless what they wanted was *the roadhouse*. Several of the Stillness's oldest comms started as sources of water seized by the strongest group in a given area, and held against all comers until a Season ended. It's the great hope of the commless in such times—that with no comm willing to take them in, they might forge their own. Still, few commless groups are organized enough, sociable enough, strong enough, to do it successfully.

And few have had to contend with an orogene who wanted the water more than they did.

"If they want to keep it," you say, and you mean it, even though this is such a small thing, you just want water, but in that moment every obstacle looms large as a mountain and *orogenes eat mountains for breakfast*, "they'd better let me have some."

The boy, whom you half-expect to run away screaming after this statement, merely gets to his feet. You purchased clothing for him at the last comm you passed, along with the peat. Now he's got good sturdy walking boots and good thick socks, two full changes of clothing, and a jacket that's remarkably similar to your own. Apart from his bizarre looks, the matching garb makes you look like you're together. That sort of thing sends unspoken messages of organization, shared focus, group membership; it's not much, but every little deterrent helps. *Such a formidable pair we are, crazy woman and changeling child.*

"Come on," you say, and start walking. He follows.

It's quiet as you approach the roadhouse. You can tell you're close by the disturbances in the meadow: Here's someone's abandoned campsite, with still-smoldering fire; there's someone's torn runny-sack, trailed by supplies grabbed and dropped in flight. There's a ring of pulled grass, campfire coals, and an abandoned bedroll that might've been yours. You scoop it up in passing and roll it up, jabbing it through the straps of your sack to tie properly later. And then, sooner than you were expecting, there is the roadhouse itself.

You think at first there's no one here. You can't hear anything but your own footsteps, and your breath. The boy is mostly silent, but his footsteps are oddly heavy against the asphalt when you step back onto the road. You glance at him, and he seems to realize it. He stops, looking intently at your feet as you keep walking. Watching how you roll from heel to toes, not so much planting a step as peeling your feet off the ground and carefully reapplying them. Then he begins doing the same thing, and if you didn't need to pay attention to your surroundings—if you weren't distracted by the racing of your own heart—you would laugh at the surprise on his little face when his own footfalls become silent. He's almost cute.

But that's when you step into the roadhouse, and realize you're not alone.

First you notice just the pump and the cement casing it's set into; that's really all the roadhouse is, a shelter for the pump. Then you see a woman, who is humming to herself as she pulls away one large canteen and sets another, empty and even larger, in its place beneath the spigot. She bustles around the casing to work the pump mechanism, busy as you please, and only sees you after she's started working the lever again. Then she freezes, and you and she stare at each other.

She's commless. No one who's suffered only recent homelessness would be so filthy. (Except the boy, a part of your mind supplies, but there's a difference between disaster filth and *unwashed* filth.) This woman's hair is matted, not in clean, well-groomed locks like yours but from sheer neglect; it hangs in moldy, uneven clumps from her head. Her skin isn't just covered in dirt; the dirt is ground in, a permanent fixture. There's iron ore in some of it and it's rusted from the moisture in her skin, tinting the pattern of her pores red. Some of her clothes are fresh—given how much you saw abandoned around the roadhouse, easy to guess where she got those—and the pack at her feet is one of three, each one fat with supplies and dangling an already-filled canteen. But her body odor is so high and ripe that you hope she's taking all that water to use for a bath.

Her eyes flick over you and Hoa, assessing just as quickly and thoroughly, and then after a moment she shrugs a little and finishes pumping, filling the large canteen in two strokes. Then she takes it, caps it, attaches it again to one of the big packs at her feet, and—so deftly that you're a little awed—scoops up all three and scuttles back. "Have at."

You've seen commless before, of course; everyone has. In cities that want cheaper labor than Strongbacks—and where the Strongbacks' union is weak—they live in shantytowns and beg on the streets. Everywhere else, they live in the spaces between comms, forests and the edges of deserts and such, where they survive by hunting game and building encampments out of scraps. The ones who don't want trouble raid fields and silos on the outskirts of comm territories; the ones who like a fight raid small, poorly defended comms and attack travelers along the lesser quartent roads. Quartent governors don't mind a little of this. Keeps everyone sharp, and reminds troublemakers of how they could end up. Too many thefts, though, or too violent an attack and militias get sent out to hunt the commless down.

None of that matters now. "We don't want any trouble," you say. "We're just here for water, same as you."

The woman, who's been looking with curiosity at Hoa, flicks

her gaze back to you. "Not like *I'm* starting any." Rather deliberately she caps another canteen she's filled. "Got more of these to fill, though, so." She jerks her chin at your pack and the canteen dangling from it. "Yours won't take long."

Hers are truly huge. They're also probably heavy as logs. "Are you waiting for others to come?"

"Nope." The woman grins, flashing remarkably good teeth. If she's commless now, she didn't start out that way; those gums haven't known much malnutrition. "Gonna kill me?"

You have to admit, you weren't expecting that.

"She must have someplace nearby," Hoa says. You're pleased to see that he's at the door, looking outward. Still on guard. Smart boy.

"Yep," says the woman, cheerfully unperturbed that they have sussed out her ostensible secret. "Gonna follow me?"

"No," you say, firmly. "We're not interested in you. Leave us be and we'll do the same."

"Solid by me."

You unsling your canteen and edge over to the pump. It's awkward; the thing is meant to be worked by one person while another holds a container.

The woman puts a hand on the pump, silently offering. You nod, and she pumps for you. You drink your fill first, and then there's tense silence while the canteen fills. Nerves make you break it. "You took a big risk coming here. Everyone else is probably coming back soon."

"A few, and not soon. And you took the same big risk."

"True."

"So." The woman nods toward her pile of filled canteens,

and belatedly you see—what is that? Atop one of the canteens' mouths is some kind of little contraption made of sticks, twisted leaves, and a piece of crooked wire. It clicks softly as you stare. "Running a test, anyway."

"What?"

She shrugs, eyeing you, and you realize it then: This woman is no more an ordinary commless than you are a still.

"That shake from the north," she says. "It was at least a niner—and that was just what we felt on the surface. It was deep, too." She pauses abruptly, actually cocking her head away from you and frowning, as if she's heard something startling, though there's nothing there but the wall. "Never seen a shake like that. Weird wave pattern to it." Then she focuses on you again, bird-quick. "Probably breached a lot of aquifers. They'll repair themselves over time, of course, but in the short term, no telling what kinds of contaminants might be around here. I mean, this is perfect land for a city, right? Flat, ready access to water, nowhere near a fault. Means there probably *was* one here, at some point. You know what kinds of nasty things cities leave behind when they die?"

You're staring at her now. Hoa is, too, but he stares at everyone like that. Then the thing in the canteen finishes clicking, and the commless woman bends over to pluck it free. It had been dangling a strip of something—tree bark?—into the water.

"Safe," she proclaims, and then belatedly seems to notice you staring. She frowns a little and holds up the little strip. "It's made from the same plant as safe. You know? The greeting tea? But I treated it with a little something extra, to catch those substances safe doesn't catch."

"There's nothing," you blurt, and then you fall silent, uneasy, when she focuses sharply on you. Now you have to finish. "I mean...there's nothing safe misses that would hurt people." That's the only reason anyone drinks it, because it tastes like boiled ass.

Now the woman looks annoyed. "That's not true. Where the rust did you learn that?" It's something you used to teach in the Tirimo creche, but before you can say this she snaps, "Safe doesn't work as well if it's in a cold solution; everybody knows that. Needs to be room temperature or lukewarm. It also doesn't catch things that kill you in a few months instead of a few minutes. Fat lot of good it'll do you to survive today, only to come down with skinpeel next year!"

"You're a geomest," you blurt. It seems impossible. You've met geomests. They're everything people think orogenes are when they're feeling charitable: arcane, unfathomable, possessed of knowledge no mortal should have, disturbing. No one but a geomest would know so many useless facts, so thoroughly.

"I am not." The woman draws herself up, almost swelling in her fury. "I know better than to pay attention to those fools at the University. I'm not *stupid*."

You stare again, in utter confusion. Then your canteen overflows and you scramble to find the cap for it. She stops pumping, then tucks the little bark contraption into a pocket among her voluminous skirts and starts to disassemble one of the smaller packs at her feet, her movements brisk and efficient. She pulls free a canteen—the same size as yours—and tosses it aside, then when the small pack's empty, she tosses that aside, too. Your eyes lock on to both items. It would be easier on you if the boy could carry his own supplies.

"You'd better grab, if you're going to," the woman says, and though she's not looking at you, you realize she intentionally set the items out for you. "I'm not staying, and you shouldn't, either."

You edge over to take the canteen and the empty small pack. The woman stands again to help you fill the new canteen before resuming her rummaging through her own stuff. While you tie on your canteen and the bedroll you grabbed earlier, and transfer a few items from your pack into the smaller one for the boy, you say, "Do you know what happened? Who did what?" You gesture vaguely in the direction of the screams that woke you up.

"I doubt it was a 'who,'" the woman says. She tosses away several packets of gone-off food, a child's set of pants that might be big enough for Hoa, and books. Who puts books in a runny-sack? Though the woman glances at the title of each before throwing it aside. "People don't react as quickly as nature to changes like this."

You attach the second canteen to your own pack for now, since you know better than to make Hoa carry too much weight. He's just a boy, and a poorly grown one at that. Since the commless woman clearly doesn't want them, you also pick up the pants from the small pile of discards that's growing beside her. She doesn't seem to care.

You ask, "What, you mean that was some kind of animal attack?"

"Didn't you see the body?"

"Didn't know there *was* a body. People screamed and started running, so we did, too."

The woman sighs. "That's not unwise, but it does lose you... opportunities." As if to illustrate her point she tosses aside another pack that she's just emptied and stands, shouldering the two that remain. One of them is more worn and obviously comfortable than the other: her own. She's used twine to lash the heavy canteens together so that they nestle against the small of her back, supported by the not-insubstantial curve of her ass, rather than hanging as most canteens do. Abruptly she glowers at you. "Don't follow me."

"Wasn't planning to." The small pack's ready to be given to Hoa. You strap on your own, check to make sure everything's secure and comfy.

"I mean it." She leans forward a little, her whole face almost feral in its fierceness. "You don't know what I'm going back to. I could live in a walled compound with fifty other rusters just like me. We might have tooth-files and a 'juicy stupid people' recipe book."

"Okay, okay." You take a step back, which seems to mollify her. Now she goes from fierce to relaxed, and resumes settling her packs for comfort. You've got what you want, too, so it's time to get out of here. The boy looks pleased by his new pack when you hand it to him; you help him put it on properly. As you do this, the commless woman passes you to leave, and some vestige of your old self makes you say, "Thanks, by the way."

"Anytime," she says airily, heading through the door—and abruptly she stops. She's staring at something. The look on her face makes all the hairs on the back of your neck prickle. Quickly you go to the door as well, to see what she's seeing.

It's a kirkhusa—one of the long-bodied, furry creatures midlatters keep as pets instead of dogs, since dogs are too expensive for anyone except the most ostentatious Equatorials. Kirkhusa look more like big land-bound otters than canines. They're trainable, cheap as anything because they eat only the leaves of low bushes and the insects that grow on them. And they're even cuter than puppies when they're small... but *this* kirkhusa isn't cute. It's big, a good hundred pounds of healthy, sleek-furred flesh. Someone's loved it dearly, at least until lately: That's a fine leather collar still round its neck. It's growling, and as it slinks out of the grass and up onto the road, you see red blooms in the fur around its mouth and on its clawed, prehensile paws.

That's the problem with kirkhusa, see. The reason everyone can afford them. They eat leaves—until they taste enough ash, which triggers some instinct within them that's normally dormant. Then they change. Everything changes during a Season.

"Shit," you whisper.

The commless woman hisses beside you, and you tense, feeling your awareness descend briefly into the earth. (You drag it back, out of habit. Not around other people. Not unless you have no other choice.) She's moved to the edge of the asphalt, where she was probably about to bolt into the meadow and toward a distant stand of trees. But not far from the road, around the place where people screamed earlier, you see the grass moving violently and hear the soft houghs and squeals of other kirkhusa—how many, you can't tell. They're busy, though. Eating.

This one used to be a pet. Maybe it remembers its human master fondly. Maybe it hesitated when the others attacked, and failed to earn more than a taste of the meat that will be its new staple diet until the Season ends. Now it will go hungry if it doesn't rethink its civilized ways. It pads back and forth on the asphalt, chittering to itself as if in indecision—but it doesn't leave. It's got you and Hoa and the commless woman boxed in while it wrestles with its conscience. Poor, poor thing.

You set your feet and murmur to Hoa—and the woman, if she feels like listening—"Don't move."

But before you can find something harmless to latch on to, a rock inclusion you can shift or a water source you can geyser that will give you an excuse to snatch the warmth from the air and the life from this overgrown squirrel, Hoa glances at you and steps forward.

"I said," you begin, grabbing his shoulder to yank him back—but he doesn't yank. It's like trying to move a rock that's wearing a jacket; your hand just slips off the leather. Underneath it, he doesn't move at all.

The protest dies in your mouth as the boy continues to move forward. He's not simply being disobedient, you realize; there's too much purpose in his posture. You're not sure he even *noticed* your attempt to stop him.

And then the boy is facing the creature, a few feet away. It's stopped prowling, and stands tensed as if—wait. What? *Not* as if it's going to attack. It lowers its head and twitches its stubby tail, once, uncertainly. *Defensively.*

The boy's back is to you. You can't see his face, but all at once his stocky little frame seems less little, and less harmless. He lifts a hand and extends it toward the kirkhusa, as if offering it to sniff. As if it's still a pet.

The kirkhusa attacks.

It's fast. They're quick animals anyway, but you see the twitch of its muscles and then it's five feet closer, its mouth is open, and its teeth have closed around the boy's hand up to the middle of his forearm. And, oh Earth, you can't watch this, a child dying in front of you as Uche did not, how could you let either happen, you are the worst person in the whole world.

But maybe—if you can concentrate, ice the animal and not the boy—you lower your gaze to try to concentrate as the commless woman gasps and the boy's blood splatters the asphalt. Watching Hoa's mauling will make it harder; what matters is saving his life, even if he loses the arm. But then—

Silence falls.

You look up.

The kirkhusa has stopped moving. It's still where it was, teeth locked on Hoa's arm, its eyes wild with…something that is more fear than fury. It's even shaking, faintly. You hear it make the most fleeting of aborted sounds, just a hollow squeal.

Then the kirkhusa's fur starts to move. (What?) You frown, squint, but it's easy to see, close as the beast is. Each individual hair of its fur waggles, seemingly in a different direction all at the same time. Then it shimmers. *(What?)* Stiffens. All at once you realize that not only are its muscles stiff, but the flesh that covers them is stiff, too. Not just stiff but…solid.

And then you notice: *The whole kirkhusa* is solid.

What.

You don't understand what you're seeing, so you keep staring, comprehending in pieces. Its eyes have become glass, its claws crystal, its teeth some sort of ocher filament. Where there was movement, now there is stillness; its muscles are rock-hard, and that is not a metaphor. Its fur was just the last part of its body to change, twisting about as the follicles underneath transformed into *something else.*

You and the commless woman both stare.

Wow.

Really. That's what you're thinking. You've got nothing better. Wow.

That's enough to get you moving, at least. You edge forward until you can see the whole tableau from a better angle, but nothing really changes. The boy still seems fine, although his arm is still halfway down the thing's gullet. The kirkhusa is still pretty damn dead. Well. Pretty, and damn dead.

Hoa glances at you, and all at once you realize how deeply unhappy he looks. Like he's ashamed. Why? He's saved all of your lives, even if the method was... You don't know what this is.

"Did you do this?" you ask him.

He lowers his eyes. "I hadn't meant for you to see this, yet."

Okay. That's... something to think about later. "What did you do?"

He presses his lips shut.

Now he decides to sulk. But then, maybe now's not the time for this conversation, given that his arm is stuck in a glass monster's teeth. The teeth have pierced his skin; there's blood welling and dripping down its no-longer-flesh lower jaw. "Your arm. Let me..." You look around. "Let me find something to break you out."

Hoa seems to remember his arm, belatedly. He glances at you again, plainly not liking that you're watching, but then sighs a little in resignation. And he flexes his arm, before you can warn him not to do anything that might wound him further.

The kirkhusa's head shatters. Great chunks of heavy stone thud to the ground; glittering dust sprays. The boy's arm is bleeding more, but free. He flexes his fingers a little. They're fine. He lowers the arm to his side.

You react to his wound, reaching for his arm because that is something you can comprehend and do something about. But he pulls away quickly, covering the marks with his other hand. "Hoa, let me—"

"I'm fine," he says, quietly. "We should go, though."

The other kirkhusa are still close, though they're busy chewing on some poor fool in the plainsgrass. That meal won't last them forever. Worse, it's only a matter of time before other desperate people make the choice to brave the roadhouse again, hoping the bad things have gone.

One of the bad things is still right here, you think, looking at the kirkhusa's topless lower jaw. You can see the rough nodules on the back of its tongue, now gleaming in crystal. Then you turn to Hoa, who is holding his bloody arm and looking miserable.

It's the misery, finally, that pushes the fear back down inside you, replaces it with something more familiar. Did he do this because he didn't know you could defend yourself? For some other, unfathomable reason? In the end, it doesn't matter. You have no idea what to do with a monster who can turn living things into statuary, but you do know how to handle an unhappy child.

Also, you have a lot of experience with children who are secretly monsters.

So you offer your hand. Hoa looks surprised. He stares at it, then at you, and there is something in his gaze that is entirely human, and grateful for your acceptance in that moment. It makes you feel a little more human, too, amazingly.

He takes your hand. His grip seems no weaker despite his wounds, so you pull him along as you turn south and start walking again. The commless woman wordlessly follows, or maybe she's walking in the same direction, or maybe she just thinks there's strength in numbers. None of you say anything because there's nothing to say.

Behind you, in the meadow, the kirkhusa keep eating.

* * *

Beware ground on loose rock. Beware hale strangers.

Beware sudden silence.

—*Tablet One, "On Survival," verse three*

11

Damaya at the fulcrum of it all

THERE'S AN ORDER TO LIFE in the Fulcrum.

Waking comes with dawn. Since that's what Damaya always did back on the farm, this is easy for her. For the other grits—and that's what she is now, an unimportant bit of rock ready to be polished into usefulness, or at least to help grind other, better rocks—waking comes when one of the instructors enters the dormitory and rings a painfully loud bell, which makes them all flinch even if they're already awake. Everyone groans, including Damaya. She likes this. It makes her feel like she's part of something.

They rise and make their beds, folding the top sheets military-style. Then they shuffle into the showers, which are white with electric lights and shining with tile, and which smell of herbal cleaners because the Fulcrum hires Strongbacks and commless from Yumenes' shantytowns to come and clean them. For this and other reasons the showers are wonderful. She's never been able to use hot water every day like this, tons of it just falling from holes in the ceiling like the most perfect rain ever. She tries not to be obvious about it, because some of the other grits are Equatorials and would laugh at her, the bumpkin overwhelmed by the novelty of easy, comfortable cleanliness. But, well, she is.

After that the grits brush their teeth and come back to the dormitory room to dress and groom themselves. Their uniforms are stiff gray fabric pants and tunics with black piping, girls and boys alike. Children whose hair is long and locked or thin enough to be combed and pulled back must do so; children whose hair is ashblow or kinky or short must make sure it's shaped neatly. Then the grits stand in front of their beds, waiting while instructors come in and move down the rows for inspection. They want to make sure the grits are actually clean. The instructors check the beds, too, to make sure no one's peed in theirs or done a shoddy job of folding the corners. Grits who aren't clean are sent back for another shower—this one cold, with the instructor standing there watching to make sure it's done right. (Damaya makes sure she'll never have to do this, because it doesn't sound fun at all.) Grits who haven't dressed and groomed themselves or tended the bed properly are sent to Discipline, where they receive punishments suited to the infraction. Uncombed hair gets cut very short; repeat offenders are shaven bald. Unbrushed teeth merit mouthwashing with soap. Incorrect dress is corrected with five switches across the naked buttocks or back, incorrect bedmaking with ten. The switches do not break the skin—instructors are trained to strike just enough—but they do leave welts, which are probably meant to chafe underneath the stiff fabric of the uniforms.

You are representatives of us all, the instructors say, if any grit dares to protest this treatment. *When you're dirty, all orogenes are dirty. When you're lazy, we're all lazy. We hurt you so you'll do the rest of us no harm.*

Once Damaya would have protested the unfairness of such judgments. The children of the Fulcrum are all different: different ages, different colors, different shapes. Some speak Sanze-mat with different accents, having originated from different parts of the world. One girl has sharp teeth because it is her race's custom to file them; another boy has no penis, though he stuffs a sock into his underwear after every shower; another girl has rarely had regular meals and wolfs down every one like she's still starving. (The instructors keep finding food hidden in and around her bed. They make her eat it, all of it, in front of them, even if it makes her sick.) One cannot reasonably expect sameness out of so much difference, and it makes no sense for Damaya to be judged by the behavior of children who share nothing save the curse of orogeny with her.

But Damaya understands now that the world is not fair. They are orogenes, the Misalems of the world, born cursed and terrible. This is what is necessary to make them safe. Anyway, if she does what she's supposed to, no unexpected things happen. Her bed is always perfect, her teeth clean and white. When she starts to forget what matters, she looks at her right hand, which twinges now and again on cold days, though the bones healed within a few weeks. She remembers the pain, and the lesson that it taught.

After inspection there is breakfast—just a bit of fruit and a piece of sausage in the Sanzed fashion, which they pick up in the dormitory foyer and eat on the way. They walk in small groups to lessons in the various courts of the Fulcrum that the older grits call crucibles, though that's not what they're supposed to be called. (There are many things the grits say to each other that they can never say to the adults. The adults know, but pretend they don't. The world is not fair, and sometimes it makes no sense.)

In the first crucible, which is roofed over, the first hours of the day are spent in chairs with a slateboard and a lecture by one of the Fulcrum's instructors. Sometimes there are oral examinations, with questions peppered at the grits one by one until someone falters. The grit who falters will have to clean the slateboards. Thus do they learn to work calmly under pressure.

"What was the name of the first Old Sanze emperor?"

"A shake in Erta emits push waves at 6:35 and seven seconds, and vibrational waves at 6:37 and twenty-seven seconds. What is the lag time?" This question becomes more complex if it is asked of older grits, going into logarithms and functions.

"Stonelore advises, 'Watch for the center of the circle.' Where is the fallacy in this statement?"

This is the question that lands on Damaya one day, so she stands to answer: "The statement explains how one may estimate the location of an orogene by map," she says. "It is incorrect—oversimplified—because an orogene's region of consumption is not *circular*, it is *toroidal*. Many people then fail to understand that the zone of effect extends downward or upward as well, and can be deformed in other three-dimensional ways by a skilled orogene."

Instructor Marcasite nods approval for this explanation, which makes Damaya feel proud. She likes being right. Marcasite continues: "And since stonelore would be harder to remember if it was full of phrases like 'watch for the inverted fulcrum of a conical torus,' we get centers and circles. Accuracy is sacrificed in the name of better poetry."

This makes the class laugh. It's not that funny, but there's a lot of nervous tension on quiz days.

After lectures there is lunch in the big open-air court set aside for that purpose. This court has a roof of oiled canvas strips on slats, which can be rolled shut on rainy days—although Yumenes, which is far inland, rarely has such days. So the grits usually get to sit at long bench-tables under a bright blue sky as they giggle and kick each other and call each other names. There's lots of food to make up for the light breakfast, all of it varied and delicious and rich, though much of it is from distant lands and Damaya does not know what some of it is called. (She eats her share anyway. Muh Dear taught her never to waste food.)

This is Damaya's favorite time of day, even though she is one of the grits who sit alone at an empty table. Many of the other children do this, she has noticed—too many to dismiss them all as those who've failed to make friends. The others have a look to them that she is rapidly learning to recognize—a certain furtiveness of movement, a hesitancy, a tension about the eyes and jawline. Some of them bear the marks of their old lives in a more obvious way. There is a gray-haired western Coaster boy who's missing an arm above the elbow, though he is deft enough at managing without it. A Sanzed girl maybe five years older has the twisting seams of old burn scars all down one side of her face. And then there is another grit even newer than Damaya, whose left hand is in a special leather binding like a glove without fingers, which fastens around the wrist. Damaya recognizes this binding because she wore it herself while her hand healed, during her first few weeks at the Fulcrum.

They do not look at each other much, she and these others who sit off to themselves.

After lunch the grits travel through the Ring Garden in long, silent lines overseen by the instructors so that they will not talk or stare too obviously at the adult orogenes. Damaya does stare, of course, because they're supposed to. It's important that they see what awaits them once they begin earning rings. The garden is a wonder, as are the orogenes themselves: adult and elderly of every conformation, all healthy and beautiful—confident, which makes them beautiful. All are starkly forbidding in their black uniforms and polished boots. Their ringed fingers flick and flash as they gesture freely, or turn the pages of books they don't *have* to read, or brush back a lover's curling hair from one ear.

What Damaya sees in them is something she does not understand at first, though she *wants* it with a desperation that surprises and unnerves her. As those first weeks pass into months and she grows familiar with the routine, she begins to understand what it is that the older orogenes display: control. They have mastered their power. No ringed orogene would ice the courtyard just because some boy shoved her. None of these sleek, black-clad professionals would bat so much as an eyelash at either a strong earthshake, or a family's rejection. They know what they are, and they have accepted all that means, and they fear nothing—not the stills, not themselves, not even Old Man Earth.

If to achieve this Damaya must endure a few broken bones, or a few years in a place where no one loves or even likes her, that is a small price to pay.

Thus she pours herself into the afternoon training in Applied Orogeny. In the practice crucibles, which are situated within the innermost ring of the Fulcrum complex, Damaya stands in a row with other grits of a similar level of experience. There, under an instructor's watchful gaze, she learns how to visualize and breathe, and to extend her awareness of the earth at will and not merely in reaction to its movements or her own agitation. She learns to control her agitation, and all the other emotions that can induce the power within her to react to a threat that does not exist. The grits have no fine control at this stage, so none of them are allowed to actually *move* anything. The instructors can tell, somehow, when they're about to—and because the instructors all have rings, they can pierce any child's developing torus in a way that Damaya does not yet understand, administering a quick, stunning slap of icy cold air as a warning. It is a reminder of the seriousness of the lesson—and it also lends credence to a rumor that the older grits have whispered in the dark after lights out. *If you make too many mistakes in the lessons, the instructors ice you.*

It will be many years before Damaya understands that when the instructors kill an errant student, it is meant not as a goad, but as a mercy.

After Applied comes dinner and free hour, a time in which they may do what they please, allowed in deference to their youth. The newest grits usually fall into bed early, exhausted by the effort of learning to control invisible, semivoluntary muscles. The older children have better stamina and more energy, so there's laughter and play around the dormitory bunks for a while, until the instructors declare lights-out. The next day, it all begins again.

Thus do six months pass.

* * *

One of the older grits comes over to Damaya at lunch. The boy is tall and Equatorial, though he doesn't look fully Sanzed. His hair has the ashblow texture, but it's backwater blond in color. He's got the broad shoulders and developing bulk of Strongback, which makes her wary at once. She still sees Zab everywhere.

The boy smiles, though, and there is no menace in his manner as he stops beside the small table she inhabits alone. "Can I sit down?"

She shrugs, because she doesn't want him to but is curious despite herself. He puts down his tray and sits. "I'm Arkete," he says.

"That's not your name," she replies, and his smile falters a little.

"It's the name my parents gave me," he says, more seriously, "and it's the name I intend to keep until they find a way to take it from me. Which they'll never do because, y'know, it's a name. But if you'd rather, I'm *officially* called Maxixe."

The highest-quality grade of aquamarine, used almost exclusively for art. It suits him; he's a handsome boy despite his obvious Arctic or Antarctic heritage (she doesn't care, but Equatorials do), and that makes him dangerous in the sharp-faceted way that handsome big boys have always been. She decides to call him Maxixe because of this. "What do you want?"

"Wow, you're really working on your popularity." Maxixe

starts eating, resting his elbows on the table while he chews. (But he checks to make sure there are no instructors around to chide him on his manners, first.) "You know how these things are supposed to work, right? The good-looking popular guy suddenly shows interest in the mousy girl from the country. Everyone hates her for it, but she starts to gain confidence in herself. Then the guy betrays her and regrets it. It's awful, but afterward she 'finds herself,' realizes she doesn't need him, and maybe there's some other stuff that happens"—he waggles his fingers in the air—"and finally she turns into the most beautiful girl ever because she likes herself. But it won't work at all if you don't stammer and blush and pretend you don't like me."

She's utterly confused by this salad of words. It annoys her so much that she says, "I *don't* like you."

"Ouch." He pantomimes being stabbed in the heart. In spite of herself, his antics do make Damaya relax a little. This makes him grin, in turn. "Ah, that's better. What, don't you read books? Or didn't you have lorists in whatever midlatter hole you came from?"

She doesn't read books, because she's not very good at reading yet. Her parents taught her enough to get by, and the instructors have assigned her a weekly regimen of additional reading to improve her skills in this area. But she's not about to admit that. "Of course we had lorists. They taught us stonelore and told us how to prepare—"

"Urgh. You had *real* lorists." The boy shakes his head. "Where I grew up, nobody listened to them except creche teachers and the most boring geomests. What everybody liked instead were the pop lorists—you know, the kind who perform in ampitheaters and bars? Their stories don't teach anything. They're just fun."

Damaya has never heard of this, but maybe it's some Equatorial fad that never made it to the Nomidlats. "But lorists tell *stonelore*. That's the whole point. If these people don't even do that, shouldn't they be called... I don't know, something else?"

"Maybe." He shrugs and reaches over to steal a piece of cheese from her plate; she's so flustered by the pop lorist thing that she doesn't protest. "The real lorists have been complaining about them to the Yumenescene Leadership, but that's all I know about it. They brought me here two years ago, and I haven't heard anything since." He sighs. "I hope the pop lorists don't go away, though. I like them, even if their stories are a little stupid and predictable. 'Course, their stories are set in real creches, not places like this." His lips twitch down at the corners as he looks around at their surroundings in faint disapproval.

Damaya knows full well what he means, but she wants to know if he'll say. "Places like this?"

His eyes slide sidelong back to hers. Flashing his teeth in a smile that probably charms more people than it alarms, he says, "Oh, you know. Beautiful, wonderful, perfect places full of love and light."

Damaya laughs, then stops herself. Then she's not sure why she did either.

"Yeah." The boy resumes eating with relish. "Took me a while to laugh after I got here, too."

She likes him, a little, after this statement.

He doesn't want anything, she realizes after a time. He makes small talk and eats her food, which is all right since she was mostly finished anyway. He doesn't seem to mind when she calls him Maxixe. She still doesn't trust him, but he just seems to want someone to talk to. Which she can understand.

Eventually he stands and thanks her—"For this scintillating conversation," which was almost entirely one-sided on his part—and then heads off to rejoin his friends. She puts it out of her mind and goes on about her day.

Except. The next day, something changes.

It starts that morning in the shower, when someone bumps into her hard enough to make her drop her washcloth. When she looks around, none of the boys or girls sharing the shower with her look in her direction, or apologize. She chalks it up to an accident.

When she gets out of the shower, however, someone has stolen her shoes. They were with her clothes, which she'd prepared before the shower and laid out on her bed to speed up the process of getting dressed. She always does this, every morning. Now they're gone.

She looks for them methodically, trying to make sure she hasn't forgotten them somewhere even though she knows she hasn't. And when she looks around at the other grits, who are carefully not looking at her as the instructors call inspection and she can do nothing but stand there in her impeccable uniform and bare feet, she knows what's happening.

She fails inspection and is punished with a scrub-brushing, which leaves her soles raw and stinging for the rest of the day inside the new shoes they give her.

This is only the beginning.

That evening at dinner, someone puts something in the juice she is given with her meal. Grits with poor table manners are given kitchen duty, which means they have access to everyone's food. She forgets this, and does not think about the odd taste of the juice until it becomes hard to focus and her head starts hurting. Even then she's not sure what's happening, as she stumbles and lurches on her way back to the dormitory. One of the instructors pulls her aside, frowning at her lack of coordination, and sniffs her breath. "How much have you had to drink?" the man asks.

Damaya frowns, confused at first because she just had a regular-sized glass of juice. The reason it takes her a while to understand is that she's drunk: Someone has slipped alcohol into her juice.

Orogenes aren't supposed to drink. Ever. The power to move mountains plus inebriation equals disaster waiting to happen. The instructor who stopped Damaya is Galena, one of the younger four-ringers, who runs the afternoon orogeny drills. He's merciless in the crucible, but for whatever reason he takes pity on her now. Galena takes her out of lineup and brings her to his own quarters, which are fortunately nearby. There he puts Damaya on a couch and commands her to sleep it off.

In the morning, as Damaya drinks water and winces at the awful taste in her mouth, Galena sits her down and says, "You need to deal with this now. If any of the seniors had caught you—" He shakes his head. It's an offense so severe that there's no standing punishment. It would be terrible; that's all either of them needs to understand.

It doesn't matter why the other grits have decided to bully

her. All that matters is that they're doing it, and that these are no harmless pranks. They're trying to get her iced. Galena's right; Damaya's got to deal with this. Now.

She decides she needs an ally.

There's another girl among the loners that she's noticed. *Everyone* notices this girl; there's something wrong with her. Her orogeny is a precarious, pent thing, a dagger constantly poised to plunge into the earth—and training has only made it worse, because now the knife is sharper. That's not supposed to happen. Selu is her name, and she hasn't yet earned or been given an orogene name, but the other grits call her *Crack* to be funny, and that is the name that has stuck. She even answers to that name, since she can't seem to stop them from using it.

Everyone's already whispering that she won't make it. Which means she's perfect.

Damaya makes her move on Crack at breakfast the next day. (She drinks only water now, which she has drawn from a nearby fountain. She has to eat the food they serve her, but she inspects it carefully before putting anything in her mouth.) "Hi," she says, setting her tray down.

Crack eyes her. "Really? Things are bad enough that you need *me*?"

It's a good sign that they can be honest with each other right off. "Yes," Damaya says, and sits since Crack hasn't really objected. "They're messing with you, too, aren't they?" Of course they are. Damaya hasn't seen whatever they're doing, but it only makes sense. There's an order to life in the Fulcrum.

Crack sighs. This makes the room reverberate faintly, or so it feels for an instant. Damaya makes herself not react, because a good partnership should not begin with a display of fear. Crack sees this and relaxes, just a little. The judder of imminent disaster fades.

"Yeah," Crack says, softly. Damaya realizes all of a sudden that Crack is *angry*, though she keeps her gaze on her plate. It's there in the way she holds her fork too tightly, and the way her expression is too blank. All at once Damaya wonders: Is Crack's control really a problem? Or is it simply that her tormentors have done their best to *make* her crack? "So what do you want to do about it?"

Damaya outlines her plan. After an initial flinch, Crack realizes she is serious. They finish eating in silence, while Crack thinks it over. At last, Crack says, "I'm in."

The plan is really quite simple. They need to find the head of the serpent, and the best way to do that is to use bait. They decide on Maxixe, because of course Maxixe must be involved. Damaya's troubles began right after his ostensibly friendly overtures. They wait until he's in the shower one morning, laughing with his friends, and then Damaya returns to her bunk. "Where are my shoes?" she asks, loudly.

The other grits look around; some of them groan, all too ready to believe that bullies would be uncreative enough to pull the same trick twice. Jasper, who's only been in the Fulcrum a few months longer than Damaya, scowls. "Nobody took your shoes this time," he says. "They're in your trunk."

"How do you know? Did *you* take them?" Damaya moves to confront him, and he bristles and meets her in the middle of the room, his shoulders back with affront.

"I didn't take your crap! If they're lost, you lost them."

"I don't lose things." She jabs him in the chest with a finger. He's a Nomidlatter like her, but thin and pale; probably from some comm close to the Arctic. He turns red when he's angry; the other kids make fun of this, but not much, because he teases other kids more loudly. (Good orogeny is deflection, not cessation.) "If you didn't take them, then you know who did." She jabs him again, and he swats her hand away.

"Don't *touch* me, you stupid little pig. I'll break your rusting finger."

"What is this?"

They all jump and fall silent and turn. In the doorway, ready to begin evening inspection, is Carnelian, one of the few seniors among the instructors. He's a big man, bearded and older and severe, with six rings; they're all afraid of him. In token of which, the grits immediately scramble into their places before the bunks, standing at attention. Damaya, in spite of herself, feels a bit of trepidation—until she catches Crack's eye, and Crack gives her a small nod. The distraction was enough.

"I said, what is this?" Carnelian comes into the room once they're assembled. He focuses on Jasper, who's still apple-red, though probably with fear rather than anger this time. "Is there some problem?"

Jasper glares at Damaya. "Not with *me*, Instructor."

When Carnelian turns to her, she is ready. "Someone stole my shoes, Instructor."

"Again?" This is a good sign. Last time, Carnelian simply berated her for losing her own shoes and making excuses. "You have proof it was Jasper who stole them?"

Here's the tricky part. She's never been good at lying. "I know it was a boy. They disappeared during the last shower, and all the girls were *in* there with me. I counted."

Carnelian sighs. "If you're trying to blame someone else for your shortcomings—"

"She's always doing that," says a red-haired eastern Coaster girl.

"She's got a *lot* of shortcomings," says a boy who looks like he comes from the same comm, if he's not a relative of hers outright. Half the grits snicker.

"Search the boys' chests." Damaya speaks over their laughter. It's something she didn't ask for last time, because she wasn't sure where the shoes would be. This time she is sure. "There wasn't much time to get rid of the shoes. They have to still be here. Look in their chests."

"That's not fair," says one tiny Equatorial boy, who looks barely old enough to be out of the toddlers' creche.

"No, it isn't," says Carnelian, his scowl deepening as he looks at her. "Be very certain before you ask me to violate your fellow trainees' privacy. If you're wrong, we won't go easy on you this time."

She still remembers the sting of brush-scrubbed feet. "I understand, Instructor."

Carnelian sighs. Then he turns to the boys' side of the dormitory room. "Open your trunks, all of you. Let's get this over with."

There's a lot of grumbling as they open their chests, and enough glares that Damaya knows she's made things worse for herself. They all hate her now. Which is fine; if they're going to hate her, she'd rather they do it for a reason. But that might change once this game has played out.

Maxixe opens his chest along with the rest, sighing mortally as he does so, and her shoes are right there on top of the folded uniforms. When Damaya sees his expression change from annoyance to confusion and then mortification, she feels bad. She doesn't like hurting people. But she watches closely, and the instant Maxixe's expression changes to fury, he swings around and glares at someone. She follows his glare, tense, ready—

—to see that he's looking at Jasper. Yes. That was what she expected. He's the one, then.

Jasper, though, has suddenly gone pale. He shakes his head as if trying to throw off Maxixe's accusatory look; it doesn't work.

Instructor Carnelian sees all of this. A muscle in his jaw flexes as he glances toward Damaya again. He looks almost angry with her. But why? He must understand that she has to do this.

"I see," he says, as if responding to her thought. Then he focuses on Maxixe. "Do you have anything to say for yourself?"

Maxixe doesn't protest his innocence. She can see by the slump of his shoulders and the shaking of his fists that he knows there's no point. But he's not going down alone. With his head down, he says, "Jasper took her shoes last time."

"I did not!" Jasper backs away from his bunk and the inspection line, into the middle of the room. He's trembling all over. Even his eyes are trembling; he looks ready to cry. "He's lying, he's just trying to pass this off on someone else—" But when Carnelian turns to Jasper, Jasper flinches and goes still. He almost spits the next words. "*She* sold them for me. Traded them to one of the cleaning commless in exchange for *liquor*."

And then he points at Crack.

Damaya inhales, everything inside her going still with shock. Crack?

Crack.

"You rusting cannibalson *whore*!" Crack clenches her fists. "You *let* that old pervert feel you up for liquor and a letter, you know full well he wouldn't give it to us just for *shoes*—"

"It was from my mother!" Jasper's definitely crying now. "I didn't want him to, to, but I couldn't...they wouldn't let me write to her..."

"You liked it," Crack sneers. "I told you I'd tell if you said anything, didn't I? Well, I saw you. He had his *fingers* in you and you moaned like it felt *good*, just like the little wannabe Breeder you are, only Breeders have *standards*—"

This is wrong. This is all wrong. Everyone's staring at each other, at Crack as she rants, at Damaya, at Jasper as he weeps, at Carnelian. The room is full of gasps and murmurings. That feeling is back: the pent, fraught, not-quite-reverberation that is Crack's orogeny unfurling itself, and everyone in the room is twitching with it. Or maybe they're twitching at the words and what they mean, because these aren't things grits should know, or do. Getting in trouble, sure, they're kids and kids do that. Getting in trouble *like this*, no.

"No!" Jasper wails the word at Crack. "I told you not to tell!" He's sobbing openly now. His mouth works but nothing more comes out that's intelligible, nothing but a low, despairing moan—or maybe it's just a continuation of the word *no*. Impossible to tell, because everyone else is making noise now, some of them hissing at Crack to shut up, some sniffing with Jasper, some of them giggling nervously at Jasper's tears, some of them stage-whispering at each other for confirmation of things they knew but didn't believe—

"*Enough.*" The room goes silent with Carnelian's quiet command, except for Jasper's soft hitching. After a moment, Carnelian's jaw flexes. "You, you, and you." He points at Maxixe, Jasper, and Crack. "Come with me."

He walks out of the room. The three grits look at each other, and it's a wonder none of them combust from the sheer hatred in these looks. Then Maxixe curses and moves to follow Carnelian. Jasper scrubs a forearm across his face and does the same, his head hanging and fists tight. Crack glares around the room, defiant—until her eyes meet Damaya's. Then Crack flinches.

Damaya stares back, because she's too stunned to look away. And because she is furious with herself. *This* is what comes of trusting others. Crack was not her friend, wasn't even someone she liked, but she'd thought they could at least help each other. Now she's found the head of the snake that's been trying to eat her, and it's halfway down the gullet of a completely different snake. The result is something too obscene to look at, let alone kill.

"Better you than me," Crack says softly, into the room's silence. Damaya hasn't said anything, hasn't demanded an explanation, but Crack gives one anyway, right there in front of everyone. No one says a word. No one even breathes loudly. "That was the idea. One more slip-up and I'm done for, but you, you're Little Citizen Perfect. Top scores on all the tests, perfect control in Applied, not a wrinkle out of place. The instructors wouldn't really do much to you, not yet. And while they were trying to figure out how their star pupil suddenly went wrong, everyone would stop waiting for me to blow up a mountain. Or trying to *make* me do it... for a while, anyway." Her smile fades, and she looks away. "That was the idea."

Damaya can't say anything. She can't even think. So after a while Crack shakes her head, sighs, and moves to follow the others after Carnelian.

The room is still. Nobody looks at anybody else.

Then there's a stir at the door as two other instructors come in and begin examining Crack's bunk and trunk. The grits watch as one woman lifts the mattress, and the other ducks under it. There's a brief ripping sound, and the instructor reappears with a big brown flask, half full, in one hand. She opens the flask and sniffs its contents, grimaces, and nods to the other woman. They both leave.

When the echoes of their steps fade, Damaya goes to Maxixe's trunk to retrieve her shoes. She closes the lid; the sound is very loud in the silence. No one moves until she goes back to her own bunk and sits down to put the shoes on.

As if this is a signal, there are several sighs, and some of the others start moving, too—retrieving books for the next lesson, filing off to first crucible, going over to the sideboard where breakfast waits. When Damaya goes to the sideboard herself, another girl glances at her, then away, quickly. "Sorry," she mutters. "I'm the one who pushed you in the shower."

Damaya looks at her and sees lurking fear making the skin around her eyes tight.

"It's okay," she says, softly. "Don't worry about it."

The other grits never give Damaya trouble again. A few days later Maxixe returns with broken hands and haunted eyes; he never speaks to Damaya again. Jasper does not return, but Carnelian tells them he's been sent to the satellite Fulcrum up in Arctic, since the Fulcrum of Yumenes holds too many bad memories for him. This was meant as a kindness, perhaps, but Damaya knows an exile when she sees one.

It could be worse, though. No one ever sees or mentions Crack again.

* * *

FUNGUS SEASON: 602 Imperial. A series of oceanic eruptions during the eastern Equatorial monsoons increased humidity in the region and obscured sunlight for six months. While this was a mild Season as such things go, its timing created perfect conditions for a fungal bloom that spread across the Equatorials into the northern and southern midlats, wiping out then-staple-crop miroq (now extinct). The resulting famine is included in the official geomestric record, extending the Season's length to four years (two years for the fungus blight to run its course, two more for agriculture and food distribution systems to recover). Nearly all affected comms were able to subsist on their own stores, thus proving the efficacy of Imperial reforms and Seasonal planning. In its aftermath, many comms of the Nomidlats and Somidlats voluntarily joined the Empire, beginning its Golden Age.

—*The Seasons of Sanze*

12

Syenite finds a new toy

My colleague is ill," Syenite tells Asael Leadership Allia as she sits facing the woman across a desk. "He sends his apologies for being unable to assist. I will clear the blockage in your harbor."

"I'm sorry to hear of your senior's illness," says Asael, with a little smile that almost makes Syen's hackles rise. Almost, because she knew it was coming and could thus brace for it. It still rankles.

"But I must ask," Asael continues, looking overly concerned. "Will you be . . . sufficient?" Her eyes flick down to Syen's fingers, where Syen has taken great care to put her rings on the four fingers a casual observer would be most likely to see. Her hands are folded, with the thumb of that hand tucked out of the way for the moment; let Asael wonder if there's a fifth one there. But when Asael's eyes meet Syen's again, Syen sees only skepticism. She is unimpressed by four rings or even five.

And this is why I will never, ever take a mission with a ten-ringer again. Like she has a choice. She feels better thinking it anyway.

Syenite forces herself to smile, though she doesn't have Alabaster's knack for exaggerated politeness. She knows her smiles just look pissed-off. "In my last mission," she says, "I was responsible for demolishing three buildings out of a block of five. This was in downtown Dibars, an area with several thousand inhabitants on a busy day, and not far from the Seventh University." She uncrosses and recrosses her legs. The geomests had driven her half mad on that mission, constantly demanding reassurances that she wouldn't create a shake any stronger than a 5.0. Sensitive instruments, important calibrations, something like that. "It took five minutes, and no rubble landed outside of the demolition zone. That was before I earned my latest ring." And she'd kept the shake to a fourer, much to the geomests' delight.

"I'm pleased to hear you're so competent," says Asael. There is a pause, which makes Syen brace herself. "With your colleague unable to contribute, however, I see no reason for Allia to pay for the services of two orogenes."

"That's between you and the Fulcrum," Syen says, dismissively. She honestly doesn't care. "I suspect you'll get an argument from them because Alabaster is mentoring me on this trip, and overseeing my work even if he isn't actually doing it."

"But if he isn't here—"

"That's irrelevant." It galls, but Syenite decides to explain. "He wears ten rings. He'll be able to observe what I'm doing, and intervene if necessary, from his hotel room. He could do it while unconscious. Moreover, he's been quelling shakes in this area for the past few days, as we've traveled through it. That's a service he provides as a courtesy to local node maintainers—or to your comm, rather, since such a remote location doesn't have a node station nearby." As Asael's expression tightens into a frown, probably at the perceived insult, Syen spreads her hands. "The biggest difference between him and me is that I'm the one who needs to see what she's doing."

"I... see." Asael sounds deeply uneasy, as she should. Syen knows that it's the job of any Fulcrum orogene to ease the fears of the stills, and here Syen has exacerbated Asael's. But she's begun to develop a nasty suspicion about who in Allia might want Alabaster dead, so it's a good idea for her to dissuade Asael—or whoever Asael knows—from that plan. This pedantic minor bureaucrat has no idea how close her little city came to being flattened last night.

In the uncomfortable silence that falls, Syenite decides it's time she asks some questions of her own. And maybe stirs the shit a little, to see what rises to the top. "I see that the governor wasn't able to make it, today."

"Yes." Asael's face goes gameswoman-blank, all polite smile and empty eyes. "I did convey your colleague's request. Unfortunately, the governor was unable to make time in his schedule."

"That's a shame." And then, because Syenite is beginning to understand why Alabaster is such an ass about this, she folds her hands. "Unfortunately, it wasn't a request. Do you have a telegraph here? I'd like to send a message to the Fulcrum, let them know we'll be delayed."

Asael's eyes narrow, because of course they have a telegraph, and of course Syenite meant that as another dig. "Delayed."

"Well, yes." Syen raises her eyebrows. She knows she's not doing a good job of looking innocent, but she tries, at least.

"How long do you think it will be before the governor is able to meet with us? The Fulcrum will want to know." And she stands, as if to leave.

Asael tilts her head, but Syenite can see the tension in her shoulders. "I thought you were more reasonable than your colleague. You're actually going to walk out of here, and not clear our harbor, in a fit of pique."

"It isn't a fit of pique." Now Syen's mad for real. Now she gets it. She looks down at Asael, who sits there, smug and secure in her big chair behind her big desk, and it's an actual fight to keep her fists from clenching, her jaw muscles from flexing. "Would you tolerate this treatment, in our position?"

"Of course I would!" Asael straightens, surprised into an actual reaction for once. "The *governor* has no time for—"

"No, you wouldn't tolerate it. Because if you were in my position, you'd be the representative of an independent and powerful organization, not some two-quartz backwater flunky. You would expect to be treated like a skilled expert who's been learning her craft since childhood. Like someone who plies an important and *difficult* trade, and who's come to perform a task that dictates your comm's livelihood."

Asael is staring at her. Syenite pauses, takes a deep breath. She must stay polite, and wield that politeness like a finely knapped glassknife. She must be cold and calm in her anger, lest a lack of self-control be dismissed as the mark of monstrosity. Once the heat behind her eyes has eased, she steps forward.

"And yet you haven't shaken our hands, Asael Leader. You didn't look us in the eye when we first met. You *still* haven't offered that cup of safe that Alabaster suggested yesterday.

Would you do that to a decreed 'mest from the Seventh University? Would you do it to a master geneer, come to repair the comm's hydro? Would you do it to a representative of the Strongbacks' Union for your own comm?"

Asael actually flinches as the analogies finally get through to her. Syenite waits in silence, letting it gather pressure. Finally Asael says, "I see."

"Maybe you do." She keeps waiting, and Asael sighs.

"What do you want? An apology? Then I apologize. You must remember, though, that most normal people have never seen an orogene, let alone had to do business with one, and—" She spreads her hands. "Isn't it understandable that we might be . . . uncomfortable?"

"Discomfort is understandable. It's the rudeness that isn't." Rust this. This woman doesn't deserve the effort of her explanation. Syen decides to save that for someone who matters. "And that's a really shitty apology. 'I'm sorry you're so abnormal that I can't manage to treat you like a human being.' "

"You're a rogga," Asael snaps, and then has the gall to look surprised at herself.

"Well." Syenite makes herself smile. "At least that's out in the open." She shakes her head and turns toward the door. "I'll come back tomorrow. Maybe you'll have had time to check the governor's schedule by then."

"You are under contract," Asael says, her voice tight enough to quaver. "You are *required* to perform the service for which we have paid your organization."

"And we will." Syenite reaches the door and stops with her hand on the handle, shrugging. "But the contract doesn't specify how long we have, upon arrival, to get it done." She's bluffing. She has no idea what's in the contract. But she's willing to bet Asael doesn't, either; a deputy governor doesn't sound important enough to know that sort of thing. "Thanks for the stay at the Season's End, by the way. The beds are very comfortable. And the food's delicious."

That, of course, does it. Asael stands as well. "Stay here. I'll go and speak with the governor."

So Syen smiles pleasantly, and sits back down to wait. Asael leaves the room, and stays gone for long enough that Syen starts to doze off. She recovers when the door opens again, and another Coaster woman, elderly and portly, comes in with a chastened-looking Asael. The governor's a man. Syenite sighs inwardly and braces herself for more weaponized politeness.

"Syenite Orogene," the woman says, and despite her rising ire Syenite is impressed by the gravity of her presence. The "orogene" after Syen's name isn't necessary, of course, but it's a nice bit of much-needed courtesy—so Syen rises, and the woman immediately steps forward and offers a hand for her to shake. Her skin is cool and dry and harder than Syenite expected. No calluses, just hands that have done their share of everyday labor. "My name is Heresmith Leadership Allia. I'm the lieutenant governor. The governor genuinely is too busy to meet with you today, but I've cleared enough time on my schedule, and I hope my greeting will be sufficient...especially as it comes with an apology for your poor treatment thus far. I can assure you that Asael will be censured for her behavior, to remind her that it's always good leadership to treat others—*all* others—with courtesy."

Well. The woman could be just playing a politician's game, or she could be lying about being the lieutenant governor; maybe Asael's found a very well-dressed janitor to play the part. Still, it's an effort at compromise, and Syen will take it.

"Thank you," she says, with genuine gratitude. "I'll convey your apology to my colleague Alabaster."

"Good. Please also tell him that Allia will pay your expenses, per our agreed-upon contract, for up to three days before and three after your clearing of the harbor." And there's an edge to her smile now, which Syenite knows she probably deserves. This woman, it seems, actually has read the contract.

Doesn't matter, though. "I appreciate the clarification."

"Is there anything else you need during your stay? Asael would be happy to provide a tour of the city, for example."

Damn. Syen *likes* this woman. She stifles the urge to smile and glances at Asael, who's managed to compose herself by this point; she gazes impassively back at Syenite. And Syen's tempted to do what Alabaster probably would, and take Heresmith up on that tacit offer of Asael's humiliation. But Syenite is tired, and this whole trip's been hellish, and the sooner it's over and she's back home at the Fulcrum, the better.

"No need," she says, and does Asael's face twitch a little in suppressed relief? "I'd actually like to get a look at the harbor, if I may, so that I can assess the problem."

"Of course. But surely you'd like refreshment first? At least a cup of safe."

Syenite can't help it now. Her lips twitch. "I don't actually *like* safe, I should probably say."

"No one does." And there's no mistaking the genuine smile on Heresmith's face. "Anything else, then, before we go?"

Now it's Syen's turn to be surprised. "You're coming with us?"

Heresmith's expression grows wry. "Well, our comm's livelihood *is* dependent on you, after all. It seems only proper."

Oh, yeah. This one's a keeper. "Then please proceed, Heresmith Leader." Syenite gestures toward the door, and they all head out.

* * *

The harbor's wrong.

They're standing on a kind of boardwalk along the western curve of the harbor's half circle. From there most of Allia can be seen, spreading up the caldera slopes that surround the waterfront. The city really is quite lovely. It's a beautiful day, bright and warm, with a sky so deep and clear that Syenite thinks the stargazing at night should be amazing. Yet it's what she can't see—under the water, along the harbor bottom—that makes her skin crawl.

"That's not coral," she says.

Heresmith and Asael turn to her, both of them looking puzzled. "Pardon?" asks Heresmith.

Syenite moves away from them, going to the railing and extending her hands. She doesn't need to gesture; she just wants them to know she's doing something. A Fulcrum orogene always reassures clients of their awareness and understanding of the situation, even when those clients have no actual idea what's going on. "The harbor floor. The *top* layer is coral." She thinks. She's never felt coral before, but it feels like what she expected: layers of wriggling bright life that she can pull from, if she needs to, to fuel her orogeny; and a solid core of ancient calcified death. But the coral heap sits atop a humped ridge in the floor of the harbor, and although it feels natural—there are usually folds like this in places where land meets sea, she's read—Syenite can tell it's not.

It's absolutely straight, for one thing. And huge; the ridge spans the width of the harbor. But more importantly, *it isn't there*.

The rock beneath the raised layers of silt and sand, that is: She can't feel it. She should be able to, if it's pushing up the seafloor like this. She can feel the weight of the water atop it, and the rock deformed by its weight and pressure underneath, and the strata around it, but not the actual obstruction itself. There might as well be a big empty hole on the bottom of the harbor... around which the entire harbor floor has shaped itself.

Syenite frowns. Her fingers spread and twitch, following the flow and curve of the sesuna. Soft slither of loose schist and sand and organic matter, cool press of solid bedrock, flow and dip. As she follows it, she belatedly remembers to narrate her explorations. "There's something *beneath* the coral, buried in the ocean floor. Not far down. The rock underneath is compressed; it must be heavy..." But why can't she feel it, if so? Why can she detect the obstruction only by its effect on everything nearby? "It's strange."

"Is it relevant?" That's Asael, maybe trying to sound professional and intelligent in order to get back into Heresmith's good graces. "All we need is for the coral blockage to be destroyed."

"Yes, but the coral's on top of it." She searches for the coral and finds it all around the edges of the harbor; a theory forms. "That's why this is the only place in the deep part of the harbor that's blocked by coral. It's growing *on top of* the thing, where the ocean floor has effectively been raised. Coral's a thing of the shallows, but it can get plenty of sun-warmed water, along this ridge."

"Rusting Earth. Does that mean the coral will just grow back?" That's one of the men who came with Asael and Heresmith. They're a bunch of clerks, as far as Syenite can tell, and she keeps forgetting they're present until they speak. "The whole *point* of this is to clear the harbor for good."

Syenite exhales and relaxes her sessapinae, opening her eyes so they'll know she's done. "Eventually, yes," she says, turning to them. "Look, here's what you're dealing with. This is your harbor." She cups her left hand in an approximate circle, two-thirds closed. Allia's harbor is more irregular than this, but they get it, she sees as they step closer to her demonstration. So she lays the thumb of her right hand across the open part of the circle, almost but not quite closing it off. "This is the position of the thing. It's slightly elevated at one end"—she wiggles the tip of her thumb—"because there's a natural incline in the substrate. That's where most of the coral is. The waters at the far end of the thing are deeper, and colder." Awkwardly she waggles her hand to indicate the heel of her thumb. "That's the open channel you've been using for port traffic. Unless this coral suddenly starts liking cold dark water, or another variety of coral shows up that does, then that part may never become occluded."

But even as she says this, it occurs to her: Coral builds on itself. New creatures grow on the bones of their predecessors; in time, that will lift even the colder part of the harbor into the zone of optimal growth. And with perfect timing Asael frowns and says, "Except that channel *has* been closing, slowly but surely, over the years. We have accounts from a few decades ago that say we used to be able to accommodate boats across the middle of the harbor; we can't, anymore."

Underfires. When Syen gets back to the Fulcrum, she's going to tell them to add rock-building marine life to the grit curriculum; ridiculous that it's not something they learn already. "If this comm's been around for many Seasons and you're only just now having this problem, then obviously this isn't the kind of coral that grows quickly."

"Allia is only two Seasons old," says Heresmith, with a pained smile at Syen. That's a respectable achievement in and of itself. In the midlats and arctics, a lot of comms don't last a single Season; the coasts are even more volatile. But of course, Heresmith thinks she's talking to a born-and-bred Yumenescene.

Syenite tries to remember the stuff she didn't sleep through in history creche. The Choking Season is the one that occurred most recently, a little over a hundred years ago; it was mild as Seasons have gone, killing mostly people in the Antarctic, near Mount Akok when it blew. Before that was the Acid Season? Or was it Boiling? She always gets those two mixed up. Whichever one it was, it was two or maybe three hundred years before Choking, and it was a bad one. Right—there were no seaside comms left after that one, so naturally Allia can only be a few decades younger, founded when the waters sweetened and receded and left the coastline habitable again.

"So that coral blocked the harbor over the course of four hundred years or so," Syenite says, thinking aloud. "Maybe with a setback during Choking..." How does coral survive a Fifth Season? She has no idea, but it clearly needs warmth and light to thrive, so it must have died back during that one. "All right, let's say it really grew into a blockage over a hundred years."

"Fire-under-Earth," says another woman, looking horrified. "You mean we might have to do this *again* in just a century?"

"We will still be paying the Fulcrum in a century," says Heresmith, sighing, and the look she throws Syenite is not resentful, just resigned. "Your superiors charge dearly for your services, I'm afraid."

Syenite resists the urge to shrug. It's true.

They all look at each other, and then they look at her, and by this Syen knows: They're about to ask her to do something stupid.

"That's a very bad idea," she says preemptively, holding up her hands. "Seriously. I've never shifted anything underwater before; that's why I had a senior assigned to me." Fat lot of good he's been. "And more importantly, *I don't know what that thing is.* It could be a massive gas or oil pocket that will poison your harbor waters for years." It's not. You know this because no oil or gas pocket is as perfectly straight and dense as this thing is, and because you can *sess* oil and gas. "It could even be the remnant of some especially stupid deadciv that seeded all its harbors with bombs." Oh, that was brilliant. They're staring at her now, horrified. She tries again.

"Commission a study," she says. "Bring in some geomests who study marine floors, maybe some geneers who know something about..." She waggles a hand, guesses wildly. "Ocean currents. Figure out all the positives and negatives. *Then* call in someone like me." She hopes it won't be her again, specifically. "Orogeny should always be your last resort, not your first."

That's better. They're listening. Two of the ones she doesn't know start murmuring quietly to each other, and Heresmith has a thoughtful look on her face. Asael looks resentful, but that doesn't necessarily mean anything bad. Asael's not very smart.

"I'm afraid we have to consider it," says Heresmith at last, looking so deeply frustrated that Syenite feels sorry for her. "We can't afford another contract with the Fulcrum, and I'm not certain we can afford a study; the Seventh University and Geneer Licensure charge almost as much as the Fulcrum for their services. But most importantly, we can't afford to have the harbor blocked any longer—as you've guessed, we're already losing business to several other Coaster ports that can accommodate the heavier-riding freight vessels. If we lose accessibility altogether, there will be no reason for this comm to continue existing."

"And I'm sympathetic," Syen begins, but then one of the men who've been murmuring in the background scowls at her.

"You're also an agent of the Fulcrum," he says, "and we contracted you to do a job."

Maybe he's not a clerk, then. "I know that. And I'll do it right now, if you want." The coral is nothing, she knows, now that she's sessed it out. She can probably do that without rocking the boats in their moorings too much. "Your harbor can be usable tomorrow, if I get rid of the coral today—"

"But you were hired to *clear* the harbor," says Asael. "Permanently, not some temporary fix. If the problem has turned out to be bigger than you think, that's no excuse for not finishing the job." Her eyes narrow. "Unless there's some reason you're so reluctant to shift the obstruction."

Syen resists the urge to call Asael one of several names. "I've explained my reasoning, Leader. If it was my intention to cheat you in some way, why would I have told you anything about the obstruction? I would've just cleared the coral and let you figure it out the hard way when the stuff grows back."

That sways some of them, she can see; both of the group's men stop looking so suspicious. Even Asael falters out of her accusatory stance, straightening a little in unease. Heresmith, too, nods and turns to the others.

"I think we'll need to discuss this with the governor," she says, finally. "Present him all the options."

"Respectfully, Leader Heresmith," says one of the other women, frowning, "I don't *see* another option. We either clear the harbor temporarily, or permanently. Either way we pay the Fulcrum the same amount."

"Or you do nothing," Syenite says. They all turn to stare at her, and she sighs. She's a fool to even mention this; Earth knows what the seniors will do to her if she scuttles this mission. She can't help it, though. These people face the economic destruction of their whole community. It's not a Season, so they can move somewhere else, try to start over. Or they can dissolve, with all the comm's families trying to find places in other communities—

—which should work except for those family members who are poor, or infirm, or elderly. Or those who have uncles or siblings or parents who turned out to be orogenes; nobody will take those. Or if the community they try to join has too many members of their use-caste already. Or.

Rust it.

"If my colleague and I go back now," Syenite continues in spite of everything, "without doing anything, then we'll be in breach of contract. You'll be within your rights to demand your commission fee back, less our expenses for travel and local accommodations." She's looking dead at Asael as she says this; Asael's jaw muscles flex. "Your harbor will still be usable, at least for a few years more. Use that time, and the money you saved, to either study what's happening and figure out what's down there . . . or move your comm to a better location."

"*That's* not an option," says Asael, looking horrified. "This is our home."

Syen cannot help thinking of a fusty-smelling blanket.

"Home is people," she says to Asael, softly. Asael blinks. "Home is what you take with you, not what you leave behind."

Heresmith sighs. "That's very poetic, Syenite Orogene. But Asael is correct. Moving would mean the loss of our comm's identity, and possibly the fracturing of our population. It would also mean losing everything we've invested in this location." She gestures around, and Syenite understands what she means: You can move people easily, but not buildings. Not infrastructure. These things are wealth, and even outside of a Season, wealth means survival. "And there's no guarantee we won't face worse problems elsewhere. I appreciate your honesty—I do. Really. But, well . . . better the volcano we know."

Syenite sighs. She tried. "What do you want to do, then?"

"It seems obvious, doesn't it?"

It does. Evil Earth, it does.

"*Can* you do it?" asks Asael. And maybe she doesn't mean it as a challenge. Maybe she's just anxious, because after all what

Syen is talking about here is the fate of the comm Asael's been raised in and trained to guide and protect. And of course, as a Leader-born child, Asael would know nothing of this comm but its potential and welcome. She would never have reason to view her community with distrust or hatred or fear.

Syen doesn't mean to resent her. But she's already in a bad mood, and she's tired because she didn't get much sleep while saving Alabaster from poisoning the night before, and Asael's question assumes that she is less than what she is. It's one time too many, throughout this whole long, awful trip.

"Yes," Syenite snaps, turning and extending her hands. "You should all step back at least ten feet."

There are gasps from the group, murmurs of alarm, and she feels them recede quickly along the unfolding map of her awareness: hot bright jittering points moving out of easy reach. They're still in slightly less easy reach. So's their whole comm, really, a cluster of motion and life all around her, so easy to grasp and devour and use. But they don't need to know that. She's a professional, after all.

So she stabs the fulcrum of her power into the earth in a sharp, deep point so that her torus will be narrow and high rather than wide and deadly. And then she probes around the local substrate again, searching for the nearest fault or perhaps a remnant bit of heat from the extinct volcano that once formed Allia's caldera. The thing in the harbor is heavy, after all; she's going to need more than ambient power to shift it.

But as she searches, something very strange—and very familiar—happens. Her awareness shifts.

Suddenly she's not in the earth anymore. Something pulls

her away, and over, and down, and *in*. And all at once she is lost, flailing about in a space of black constricting cold, and the power that flows into her is not heat or motion or potential but something entirely else.

Something like what she felt last night when Alabaster comandeered her orogeny. But *this isn't Alabaster.*

And she's still in control, sort of. That is, she can't stop what's happening—she's taken in too much power already; if she tries to let it go, she'll ice half the comm and set off a shake that makes the shape of the harbor academic. But she can *use* the flood of power. She can steer it, for example, into the rock bed underneath the thing she can't see. She can push up, which lacks finesse and efficiency but gets the rusting job done, and she can feel the enormous *blankness* that is the object rise in response. If Alabaster's observing from his inn room, he must be impressed.

But where's the power coming from? How am I—

She can realize, belatedly and with some horror, that water moves much like rock in response to a sudden infusion of kinetic energy—but it's much, much faster to react. And she can react herself, faster than she's ever done before because she's *brimming* with strength, it's practically coming out of her pores and, Earthfire, it feels unbelievably good, it is child's play to stop the massive wave that's building and about to swamp the harbor. She just disippates its force, sending some back out to sea, channeling the rest into soothing the waters as the thing from the ocean floor breaks free of its encumbering sediment—and the coral, which just slides off and shatters—and begins to rise.

But.

But.

The thing isn't doing what she wants it to do. She'd intended to just shunt it to the side of the harbor; that way if the coral grows back, it still won't block the channel. Instead—

—Evil Earth—what the rust—instead—

Instead, it's *moving on its own.* She can't hold it. When she tries, all the power that she held just trickles away, sucked off somewhere as quickly as it infused her.

Syen falls back into herself then, gasping as she sags against the wooden railing of the boardwalk. Only a few seconds have passed. Her dignity will not allow her to fall to her knees, but the railing's the only thing keeping her up. And then she realizes no one will notice her weakness, because the boards beneath her feet, and the railing she's clinging to, are all rattling in an ominous sort of way.

The shake siren begins wailing, deafeningly loud, from a tower right behind her. People are running on the quays below the boardwalk and the streets around it; if not for the siren, she would probably hear screams. With an effort Syen lifts her head to see Asael, Heresmith, and their party hurrying away from the boardwalk, keeping well away from any buildings, their faces stark with fear. Of course they leave Syenite behind.

But that is not the thing that finally pulls Syen out of self-absorption. What does is a sudden spray of seawater that wafts across the quays like rain, followed by a shadow that darkens this whole side of the harbor. She turns.

There, rising slowly from the water and shedding the remnants of its earthen shell as it begins to hum and turn, is an obelisk.

It's different from the one Syen saw last night. That one, the purple one, she thinks is still a few miles off coast, though she doesn't look that way to confirm its presence. The one before her dominates all her vision, all her thought, because it's rusting *huge* and it's not even completely out of the water yet. Its color is the deep red of garnets, its shape a hexagonal column with a sharp-pointed, irregular tip. It is completely solid, not shimmering or flickering in the half-real way of most obelisks; it is wider than several ships put end to end. And of course it is long enough, as it continues to rise and turn, to nearly block off the whole harbor. A mile from tip to tip.

But something's wrong with it, which becomes clear as it rises. At the midpoint of the shaft, the clear, crystalline beauty of the thing gives way to cracks. Massive ones, ugly and black-tinged, as if some contaminant from the ocean floor has seeped in during all the centuries that the thing must have lain down there. The jagged, spidering lines spread across the crystal in a radiant pattern. Syenite can *feel* how the obelisk's hum jitters and stutters here, incomprehensible energies struggling through the place of damage.

And at the center of the radiating cracks, she can see some kind of occlusion. Something small. Syenite squints, leaning harder on the railing as she cranes her neck to follow the rising mote. Then the obelisk turns a little more as if to face her, and all at once her blood ices over as she realizes what she's seeing.

A person. There's someone *in* the thing, stuck like a bug in amber, limbs splayed and still, hair a frozen spray. She can't make out the face, not quite, but in her imagination the eyes are wide, the mouth open. Screaming.

That's when she realizes she can make out an odd marbling along the figure's skin, black-bruised through the dark red of the shaft. The sunlight flickers and she realizes its hair is clear, or at least translucent enough to be lost in the garnet around it. And there's just something *about* what she's seeing, something maybe she knows because for a moment she was a part of this obelisk, that's where the power was coming from, something she won't question too deeply because, Evil Earth, she can't *take* this. The knowledge is there in her mind, impossible to deny no matter how much she might want to. When the reasoning mind is forced to confront the impossible again and again, it has no choice but to adapt.

So she accepts that what she is looking at is a broken obelisk that has lain unknown on the floor of Allia's harbor for Earth knows how long. She accepts that what is trapped at its heart, what has somehow *broken* this massive, magnificent, arcane thing... is a stone eater.

And it's dead.

* * *

Father Earth thinks in ages, but he never, ever sleeps.

Nor does he forget.

—*Tablet Two, "The Incomplete Truth," verse two*

13

you're on the trail

THIS IS WHAT YOU ARE at the vein, this small and petty creature. This is the bedrock of your life. Father Earth is right to despise you, but do not be ashamed. You may be a monster, but you are also great.

* * *

The commless woman is called Tonkee. That's the only name she gives you: no use name, no comm name. You're sure she is, despite her protestations, a geomest; she admits it—sort of—when you ask her why she's following you. "He's just too damn interesting," Tonkee says, jerking her chin toward Hoa. "If I didn't try to figure him out, my old masters at the uni would hire assassins to hunt me down. Not that they haven't done that already!" She laughs like a horse, all bray and big white teeth. "I'd love a sample of his blood, but fat lot of good that will do me without proper equipment. So I'll settle for observation."

(Hoa looks annoyed at this, and pointedly makes an effort to keep you between himself and Tonkee as you walk.)

"The uni" she referred to, you are certain, is the Seventh

University in Dibars—the most famous center of learning for 'mests and lorists in all the Stillness, located in the second-largest city of the Equatorials. And if that prestitious place is where Tonkee trained, rather than at some jumped-up regional creche for adults, or at the knee of some local tinkerer, then she has fallen very far indeed. But you're too polite to say this aloud.

Tonkee does not live in an enclave of cannibals, despite her creative threats. You discover this when she leads you to her home that afternoon. Her home is a cave situated in a vesicle—the ancient fallen-in remains of a solidified lava bubble, this one once as big as a small hill. Now it's a secluded glen in a pocket of forest, with curving columns of gleaming black glass interspersed among the trees. There are all sorts of odd little cavelets tucked into its sides, where smaller bubbles must've nestled against the larger, and Tonkee warns you that some of the ones on the far side of the vesicle are home to forest cats and other animals. Most of them are no threat, normally, but everything changes in a Season, so you're careful to follow Tonkee's lead.

Tonkee's cavern is full of contraptions, books, and junk she's scavenged, amid a lot of actually useful things like lanterns and storecache food. The cavern smells of fragrant resins from the fires she's burned, but it quickly takes on Tonkee's stench once she's in and bustling about. You resign yourself to endure it, though Hoa doesn't seem to notice or maybe care; you envy his stoicism. Fortunately it turns out that Tonkee did indeed bring all that water with her for a bath. She does this in front of you, shamelessly stripping down and squatting by a wooden basin to scrub at her pits and crotch and the rest. You're a little surprised to notice a penis somewhere amid this process, but, well, not like any comm's going to make her a Breeder. She finishes up by rinsing her clothes and hair with a murky green solution that she claims is antifungal. (You have your doubts.)

Anyway, the place smells much better when she's done, so you spend a remarkably pleasant and cozy night there on your bedroll—she's got spares, but you don't want to risk lice—and even let Hoa curl up against you, though you turn your back to him so he won't cuddle. He does not try.

The next day you resume the journey south, with Tonkee the commless geomest and Hoa the... whatever he is. Because you're pretty sure by now that he's not human. That doesn't bother you; officially speaking, you're not human, either. (Per the Second Yumenescene Lore Council's *Declaration on the Rights of the Orogenically Afflicted*, a thousand-ish years ago.) What does bother you is that Hoa won't talk about it. You ask about what he did to the kirkhusa and he refuses to answer. You ask him why he won't answer, and he just looks miserable and says, "Because I want you to like me."

It almost makes you feel normal, traveling with these two. The road demands most of your attention, in any case. The ashfall only gets heavier over the next few days, until you finally do pull the masks out of your runny-sack—you have four, fortunately, horribly—and hand them around. It's clumpy ash for now, not the floating haze of death that stonelore warns against, but no sense being incautious. Other people have broken out their masks, too, you see when they materialize out of the grayness, their skin and hair and clothing hardly distinguishable from the ash-painted landscape, their eyes grazing over you and away. The masks make everyone equally unknown and unknowable, which is good. No one pays attention to you or Hoa or Tonkee, not anymore. You're happy to join the indistinct masses.

By the end of a week, the crowds of people traveling along the road have begun to thin into knots and, occasionally, trickles. Everyone who has a comm is hurrying back there, and the thinning crowds mean most of them are finding somewhere to settle in. Now only those journeying farther than usual remain on the road, or people who don't have a home to return to—like the hollow-eyed Equatorials you've seen, many of them sporting terrible burns or injuries that come from falling debris. The Equatorials are a brewing problem, because there's a lot of them on the road even if the injured ones are mostly getting sick with infection and starting to die. (You pass at least one or two people every day who just sit there on the edges of the road, pale or flushed, curled up or shaking, waiting for the end to come.) There's plenty left who seem hale enough, though, and they're commless now. That's always a problem.

You talk to a small group of these folk at the next roadhouse: five women of wildly varied ages and a very young, uncertain-looking man. This lot have removed most of the flowing, uselessly pretty garments that people in the Equatorial cities used to consider fashionable, you notice; somewhere along the way they've stolen or traded for sturdy clothes and proper travel gear. But each of them sports some remnant of the old life: The oldest woman wears a headscarf of frilly, stained blue satin; the youngest has gauzy sleeves poking out from under the heavier, more practical cloth of her tunic; the young man has a sash around his waist that is soft and peach colored and there solely for decoration, as far as you can tell.

Except it's not really decoration. You notice how they look at you when you walk up: a sweep of the eyes, an inspection of your wrists or neck or ankles, a frown as you are found wanting. The impractical cloth has one very practical use: It is the marker of a new tribe in the process of being born. A tribe to which you do not belong.

Not a problem. Yet.

You ask them what happened in the north. You know, but being aware of a geological event and knowing what that event *means* in the real human sense are two very different things. They tell you, once you've held up your hands and made it clear you offer no (visible) threat.

"I was on my way home from a concert," says one of the younger women, who does not introduce herself but should be—if she is not already—a Breeder. She's what Sanzed women are supposed to look like, tall and strong and bronze and almost offensively healthy, with nice even features and wide hips, all of it crowned with a shock of gray ashblow hair that's almost like a pelt about her shoulders. She jerks her head toward the young man, who lowers his gaze demurely. Just as pretty; probably a Breeder, too, though a bit on the scrawny side. Well, he'll beef up if he's got five women to service for his keep. "He was playing at the improvisation hall on Shemshena Street; this was in Alebid. The music was so beautiful..."

She trails off, and for a moment you see her detach from the here and now. You know Alebid is—was—a mid-sized city comm, known for its art scene. Then she snaps back, because of course she is a good Sanzed girl, and Sanzeds hold little truck with daydreamers.

She continues: "We saw something sort of—*tear*, off to the north. Along the horizon, I mean. We could see this . . . red light flare up at one point, then it spread off to the east and west. I couldn't tell how far away, but we could see it reflected on the underside of the clouds." She's drifting again, but remembering something terrible this time, and so her face is hard and grim and angry. That's more socially acceptable than nostalgia. "It spread *fast*. We were just standing in the street, watching it grow and trying to figure out what we were seeing, and sessing, when the ground started to shake. Then something—a cloud—obscured the red, and we realized it was coming toward us."

It had not been a pyroclastic cloud, you know, or she wouldn't be here talking to you. Just an ash storm, then. Alebid is well south of Yumenes; all they got was the dregs of whatever more northerly comms did. And that's good, because those dregs alone almost broke the much-further-south Tirimo. By rights Alebid should have been pebbles.

An orogene saved this girl, you suspect. Yes, there's a node station near Alebid, or there was.

"Everything was still standing," she says, confirming your guess. "But the ash that followed—no one could breathe. The ash was getting in people's mouths, into their lungs, turning into cement. I tied my blouse around my face; it was made of the same stuff as a mask. That's the only thing that saved me. Us." She glances at her young man, and you realize the scrap around his wrist is part of what used to be a woman's garment, by the color. "It was evening, after a beautiful day. It's not like anybody had their runny-sacks with them."

Silence falls. This time everyone in the group lets it go on, and drifts with her for a moment. The memory's just that bad. You remember, too, that not many Equatorials even have runny-sacks. The nodes have been more than enough to keep the biggest cities safe for centuries.

"So we ran," the woman concludes abruptly, with a sigh. "And we haven't stopped."

You thank them for the information, and leave before they can ask questions in return.

As the days pass, you hear other, similar, stories. And you notice that none of the Equatorials you meet are from Yumenes, or any comms from the same approximate latitude. Alebid is as far north as the survivors run.

Doesn't matter, though. You're not going north. And no matter how much it bothers you—what's happened, what it means—you know better than to dwell too much on it. Your head's crowded enough with ugly memories.

So you and your companions keep going through the gray days and ruddy nights, and all that really concerns you is keeping your canteen filled and your food stores topped up, and replacing your shoes when they start to wear thin. Doing all this is easy, for now, because people are still hoping this will be just a brief Season—a year without a summer, or two, or three. That's how most Seasons go, and comms that remain willing to trade during such times, profiting off others' poor planning, generally come out of it wealthy. You know better—this Season will be much, much longer than anyone could have planned for—but that won't stop you from taking advantage of their misconception.

Now and again you stop at comms you pass on the road, some of them huge and sprawling with granite walls that loom overhead, some of them protected merely by fencewire, sharpened sticks, and poorly armed Strongbacks. The prices are beginning to go strange. One comm will take currency, and you use up nearly all of yours buying Hoa his own bedroll. The next won't take currency at all, but they will take useful tools, and you've got one of Jija's old knapping hammers at the bottom of your bag. That buys you a couple weeks' worth of cachebread and three jars of sweet nut paste.

You share the food out among the three of you, because that's important. Stonelore's full of admonitions against hoarding within a group—and you are a group by now, whether you want to admit it or not. Hoa does his part, staying up most of the night to keep watch; he doesn't sleep much. (Or eat anything. But after a while you try not to notice that, the same way you try not to think about him turning a kirkhusa into stone.) Tonkee doesn't like approaching comms, even though with fresh clothing and no-worse-than-usual body odor she can pass for just another displaced person rather than a commless. So that part's on you. Still, Tonkee helps where she can. When your boots wear out and the comm you've approached won't take anything you offer, Tonkee surprises you by holding out a compass. Compasses are priceless, with the sky clouded over and no visibility through the ashfall. You ought to be able to get ten pairs of boots for it. But the woman doing the comm's trading has you over a barrel and she knows it, so you get only two pairs of boots, one for you and another for Hoa, since his are already starting to look worn. Tonkee, who has her own spare boots dangling from her pack, dismisses the price when you complain about it later. "There are other ways to find our way," she says, and then she stares at you in a way that makes you uneasy.

You don't *think* she knows you're a rogga. But who can really say, with her?

The miles roll on. The road forks often because there are a lot of big comms in this part of the midlats, and also because the Imperial Road intersects comm roads and cowpaths, rivers and old metal tracks that were used for transportation in some way or another by some ancient deadciv or another. These intersections are why they put Imperial Roads where they do; roads have always been the lifeblood of Old Sanze. Unfortunately that means it's easy to get lost if you don't know where you're going—or if you don't have a compass, or a map, or a sign saying *filicidal fathers this way*.

The boy is your savior. You're willing to believe that he can somehow sense Nassun because for a while he's better than a compass, pointing unerringly in the direction that you should go whenever you reach a crossroads. For the most part you follow the Imperial Road—this one is Yumenes-Ketteker, though Ketteker's all the way in the Antarctics and you pray you won't have to go that far. At one point Hoa takes you down a comm road that cuts between Imperial segments and probably saves you a lot of time, especially if Jija just stayed on the main roads the whole way. (The shortcut is a problem because the comm that built it is bristling with well-armed Strongbacks who shout and fire crossbow warning shots when they see you. They do not open their gates to trade. You feel their sights on you long after you've passed by.) When the road meanders away from due south, though, Hoa's less certain. When you ask, he says that he knows the direction in which Nassun is traveling, but he cannot sense the specific route she and Jija took. He can only point out the path that's most likely to get you there.

As the weeks pass, he begins to have trouble with even that. You stand with Hoa at one crossroads for a full five minutes while he chews his lip, until finally you ask him what's wrong.

"There are a lot of you in one place now," he says uneasily, and you change the subject quickly because if Tonkee doesn't know what you are, then she will after a conversation like that.

A lot of you, though. People? No, that doesn't make sense. Roggas? Gathering together? That makes even less sense. The Fulcrum died with Yumenes. There are satellite Fulcrums in Arctic—far north, past the now-impassible central latitude of the continent—and Antarctic, but you're months away fom the latter. Any orogenes left on the roads now are people like her, hiding what they are and trying to survive same as the rest. It wouldn't make sense for them to gather into a group; that would increase the chance of discovery.

At the crossroads Hoa picks a path, and you follow, but you can tell by the frown on his face that it's a guess.

"It's nearby," Hoa finally tells you, one night while you're eating cachebread and nut paste and trying not to wish it was something better. You're starting to crave fresh vegetables, but those are going to be in short supply very soon if they aren't already, so you try to ignore the craving. Tonkee is off somewhere, probably shaving. She's run out of something in the past few days, some biomest potion she keeps in her pack and tries not to let you see her drinking even though you don't care, and she's been sprouting beard stubble every few days because of the lack. It's made her irritable.

"The place with all the orogenes," Hoa continues. "I can't find anything past them. They're like... little lights. It's easy to see just one by itself, Nassun, but together they make one very bright light, and she passed close to it or through it. Now I can't—" He seems to grope for the words. There are no words for some things. "I can't, uh—"

"Sess?" you suggest.

He frowns. "No. That isn't what I do."

You decide not to ask what he does.

"I can't... I can't *know* anything else. The bright light keeps me from focusing on any little light."

"How many"—you leave out the word, in case Tonkee's coming back—"are there?"

"I can't tell. More than one. Less than a town. But more are heading there."

This worries you. They can't all be chasing stolen daughters and murderous husbands. "Why? How do they know to go there?"

"I don't know."

Well, that's helpful.

All you know for sure is that Jija headed south. But "south" covers a lot of territory—more than a third of the continent. Thousands of comms. Tens of thousands of square miles. Where's he going? You don't know. What if he turns east, or west? What if he stops?

There's a notion. "Could they have stopped there? Jija and Nassun, in that place?"

"I don't know. They went that way, though. I didn't lose them until here."

So you wait till Tonkee comes back, and you tell her where you're going. You don't tell her why, and she doesn't ask. You don't tell her what you're going into, either—because, really, you don't know. Maybe someone's trying to build a new Fulcrum. Maybe there was a memo. Regardless, it's good to have a clear destination again.

You ignore the feeling of unease as you start down the road that—hopefully—Nassun traveled.

* * *

Judge all by their usefulness: the leaders and the hearty,
the fecund and the crafty, the wise and the deadly, and
a few strong backs to guard them all.

—*Tablet One, "On Survival," verse nine*

14

Syenite breaks her toys

Remain at location. Await instructions, reads the telegram from Yumenes.

Syenite offers this to Alabaster wordlessly, and he glances at it and laughs. "Well, well. I'm beginning to think you've just earned yourself another ring, Syenite Orogene. Or a death sentence. I suppose we'll see when we get back."

They're in their room at the Season's End Inn, naked after their usual evening fuck. Syenite gets up, naked and restless and annoyed, to pace around the room's confines. It's a smaller room than the one they had a week ago, since their contract with Allia is now fulfilled and the comm will no longer pay for their boarding.

"When we get back?" She glares at him as she paces. He is completely relaxed, a long-boned positive space against the bed's negative whiteness, in the dim evening light. She cannot help thinking of the garnet obelisk when she looks at him: He is just as should-not-be, just as not-quite-real, just as frustrating. She cannot understand why he's not upset. "What is this 'remain at location' bullshit? Why won't they let us come back?"

He "tsks" at her. "Language! You were such a proper thing back at the Fulcrum. What happened?"

"I met you. Answer the question!"

"Maybe they want to give us a vacation." Alabaster yawns and leans over to take a piece of fruit from the bag on the nightstand. They've been buying their own food for the past week. At least he's eating without being reminded, now. Boredom is good for him. "What does it matter whether we waste our time here, or on the road back to Yumenes, Syen? At least here we can be comfortable. Come back to bed."

She bares her teeth at him. "No."

He sighs. "To *rest*. We've done our duty for the night. Earthfires, do you want me to leave for a while so you can masturbate? Will that put you in a better mood?"

It would, actually, but she won't admit that to him. She does come back to the bed, finally, for lack of anything better to do. He hands her an orange slice, which she accepts because they're her favorite fruit and they're cheap here. There's a lot to be said for living in a Coaster comm, she's thought more than once since coming here. Mild weather, good food, low cost of living, meeting people from every land and region as they flow through the port for travel and trade. And the ocean is a beautiful, entrancing thing; she has stood at the window and stared out at it for hours. If not for the tendency of Coaster comms to be wiped off the map every few years by tsunami… well.

"I just don't understand," she says, for what feels like the ten thousandth time. 'Baster's probably getting tired of her complaining, but she's got nothing else to do, so he'll have to endure it. "Is this some kind of punishment? Was I not supposed to find a giant floating whatevertherust hidden at the bottom of a harbor during a routine coral-clearing job?" She throws up her hands. "As if anyone could've anticipated that."

"Most likely," Alabaster says, "they want you on hand for whenever the geomests arrive, in case there's more potential business for the Fulcrum in it."

He's said this before, and she knows it's probably true. Geomests have already been converging on the city, in fact—and archaeomests, and lorists, and biomests, and even a few doctors who are concerned about the effect that an obelisk so close will have on Allia's populace. And the charlatans and cranks have come, too, of course: metallorists and astronomests and other junk science practitioners. Anyone with a bit of training or a hobby, from every comm in the quartent and neighboring ones. The only reason Syenite and Alabaster have even gotten a room is that they're the ones who discovered the thing, and because they got in early; otherwise, every inn and lodging-house in the quartent is full to brimming.

No one's really cared about the damn obelisks before now. Then again, no one's ever seen one hovering so close, clearly visible and stuffed with a dead stone eater, above a major population center.

But beyond interviewing Syenite for her perspective on the raising of the obelisk—she's already starting to wince every time a stranger is introduced to her as *Somefool Innovator*

Wherever—the 'mests haven't wanted anything from her. Which is good, since she's not authorized to negotiate on behalf of the Fulcrum. Alabaster might be, but she doesn't want him bargaining with anyone for her services. She doesn't *think* he'd intentionally sign her up for anything she doesn't want; he's not a complete ass. It's just the principle of the thing.

And worse, she doesn't quite believe Alabaster. The politics of being left here don't make sense. The Fulcrum should want her back in the Equatorials, where she can be interviewed at Seventh by Imperial Scholars, and where the seniors can control how much the 'mests have to pay for access to her. They should want to interview her themselves, and better understand that strange power she's now felt three times, and which she finally understands is somehow coming from obelisks.

(And the Guardians should want to talk to her. They always have their own secrets to keep. It disturbs her most of all that they've shown no interest.)

Alabaster has warned her not to talk about this part of it. *No one needs to know that you can connect to the obelisks,* he said, the day after the incident. He was still weak then, barely able to get out of bed after his poisoning; turns out he'd been too orogenically exhausted to do anything when she raised the obelisk, despite her boasting to Asael about his long-distance skill. Yet weak as he was, he'd grabbed her hand and gripped it hard to make sure she listened. *Tell them you just tried to shift the strata and the thing popped up on its own, like a cork underwater; even our own people will believe that. It's just another deadciv artifact that doesn't make any sense; nobody will question you about it if you don't give them a reason to. So don't* talk *about it. Not even to me.*

Which of course makes her want to talk about it even more. But the one time she tried after 'Baster recovered, he glared at her and said nothing, until she finally took the hint and went to go do something else.

And that pisses her off more than anything else.

"I'm going for a walk," she says finally, and gets to her feet.

"Okay," says Alabaster, stretching and getting up; she hears his joints pop. "I'll go with you."

"I didn't ask for company."

"No, you didn't." He's smiling at her again, but in that hard-edged way she's beginning to hate. "But if you're going out alone, at night, in a strange comm *where someone's already tried to kill one of us,* then you're rusting well going to have company."

At this, Syenite flinches. "Oh." But that's the other subject they can't talk about, not because Alabaster's forbidden it but because neither of them knows enough to do more than speculate. Syenite wants to believe that the simplest explanation is the most likely: Someone in the kitchen was incompetent. Alabaster has pointed out the flaw in this, however: No one else at the inn, or in the city, has gotten sick. Syenite thinks there might be a simple explanation for this, too—Asael told the kitchen workers to contaminate only Alabaster's food. That's the kind of thing angry Leaders tend to do, at least in all the stories about them, which abound with poisonings and convoluted, indirect viciousness. Syen prefers stories about Resistants overcoming impossible odds, or Breeders saving lives through clever political marriages and strategic reproduction, or Strongbacks tackling their problems with good honest violence.

Alabaster, being Alabaster, seems to think there was more to his near-death brush. And Syenite doesn't want to admit that he might be right.

"Fine, then," she says, and gets dressed.

It's a pleasant evening. The sun's just setting as they walk down a sloping avenue that leads toward the harbor. Their shadows stretch long before them, and the buildings of Allia, which are mostly stuccoed sandy-pale in color, briefly bloom with deeper jewel tones of red and violet and gold. The avenue they're on intersects a meandering side street that ends at a small cove off the harbor's busier area; when they stop here to take in the view, Syen can see a group of the comm's adolescents playing and laughing along the black-sand beach. They are all lean and brown and healthy, and obviously happy. Syen finds herself staring, and wondering if that is what it's like to grow up normal.

Then the obelisk—which is easily visible at the end of the avenue they're standing on, where the thing hovers perhaps ten or fifteen feet above the harbor waters—emits another of the low, barely perceptible pulses that it's been spitting out since Syenite raised it, and that makes her forget about the kids.

"Something's wrong with that thing," Alabaster says, very softly.

Syenite looks at him, annoyed and on the brink of saying, *What, now you want to talk about it?* when she notices that he's not looking at it. He's scuffing the ground with one foot, his hands in his pockets, appearing—oh. Syen almost laughs. Appearing, for the moment, like a bashful young man who's about to suggest something naughty to his pretty female companion. The facts that he is not young, or bashful, and that it doesn't matter if she's pretty or he's naughty because they're already fucking, aside. A casual observer would not realize he was paying any attention to the obelisk.

Which abruptly makes Syenite realize: *No one sesses its pulse but them.* The pulse is not a pulse, exactly. It's not brief, or rhythmic; more a momentary throb that she sesses now and again, at random and ominously, like a toothache. But if the other people of the comm had sessed that last one, they wouldn't be laughing and playing and winding down comfortably at the end of a long golden day. They would all be out here watching this massive, looming thing to which Syenite is increasingly beginning to apply the adjective *dangerous* in her head.

Syen takes a clue from 'Baster and reaches for his arm, cuddling close as if she actually likes him. She keeps her voice to a murmur, even though she has no clue who or what he's trying to conceal the conversation from. There are people out on the street as the city's business day winds down, but nobody's nearby, or paying attention to them for that matter. "I keep waiting for it to rise, like the others."

Because it's hanging far, far too close to the ground, or the water's surface as it were. Every other obelisk Syen has ever seen—including the amethyst that saved Alabaster's life, and which is still drifting a few miles offshore—floats amid the lowest layer of clouds, or higher.

"It's listing to one side, too. Like it's barely able to stay up at all."

What? And she cannot help looking up at it, though 'Baster immediately squeezes her arm to make her look away again. But that brief glimpse was enough to confirm what he said: The obelisk is indeed listing, just a little, its top end tilted toward the south. It must wobble, very slowly, as it turns. The slant is so slight that she wouldn't have noticed it at all if they hadn't been standing on a street surrounded by straight-walled buildings. Now she can't unsee it.

"Let's go this way," she suggests. They've lingered here too long. Alabaster obviously agrees, and they start down the side street to the cove, strolling casually.

"It's why they're keeping us here."

Syen's not paying attention to him when he says this. In spite of herself she's distracted by the beauty of the sunset, and the long, elegant streets of the comm itself. And another couple, passing on the sidewalk; the taller woman nods to them even though both Syen and 'Baster are wearing their black uniforms. It's strange, that little gesture. And nice. Yumenes is a marvel of human achievement, the pinnacle of ingenuity and geneering; if it lasts a dozen Seasons, this paltry little Coaster comm will never even come close to matching it. But in Yumenes, no one would ever have deigned to nod to a rogga, no matter how pleasant the day.

Then Alabaster's last words penetrate her ruminations. "What?"

He keeps his pace easy, matching hers despite his naturally longer gait. "We can't talk in the room. It's risky even to talk out here. But you wanted to know why they're keeping us here, telling us not to come back: That's why. That obelisk is failing."

That much is obvious, but... "What's that got to do with us?"

"You raised it."

She scowls before she remembers to school her expression.

"It raised itself. I just moved all the crap that was holding it down, and maybe woke it up." That her mind insists *it was sleeping* before is not something she's willing to question too deeply.

"And that's more control over an obelisk than anyone has ever managed in nearly three thousand years of Imperial history." 'Baster shrugs a little. "If *I* were a jumped-up little five-ring pedant reading a telegram about this, it's what I'd think, and it's how I'd react: by trying to control the person who can control that." His eyes flick toward the obelisk. "But it's not the jumped-up pedants at the Fulcrum we have to worry about."

Syen doesn't know what the rust he's on about. It isn't that his words don't ring true; she can completely imagine someone like Feldspar pulling something like this. But why? To reassure the local population, by keeping a ten-ringer on hand? The only people who know 'Baster's here are a bunch of bureaucrats who are probably too busy dealing with the sudden influx of 'mests and tourists to care. To be able to do something, should the obelisk suddenly...do something? That makes no sense. And who else is she supposed to worry about? Unless—

She frowns.

"You said something, earlier." Something about...connecting to an obelisk? What did that mean? "And—and you did something, that night." She throws an uneasy look at him, but he doesn't glare at her this time. He's gazing down at the cove, as if entranced by the view, but his eyes are sharp and serious. He knows what she's talking about. She hesitates a moment more, then says, "You *can* do something with those things, can't you?" Oh Earth, she's a fool. "*You* can control them! Does the Fulcrum know that?"

"No. And you don't know it, either." His dark eyes slide to hers for a moment, then away.

"Why are you being so—" It's not even secretive. He's talking to her. But it's as if he suspects someone of listening to them, somehow. "No one could hear us in the room." And she nods pointedly toward a gaggle of children running past, one of them jostling Alabaster and apologizing; the street's narrow. Apologizing. Really.

"You don't know that. The building's main support column is whole-hewn granite, didn't you notice? The foundation looks to be the same. If it sits directly on the bedrock..." His expression grows momentarily uneasy, and then he blanks his face.

"What's that got to do with—" And then she understands. Oh. *Oh*. But—no, that can't be right. "You're saying someone could hear us *through the walls*? Through the, the stone itself?" She's never heard of anything like that. It makes sense, of course, because it's how orogeny works; when Syen is anchored in the earth, she can sess not only the stone that her awareness is tied to, but anything that touches it. Even if she can't perceive the thing itself, as with the obelisk. Still, to feel not just tectonic vibrations, but *sound*? It can't be true. She's never heard of a rogga with that kind of fine sensitivity.

He looks at her directly for a long moment. "I can." When she stares back, he sighs. "I always could. You can, too, probably—it just isn't clear, yet. It's just minute vibrations to you now. Around my eighth or ninth ring is when I started to distinguish patterns amid the vibrations. Details."

She shakes her head. "But you're the only ten-ringer."

"Most of my children have the potential to wear ten rings."

Syenite flinches, suddenly remembering the dead child in the node station near Mehi. Oh. The Fulcrum controls all the node maintainers. What if they have some way to force those poor damaged children to listen, and to spit back what they listen to, like some kind of living telegraph receivers? Is that what he fears? Is the Fulcrum like a spider, perching in Yumenes's heart and using the web of nodes to listen in on every conversation in the Stillness?

But she is distracted from these speculations by something that niggles at the back of her mind. Something Alabaster just said. His damn influence, making her question all the assumptions she's grown up with. *Most of my children have the potential to wear ten rings*, he'd said, but there are no other ten-ringers in the Fulcrum. Rogga children are sent to the nodes only if they can't control themselves. Aren't they?

Oh.

No.

She decides not to mention this epiphany aloud.

He pats her hand, perhaps playacting again, perhaps really trying to soothe her. Of course he knows, probably better than she, what they've done to his children.

Then he repeats: "The seniors at the Fulcrum aren't who we have to worry about."

Who else could he mean? The seniors are a mess, granted. Syen keeps an eye on their politics, because one day she'll be among them and it's important to understand who holds power and who only looks like they do. There are at least a dozen factions, along with the usual rogues: brown-nosers and idealists and those who would glassknife their own mothers to get ahead. But all at once it occurs to Syenite to consider who they answer to.

The Guardians. Because no one would really trust a group of filthy roggas to manage their own affairs, any more than Shemshena would have trusted Misalem. No one in the Fulcrum talks about the Guardians' politics, probably because no one in the Fulcrum understands them. The Guardians keep their own counsel, and they object to inquiries. Vehemently.

Not for the first time Syenite wonders: To whom do the Guardians answer?

As Syen's considered this, they've reached the cove, and stopped at its railed boardwalk. The avenue ends here, its cobbles vanishing beneath a drift of sand and then the raised wooden walkway. Not far off there's a different sandy beach from the one they saw earlier. Children run up and down the boardwalk's steps, squealing in play, and beyond them Syen can see a gaggle of old women wading nude in the harbor's waters. She notices the man who sits on the railing, a few feet down from where they stand, only because he's shirtless, and because he's looking at them. The former gets her attention for a moment—then she's polite and looks away—because Alabaster's not much to look at and it's been a while since she had sex she actually enjoyed. The latter is something she would ignore, ordinarily, because in Yumenes she gets stared at by strangers all the time.

But.

She's standing at the railing with 'Baster, relaxed and more comfortable than she's been in a while, listening to the children play. It's hard to keep her mind on the cryptic stuff they're discussing. The politics of Yumenes seem so very far from here, mysterious but unimportant, and untouchable. Like an obelisk.

But.

But. She notices, belatedly, that 'Baster has gone stiff beside her. And although his face is turned toward the beach and the children, she can tell that he's not paying attention to them. That is when it finally occurs to her that people in Allia *don't stare,* not even at a couple of blackjackets out for an evening stroll. Asael aside, most of the people she's met in this comm are too well-mannered for something like that.

So she looks back at the man on the railing. He smiles at her, which is kind of nice. He's older, maybe by ten years or so, and he's got a gorgeous body. Broad shoulders, elegant deltoids under flawless skin, a perfectly tapered waist.

Burgundy pants. And the shirt that hangs over the railing beside him, which he has ostensibly taken off in order to soak up some of the sunlight, is also burgundy. Only belatedly does she notice the peculiar, familiar buzz at the back of her sessapinae that warns of a Guardian's presence.

"Yours?" asks Alabaster.

Syenite licks her lips. "I was hoping he was yours."

"No." And then Alabaster makes a show of stepping forward to rest his hands against the railing, bowing his head as if he means to lean on it and stretch his shoulders. "Don't let him touch you with his bare skin."

This is a whisper; she barely catches it. And then Alabaster straightens and turns to the young man. "Something on your mind, Guardian?"

The Guardian laughs softly and hops down from the railing. He's at least part Coaster, all-over brown and kinky-haired; a bit on the pale side, but aside from this he fits right in among the citizens of Allia. Well. No. He blends in superficially, but there's that indefinable *something* about him that's in every Guardian Syenite's had the misfortune to interact with. No one in Yumenes ever mistakes a Guardian for an orogene—or for a still, for that matter. There's just something different about them, and everyone notices.

"Yes, actually," the Guardian says. "Alabaster Tenring. Syenite Fourring." That alone makes Syenite grind her teeth. She would prefer the generic *Orogene*, if she has to be called anything besides her name. Guardians, of course, understand perfectly well the difference between a four-ringer and a ten-ringer. "I am Edki Guardian Warrant. My, but you've both been busy."

"As we should be," says Alabaster, and Syenite cannot help looking at him in surprise. He's tensed in a way she's never seen, the cords of his neck taut, his hands splayed and—ready? ready for what? she does not know why the word *ready* even occurred to her—at his sides. "We've completed our assignment for the Fulcrum, as you can see."

"Oh, indeed. A fine job." Edki glances off then, almost casually, toward that listing, throbbing accident of an obelisk. Syenite is watching his face, however. She sees the Guardian's smile vanish as if it were never there. That can't be good. "Would that you had done *only* the job you were told to do, however. Such a willful creature you are, Alabaster."

Syenite scowls. Even here, she is condescended to. "*I* did this job, Guardian. Is there some problem with my work?"

The Guardian turns to look at her in surprise, and that's when Syenite realizes she's made a mistake. A big one, because his smile doesn't return. "Did you, now?"

Alabaster hisses and—Evil Earth, she *feels* it when he stabs his awareness into the strata, because it goes so unbelievably deep. The strength of him makes her whole body reverberate, not just her sessapinae. She can't follow it; he's past her range in the span of a breath, easily piercing to the magma even though it's miles down. And his control of all that pure earth energy is perfect. Amazing. He could shift a mountain with this, easily.

But *why*?

The Guardian smiles, suddenly. "Guardian Leshet sends her regards, Alabaster."

While Syenite is still trying to parse this, and the fact that Alabaster is *about to fight a Guardian*, Alabaster stiffens all over. "You found her?"

"Of course. We must talk of what you did to her. Soon."

Suddenly—Syenite does not know when he drew it, or where from—there is a black glassknife in his hand. Its blade is wide, but ridiculously short, maybe only two inches in length. Barely enough to be called a knife at all.

What the rust is he going to do with that, pare our nails?

And why is he drawing a weapon on two Imperial Orogenes in the first place? "Guardian," she tries, "maybe there's been some kind of misun—"

The Guardian does something. Syenite blinks, but the tableau is as before: She and Alabaster face Edki on a boardwalk stark with shadows and bloody sunset light, with children and old ladies playing beyond them. But something has changed. She's not sure what, until Alabaster makes a choking sound and lunges at her, knocking her to the ground a few feet away.

How such a skinny man has the weight to throw her, Syenite will never know. She hits the planks hard enough to jar the breath out of herself; through a blur she sees some of the children who had been playing nearby stop and stare. One of them laughs. Then she struggles up, furious, her mouth already opening to curse Alabaster to Earth and back.

But Alabaster is on the ground, too, only a foot or two away. He's lying on his belly, his eyes fixed on her, and—and he's making a strange sound. Not much of one. His mouth's open wide, but the noise that comes out of it is more like the squeak of a child's toy, or a metallorist's air bladder. And he's shivering all over, as if he can't move more than that, which doesn't make sense because nothing's wrong with him. Syen's not sure what to think until, belatedly, she realizes—

—he's *screaming.*

"Why did you think I would aim at her?" Edki is staring at Alabaster, and Syenite shivers because the look on his face is *gleeful,* it is *delighted,* even as Alabaster lies there shuddering helplessly...with the knife that Edki once held now buried in the hollow of Alabaster's shoulder. Syen stares at it, stunned that she missed it before. It stands out starkly even against the black of 'Baster's tunic. "You have always been a fool, Alabaster."

And there is a new glassknife in Edki's hand now. This one is long and viciously narrow: a chillingly familiar poniard.

"Why—" Syenite can't think. Her hands ache as she scrabbles backward along the boardwalk planks, trying to get to her feet and away all at once. Instinctively she reaches for the earth beneath her and that's when she finally realizes what the Guardian has done, because there's *nothing in her that can reach.* She cannot sess the earth past a few feet below her hands and backside; nothing but sand and salty dirt and earthworms. There is an unpleasant ringing ache in her sessapinae when she tries to reach farther. It's like when she hits her elbow and shuts off all the sensation from there to the tips of her fingers; like that part of her mind has gone to sleep. It's tingling, coming back. But for now, there's nothing there.

She has heard grits whisper of this after lights-out. All Guardians are strange, but this is what makes them what they are: Somehow, they can stop orogeny with a flick of their will. And some of them are especially strange, *specialized to be* stranger than the rest. Some of them do not have orogene charges and are never allowed near untrained children, because they are dangerous merely by proximity. These Guardians do nothing but track down the most powerful rogue orogenes, and when they find them . . . well. Syenite never particularly wanted to know what they did, before now, but it seems she's about to find out. Underfires, she's as numb to the earth as the most rust-brained elder. Is this what it's like for stills? Is this all they feel? She has envied their normalcy her whole life, until now.

But. As Edki walks toward her with the poniard ready, there is a tightness around his eyes, a grim set to his mouth, which makes her think of how she feels when she has a bad headache. This is what makes her blurt: "A-are you, ah, all right?" She has no idea why she asks this.

At this, Edki cocks his head; the smile returns to his face, gentle and surprised. "How kind you are. I'm fine, little one. Just fine." But he's still coming at her.

She scrambles backward again, tries to get to her feet again, tries again to reach for power, and fails in all three efforts. Even if she could succeed, though—he's a Guardian. It's her duty to obey. It's her duty to *die*, if he wills it.

This is not right.

"Please," she says, desperate, wild with it. "Please, we haven't done anything wrong, I don't understand, I don't . . ."

"You need not understand," he says, with perfect kindness. "You need do only one thing." And then he lunges, aiming the poniard at her chest.

Later she will understand the sequence of events.

Later she will realize everything occurred in the span of a gasp. For now, however, it is slow. The passage of time becomes meaningless. She is aware only of the glassknife, huge and sharp, its facets gleaming in the fading dusk. It seems to come at her gradually, gracefully, drawing out her duty-bound terror.

This has *never been* right.

She is aware only of the gritty wood beneath her fingers, and the useless pittance of warmth and movement that is all she can sess beneath that. Can't shift much more than a pebble with that.

She is aware of Alabaster, twitching because he is *convulsing*, how did she not realize this before, he is not in control of his own body, there is something about the glassknife in his shoulder that has rendered him helpless for all his power, and the look on his face is of helpless fear and agony.

She becomes aware that she is *angry*. Furious. Duty be

damned. What this Guardian is doing, what all Guardians do, is *not right.*

And then—

And then—

And then—

She becomes aware of the obelisk.

(Alabaster, twitching harder, opens his mouth wider, his eyes fixing on hers despite the uncontrollability of the rest of his flesh. The fleeting memory of his warning rings in her mind, though in that instant she cannot recall the words.)

The knife is halfway to her heart. She is very very aware of this.

We are the gods in chains and this is not. Rusting. Right.

So she reaches again, not down but up, not straight but to the side—

No, Alabaster is shaping his mouth to say, through his twitches.

—and the obelisk draws her into its shivering, jittering bloodred light. She is falling up. She is being *dragged* up, and in. She is completely out of control, oh Father Earth, Alabaster was right, this thing is too much for her—

—and she screams because she has forgotten that this obelisk is *broken.* It hurts as she grinds across the zone of damage, each of the cracks seaming through her and shattering her and splitting her into pieces, until—

—until she stops, hovering and curled in agony, amid the cracked redness.

It isn't real. It cannot be real. She feels herself also lying on sandy wooden boards with fading sunlight on her skin. She does not feel the Guardian's glassknife, or at least not yet. But she is here, too. And she *sees*, though sessapinae are not eyes and the "sight" is all in her imagination:

The stone eater at the core of the obelisk floats before her.

It's her first time being close to one. All the books say that stone eaters are neither male nor female, but this one resembles a slender young man formed of white-veined black marble, clothed in smooth robes of iridescent opal. Its—his?—limbs, marbled and polished, splay as if frozen in mid-fall. His head is flung back, his hair loose and curling behind him in a splash of translucence. The cracks spread over his skin and the stiff illusion of his clothing, *into* him, through him.

Are you all right? she wonders, and she has no idea why she wonders it, even as she herself cracks apart. His flesh is so terribly fissured; she wants to hold her breath, lest she damage him further. But that is irrational, because she isn't here and this isn't real. She is on a street about to die, but this stone eater has been dead for an age of the world.

The stone eater closes his mouth, and opens his eyes, and lowers his head to look at her. "I'm fine," he says. "Thank you for asking."

And then

the obelisk

shatters.

15

you're among friends

You reach "the place with all the orogenes," and it's not at all what you were expecting. It's abandoned, for one thing. It's not a comm, for another.

Not in any real sense of the word. The road gets wider as you approach, flattening into the land until it vanishes completely near the middle of town. A lot of comms do this, get rid of the road to encourage travelers to stop and trade, but those comms usually have some place to trade *in*, and you can't see anything here that looks like a storefront or marketplace or even an inn. Worse, it doesn't have a wall. Not a stone pile, not a wire fence, not even a few sharpened sticks jabbed into the ground around the town perimeter. There's *nothing* to separate this community from the land around it, which is forested and covered in scraggly underbrush that makes perfect cover for an attacking force.

But in addition to the town's apparent abandonment, and lack of a wall, there are other oddities. Lots of them, you notice as you and the others look around. There aren't enough fields, for one. A comm that can hold a few hundred people, as this one seems to be able to do, should have more than the single (stripped bare) hectare of scraggly choya stalks that you noticed on the way in. It should have a bigger pasture than the small plot of dried-out green you see near the town's center. You don't see a storehouse, either, elevated or otherwise. Okay, maybe that's hidden; lots of comms do that. But then you notice that all the buildings are in wildly varied styles: this one tall and city-narrow, that one wide and flat to the ground like something from a warmer climate, yet another that looks to be a sod-covered dome half set into the earth like your old house in Tirimo. There's a reason most comms pick a style and stick to it: Uniformity sends a visual message. It warns potential attackers that the comm's members are equally unified in purpose and the willingness to defend themselves. This comm's visual message is . . . confused. Uncaring, maybe. Something you can't interpret. Something that makes you more nervous than if the comm had been teeming with hostile people instead.

You and the others proceed warily, slowly, through the empty streets of the town. Tonkee's not even pretending to be at ease. She's got twin glassknives in her hands, stark and black-bladed; you don't know where she's been hiding them although that skirt of hers could conceal an army. Hoa seems calm, but who can really tell what Hoa feels? He seemed calm when he turned a kirkhusa into a statue, too.

You don't pull your knife. If there really are lots of roggas here, there's only one weapon that will save you if they take exception to your presence.

"You sure this is the right place?" you say to Hoa.

Hoa nods emphatically. Which means that there are lots of people here; they're just hiding. But why? And how could they have seen you coming through the ashfall?

"Can't have been gone long," Tonkee mutters. She's staring at a dead garden near one of the houses. It's been picked over by travelers or the former inhabitants, anything edible among its dried stalks gone. "These houses look in good repair. And that garden was healthy until a couple of months ago."

You're momentarily surprised to realize you've been on the road for two months. Two months since Uche. A little less since the ash started to fall.

Then, swiftly, you focus on the here and now. Because after the three of you stop in the middle of town and stand there awhile in confusion, the door of one of the nearby buildings opens, and three women come out on the porch.

The first one you pay attention to has a crossbow in her hands. For a minute that's all you see, same as that last day in Tirimo, but you don't immediately ice her because the crossbow isn't aimed at you. She's just got it leaned against one arm, and although there's a look on her face that warns you she has no problem using it, you also think she won't do it without provocation. Her skin is almost as white as Hoa's, although thankfully her hair is simply yellow and her eyes are a nice normal brown. She's petite, small-boned and poorly fleshed and narrow-hipped in a way that would prompt the average Equatorial to make snide remarks about bad breeding. An Antarctic, probably from a comm too poor to feed its kids well. She's a long way from home.

The one who draws your eye next is nearly her opposite, and quite possibly the most intimidating woman you've ever seen.

It has nothing to do with her looks. Those are just Sanzed: the expected pouf of slate-gray hair and the expected deep brown skin and the expected size and visible strength of build. Her eyes are shockingly black—shocking not because black eyes are particularly rare, but because she's wearing smoky gray eyeshadow and dark eyeliner to accentuate them further. Makeup, while the world is ending. You don't know whether to be awed or affronted by that.

And she wields those black-clad eyes like piercing weapons, holding each of your gazes at eyepoint for an instant before finally examining the rest of your gear and clothing. She's not quite as tall as Sanzeds like their women—shorter than you—but she's wearing a thick brown-fur vest that hangs to her ankles. The vest sort of makes her look like a small, yet fashionable, bear. There's something in her face, though, that makes you flinch a little. You're not sure what it is. She's grinning, showing all her teeth; her gaze is steady, neither welcoming nor uneasy. It's the steadiness that you recognize, finally, from seeing it a few times before: confidence. That kind of utter, unflinching embrace of self is common in stills, but you weren't expecting to see it here.

Because she's a rogga, of course. You know your own when you sess it. And she knows you.

"All right," the woman says, putting her hands on her hips. "How many in your party, three? I assume you don't want to be parted."

You sort of stare at her for a breath or two. "Hello," you say at last. "Uh."

"Ykka," she says. You realize it's a name. Then she adds, "Ykka Rogga Castrima. Welcome. And you are?"

You blurt: "*Rogga?*" You use this word all the time, but hearing it like this, as a use name, emphasizes its vulgarity. Naming yourself *rogga* is like naming yourself *pile of shit*. It's a slap in the face. It's a statement—of what, you can't tell.

"That, ah, isn't one of the seven common use names," says Tonkee. Her voice is wry; you think she's trying to make a joke to cover nerves. "Or even one of the five lesser-accepted ones."

"Let's call this one new." Ykka's gaze flickers over each of your companions, assessing, then back to you. "So your friends know what you are."

Startled, you look at Tonkee, who's staring at Ykka the way she stares at Hoa when Hoa isn't hiding behind you—as if Ykka is a fascinating new mystery to maybe get a blood sample from. Tonkee meets your gaze for a moment with such an utter lack of surprise or fear that you realize Ykka's right; she probably figured it out sometime ago.

"Rogga as a use name." Tonkee's thoughtful as she focuses on Ykka again. "So many implications to that one. And Castrima; that's not one of the Imperial Registry-listed Somidlats comm names, either, although I'll admit I might just have forgotten it. There's hundreds, after all. I don't think I have, though; I've got a good memory. This a newcomm?"

Ykka inclines her head, partly in affirmation and partly in ironic acknowledgment of Tonkee's fascination. "Technically. This version of Castrima has been around for maybe fifty years. It isn't really a comm at all, officially—just another lodging stop for people heading along the Yumenes–Mecemera and Yumenes–Ketteker routes. We get more business than most because there are mines in the area."

She pauses then, gazing at Hoa, and for a moment her expression tightens. You look at Hoa, too, puzzled, because granted, he's strange-looking, but you're not sure what he's done to merit that kind of tension from a stranger. That's when you finally notice that Hoa has gone utterly still, and his little face has sharpened from its usual cheerfulness into something taut and angry and almost feral. He's glaring at Ykka like he wants to kill her.

No. Not Ykka. You follow his gaze to the third member of Ykka's party, who's stayed slightly behind the other two till now, and whom you haven't really paid attention to because Ykka's so eye-catching. A tall, slender woman—and then you stop, frowning, because all at once you're not sure about that designation. The female part, sure; her hair is Antarctic-lank and deep red in color, decoratively long, framing features that are finely lined. It's clear she means to be read as a woman, though she's only wearing a long, loose sleeveless gown that should be far too thin for the cooling air.

But her skin. You're staring, it's rude, not the best way to start things off with these people, but you can't help it. Her skin. It's not just smooth, it's...glossy, sort of. Almost polished. She's either got the most amazing complexion you've ever seen, or—or that isn't skin.

The red-haired woman smiles, and the sight of her teeth confirms it even as you shiver to your bones.

Hoa hisses like a cat in reply to that smile. And as he does so, finally, terribly, you see his teeth clearly for the first time. He never eats in front of you, after all. He never shows them when he smiles. They're colored in where hers are transparent, enamel-white as a kind of camouflage—but not so different from the red-haired woman's in shape. Not squared but *faceted.* Diamondine.

"Evil Earth," mutters Tonkee. You feel that she speaks for the both of you.

Ykka glances sharply at her companion. "No."

The red-haired woman's eyes flick toward Ykka. No other part of her moves, the rest of her body remaining stock-still. *Statue*-still. "It can be done without harm to you or your companions." Her mouth doesn't move, either. The voice sounds oddly hollow, echoing up from somewhere inside her chest.

"I don't want anything 'done.'" Ykka puts her hands on her hips. "This my place, and you've agreed to abide by my rules. *Back off.*"

The blond woman shifts a little. She doesn't bring the crossbow up, but you think she's ready to do so at a moment's notice. For whatever good that will do. The red-haired woman doesn't move for a moment, and then she closes her mouth to hide those awful diamond teeth. As she does this, you realize several things at once. The first is that she wasn't actually smiling. It was a threat display, like the way a kirkhusa draws back its lips to bare its fangs. The second is that with her mouth closed and that placid expression, she looks far less unnerving.

The third realization you have is that Hoa was making the same threat display. But he relaxes, and closes his mouth, as the red-haired woman eases back.

Ykka exhales. She focuses on you again.

"I think perhaps," she says, "you'd better come inside."

"I'm not sure that's the best idea in the world," Tonkee says to you, pleasantly.

"Neither am I," says the blond woman, glaring at Ykka's head. "You sure about that, Yeek?"

Ykka shrugs, though you think she's not nearly as nonchalant as she seems. "When am I sure about anything? But it seems like a good idea, for now."

You're not sure you agree. Still—strange comm or not, mythical creatures or not, unpleasant surprises or not, you came here for a reason.

"Did a man and a girl come through here?" you ask. "Father and daughter. The man would be about my age, the girl eight—" Two months. You've almost forgotten. "*Nine* years old. She—" You falter. Stutter. "Sh-she looks like me."

Ykka blinks, and you realize you've genuinely surprised her. Clearly she was braced for entirely different questions. "No," she says, and—

—and there's a sort of skip inside you.

It *hurts* to hear that simple "no." It hits like a hachet blow, and the salt in the wound is Ykka's look of honest perplexity. That means she's not lying. You flinch and sway with the impact, with the death of all your hopes. It occurs to you through a haze of floating not-quite-thought that you've been *expecting* something since Hoa told you about this place. You were beginning to think you would find them here, have a daughter again, be a mother again. Now you know better.

"S—Essun?" Hands grasp your forearms. Whose? Tonkee. Her hands are rough with hard living. You hear her calluses rasp on the leather of your jacket. "Essun—oh, rust, don't."

You've always known better. How dare you expect anything else? You're just another filthy, rusty-souled rogga, just another agent of the Evil Earth, just another mistake of sensible breeding practices, just another mislaid tool. You should never have had children in the first place, and you shouldn't have expected to keep them once you did, and why's Tonkee pulling on your arms?

Because you've lifted your hands to your face. Oh, and you've burst into tears.

You should have told Jija, before you ever married him, before you slept with him, before you even looked at him and thought *maybe*, which you had no right to ever think. Then if the urge to kill a rogga had hit him, he would've inflicted it on you, not Uche. You're the one who deserves to die, after all, ten thousand times the population of two comms.

Also, you might be screaming a little.

You shouldn't be screaming. You should be dead. You should have died before your children. You should have died at birth, and never lived to bear them.

You should have—

You should have—

Something sweeps through you.

It feels a little like the wave of force that came down from the north, and which you shunted away, on that day the world changed. Or maybe a little like the way you felt when you walked into the house after a tiring day and saw your boy lying on the floor. A waft of potential, passing on unutilized. The brush of something intangible but meaningful, there and gone, as shocking by its absence as its existence in the first place.

You blink and lower your hands. Your eyes are blurry and they hurt; the heels of your hands are wet. Ykka is off the porch and standing in front of you, just a couple of feet away. She's not touching you, but you stare at her anyway, realizing she just did—something. Something you don't understand. Orogeny, certainly, but deployed in a way you've never experienced before.

"Hey," she says. There's nothing like compassion on her face. Still, her voice is softer as she speaks to you—though maybe that's only because she's closer. "Hey. You okay now?"

You swallow. Your throat hurts. "No," you say. (That word again! You almost giggle, but you swallow and the urge vanishes.) "No. But I'm . . . I can keep it together."

Ykka nods slowly. "See that you do." Beyond her, the blond woman looks skeptical about the possibility of this.

Then, with a heavy sigh, Ykka turns to Tonkee and Hoa—the latter of whom looks deceptively calm and normal now. Normal by Hoa standards, anyway.

"All right, then," she says. "Here's how it is. You can stay or you can go. If you decide to stay, I'll take you into the comm. But you need to know up front: Castrima is something unique. We're trying something very different here. If this Season turns out to be short, then we're going to be up a lava lake when Sanze comes down on us. But I don't think this Season will be short."

She glances at you, sidelong, not quite for confirmation. *Confirmation*'s not the word for it, since there was never doubt. Any rogga knows it like they know their own name.

"This Season won't be short," you agree. Your voice is hoarse, but you're recovering. "It will last decades." Ykka lifts an eyebrow. Yeah, she's right; you're trying to be gentle for the sake of your companions, and they don't need gentleness. They need truth. "Centuries."

Even that's an understatement. You're pretty sure this one will last at least a thousand years. Maybe a *few* thousand.

Tonkee frowns a little. "Well, everything does point to either a major epeirogenic deformation, or possibly just a simple disruption of isostasy throughout the entire plate network. But the amount of orogenesis needed to overcome that much inertia is . . . prohibitive. Are you sure?"

You're staring at her, grief momentarily forgotten. So's Ykka, and the blond woman. Tonkee grimaces in irritation, glowering particularly at you. "Oh, for rust's sake, stop acting all surprised. The secrets are done now, right? You know what I am and I know what you are. Do we have to keep pretending?"

You shake your head, though you're not really responding to her question. You decide to answer her other question instead. "I'm sure," you say. "Centuries. Maybe more."

Tonkee flinches. "No comm has stores enough to last that long. Not even Yumenes."

Yumenes's fabled vast storecaches are slag in a lava tube somewhere. Part of you mourns the waste of all that food. Part of you figures, well, *that much quicker and more merciful an end for the human race*.

When you nod, Tonkee falls into a horrified silence. Ykka looks from you to Tonkee, and apparently decides to change the subject.

"There are twenty-two orogenes here," she says. You flinch. "I expect there will be more as time passes. You all right with that?" She looks at Tonkee in particular.

As subject changes go, it's perfect for distracting everyone. "How?" asks Tonkee at once. "How are you making them come here?"

"Never mind that. Answer the question."

You could've told Ykka not to bother. "I'm fine with it," Tonkee says immediately. You're surprised she's not visibly salivating. So much for her shock over the inevitable death of humanity.

"All right." Ykka turns to Hoa. "And you. There are a few others of your kind here, too."

"More than you think," Hoa says, very softly.

"Yeah. Well." Ykka takes this with remarkable aplomb. "You heard how it is. If you want to stay here, you follow the rules. No fighting. No—" She waggles her fingers and bares her teeth. This is surprisingly comprehensible. "And you do as I say. Got it?"

Hoa cocks his head a little, his eyes glittering in pure menace. It's as shocking to see as his diamond teeth; you'd started thinking of him as a rather sweet creature, if a bit eccentric. Now you're not sure what to think. "You don't command me."

Ykka, to your greater amazement, leans over and puts her face right in front of his.

"Let me put it this way," she says. "You can keep doing what you've obviously been doing, trying to be as avalanche-subtle as your kind ever gets, or I can start telling everyone what all of you are *really* up to."

And Hoa...flinches. His eyes—only his eyes—flick toward the not-woman on the porch. The one on the porch smiles again, though she doesn't show her teeth this time, and there's a rueful edge to it. You don't know what any of this means, but Hoa seems to sag a little.

"Very well," he says to Ykka, with an odd formality. "I agree to your terms."

Ykka nods and straightens, letting her gaze linger on him for a moment longer before she turns away.

"What I was going to say before your little, ah, moment, was that we've taken in a few people," she says to you. She says this over her shoulder, as she turns and walks back up the steps of the house. "No men traveling with girls, I don't think, but other travelers looking for a place, including some from Cebak Quartent. We adopted them if we thought they were useful." It's what any smart comm does at times like these: kicking out the undesirable, taking in those with valuable skills and attributes. The comms that have strong leaders do this systematically, ruthlessly, with some degree of cold humanity. Less well-run comms do it just as ruthlessly but more messily, like the way Tirimo got rid of you.

Jija's just a stoneknapper. Useful, but knapping's not exactly a rare skill. Nassun, though, is like you and Ykka. And for some reason, the people of this comm seem to *want* orogenes around.

"I want to meet those people," you say. There's a slim chance that Jija or Nassun is in disguise. Or that someone else might have seen them, on the road. Or that . . . well. It really is a slim chance.

You'll take it, though. She's your daughter. You'll take anything, to find her.

"All right, then." Ykka turns and beckons. "Come on in, and I'll show you a marvel or three." As if she hasn't already done so. But you move to follow her, because neither myths nor mysteries can hold a candle to the most infinitesimal spark of hope.

* * *

The body fades. A leader who would last relies on more.

—*Tablet Three, "Structures," verse two*

16

Syen in the hidden land

Syenite wakes up cold on one side of her body. It's her left side—hip and shoulder and most of her back. The source of the cold, a sharp wind, blows almost painfully through the hair all along the back of her skull, which means her hair must have come loose from its Fulcrum-regulation bun. Also, there's a taste like dirt in her mouth, though her tongue is dry.

She tries to move and hurts all over, dully. It's a strange kind of pain, not localized, not throbbing or sharp or anything that specific. More like her whole body is one big bruise. She groans inadvertently as she wills a hand to move and finds hard ground beneath it. She pushes against it enough to feel like she's in control of herself again, though she doesn't actually manage to get up. All she does successfully is open her eyes.

Crumbling silvery stone beneath her hand and in front of her face: monzonite, maybe, or one of the lesser schists. She can never remember the subvolcanic rocks because the grit instructor for geomestry back at the Fulcrum was unbelievably boring. A few feet away, the whatever-it-is stone is broken by clovers and a scraggle of grass and some kind of bushy-leafed weed. (She paid even less attention in biomestry.) The plants stir restlessly in the wind, though not much, because her body shields them from the worst of it.

Blow that, she thinks, and is pushed awake by mild shock at her own mental crudeness.

She sits up. It hurts and it's hard to do, but she does it, and this allows her to see that she's lying on a gentle slope of rock, surrounded by more weeds. Beyond that is the unbroken expanse of the lightly clouded sky. There's an ocean smell, but it's different from what she's gotten used to in the past few weeks: less briny, more rarefied. The air is drier. The sun's position makes it late morning, and the cold feels like late winter.

But it should be late afternoon. And Allia is Equatorial; the temperature should be balmy. And the cold, hard ground she's lying on should be warm, sandy ground. So where the burning rusty fuck is she?

Okay. She can figure this out. The rock she's lying on sesses high above sea level, relatively close to a familiar boundary: That's the edge of the Maximal, one of the two main tectonic plates that make up the Stillness. The Minimal's way up north. And she's sessed this plate edge before: They're not far from Allia.

But they're not *in* Allia. In fact, they're not on the continent at all.

Reflexively Syenite tries to do more than just sess, reaching toward the plate edge as she's done a few times before—

—and nothing happens.

She sits there for a moment, more chilled than the wind can account for.

But she is not alone. Alabaster lies curled nearby, his long limbs folded fetal, either unconscious or dead. No; his side rises and falls, slowly. Okay, that's good.

Beyond him, at the top of the slope, stands a tall, slender figure clad in a white flowing robe.

Startled, Syen freezes for a moment. "Hello?" Her voice is a croak.

The figure—a woman, Syen guesses—does not turn. She's looking away, at something over the rise that Syenite cannot see. "Hello."

Well, that's a start. Syen forces herself to relax, although this is difficult when she cannot reach toward the earth for the reassurance of power. There's no reason to be alarmed, she chides herself; whoever this woman is, if she'd wanted to harm them, she could have easily done so by now. "Where are we?"

"An island, perhaps a hundred miles off the eastern coast."

"An *island?*" That's terrifying. Islands are death traps. The only worse places to live are atop fault lines and in dormant-but-not-extinct volcano calderas. But yes, now Syenite hears the distant sough of waves rolling against rocks, somewhere below the slope on which they lie. If they're only a hundred miles from the Maximal's edge, then that puts them entirely too close to an underwater fault line. Basically on top of it. This is why people don't live on islands, for Earth's sake; they could die in a tsunami any minute.

She gets to her feet, suddenly desperate to see how bad the situation is. Her legs are stiff from lying on stone, but she stumbles around Alabaster anyway until she's standing on the slope beside the woman. There she sees:

Ocean, as far as the eye can see, open and unbroken. The rock slope drops off sharply a few feet from where she's standing, becoming a sheer jagged cliff that stands some few hundred feet above the sea. When she eases up to that edge and looks down, froth swirls about knifelike rocks far below; falling means death. Quickly she steps back.

"How did we get here?" she whispers, horrified.

"I brought you."

"You—" Syenite rounds on the woman, anger already spiking through shock. Then the anger dies, leaving the shock to reign uncontested.

Make a statue of a woman: not tall, hair in a simple bun, elegant features, a graceful pose. Leave its skin and clothing the color of old warm ivory, but dab in deeper shading at irises and hair—black in both cases—and at the fingertips. The color here is a faded and rusty gradient, ground in like dirt. Or blood.

A stone eater.

"Evil Earth," Syenite whispers. The woman does not respond.

There is a groan behind them that forestalls anything else Syenite might have said. (But what can she say? What?) She tears her eyes from the stone eater and focuses on Alabaster, who's stirring and clearly feeling no better than Syenite about it. But she ignores him for the moment as she finally thinks of something to say.

"Why?" she asks. "Why did you bring us here?"

"To keep him safe."

It's just like the lorists say. The stone eater's mouth doesn't open when she speaks. Her eyes don't move. She might as well be the statue she appears to be. Then sense reasserts itself, and

Syenite notices what the creature has said. "To keep... *him* safe?" Again, the stone eater does not reply.

Alabaster groans again, so Syenite finally goes to him, helping him sit up as he begins to stir. His shirt pulls at the shoulder and he hisses, and belatedly she remembers the Guardian's throwing knife. It's gone now, but the shallow wound is stuck to the cloth of his shirt with dried blood. He swears as he opens his eyes. "*Decaye, shisex unrelabbemet.*" It's the strange language she's heard him use before.

"Speak Sanze-mat," she snaps, though she's not really irritated with him. She keeps her eyes on the stone eater, but the stone eater continues not to move.

"...Flaking, fucking *rust*," he says, grabbing at the injured area. "Hurts."

Syenite swats his hand away. "Don't bother it. You might reopen the wound." And they are hundreds of miles from civilization, separated from it by water as far as the eye can see in most directions. At the mercy of a creature whose race is the very definition of *enigmatic*, and also *deadly*. "We've got company."

Alabaster comes fully awake, blinking at Syenite and then looking beyond her; his eyes widen a little at the sight of the stone eater. Then he groans. "Shit. *Shit*. What have you done this time?"

Somehow, Syenite is not entirely surprised to realize Alabaster knows a stone eater.

"I've saved your life," the stone eater says.

"What?"

The stone eater's arm rises, so steadily that the motion surpasses *graceful* and edges into *unnatural*. No other part of her moves. She's pointing. Syenite turns to follow the gesture and sees the western horizon. But this horizon is broken, unlike the rest: There's a flat line of sea and sky to the left and right, but at the midpoint of this line is a pimple, fat and red-glowing and smoky.

"Allia," says the stone eater.

* * *

There's a village on the island, it turns out. The island is nothing but rolling hills and grass and solid rock—no trees, no topsoil. An utterly useless place to live. And yet as they reach the other side of the island, where the cliffs are a bit less jagged, they see another semicircular cove not unlike the one at Allia. (Not unlike the one that *was* at Allia.) The similarity stops there, however—because this harbor is much smaller, and this village is carved directly into the sheer cliff face.

It's hard to tell at first. Initially Syen thinks that what she's seeing are the mouths of caverns, irregularly dotting the jagged rock face. Then she realizes the cave mouths are all uniformly shaped, even if they vary in size: straight lines across the bottom of the opening and up its sides, arching to a graceful point across the top. And around each opening, someone has carved out the facade of a building: elegant pillars, a beveled rectangle of a doorway, elaborate corbels of curled flowers and cavorting animals. She's seen stranger. Not much, granted—but living in Yumenes, in the shadow of the Black Star and the Imperial Palace that crowns it, and in the Fulcrum with its walls of molded obsidian, makes one inured to oddities of art and architecture.

"She doesn't have a name," Alabaster tells her as they walk

down a set of railed stone steps they've found, which seem to wend toward the village. He's talking about the stone eater, who left them at the top of the steps. (Syen looked away for a moment and when she glanced back the stone eater was gone. Alabaster has assured her that she is still nearby. How he knows this, Syen isn't sure she wants to know.)

"I call her Antimony. You know, because she's mostly white? It's a metal instead of stone, because she's not a rogga, and anyway 'Alabaster' was taken."

Cute. "And she—it—answers to that."

"She does." He glances back at Syenite, which is a precarious sort of thing to do considering the steps here are very, very sheer. Even though there's a railing, anyone who takes a header down these stairs is likely to just flip over the railing and fall to a messy death down the rock face. "She doesn't mind it, anyway, and I figure she'd object if she did."

"Why did she bring us here?" To save them. All right, they can see Allia smoking, over the water. But Antimony's kind usually ignores and avoids humankind, unless humans piss them off.

Alabaster shakes his head, focusing on his footing again. "There's no 'why' to anything they do. Or if there is, they never bother telling us. I've stopped asking, frankly; waste of breath. Antimony has been coming to me for the past, hmm, five years? Usually when no one else is around." He makes a soft, rueful sound. "I used to think I was hallucinating her."

Yes, well. "And she doesn't tell you anything?"

"She just says she's here for me. I can't decide whether it's a supportive statement—you know, 'I'm here for you, 'Baster, I'll always love you, never mind that I'm a living statue that only looks like a pretty woman, I've got your back'—or something more sinister. Does it matter, though? If she saved our lives?"

Syen supposes not. "And where is she now?"

"Gone."

Syen resists the urge to kick him down the steps. "Into, ah—" She knows what she's read, but it does seem sort of absurd to say it aloud. "Into the earth?"

"I suppose so. They move through rock like it's air; I've seen them do it." He pauses on one of the stairs' frequent landings, which almost makes Syenite run into the back of him. "You *do* know that's probably how she got us here, right?"

It's something Syen's been trying not to think about. Even the idea of being touched by the stone eater is unnerving. To think further of being carried by the creature, dragged down beneath miles of solid rock and ocean: She cannot help shuddering. A stone eater is a thing that defies reason—like orogeny, or deadciv artifacts, or anything else that cannot be measured and predicted in a way that makes sense. But where orogeny can be understood (somewhat) and controlled (with effort), and where deadciv artifacts can at least be avoided until they rise from the rusting ocean right in front of you, stone eaters do as they please, go where they will. Lorists' tales are generous with warnings regarding these creatures; no one tries to stop them.

This thought makes Syen herself stop, and Alabaster continues for another flight before he realizes she's not following. "The stone eater," she says, when he turns back to her with an annoyed look. "The one in the obelisk."

"Not the same one," he says, with the sort of patience one reserves for people who are being particularly stupid but don't deserve to be told that to their faces because they've had a hard day. "I told you, I've known this one awhile."

"That isn't what I meant." *You idiot.* "The stone eater that was in the obelisk looked at me, before... before. It moved. It wasn't dead."

Alabaster stares at her. "When did you see this?"

"I..." She gestures, helplessly. There aren't words for it. "There was... it was when I... I *think* I saw it." Or maybe she hallucinated it. Some kind of life-flashing-before-her-eyes vision, triggered by the Guardian's knife? It felt so real.

Alabaster regards her for a long moment, his mobile face still in that way she is beginning to associate with his disapproval. "You did something that should've killed you. It didn't, but only because of sheer dumb luck. If you... saw things... I'm not surprised."

Syenite nods, not protesting his assessment. She felt the obelisk's power in those moments. It *would* have killed her, had it been whole. As it is, she feels... burned, sort of numb, in its wake. Is that why she can't work orogeny anymore? Or is that the lingering effect of whatever the Guardian did?

"What happened back there?" she asks him, frustrated. There's so much that makes no sense in all of this. Why did someone try to kill Alabaster? Why did a Guardian come to finish the job? What did any of that have to do with the obelisk? Why are they here, on a death-trap island in the middle of the rusting sea? "What's happening *now*? 'Baster, Earth eat us, you know more than you're saying."

His expression grows pained, but he finally sighs and folds his arms. "I don't, you know. Whatever you might think, I really don't have all the answers. I have no idea why you think I do."

Because he knows so much else that she doesn't. And because he's a ten-ringer: He can do things she can't imagine, can't even describe, and some part of her thinks he can probably *understand* things she can't, too. "You knew about that Guardian."

"Yes." Now he looks angry, though not at her. "I've run into that kind before. But I don't know why he was there. I can only guess."

"That's better than nothing!"

He looks exasperated. "Okay, then. A guess: Someone, or many someones, knew about that broken obelisk in Allia's harbor. Whoever that was, they also knew that a ten-ringer would likely notice the thing the instant he started sessing around down there. And since all it took to reactivate it was a *four-ringer* sessing around, it stands to reason that these mysterious Someones had no idea just how sensitive, or how dangerous, the obelisk really was. Or neither you nor I would ever have made it to Allia alive."

Syenite frowns, putting a hand on the railing to steady herself when an especially harsh gust of wind soughs up the cliff walls. "Someones."

"Groups. Factions, in some conflict we know nothing about and have only blundered into through sheer dumb luck."

"Factions *of Guardians*?"

He snorts derisively. "You say that like it's impossible. Do all roggas have the same goals, Syen? Do all stills? Even the stone eaters probably have their spats with one another."

And Earth only knows what that's like. "So one of these, ah, factions, dispatched that—Guardian—to kill us." No. Not once Syenite had told the Guardian that she'd been the one to activate the obelisk. "To kill *me*."

Alabaster nods, somber. "I imagine he's the one who poisoned me, too, thinking I'd be the one to trigger the obelisk. Guardians don't like to discipline us where the stills can see, if they can avoid it; might earn us inappropriate public sympathy. That broad-daylight attack was a last resort." He shrugs, frowning as he considers it. "I guess we're lucky he didn't try to poison you instead. Even for me, it should've worked. Paralysis of any kind tends to affect the sessapinae, too; I would've been completely helpless. If."

If he hadn't been able to summon power from the amethyst obelisk, harnessing Syenite's sessapinae to do what his could not. Now that Syen better understands what he did that night, it's somehow worse. She cocks her head at him. "No one really knows what you're capable of, do they?"

Alabaster sighs a little, looking away. "*I* don't even know what I'm capable of, Syen. The things the Fulcrum taught me… I had to leave them behind, past a certain point. I had to make my own training. And sometimes, it seems, if I can just *think* differently, if I can shed enough of what they taught me and try something new, I might…" He trails off, frowning in thought. "I don't know. I really don't. But I guess it's just as well that I don't, or the Guardians would've killed me a long time ago."

It's half-babble, but Syenite sighs in understanding. "So who has the ability to send killer Guardians out to, to…" Hunt down ten-ringers. Scare the piss out of four-ringers.

"All Guardians are killers," he snaps, bitterly. "As for who has the power to command a Guardian forth, I have no idea." Alabaster shrugs. "Rumor has it the Guardians answer to the Emperor—supposedly the Guardians are the last bit of power he possesses. Or maybe that's a lie, and the Yumenes Leadership families control them like they do everything else. Or are they controlled by the Fulcrum itself? No idea."

"I heard they controlled themselves," Syen says. It's probably just grit gossip.

"Maybe. The Guardians are certainly as quick to kill stills as roggas when it comes to maintaining their secrets, or if a still just gets in their way. If they have a hierarchy, only the Guardians themselves recognize it. As for how they do what they do . . ." He takes a deep breath. "It's some sort of surgical procedure. They're all the children of roggas, but not roggas themselves, because there's something about their sessapinae that makes this procedure work better on them. There's an implant involved. Into the brain. Earth knows how they learned that, or when they started doing it, but it gives them the ability to negate orogeny. And other abilities. Worse ones."

Syenite flinches, remembering the sound of ripping tendons. The palm of her hand stings sharply.

"He didn't try to kill you, though," she says. She's looking at his shoulder, which is still visibly darker colored than the cloth around it, though the walk has probably loosened the dried blood so it no longer sticks to the wound. There's a bit of fresh dampness there; it's bleeding again, but thankfully not much. "That knife—"

Alabaster nods grimly. "A Guardian specialty. Their knives

look like ordinary blow glass, but they aren't. They're like the Guardians themselves, somehow disrupting whatever it is in an orogene that makes us what we are." He shudders. "Never knew how it felt before; it hurt like Earthfire. And no," he says quickly, forestalling Syen's open mouth, "I don't know *why* he hit me with it. He'd already stilled us both; I was just as helpless as you."

And that. Syenite licks her lips. "Can you ... are you still ..."

"Yes. It goes away after a few days." He smiles at her look of relief. "I told you, I've run into Guardians like that before."

"Why did you tell me not to let him touch me? With his skin?"

Alabaster goes silent. Syenite thinks at first he's just being stubborn again, then she really looks at his expression and sees the shadows in it. After a moment, he blinks. "I knew another ten-ringer, when I was younger. When I was ... He was a mentor, sort of. Like Feldspar is, for you."

"Feldspar isn't—never mind."

He ignores her anyway, lost in memory. "I don't know why it happened. But one day we were walking the Ring, just out enjoying a nice evening ..." He falters abruptly, then looks at her with a wry, if pained, expression. "We were looking for someplace to be alone."

Oh. Maybe that explains a few things. "I see," she says unnecessarily.

He nods, unnecessarily. "Anyway, this Guardian shows up. Shirtless, like the one you saw. He didn't say anything about why he'd come, either. He just ... attacked. I didn't see—it happened fast. Like in Allia." 'Baster rubs a hand over his face. "He put Hessionite in a choke hold, but not hard enough to actually choke him. The Guardian needed skin-to-skin contact. Then he just held Hess, and, and *grinned* while it happened. Like it was the most beautiful thing in the world, the sick fuck."

"What?" She almost doesn't want to know, and yet she does. "What does the Guardian's skin do?"

Alabaster's jaw flexes, the muscles knotting. "It turns your orogeny inward. I guess. I don't know a better way to explain it. But everything inside us that can move apart plates and seal faults and so on, all that power we're born with… Those Guardians turn it back on us."

"I, I don't…" But orogeny doesn't work on flesh, not directly. If it did—

…Oh.

He falls silent. Syenite does not prompt him to go on, this time.

"Yeah. So." Alabaster shakes his head, then glances toward the stone-cut cliff village. "Shall we go on?"

It's hard to talk, after that story. "'Baster." She gestures at herself, at her uniform, which is dusty but still plainly an Imperial Orogene's blackjacket. "Neither of us can so much as shake a pebble right now. We don't know these people."

"I know. But my shoulder hurts, and I'm thirsty. You see any free-flowing water around here?"

No. And no food. And there's no way to swim back to the mainland, not across such a long expanse. That's if Syenite knew how to swim, which she doesn't, and if the ocean wasn't teeming with monsters like the tales say, which it probably is.

"Fine, then," she says, and pushes past him to lead the way. "Let me talk to them first, so you don't get us killed." Crazy ruster.

Alabaster chuckles a little as if he's heard her unvoiced thought, but he does not protest, resuming the descent in her wake.

The stairs level out, eventually, into a smooth-carved walkway that curves along the cliff wall some hundred feet above the highest waterline. Syen figures that means the comm is safe from tsunami because of its elevation. (She can't be sure, of course. All this *water* is still strange to her.) It also almost makes up for the lack of a protective wall—although, all things considered, the ocean makes for a pretty effective barrier between these people and anyone from outside their...comm, if it can be called that. There are a dozen or so boats docked below, bobbing at jetties that look as though they're made of piled stone overlaid haphazardly with boards—ugly and primitive in comparison with Allia's neat piers and pylons, but effective. And the boats are strange-looking too, at least compared to the boats she's seen: Some are simple, elegant things that look as if they might have been carved whole from tree trunks, braced on each side by some sort of strut. Some are larger and have sails, but even these are of a completely foreign design to what she's used to seeing.

There are people at and around the boats, some of them carting baskets to and fro, others working on an elaborate rigging of sails on one of them. They don't look up; Syenite resists the urge to call down to them. She and Alabaster have already been seen, anyhow. At the first of the cavern mouths up ahead—each of which is huge, now that they're on the "ground" level and can get a good look—a knot of people has begun to gather.

Syenite licks her lips and takes a deep breath as they draw

near. They don't look hostile. "Hello," she ventures, and then waits. No one tries to kill her immediately. So far, so good.

The twenty or so people waiting for them mostly look bemused at the sight of her and Alabaster. The group is mostly children of varying ages, a few younger adults, a handful of elders, and a leashed kirkhusa that seems friendly, to judge by the wag of its stubby tail. The people are definitely Eastcoasters, mostly tall and dark like Alabaster though with a sprinkling of paler citizens, and she spots at least one pouf of ashblow hair lifting in the constant breeze. They also don't look alarmed, which is good, though Syen gets the distinct impression they're not used to surprise visitors.

Then an older man with an air of Leadership, or maybe just leadership, steps forward. And says something completely incomprehensible.

Syen stares at him. She can't even tell what language that is, although it's familiar somehow. Then—oh, of rusting *course*—Alabaster sort of jerks and says something back in the same tongue, and all at once everyone chuckles and murmurs and relaxes. Except Syenite.

She glares at him. "Translation?"

"I told them you were afraid I'd get us killed if I spoke first," he says, and she considers killing him right then and there.

So it goes. They start talking, the people of this strange village and Alabaster, while Syen can't do anything but stand there trying not to look frustrated. Alabaster pauses to translate when he can, though he stumbles over some of what the strangers are saying; they're all talking really fast. She gets the impression that he's summarizing. A lot. But it turns out that the comm is called Meov, and the man who has stepped forward is Harlas, their headman.

Also, they're pirates.

* * *

"There's no way to grow food here," Alabaster explains. "They do what they have to do, to get by."

This is later, after the people of Meov have invited them into the vaulted halls which make up their comm. It's all inside the cliff—unsurprising since the island consists of little more than a straight column of undifferentiated rock—with some of the caverns natural and others carved by unknown means. All of it is surprisingly beautiful, too, with artfully vaulted ceilings, aqueduct arches running along many walls, and enough torch and lantern light that none of it feels claustrophobic. Syen doesn't like the feel of all that rock hovering overhead and waiting to crush them next time there's a shake, but if she must be stuck inside a death trap, at least this one is cozy.

The Meovites have put them up in a guesthouse—or rather, a house that's been abandoned for a while and isn't in too much disrepair. She and Alabaster have been given food from the communal fires, access to the communal baths, and a couple of changes of clothing in the local style. They've even been allotted a modicum of privacy—though this is difficult, as curious children keep peeking through their carved, curtainless windows to giggle at them and then run away. It's almost cute.

Syen sits now on a pile of folded blankets, which seem to have been made for the purpose of sitting, watching as Alabaster winds a length of clean rag around his injured shoulder, holding the other end in his teeth for a moment to tighten it into a bandage. He could ask her for help, of course, but he doesn't, so she doesn't offer.

"They don't trade much with the mainland," he continues as he works. "All they've really got to offer is fish, and the mainland Coaster comms have plenty of that. So Meov raids. They attack vessels along the main trading routes, or extort comms for protection from attacks—yes, *their* attacks. Don't ask me how it works; that's just what the headman told me."

It sounds... precarious. "What are they even doing here?" Syen looks around at the rough-carved walls and ceiling. "It's an *island*. I mean, these caverns are nice, sort of, until the next shake or tsunami wipes the whole thing off the map. And like you said, there's no way to grow food. Do they even have storecaches? What happens if there's a Season?"

"Then they'll die, I guess." 'Baster shrugs, mostly to settle his newly tied bandage. "I asked them that, too, and they just sort of laughed the question off. You notice this island sits on top of a hot spot?"

Syen blinks. She hadn't noticed, but then her orogeny is as numb as a hammered finger. His is, too, but the numbness is relative, apparently. "How deep?"

"Very. It's unlikely to blow anytime soon, or ever—but if it ever does, there will be a crater here instead of islands." He grimaces. "'Course, that's if a tsunami doesn't get the island first, close as we are to the plate boundary here. There're so *many* ways to die in this place. But they know about all of them—seriously—and as far as I can tell, they don't care. At least they'll die free, they say."

"Free of what? Living?"

"Sanze." Alabaster grins when Syen's mouth falls open. "According to Harlas, this comm's part of a string of small island comms all along the archipelago—that's the word for a group of islands, if you didn't know—that extends from here down almost to the Antarctic, created by that hot spot. Some of the comms in that chain, this one included, have been around ten Seasons or longer—"

"Bullshit!"

"—and they don't even remember when Meov was founded and, uh, carved, so maybe it's older than that. They've been around since *before Sanze.* And as far as they know, Sanze either doesn't know or doesn't care that they're here. They were never annexed." He shakes his head. "The Coaster comms are always accusing each other of hosting the pirates, and no one with sense sails this far out; maybe nobody knows these island comms are out here. I mean, they probably know the islands exist, but they must not think anyone would be stupid enough to live on them."

No one should be. Syen shakes her head, amazed at these people's audacity. When another comm child pokes her head above the windowsill, blatantly staring at them, Syen can't help smiling, and the girl's eyes grow round as saucers before she bursts out laughing, babbles something in their choppy language, and then gets pulled away by her comrades. Brave, crazy little thing.

Alabaster chuckles. "She said, 'The mean one actually smiles!'"

Rusting brat.

"I can't believe they *are* crazy enough to live here," she says, shaking her head. "I can't believe this island hasn't shaken apart, or been blown to slag, or been swamped a hundred times over."

Alabaster shifts a little, looking cagey, and by this Syen knows to brace herself. "Well, they survive in large part because they live on fish and seaweed, see. The oceans don't die during a Season the way the land or a smaller body of water does. If you can fish, there's always food. I don't think they even have storecaches." He looks around, thoughtful. "If they can keep the place stable against shakes and blows, then I guess it *would* be a good place to live."

"But how could they—"

"Roggas." He looks at her and grins, and she realizes he's been waiting to tell her this. "That's how they've survived all this time. They don't kill their roggas, here. They put them *in charge*. And they're really, really, glad to see us."

* * *

The stone eater is folly made flesh. Learn the lesson of its creation, and beware its gifts.

—*Tablet Two, "The Incomplete Truth," verse seven*

17

Damaya, in finality

THINGS CHANGE. THERE IS AN order to life in the Fulcrum, but the world is never still. A year passes.

After Crack disappears, Maxixe never speaks to Damaya again. When he sees her in the corridors, or after inspection, he simply turns away. If he catches her looking at him, he scowls. He doesn't catch her often, though, because she doesn't look at him often. She doesn't mind that he hates her. He was only a *potential* friend, anyway. She knows better, now, than to want such a thing, or to believe that she will ever deserve one.

(Friends do not exist. The Fulcrum is not a school. Grits are not children. Orogenes are not people. Weapons have no need of friends.)

Still, it's hard, because without friends she's bored. The instructors have taught her to read as her parents did not, but she can only do so much of that before the words start to flip and jitter on the page like pebbles during a shake. The library doesn't have a lot of books that are just for fun and not utilitarian, anyway. (Weapons do not need fun, either.) She's only allowed to practice her orogeny during Applied, and even though she sometimes lies in her bunk and imagines the lessons over again for extra practice—an orogene's power is in her focus, after all—there's only so much of that she can do, too.

So to occupy her Free Hour, and any other hour when she isn't busy or sleeping, she wanders around the Fulcrum.

No one stops grits from doing this. No one guards the grit dormitory during Free Hour or afterward. The instructors do not enforce a curfew; Free Hour can be Free Night, if a grit's willing to struggle through the next day sleepy. Nor do the adults do anything to prevent the grits from leaving the building. Any child caught in the Ring Garden, which is off-limits to the unringed, or approaching the gates that lead out of the Fulcrum, will have to answer to the seniors. But anything less and the sanctions will be mild, bearable; the usual punishment befitting the crime. That's it.

No one gets expelled from the Fulcrum, after all. Dysfunctional weapons are simply removed from the stockpile. And functional weapons should be smart enough to take care of themselves.

Thus Damaya keeps to the Fulcrum's least interesting areas in her wanderings—but this leaves plenty to explore, because the Fulcrum complex is huge. Apart from the Garden and the grit training grounds there are clusters of living quarters that house the ringed orogenes, libraries and theaters, a hospital, and places where all the adult orogenes do their work when they're not off on assignments beyond the Fulcrum. There are also miles of obsidian-paved walkways and greenland that hasn't been left fallow or kept prepared for a possible Fifth Season;

instead, it's landscaped. It's just there to be pretty. Damaya figures that means someone should look at it.

So it is through all this that Damaya walks, in the late hours of the evening, imagining where and how she will live once she joins the ranks of the ringed. The adults in this area mostly ignore her, coming and going about their business, talking with each other or muttering to themselves alone, focused on their adulty things. Some of them notice her, but then shrug and keep walking. They were grits once. Only on one occasion does a woman stop and ask, "Are you supposed to be here?" Damaya nods and walks past her, and the woman does not pursue.

The administrative buildings are more interesting. She visits the large practice chambers that the ringed orogenes use: great ampitheater-like halls, roofless, with mosaic rings etched into the bare ground in concentric circles. Sometimes there are huge blocks of basalt lying about, and sometimes the ground is disturbed, but the basalt is gone. Sometimes she catches adults in the chambers, practicing; they shift the blocks around like children's toys, pushing them deep into the earth and raising them again by will alone, blurring the air around themselves with deadly rings of cold. It is exhilarating, and intimidating, and she follows what they're doing as best she can, though that isn't much. She's got a long way to go before she can even begin to do some of these things.

It's Main that fascinates Damaya most. This building is the core of the Fulcrum complex: a vast domed hexagon larger than all the other buildings combined. It is in this building that the business of the Fulcrum gets done. Here ringed orogenes occupy the offices and push the papers and pay the bills, because of course they must do all of these things themselves. No one will have it said that orogenes are useless drains on the resources of Yumenes; the Fulcrum is fiscally and otherwise self-sufficient. Free Hour is after the main working hours for the building, so it's not as busy as it must be during the day, but whenever Damaya wanders the place, she notices that many of the offices are still lit with candles and the occasional electric lantern.

The Guardians have a wing in Main, too. Now and again Damaya sees burgundy uniforms amid the clusters of black, and when she does, she turns the other way. Not out of fear. They probably see her, but they don't bother her, because she's not doing anything she's been told not to do. It is as Schaffa told her: One need only fear Guardians in specific, limited circumstances. She avoids them, however, because as she grows more skilled, she begins to notice a strange sensation whenever she's in a Guardian's presence. It is a . . . a buzzy feeling, a jagged and *acrid* sort of thing, something more heard and tasted than sessed. She does not understand it, but she notices that she is not the only orogene to give the Guardians a wide berth.

In Main, there are the wings that have fallen into disuse because the Fulcrum is larger than it needs to be, or so Damaya's instructors have told her when she asks them about this. No one knew how many orogenes there were in the world before the Fulcrum was built, or perhaps the builders thought that more orogenes would survive childhood to be brought here than has proven true over time. Regardless, the first time Damaya pushes open a conspicuous-looking door that no one seems to be using and finds dark, empty hallways beyond it, she is instantly intrigued.

It's too dark to see very far within. Nearby she can make out discarded furniture and storage baskets and the like, so she decides against exploring immediately. The chance that she could hurt herself is too great. Instead she heads back to the grit dorms, and all through the next few days, she prepares. It's easy to take a small glassknife used for cutting meat from one of the meal trays, and the dorm has plenty of oil lanterns that she can appropriate without anyone caring, so she does. She makes a knapsack out of a pillowcase that she nabs while on laundry duty—it has a tattered edge and was in the "discard" pile—and finally when she feels ready, she sets forth.

It's slow going, at first. With the knife she marks the walls here and there so she won't get lost—until she realizes this part of Main has exactly the same structure as the rest of Main: a central corridor with periodic stairwells, and doors on either side leading into rooms or suites of rooms. It's the rooms that she likes most, though many of them are boring. Meeting rooms, more offices, the occasional space large enough to serve as a lecture hall, though mostly these seem to be used for storage of old books and clothing.

But the books! A good many of them are the frivolous sort of tales that the library has so few of—romances and adventures and bits of irrelevant lore. And sometimes the doors lead to amazing things. She discovers a floor that was once apparently used as living quarters—perhaps in some boom year when there were too many orogenes to house comfortably in the apartment buildings. For whatever reason, however, it appears that many of the inhabitants simply walked off and left their belongings behind. Damaya discovers long, elegant dresses in the closets, dry-rotted; toys meant for toddlers; jewelry that her mother would have salivated to wear. She tries on some of it and giggles at herself in the flyspecked mirror, and then stops, surprised by the sound of her own laughter.

There are stranger things. A room full of plush, ornate chairs—worn and moth-eaten now—all arranged in a circle to face each other: why, she can only imagine. A room she does not understand until later, after her explorations have taken her into the buildings of the Fulcrum that are dedicated to research: Then she knows that what she has found is a kind of laboratory, with strange containers and contraptions that she eventually learns are used for analysis of energy and manipulation of chemicals. Perhaps geomests do not deign to study orogeny, and orogenes are left to do that for themselves, too? She can only guess.

And there is more, endlessly more. It becomes the thing she looks forward to the most in any given day, after Applied. She gets in trouble now and again in learning creche because sometimes she daydreams of things she's found, and misses questions during quizzes. She takes care not to slack off so much that the teachers question her, even though she suspects they know about her nighttime explorations. She's even seen a few of them while she wanders, lounging about and seeming oddly human in their off-hours. They don't bother her about it, though, which pleases her mightily. It's nice to feel as if she has a secret to share with them, even though she doesn't really. There is an order to life in the Fulcrum, but this is *her* order; she sets it, and no one else disrupts it. It is good to have something she keeps for herself.

And then, one day, everything changes.

* * *

The strange girl slips into the line of grits so unobtrusively that Damaya almost doesn't notice. They're walking through the Ring Garden again, on their way back to the grit dormitory after Applied, and Damaya is tired but pleased with herself. Instructor Marcasite praised her for only icing a two-foot torus around herself while simultaneously stretching her zone of control to an approximate depth of one hundred feet. "You're almost ready for the first ring test," he told her at the end of the lesson. If this is true, she could end up taking the test a year earlier than most grits, and first of any in her year group.

Because Damaya is so caught up in the glow of this thought, and because it's the evening of a long day and everyone's weary and the Garden is sparsely populated and the instructors are chatting with each other, almost no one sees the strange girl slip into line just ahead of Damaya. Even Damaya almost misses it, because the girl has cleverly waited until they're turning a curve round a hedge; between one step and another she is there, matching their pace, keeping her gaze forward as most of the others do. But Damaya knows she was not there before.

For a moment Damaya is taken aback. She doesn't know all the other grits *well*, but she does know them on sight, and this girl isn't one of them. Who is she, then? She wonders whether she should say something.

Abruptly the girl glances back and catches Damaya staring. She grins and winks; Damaya blinks. When the girl turns away again, she keeps following, too flustered now to tattle.

They proceed through the Garden and into the barracks and then the instructors depart for the evening, leaving the grits to

Free Hour before bedtime. The other kids disperse, some going to fetch food from the sideboard, the newer ones dragging off to bed. A few of the more energetic grits immediately start some sort of silly game, chasing each other round the bunk beds. As usual they ignore Damaya and anything Damaya is doing.

So Damaya turns to the grit who is not a grit. "Who are you?"

"Is that really what you want to ask?" The girl looks honestly puzzled. She is Damaya's age, tall and lanky and more sallow-skinned than most young Sanzeds, and her hair is curled and dark instead of stiff and gray. She's wearing a grit's uniform, and she's actually tied her hair back the same way the other grits with loose hair have done. Only the fact that she's a total stranger breaks the illusion.

"I mean, you don't actually care who I am, do you?" the girl continues, still looking almost offended by Damaya's first question. "If I were you, I'd want to know what I was doing here."

Damaya stares at her, speechless. In the meantime, the girl looks around, frowning a little. "I thought a lot of other people would notice me. There aren't that many of you—what, thirty in this room? That's less than in my creche, and *I* would notice if somebody new suddenly popped in—"

"*Who are you?*" Damaya demands, half-hissing the words. Instinctively, though, she keeps her voice down, and for added measure grabs the girl's arm, hauling her over to an out-of-the-way corner where people are less likely to notice. Except everyone's had years of practice at paying no attention to Damaya, so they don't. "Tell me or I yell for the instructors."

"Oh, that's better." The girl grins. "Much more what I was expecting! But it's still weird that you're the only one—" And then her expression changes to one of alarm when Damaya inhales and opens her mouth, clearly preparing to shout. Quickly she blurts, "My name's Binof! Binof! And you are?"

It's such a commonplace sort of thing to say, the pattern of courtesy that Damaya used for most of her life before coming to the Fulcrum, that she answers automatically. "Damaya Strong—" She has not thought of her use name, or the fact that it no longer applies to her, in so long that she is shocked to almost hear herself say it. "Damaya. What are you doing here? Where did you come from? Why are you—" She gestures helplessly at the girl, encompassing the uniform, the hair, Binof's existence.

"Shhh. *Now* you want to ask a million questions?" Binof shakes her head. "Listen, I'm not going to stay, and I'm not going to get you in trouble. I just need to know—have you seen anything weird around here somewhere?" Damaya stares at her again, and Binof grimaces. "A place. With a shape. Sort of. A big—a thing that—" She makes a series of complicated gestures, apparently trying to pantomime what she means. It is completely nonsensical.

Except, it isn't. Not entirely.

The Fulcrum is circular. Damaya knows this even though she can only get a sense of it when she and the other grits transit the Ring Garden. The Black Star looms to the west of the Fulcrum's grounds, and to the north Damaya has seen a cluster of buildings tall enough to peek over the obsidian walls. (She often wonders what the inhabitants of those buildings think, looking down on Damaya and her kind from their lofty windows and rooftops.) But more significantly, *Main* is circular, too—almost. Damaya has wandered its dark hallways often enough by now, with only a lantern and her fingers and sessapinae to guide her, that when she sees Binof make a hexagonal shape with her hands, she knows at once what the strange girl means.

See, Main's walls and corridors aren't wide enough to account for all the space the building occupies. The building's roof covers an area at its heart, into which its working and walking spaces do not extend; there must be a huge empty chamber within. Courtyard, maybe, or a theater, though there are other theaters in the Fulcrum. Damaya has found the walls around this space, and followed them, and they are not circular; there are planes and angles. Six of each. But if there is a door that opens into this hexagonal central room, it isn't anywhere in the unused wings—not that she's found yet.

"A room without doors," Damaya murmurs, without thinking. It is what she started calling the unseen chamber in her head, on the day she realized it must exist. And Binof inhales and leans forward.

"Yes. *Yes.* Is that what it's called? Is it in that big building at the center of the Fulcrum complex? That's where I thought it might be. Yes."

Damaya blinks and scowls. "Who. *Are.* You." The girl's right; that's not really what she means to say. Still, it covers all the salient questions at once.

Binof grimaces. She glances around, thinks a moment, sets her jaw, and finally says, "Binof Leadership Yumenes."

It almost means nothing to Damaya. In the Fulcrum, no one has use names or comm names. Anyone who was Leadership, before being taken by the Guardians, isn't anymore. The grits who were born here or brought in young enough have a rogga name, and anyone else is required to take one when they earn their first ring. That's all they get.

But then intuition turns a key here and makes various clues click together there, and suddenly Damaya realizes Binof is not merely expressing misplaced loyalty to a social convention that no longer applies. It *does* apply to Binof, because *Binof is not an orogene.*

And Binof's not just any still: she's a Leader, and she's from Yumenes, which makes her a child of one of the most powerful families in the Stillness. *And she has snuck into the Fulcrum, pretending to be an orogene.*

It's so impossible, so insane, that Damaya's mouth falls open. Binof sees that she understands, and edges closer, dropping her voice. "I told you, I'm not going to get you into trouble. I'll go, now, and find that room, and all I ask is that you don't tell anyone yet. But you wanted to know why I'm here. *That's* why I'm here. That room is what I'm looking for."

Damaya closes her mouth. "Why?"

"I can't tell you." When Damaya glares, Binof holds up her hands. "That's for your safety, and mine. There's things only Leaders are supposed to know, and I'm not even supposed to know them yet. If anyone learns I told you, then—" She hesitates. "I don't know what they would do to either of us, but I don't want to find out."

Crack. Damaya nods, absently. "They'll catch you."

"Probably. But when they do, I'll just tell them who I am." The girl shrugs, with the ease of someone who has never known true fear in her life. "They won't know why I'm here. Someone will call my parents and I'll be in trouble, but I get in trouble all the time anyway. If I can find out the answers to some questions first, though, it'll be worth it. Now, where's that room without doors?"

Damaya shakes her head, seeing the trap at once. "*I* could get in trouble for helping you." She isn't a Leader, or a person; no one will save her. "You should leave, however you got here. Now. I won't tell anyone, if you do."

"No." Binof looks smug. "I went to a lot of trouble to get in here. And anyway, you're already in trouble, because you didn't shout for an instructor the minute you realized I wasn't a grit. Now you're my accomplice. Right?"

Damaya starts, her stomach constricting as she realizes the girl is right. She's also furious, because Binof is trying to manipulate her, and she hates that. "It's better if I shout now than let you blunder off and get caught later." And she gets up and heads for the dormitory door.

Binof gasps and trots after her quickly, catching her arm and speaking in a harsh whisper. "Don't! Please—look, I have money. Three red diamond chips and a whole alexandrite! Do you want money?"

Damaya's growing angrier by the minute. "What the rust would I need with money?"

"Privileges, then. The next time you leave the Fulcrum—"

"*We don't leave.*" Damaya scowls and yanks her arm out of Binof's grip. How did this fool of a still even get in here? There are guards, members of the city militia, at all the doors that lead out of the Fulcrum. But those guards are there to keep orogenes in, not stills out—and perhaps this Leader girl with her money and her *privileges* and her fearlessness would have found a way in even if the guards had tried to stop her. "We're here because it's the only place we can be safe from people like *you*. *Get out*."

Suddenly Damaya has to turn away, clenching her fists and concentrating hard and taking quick deep breaths, because she's so angry that the part of herself that knows how to shift fault lines is starting to wander down into the earth. It's a shameful breach of control, and she prays none of the instructors sense it, because then she will no longer be thought of as almost ready for the first ring test. Not to mention that she might end up icing this girl.

Infuriatingly, Binof leans around her and says, "Oh! Are you angry? Are you doing orogeny? What does it feel like?"

The questions are so ridiculous, her lack of fear so nonsensical, that Damaya's orogeny fizzles. She's suddenly not angry anymore, just astonished. Is this what all Leaders are like as children? Palela was so small that it didn't have any; people of the Leader use-caste generally prefer to live in places that are worth leading. Maybe this is just what *Yumenescene* Leaders are like. Or maybe this girl is just ridiculous.

As if Damaya's silence is an answer in itself, Binof grins and dances around in front of her. "I've never had a chance to meet an orogene before. The grown-ups, I mean, the ones with rings who wear the black uniforms, but not a kid like me. You're not as scary as the lorists said you would be. But then, lorists lie a lot."

Damaya shakes her head. "I don't understand anything about you."

To her surprise, Binof sobers. "You sound like my mom." She looks away for a moment, then presses her lips together and glowers at Damaya in apparent determination. "Will you help me find this room, or not? If you won't help, at least don't say anything."

In spite of everything, Damaya is intrigued—by the girl, by the possibility of finding a way into the room without doors, by the novelty of her own intrigue. She has never gone exploring *with* someone, before. It is... exciting. She shifts and looks around uncomfortably, but a part of her has already decided, hasn't it? "Okay. But I've never found a way in, and I've been exploring Main for months."

"Main, is that what the big building is called? And yes, I'm not surprised; there probably isn't an *easy* way in. Or maybe there was once, but it's closed off now." Oblivious as Damaya stares again, Binof rubs her chin. "I have an idea of where to look, though. I've seen some old structural drawings... Well, anyway, it would be on the southern side of the building. Ground level."

That is not in the unused wing, inconveniently. Still, she says, "I know the way," and it's heartening to see Binof brighten at these words.

She leads Binof the way she usually goes, walking the way she usually walks. Strangely, perhaps because she is nervous this time, she notices more people noticing her. There are more double takes than usual, and when she spies Instructor Galena by chance on her way past a fountain—Galena, who once caught her drunk and saved her life by not reporting it—he actually smiles before turning his attention back to his chatty companion. That's when Damaya finally realizes *why* people are looking: because they know about the strange quiet grit who goes wandering all the time. They've probably heard about Damaya via rumors or something, and they *like* that she's finally brought someone else with her. They think she's made a friend. Damaya would laugh, if the truth weren't so unfunny.

"Strange," says Binof as they walk one of the obsidian paths through one of the lesser gardens.

"What?"

"Well, I keep thinking everyone's going to notice me. But instead, almost no one's paying attention. Even though we're the only kids out here."

Damaya shrugs, and keeps walking.

"You'd think someone would stop us and ask questions, or something. We could be doing something unsafe."

Damaya shakes her head. "If one of us gets hurt and someone finds us before we bleed out, they'll take us to the hospital." And then Damaya will have a mark on her record that might prevent her from taking the ring test. Everything she does right now could interfere with that. She sighs.

"That's nice," says Binof, "but maybe it's a better idea to stop kids *before* they do things that might get them hurt."

Damaya stops in the middle of the lawn path and turns to Binof. "We aren't kids," she says, annoyed. Binof blinks. "We're grits—Imperial Orogenes in training. That's what you look like, so that's what everyone assumes you are. Nobody gives a damn whether a couple of orogenes get hurt."

Binof is staring at her. "Oh."

"And you're talking too much. Grits don't. We only relax in the dorms, and only when there are no instructors around. If you're going to pretend to be one of us, get it *right*."

"All right, all right!" Binof holds up both hands as if to

appease her. "I'm sorry, I just..." She grimaces as Damaya glares at her. "Right. No more talking."

She shuts up, so Damaya resumes walking.

They reach Main and head inside the way Damaya always does. Only this time she turns right instead of left, and heads downstairs instead of up. The ceilings are lower in this corridor, and the walls are decorated in a way she has never seen before, with little frescoes painted at intervals that depict pleasant, innocuous scenes. After a while she begins to worry, because they're getting closer and closer to a wing that she has never explored and doesn't want to: the Guardians'. "Where on the south side of the building?"

"What?" Preoccupied with looking around—which makes her stand out even more than the endless talking did—Binof blinks at Damaya in surprise. "Oh. Just...somewhere on the south side." She grimaces at Damaya's glare. "I don't know where! I just know there was a door, even if there isn't one anymore. Can't you—" She waggles her fingers. "Orogenes are supposed to be able to do things like that."

"What, find doors? Not unless they're *in the ground.*" But even as Damaya says this, she frowns, because...well. She *can* sort of sess where doors are, by inference. Load-bearing walls feel much like bedrock, and door frames feel like gaps in strata—places where the pressure of the building against the ground is lesser. If a door somewhere on this level has been covered over, would its frame have been removed, too? Maybe. But would that place not feel different from the walls around it?

She's already turning, splaying her fingers the way she tends to do when she's trying to stretch her zone of control farther.

In the Applied crucibles there are markers underground—small blocks of marble with words etched into one surface. It takes a very fine degree of control to not only find the blocks but determine the word; it's like tasting a page of a book and noticing the minute differences between the ink and the bare page and using that to read. But because she has been doing this over and over and over under the instructors' watchful eye, she realizes that the same exercise works for this purpose.

"Are you doing orogeny?" Binof asks eagerly.

"Yes, so shut *up* before I ice you by accident." Thankfully Binof actually obeys, even though sessing isn't orogeny and there's no danger of icing anyone. Damaya's just grateful for the silence.

She gropes along the walls of the building. They are like shadows of force compared to the stolid comfort of rock, but if she's delicate, she can trace them. And *there* and *there* and *there* along the building's inner walls, the ones that enclose that hidden chamber, she can feel where the walls are... interrupted. Inhaling, Damaya opens her eyes.

"Well?" Binof's practically salivating.

Damaya turns, walking along the wall a ways. When she gets to the right place and stops, there's a door there. It's risky opening doors in occupied wings; this is probably someone's office. The corridor is quiet, empty, but Damaya can see lights underneath some of the doors, which means that at least a few people are working late. She knocks first. When there is no answer, she takes a deep breath and tries the latch. Locked.

"Hang on," Binof says, rummaging in her pockets. After a moment she holds up something that looks like a tool Damaya once used to pick bits of shell out of the kurge nuts that grew on her family's farm. "I read about how to do this. Hopefully it's a simple lock." She begins fiddling with the tool in the lock, her face set in a look of concentration.

Damaya waits awhile, leaning casually against the wall and listening with both ears and sessapinae for any vibration of feet or approaching voices—or worse, the buzz of an approaching Guardian. It's after midnight by now, though, and even the most dedicated workers are either planning to sleep in their offices or have left for the night, so no one troubles them during the agonizingly long time it takes for Binof to figure out how to use the thing.

"That's enough," Damaya says after an eternity. If anyone comes along and catches them here, Damaya won't be able to play it off. "Come back tomorrow and we'll try this again—"

"I *can't*," says Binof. She's sweating and her hands are shaking, which isn't helping matters. "I gave my nurses the slip for one night, but that won't work again. I almost got it last time. Just give me another minute."

So Damaya waits, growing more and more anxious, until finally there is a click and Binof gasps in surprise. "Was that it? I think that was it!" She tries the door, and it swings open. "Earth's flaming *farts*, it worked!"

The room beyond is indeed someone's office: There's a desk and two high-backed chairs, and bookcases line the walls. The desk is bigger than most, the chairs more elaborate; whoever works here is someone important. It is jarring for Damaya to see an office that's still in use after so many months of seeing the disused offices of the old wings. There's no dust, and the lanterns are already lit, though low-wick. So strange.

Binoff looks around, frowning; no sign of a door within the

office. Damaya brushes past her, going over to what looks like a closet. She opens it: brooms and mops, and a spare black uniform hanging on the rod.

"That's it?" Binof curses aloud.

"No." Because Damaya can sess that this office is too short, from door to far wall, to match the width of the building. This closet isn't deep enough to account for the difference.

Tentatively she reaches past the broom and pushes on the wall. Nothing; it's solid brick. Well, that was an idea.

"Oh, *right*." Binof shoulders in with her, feeling the walls all over the closet and shoving the spare uniform out of the way. "These old buildings always have hidden doors, leading down into the storecaches or—"

"There aren't any storecaches in the Fulcrum." Even as she says it, she blinks, because she's never thought about this before. What are they supposed to do if there's a Season? Somehow she doesn't think the people of Yumenes will be willing to share their food with a bunch of orogenes.

"Oh. Right." Binof grimaces. "Well, still, this is Yumenes, even if it is the Fulcrum. There's always—"

And she freezes, her eyes widening as her fingers trip over a brick that's loose. She grins, pushes at one end until the other end pops out; using this, she pulls it loose. There's a latch underneath, made of what looks like cast iron.

"—There's always something going on beneath the surface," Binof breathes.

Damaya draws near, wondering. "Pull it."

"*Now* you're interested?" But Binof indeed wraps her hand around the latch, and pulls.

That whole wall of the closet swings loose, revealing an opening beyond lined with the same brick. The narrow tunnel there curves out of sight almost immediately, into darkness.

Damaya and Binof both stare into it, neither taking that first step.

"What's in there?" Damaya whispers.

Binof licks her lips, staring into the shadowed tunnel. "I'm not sure."

"Bullshit." It's a shameful thrill to talk like this, like one of the ringed grown-ups. "You came here hoping to find *something*."

"Let's go see first—" Binof tries to push past her, and Damaya catches her arm. Binof jumps, arm tightening beneath Damaya's hand; she glares down at it as if in affront. Damaya doesn't care.

"*No*. Tell me what you're looking for, or I'll shut this door after you and start a shake to bring the wall down and trap you in there. Then I'll go tell the Guardians." This is a bluff. It would be the stupidest thing on Father Earth to use unauthorized orogeny right under the noses of the Guardians, and then to go tell them she's done it. But Binof doesn't know that.

"I told you, only Leaders can know this!" Binof tries to shake her off.

"You're a Leader; change the rule. Isn't that also what you're supposed to do?"

Binof blinks and stares at her. For a long moment she is silent. Then she sighs, rubs her eyes, and the tension goes out of her thin arm. "Fine. Okay." She takes a deep breath. "There's something, an artifact, at the heart of the Fulcrum."

"What kind of artifact?"

"I'm not sure. I'm really not!" Binof raises her hands quickly, shaking off Damaya in the process, but Damaya's not trying to hold her anymore. "All I know is that...something's missing from the history. There's a hole, a gap."

"What?"

"In *history*." Binof glares at Damaya as if this is supposed to mean something. "You know, the stuff the tutors teach you? About how Yumenes was founded?"

Damaya shakes her head. Beyond a line she barely remembers in creche about Yumenes being the first city of the Old Sanze Empire, she cannot remember ever hearing about its founding. Perhaps Leaders get a better education.

Binof rolls her eyes, but explains. "There was a Season. The one right before the Empire was founded was Wandering, when north suddenly shifted and crops failed because birds and bugs couldn't find them. After that warlords took over in most areas—which is what always used to happen, after a Season. There was nothing but stonelore to guide people then, and rumors, and superstition. And it was because of rumors that no one settled in this region for a really long time." She points down, at their feet. "Yumenes was the perfect place for a city: good weather, in the middle of a plate, water but nowhere near the ocean, all that. But people were afraid of this place and had been for ages, because *there was something here*."

Damaya's never heard anything like this. "What?"

Binof looks annoyed. "That's what I'm trying to find out! That's what's missing. Imperial history takes over after the Wandering Season. The Madness Season happened only a little while afterward, and Warlord Verishe—Emperor Verishe, the first Emperor—started Sanze then. She founded the Empire here, on land that everyone feared, and built a city around the thing they were all afraid of. That actually helped keep Yumenes safe in those early years. And later, after the Empire was more established, somewhere between the Season of Teeth and the Breathless Season, the Fulcrum was founded on this site. On purpose. *On top of* the thing they were all afraid of."

"But what—" Damaya trails off, understanding at last. "The histories don't say what they were afraid of."

"Precisely. And I think it's in there." Binof points toward the open door.

Damaya frowns. "Why are only Leaders supposed to know this?"

"I don't *know*. That's why I'm *here*. So are you coming in with me, or not?"

Instead of answering, Damaya walks past Binof and into the brick-lined corridor. Binof curses, then trots after her, and because of that, they enter together.

The tunnel opens out into a huge dark space. Damaya stops as soon as she feels airiness and breadth around her; it's pitch black, but she can feel the shape of the ground ahead. She catches Binof, who's blundering forward in a determined sort of way despite the dark—the fool—and says, "Wait. The ground's pressed down up ahead." She's whispering, because that's what one does in the dark. Her voice echoes; the echo takes a while to return. It's a big space.

"Pressed—what?"

"Pressed down." Damaya tries to explain it, but it's always so hard to tell stills things. Another orogene would just *know*. "Like... like there's been something really heavy here."

Something like a mountain. "The strata are deformed, and—there's a depression. A big hole. You'll fall."

"Rusting fuck," Binof mutters. Damaya almost flinches, though she's heard worse from some of her cruder fellow grits when the instructors weren't around. "We need some light."

Lights appear on the ground up ahead, one by one. There is a faint clicking sound—which echoes as well—as each activates: small round white ones near their feet and in twin lines as they march forward, and then much larger ones that are rectangular and butter-yellow, spreading outward from the walkway lights. The yellow panels continue to activate in sequence, and spread, slowly forming an enormous hexagon and gradually illuminating the space in which they stand: a cavernous atrium with six walls, enclosed by what must be the roof of Main high above. The ceiling is so distant they can barely make out its radiating spoke of supports. The walls are featureless, the same plain stone that comprises the rest of Main, but most of the floor of this chamber has been covered over in asphalt, or something very like it—smooth, stonelike but not stone, slightly rough, durable.

At the core of it, however, there is indeed a depression. That is an understatement: It's a huge, tapering pit with flat-sided walls and neat, precise edges—six of them, cut as finely as one cuts a diamond. "Evil Earth," Damaya whispers as she edges forward along the walkway to where the yellow lights limn the shape of the pit.

"Yeah," says Binof, sounding equally awed.

It is stories deep, this pit, and steep. If she fell in, she would roll down its slopes and probably break every bone in her body at the bottom. But the shape of it nags at her, because it is *faceted.*

Tapering to a point at the very bottom. No one digs a pit in that shape. Why would they? It would be almost impossible to get out of, even with a ladder that could reach so far.

But then, no one has *dug* this pit. She can sess that: Something monstrously heavy *punched* this pit into the earth, and sat in the depression long enough to make all the rock and soil beneath it solidify into these smooth, neat planes. Then whatever-it-was lifted away, clean as a buttered roll from a pan, leaving nothing but the shape of itself behind.

But wait; the walls of the pit are not wholly smooth. Damaya crouches for a closer look, while beside her, Binof just stares.

There: Along every smooth slope, she can see thin, barely visible sharp objects. Needles? They push up through fine cracks in the smooth walls, jagged and random, like plant roots. The needles are made of iron; Damaya can smell the rust in the air. Scratch her earlier guess: If she fell into this pit, she would be shredded long before she ever hit the bottom.

"I wasn't expecting this," Binof breathes at last. She's speaking in a hush, maybe out of reverence, or fear. "Many things, but . . . not this."

"What is it?" asks Damaya. "What's it for?"

Binof shakes her head slowly. "It's *supposed* to be—"

"Hidden," says a voice behind them, and they both jump and whirl in alarm. Damaya is standing closer to the edge of the pit, and when she stumbles there is a terrible, vertiginous moment in which she's absolutely certain she's going to fall in. In fact she relaxes, and doesn't try to lean forward or rebalance herself or do any of the things that she would do if she had a chance of *not* falling. She is all-over heavy, and the pit yawns with inevitability behind her.

Then Binof grabs her arm and yanks her forward, and abruptly she realizes she was still a good two or three feet from the edge. She would only have fallen in if she'd *let* herself fall in. This is such a strange thing that she almost forgets *why* she nearly fell, and then the Guardian comes down the walkway.

The woman is tall and broad and bronze, pretty in a carved sort of way, with ashblow hair shorn into a bristly cap. She feels older than Schaffa, though this is difficult to tell; her skin is unmarked, her honey-colored eyes undented by crow's feet. She just feels...heavier, in presence. And her smile is the same unnerving combination of peaceable and menacing as that of every Guardian Damaya has ever seen.

Damaya thinks, *I only need to be afraid if she thinks I'm dangerous.*

Here is the question, though: Is an orogene who goes where she knows she should not dangerous? Damaya licks her lips and tries not to look afraid.

Binof doesn't bother, darting a look between Damaya and the woman and the pit and the door. Damaya wants to tell her not to do whatever she's thinking of—making a break for it, likely. Not with a Guardian here. But Binof is not an orogene; maybe that will protect her, even if she does something stupid.

"Damaya," the woman says, though Damaya has never met her before. "Schaffa will be disappointed."

"She's with me," Binof blurts, before Damaya can reply. Damaya looks at her in surprise, but Binof's already talking, and now that she's started, it seems as though nothing will stop her. "I brought her here. Ordered her here. She didn't even know about the door and this—place—until I told her."

That isn't true, Damaya wants to say, because she'd guessed that the place existed, just hadn't known how to find it. But the Guardian is looking at Binof curiously, and that's a positive sign because nobody's hands have been broken yet.

"And you are?" The Guardian smiles. "Not an orogene, I gather, despite your uniform."

Binof jumps a little, as if she's forgotten that she's been playing little lost grit. "Oh. Um." She straightens and lifts her chin. "My name is Binof Leadership Yumenes. Your pardon for my intrusion, Guardian; I had a question that required an answer."

Binof's talking differently, Damaya realizes suddenly: her words evenly spaced and voice steady, her manner not so much haughty as grave. As if the world's fate depends upon her finding the answer to her question. As if she isn't just some spoiled girl from a powerful family who decided on a whim to do something incredibly stupid.

The Guardian stops, cocking her head and blinking as her smile momentarily fades. "Leadership Yumenes?" Then she beams. "How lovely! So young, and already you have a comm name. You are quite welcome among us, Binof Leader. If you had but told us you were coming, we could have *shown* you what you wanted to see."

Binof flinches minutely at the rebuke. "I had a wish to see it for myself, I'm afraid. Perhaps that was not wise—but my parents are likely by now aware that I have come here, so please feel free to speak to them about it."

It's a smart thing to do, Damaya is surprised to realize, because before now she has not thought of Binof as smart. Mentioning that others know where she's gone.

"I shall," says the Guardian, and then she smiles at Damaya, which makes her stomach tighten. "And I shall speak to your Guardian, and we shall all speak together. That would be lovely, yes? Yes. Please." She steps aside and bows a little, gesturing for them to precede her, and as polite as it looks, they both know it's not a request.

The Guardian leads them out of the chamber. As they all step into the brick tunnel again, the lights go out behind them. When the door is shut and the office is locked and they have proceeded into the Guardians' wing, the woman touches Damaya's shoulder to stop her while Binof keeps walking for a step or two. Then when Binof stops, looking at them in confusion, the Guardian says to Damaya, "Please wait here." Then she moves to rejoin Binof.

Binof looks at her, perhaps trying to convey something with her eyes. Damaya looks away, and the message fails as the Guardian leads her farther down the hall and into a closed door. Binof has already done enough harm.

Damaya waits, of course. She's not stupid. She's standing in front of the door to a busy area; despite the hour, other Guardians emerge now and again, and look at her. She doesn't look back, and something in this seems to satisfy them, so they move on without bothering her.

After a few moments, the Guardian who caught them in the pit chamber returns and leads her through the door, with a gentle hand on her shoulder. "Now. Let's just talk a bit, why don't we? I've sent for Schaffa; fortunately he's in the city right now, and not out on circuit as usual. But until he gets here..."

There's a large, handsomely apportioned, carpeted area

beyond the door, with many small desks. Some are occupied and some not, and the people who move between them wear a mix of black and burgundy uniforms. A very few aren't wearing uniforms at all, but civilian clothing. Damaya stares at all of it in fascination until the Guardian puts a hand on her head and gently, but inexorably, steers her gaze away.

Damaya is led into a small private office at the end of this chamber. The desk here is completely empty, however, and the room has a disused air. There's a chair on either side of the desk, so Damaya takes the one meant for guests.

"I'm sorry," she says as the Guardian sits down behind the desk. "I-I didn't think."

The Guardian shakes her head, as if this doesn't matter. "Did you touch any of them?"

"What?"

"In the socket." The Guardian's still smiling, but they always smile; this means nothing useful. "You saw the extrusions from the socket walls. Weren't you curious? There was one only an arm's length below where you stood."

Socket? Oh, and the iron bits poking out of the walls. "No, I didn't touch any of them." *Socket for what?*

The Guardian sits forward, and abruptly her smile vanishes. It doesn't fade, and she doesn't frown to replace it. All the expression just stops, in her face. "Did it call to you? Did you answer?"

Something's wrong. Damaya feels this suddenly, instinctively, and the realization dries the words from her mouth. The Guardian even sounds different—her voice is deeper, softer, almost hushed, as if she's saying something she doesn't want the others to hear.

"What did it say to you?" The Guardian extends her hand, and even though Damaya puts her hand out immediately in obedient response, she does not want to. She does it anyway because Guardians are to be obeyed. The woman takes Damaya's hand and holds it palm up, her thumb stroking the long crease. The lifeline. "You can tell me."

Damaya shakes her head in utter confusion. "What did *what* say to me?"

"It's angry." The woman's voice drops lower, going monotonous, and Damaya realizes she's not trying to go unheard anymore. The Guardian is talking differently because *that's not her voice*. "Angry and... afraid. I hear both gathering, growing, the anger and the fear. Readying, for the time of return."

It's like... like someone else is inside the Guardian, and *that* is who's talking, except using the Guardian's face and voice and everything else. But as the woman says this, her hand begins to tighten on Damaya's. Her thumb, which rests right on the bones that Schaffa broke a year and a half ago, begins to press in, and Damaya feels faint as some part of her thinks, *I don't want to be hurt again.*

"I'll tell you whatever you want," she offers, but the Guardian keeps pressing. It's like she doesn't even hear.

"It did what it had to do, last time." Press and tighten. This Guardian, unlike Schaffa, has longer nails; the thumbnail begins to dig into Damaya's flesh. "It seeped through the walls and tainted their pure creation, exploited them before they could exploit it. When the arcane connections were made, it *changed* those who would control it. Chained them, fate to fate."

"Please don't," Damaya whispers. Her palm has begun to

bleed. In almost the same moment there is a knock at the door. The woman ignores both.

"It made them a part of it."

"I don't *understand*," Damaya says. It hurts. It *hurts*. She's shaking, waiting for the snap of bone.

"It hoped for communion. Compromise. Instead, the battle... escalated."

"I don't understand! You're not making any sense!" It's wrong. Damaya's raising her voice to a Guardian, and she *knows* better, but this isn't right. Schaffa promised that he would hurt her only for a good reason. All Guardians operate on this principle; Damaya has seen the proof of it in how they interact with her fellow grits and the ringed orogenes. There is an order to life in the Fulcrum and this woman is *breaking it*. "Let go of me! I'll do whatever you want, just let go!"

The door opens and Schaffa flows in. Damaya's breath catches, but he doesn't look at her. His gaze is fixed on the Guardian who holds Damaya's hand. He isn't smiling as he moves to stand behind her. "Timay. Control yourself."

Timay's not home, Damaya thinks.

"It speaks only to warn, now," she continues in a drone. "There will be no compromise next time—"

Schaffa sighs a little, then jabs his fingers into the back of Timay's skull.

It's not clear at first, from Damaya's angle, that this is what he's done. She just sees him make a sudden sharp, violent movement, and then Timay's head jerks forward. She makes a sound so harsh and guttural that it is almost vulgar, and her eyes go wide. Schaffa's face is expressionless as he does something, his arm flexing, and that's when the first blood-lines wend around Timay's neck, beginning to sink into her tunic and patter into her lap. Her hand, on Damaya's, relaxes all at once, and her face goes slack.

That is also when Damaya begins to scream. She keeps screaming as Schaffa twists his hand again, nostrils flaring with the effort of whatever he's doing, and the sound of crunching bone and popping tendon is undeniable. Then Schaffa lifts his hand, holding something small and indistinct—too covered in gore—between his thumb and forefinger. Timay falls forward then, and now Damaya sees the ruin that was once the base of her skull.

"Be silent, little one," Schaffa says, mildly, and Damaya shuts up.

Another Guardian comes in, looks at Timay, looks at Schaffa, and sighs. "Unfortunate."

"Very unfortunate." Schaffa offers the blood-covered thing to this man, who cups his hands to receive it, carefully. "I would like this removed." He nods toward Timay's body.

"Yes." The man leaves with the thing Schaffa took from Timay, and then two more Guardians come in, sigh as the first one did, and collect her body from its chair. They drag her out, one of them pausing to mop up with a handkerchief the drops of blood from the table where Timay fell. It's all very efficient. Schaffa sits down in Timay's place, and Damaya jerks her eyes to him only because she must. They gaze at each other in silence for a few moments.

"Let me see," Schaffa says gently, and she offers him her hand. Amazingly, it does not shake.

He takes it with his left hand—the one that is still clean

because it did not rip out Timay's brain stem. He turns her hand, examining it carefully, making a face at the crescent of blood where Timay's thumbnail broke the skin. A single drop of Damaya's blood rolls off the edge of her hand, splatting onto the table right where Timay's blood had been a moment before. "Good. I was afraid she'd hurt you worse than this."

"Wh—" Damaya begins. She can't muster any more than that.

Schaffa smiles, though this is edged with sorrow. "Something you should not have seen."

"*What.*" This takes a ten-ringer's effort.

Schaffa considers a moment, then says, "You are aware that we—Guardians—are . . . different." He smiles, as if to remind her of how different. All Guardians smile a lot.

She nods, mute.

"There is a . . . procedure." He lets go of her hand for a moment, touches the back of his own skull, beneath the fall of his long black hair. "A thing is done to make us what we are. An implantation. Sometimes it goes wrong and must then be removed, as you saw." He shrugs. His right hand is still covered in gore. "A Guardian's connections with his assigned orogenes can help to stave off the worst, but Timay had allowed hers to erode. Foolish."

A chilly barn in the Nomidlats; a moment of apparent affection; two warm fingers pressed to the base of Damaya's skull. *Duty first,* he had said then. *Something that will make me more comfortable.*

Damaya licks her lips. "Sh-she was. Saying things. Not making. Sense."

"I heard some of what she said."

"She wasn't. *Her.*" Now Damaya's the one not making sense.

"She wasn't who she was anymore. I mean, she was someone else. Talking as if... someone else was there." In her head. In her mouth, speaking through it. "She kept talking about a socket. And 'it' being angry."

Schaffa inclines his head. "Father Earth, of course. It is a common delusion."

Damaya blinks. What? *It's angry.* What?

"And you're right; Timay wasn't herself any longer. I'm sorry she hurt you. I'm sorry you had to see that. I'm so sorry, little one." And there is such genuine regret in his voice, such compassion in his face, that Damaya does what she has not since a cold dark night in a Nomidlats barn: She begins to cry.

After a moment Schaffa gets up and comes around the table and picks her up, sitting in the chair and letting her curl in his lap to weep on his shoulder. There is an order to life in the Fulcrum, see, and it is this: If one has not displeased them, the Guardians are the closest thing to safety a rogga will ever have. So Damaya cries for a long time—not just because of what she's seen tonight. She cries because she has been inexpressibly lonely, and Schaffa... well. Schaffa loves her, in his tender and terrifying way. She does not pay attention to the bloody print his right hand leaves on her hip, or the press of his fingers—fingers strong enough to kill—against the base of her skull. Such things are irrelevant, in the grand scale.

When the storm of weeping subsides, though, Schaffa strokes her back with his clean hand. "How are you feeling, Damaya?"

She does not lift her head from his shoulder. He smells of sweat and leather and iron, things that she will forever associate with comfort and fear. "I'm all right."

"Good. I need you to do something for me."

"What?"

He squeezes her gently, encouraging. "I'm going to take you down the hall, to one of the crucibles, and there you will face the first ring test. I need you to pass it for me."

Damaya blinks, frowning, and lifts her head. He smiles at her, tenderly. By this she understands, in a flash of intuition, that this is a test of more than her orogeny. After all, most roggas are told of the test in advance, so that they can practice and prepare. This is happening for her now, without warning, because it is her only chance. She has proven herself disobedient. Unreliable. Because of this, Damaya will need to also prove herself useful. If she cannot…

"I need you to live, Damaya." Schaffa touches his forehead to her own. "My compassionate one. My life is so full of death. Please; pass this test for me."

There are so many things she wants to know. What Timay meant; what will happen to Binof; what is the *socket* and why was it hidden; what happened to Crack last year. Why Schaffa is even giving her this much of a chance. But there is an order to life in the Fulcrum, and her place within it is not to question a Guardian's will.

But…

But…

But. She turns her head, and looks at that single drop of her blood on the table.

This is not right.

"Damaya?"

It isn't right, what they're doing to her. What this place does to everyone within its walls. What he's making her do, to survive.

"Will you do it? For me?"

She still loves him. That isn't right, either.

"If I pass." Damaya closes her eyes. She can't look at him and say this. Not without letting him see the *it isn't right* in her eyes. "I, I picked a rogga name."

He does not chide her on her language. "Have you, now?" He sounds pleased. "What?"

She licks her lips. "Syenite."

Schaffa sits back in the chair, sounding thoughtful. "I like it."

"You do?"

"Of course I do. You chose it, didn't you?" He's laughing, but in a good way. With her, not at her. "It forms at the edge of a tectonic plate. With heat and pressure it does not degrade, but instead grows stronger."

He *does* understand. She bites her lip and feels fresh tears threaten. It isn't right that she loves him, but many things in the world are not right. So she fights off the tears, and makes her decision. Crying is weakness. Crying was a thing Damaya did. Syenite will be stronger.

"I'll do it," Syenite says, softly. "I'll pass the test for you, Schaffa. I promise."

"My good girl," Schaffa says, and smiles, holding her close.

* * *

[obscured] those who would take the earth too closely
unto themselves. They are not masters of themselves;
allow them no mastery of others.

—*Tablet Two, "The Incomplete Truth," verse nine*

18

you discover wonders down below

Ykka takes you into the house from which she and her companions emerged. There's little furniture inside, and the walls are bare. There's scuffing on the floor and walls, a lingering smell of food and stale body musk; someone *did* live here, until recently. Maybe until the Season began. The house is only a shell now, though, as you and the others cut through to a cellar door. At the bottom of the steps you find a large, empty chamber lit only by wood-pitch torches.

Here's where you first start to realize this is more than just a bizarre community of people and not-people: The walls of the cellar are solid granite. Nobody quarries into granite just to build a cellar, and . . . and you're not sure anyone *dug* this. Everyone stops while you go to one of the walls and touch it. You close your eyes and *reach*. Yes, there is the feel of something familiar here. Some rogga shaped this perfectly smooth wall, using will and a focus finer than you can imagine. (Though not the *finest* focus you've ever sessed.) You've never heard of anyone doing anything like this with orogeny. It's not for building.

Turning, you see Ykka watching you. "Your work?"

She smiles. "No. This and other hidden entrances have been around for centuries, long before me."

"The people in this comm have worked with orogenes for that long?" She'd said the comm was only fifty years old.

Ykka laughs. "No, I just mean that this world has passed through many hands down the Seasons. Not all of them were quite as stupid as ours about the usefulness of orogenes."

"We aren't stupid about it now," you say. "Everyone understands perfectly well how to *use* us."

"Ooh." Ykka grimaces, pityingly. "Fulcrum trained? The ones who survive it always seem to sound like you."

You wonder how many Fulcrum-trained orogenes this woman has met. "Yes."

"Well. Now you'll see how much more we're capable of when we're willing." And Ykka gestures toward a wide opening in the wall a few feet beyond her, which you hadn't noticed in your fascination with the cellar's construction. A faint draft wafts into the cellar from beyond it. There're also three people loitering at the mouth of the opening, watching you with varied expressions of hostility, wariness, amusement. They're not carrying any weapons—those are propped against the wall nearby—and they're not conspicuous about it, but you realize these are the gate guards this comm should have, for the gate this comm doesn't have. Here, in this cellar.

The blond woman speaks quietly with one of the guards; this emphasizes even more how tiny she is, a foot shorter and probably a hundred pounds lighter than the smallest of them. Her ancestors really should've done her a few favors and slept with a

Sanzed or two. Anyway, then you move on and the guards stay behind, two taking seats on chairs nearby, the third heading back up the steps, presumably to keep a lookout from within the empty buildings topside.

You make the paradigm shift then: The abandoned village up there *is* this comm's wall. Camouflage rather than a barrier.

Camouflage for what, though? You follow Ykka through the opening and into the dark beyond.

"The core of this place has always been here," she explains as you walk down a long dark tunnel that might be an abandoned mine shaft. There's tracks for carts, though they're so old and sunken into the gritty stone that you can't really see them. Just awkward ridges beneath your feet. The wooden bracers of the tunnel look old, as do the wall sconces that hold cord-strung electric lights—they look like they were originally made to hold wooden torches and got retrofitted by some geneer. The lights are still working, which means the comm's got functional geo or hydro or both; better than Tirimo already. It's warm in the shaft, too, but you don't see any of the usual heating pipes. It's just warm, and getting warmer as you follow the gently sloping floor downward.

"I told you there were mines in the area. That's how they found these, back in the day. Someone cracked a wall they shouldn't have and blundered into a whole warren of tunnels nobody knew were there." Ykka falls silent for a long while as the shaft widens out, and you all go down a set of dangerous-looking metal steps. There's a lot of them. They look old, too—and yet strangely, the metal doesn't seem distressed or rusted out. It's smooth and shiny and all-over whole. The steps aren't shaky at all.

After a time you notice, belatedly, that the red-haired stone eater is gone. She didn't follow you down into the shaft. Ykka doesn't seem to notice, so you touch her arm. "Where's your friend?" Though you sort of know.

"My—oh, that one. Moving the way we do is hard for them, so they've got their own ways of getting about. Including ways I would never have guessed." She glances at Hoa, who's come down the steps with you. He looks back at her, coldly, and she breathes out a laugh. "Interesting."

At the bottom of the stairs there's another tunnel, though it looks different for some reason. Curved at its top rather than squared, and the supports are some sort of thick, silvery stone columns, which arch partway up the walls like ribs. You can almost taste the age of these corridors through the pores of your skin.

Ykka resumes. "Really, all the bedrock in this area is riddled with tunnels and intrusions, mines on top of mines. One civilization after another, building on what went before."

"Aritussid," says Tonkee. "Jyamaria. The lower Ottey States."

You've heard of Jyamaria, from the history you used to teach in creche. It was the name of a large nation, the one that started the road system Sanze later improved upon, and which once spread over most of what is now the Somidlats. It died around ten Seasons ago. The rest of the names are probably those of other deadcivs; that seems like the sort of thing geomests would care about, even if no one else does.

"Dangerous," you say, as you try not to be too obvious with your unease. "If the rock here's been compromised so much—"

"Yes, yes. Though that's a risk with any mining, as much because of incompetence as shakes."

Tonkee is turning and turning as she walks, taking it all in and still not bumping into anyone; amazing. "That northern shake was severe enough that even this should have come down," she says.

"You're right. That shake—we're calling it the Yumenes Rifting, since nobody's come up with a better name yet—was the worst the world's seen in an age. I don't think I'm exaggerating by saying so." Ykka shrugs and glances back at you. "But of course, the tunnels didn't collapse, because I was here. I didn't *let* them."

You nod, slowly. It's no different than what you did for Tirimo, except Ykka must have taken care to protect more than just the surface. The area must be relatively stable anyway, or these tunnels would've all collapsed ages ago.

But you say: "You won't always be around."

"When I'm not, someone else will do it." She shrugs. "Like I said, there's a lot of us here now."

"About that—" Tonkee pivots on one foot and suddenly her whole attention is on Ykka. Ykka laughs.

"Kind of single-minded, aren't you?"

"Not really." You suspect Tonkee is still simultaneously taking note of the supports and wall composition, counting your paces, whatever, all while she talks. "So how are you doing it? Luring orogenes here."

"Luring?" Ykka shakes her head. "It's not that sinister. And it's hard to describe. There's a . . . a thing I do. Like—" She falls silent.

And all at once, you stumble while you're walking. There's no obstruction on the floor. It's just suddenly difficult to walk in a straight line, as if the floor has developed an invisible downward slope. Toward Ykka.

You stop and glare at her. She stops as well, turning to smile at you. "How are you doing that?" you demand.

"I don't know." She spreads her hands at your disbelieving look. "It's just something I tried, a few years ago. And not too long after I started doing it, a man came to town and said he'd felt me from miles away. Then two kids showed up; they didn't even realize what they were reacting to. Then another man. I've kept doing it since."

"Doing what?" Tonkee asks, looking from you to Ykka.

"Only roggas feel it," Ykka explains, though by this point you've figured that out for yourself. Then she glances at Hoa, who is watching both of you, utterly still. "And *them*, I realized later."

"About that," Tonkee blurts.

"Earthfires and rustbuckets, you ask too many questions." This comes from the blond woman, who shakes her head and gestures for all of you to keep walking.

There are faint occasional noises up ahead now, and the air is moving, noticeably. But how can that be? You must be a mile down, maybe twice that. The breeze is warm and tinged with scents you've almost forgotten after weeks of breathing sulfur and ash through a mask. A bit of cooking food here, a waft of rotting garbage there, a breath of burning wood. People. You're smelling people. Lots of them. And there's a light—much stronger than the strings of electric lights along the walls—straight ahead.

"An *underground* comm?" Tonkee says what you're thinking,

though she sounds more skeptical. (You know more about impossible things than she does.) "No, nobody's that stupid."

Ykka only laughs.

Then as the peculiar light starts to brighten the shaft around you, and the air moves faster and the noise grows, there's a place where the tunnel opens out and becomes a wide ledge with a metal railing for safety. A scenic viewpoint, because some geneer or Innovator understood exactly how newcomers would react. You do exactly as that long-ago designer intended: You stare in openmouthed, abject wonder.

It's a *geode*. You can sess that, the way the rock around you abruptly changes to something else. The pebble in the stream, the warp in the weft; countless aeons ago a bubble formed in a flow of molten mineral within Father Earth. Within that pocket, nurtured by incomprehensible pressures and bathed in water and fire, crystals grew. This one's the size of a city.

Which is probably why *someone built a city in this one.*

You stand before a vast, vaulted cavern that is full of glowing crystal shafts the size of tree trunks. *Big* tree trunks. Or buildings. Big buildings. They jut forth from the walls in an utterly haphazard jumble: different lengths, different circumferences, some white and translucent and a few smoky or tinged with purple. Some are stubby, their pointed tips ending only a few feet away from the walls that grew them—but many stretch from one side of the vast cavern into the indistinct distance. They form struts and roads too steep to climb, going in directions that make no sense. It is as if someone found an architect, made her build a city out of the most beautiful materials available, then threw all those buildings into a box and jumbled them up for laughs.

And they're definitely living in it. As you stare, you notice narrow rope bridges and wooden platforms everywhere. There are dangling lines strung with electric lanterns, ropes and pulleys carrying small lifts from one platform to another. In the distance a man walks down a wooden stairway built around a titanic slanted column of white; two children play on the ground far below, in between stubby crystals the size of houses.

Actually, some of the crystals *are* houses. They have holes cut in them—doors and windows. You can see people moving around inside some of them. Smoke curls from chimney holes cut in pointed crystal tips.

"Evil, eating *Earth*," you whisper.

Ykka stands with hands on her hips, watching your reaction with something like pride in her expression. "We didn't do most of this," she admits. "The recent additions, the newer bridges, yes, but the shaft-hollowing had already been done. We don't know how they managed it without shattering the crystals. The walkways that are made of metal—it's the same stuff as the steps in the tunnels we just passed through. The geneers have no idea how it's made; metallorists and alchemists have orgasms when they see it. There are mechanisms up there"—She points toward the barely visible ceiling of the cavern, hundreds of feet above your heads. You barely hear her, your mind numb, your eyes beginning to ache from staring without blinking—"that pump bad air into a layer of porous earth that filters and disperses it back onto the surface. Other pumps bring in good air. There are mechanisms just outside the geode that divert water from an underground hot spring a ways off, through a turbine that gives us electric power—took ages to figure that part out—and also bring it in for day-to-day use." She sighs. "But to be really honest, we don't know how half the stuff we've found here works. All of it was built long ago. Long before Old Sanze ever existed."

"Geodes are unstable once their shells are breached." Even Tonkee sounds floored. In your peripheral vision she is still for the first time since you met her. "It doesn't make sense to even think of building inside one. And why are the crystals *glowing*?"

She's right. They are.

Ykka shrugs, folding her arms. "No idea. But the people who built this wanted it to last, even through a shake, so they did things to the geode to make sure that would happen. And it did...but *they* didn't. When people from Castrima found this, it was full of skeletons—some so old they turned to dust as soon as we touched them."

"So your comm forebears decided to move everyone into a giant deadciv artifact that killed the last few people who risked it," you drawl. It's weak snark, though. You're too shaken to really get the tone right. "Of course. Why *not* repeat a colossal mistake?"

"Believe me, it's been an ongoing debate." Ykka sighs and leans against the railing, which makes you twitch. It's a long way down if she slips, and some of the crystals on the geode floor are sharp-looking. "No one was willing to live here for a long time. Castrima used this place and the tunnels leading to it as a storecache, though never for essentials like food or medicine. But in all that time, there's never been so much as a crack in the walls, even after shakes. We were further convinced by history: The comm that controlled this area during the last Season—a real, proper comm, with walls and everything—got overrun by a commless band. The whole comm was burned to the ground, all their vital stores taken. The survivors had a choice between moving down here, and trying to survive up there with no heat and no walls and every bunch of scavengers around homing in on the easy pickings left. So they were our precedent."

Necessity is the only law, says stonelore.

"Not that it went well." Ykka straightens and gestures for you to follow her again. All of you start down a broad, flat ramp that gently slopes toward the floor of the cavern. You realize only belatedly that it's a crystal, and you're walking down its side. Someone's paved the thing with concrete for traction, but past the edges of the gray strip you can see softly glowing white. "Most of the people who moved down here during that Season died, too. They couldn't make the air mechanisms work; staying here for more than a few days at a time meant suffocation. And they didn't have any food, so even though they were warm and safe and had plenty of water, most of them starved before the sun returned."

It's an old tale, freshened only by the unique setting. You nod absently, trying not to stumble as your attention is caught by an older man riding across the cavern while suspended from a pulley and cable, his butt snuggly tucked into a loop of rope. Ykka pauses to wave; the man waves back and glides on.

"The survivors of that nightmare started the trading post that eventually became Castrima. They passed down stories about this place, but still, no one wanted to live here... until my great-grandmother realized why the mechanisms didn't work. Until *she* got them working, just by walking through that entrance." Ykka gestures back the way you came. "Worked for me, too, when I first came down here."

You stop. Everyone goes on without you for a moment. Hoa is the first to notice that you're not following. He turns and looks at you. There is something guarded in his expression that was not there before, you notice distantly, through horror and wonder. Later, when you've had time to get past this, you and he will have to talk. Now there are more important considerations.

"The mechanisms," you say. Your mouth is dry. "They run on *orogeny*."

Ykka nods, half-smiling. "That's what the geneers think. Of course, the fact that it's all working now makes the conclusion obvious."

"Is it—" You grope for the words, fail. "*How?*"

Ykka laughs, shaking her head. "I have no idea. It just works."

That, more than everything else she's shown you, terrifies you.

Ykka sighs and puts her hands on her hips. "Essun," she says, and you twitch. "That's your name, right?"

You lick your lips. "Essun Resis—" And then you stop. Because you were about to give the name you gave to people in Tirimo for years, and that name is a lie. "Essun," you say again, and stop there. Limited lying.

Ykka glances at your companions. "Tonkee Innovator Dibars," says Tonkee. She throws an almost embarrassed look at you, then looks down at her feet.

"Hoa," says Hoa. Ykka gazes at him a moment longer, as if she expects more, but he offers nothing.

"Well, then." Ykka opens her arms, as if to encompass the

whole geode; she gazes at all of you with her chin lifted, amost in defiance. "This is what we're trying to do here in Castrima: survive. Same as anyone. We're just willing to *innovate* a little." She inclines her head to Tonkee, who chuckles nervously. "We might all die doing it, but rust, that might happen anyway; it's a Season."

You lick your lips. "Can we leave?"

"What the rust do you mean, can we leave? We've barely had time to explore—" Tonkee begins, looking angry, and then abruptly she realizes what you mean. Her sallow face grows more so. "Oh."

Ykka's smile is sharp as diamond. "Well. You're not stupid; that's good. Come on. We've got some people to meet."

She beckons for you to follow again, resuming her walk down the slope, and she does not answer your question.

* * *

In actual practice the sessapinae, paired organs located at the base of the brain stem, have been found to be sensitive to far more than local seismic movements and atmospheric pressure. In tests, reactions have been observed to the presence of predators, to others' emotions, to distant extremes of heat or cold, and to the movements of celestial objects. The mechanism of these reactions cannot be determined.

—Nandvid Innovator Murkettsi, "Observations of sesunal variation in overdeveloped individuals," Seventh University biomestry learning-comm. With appreciation to the Fulcrum for cadaver donation.

19

Syenite on the lookout

THEY'VE BEEN IN MEOV FOR three days when something changes. Syenite has spent those three days feeling very much out of place, in more ways than one. The first problem is that she can't speak the language—which Alabaster tells her is called Eturpic. A number of Coaster comms still speak it as a native tongue, though most people also learn Sanze-mat for trading purposes. Alabaster's theory is that the people of the islands are mostly descended from Coasters, which seems fairly obvious from their predominant coloring and common kinky hair—but since they raid rather than trade, they had no need to retain Sanze-mat. He tries to teach Eturpic to her, but she's not really in a "learn something new" sort of mood. That's because of the second problem, which Alabaster points out to her after they've had enough time to recover from their travails: They can't leave. Or rather, they've got nowhere to go.

"If the Guardians tried to kill us once, they'll try again," he explains. This is as they stroll along one of the arid heights of the island; it's the only way they can get any real privacy, since otherwise hordes of children follow them around and try to imitate the strange sounds of Sanze-mat. There's plenty to do here—the children are in creche most of the evenings, after everyone's done fishing and crabbing and whatnot for the day—but it's clear that there's not a lot of entertainment.

"Without knowing what it is we've done to provoke the Guardians' ire," Alabaster continues, "it would be folly itself to go back to the Fulcrum. We might not even make it past the gates before somebody throws another disruption knife."

Which is obvious, now that Syenite thinks it through. Yet there's something else that's obvious, whenever she looks at the horizon and sees the smoking hump that is what's left of Allia. "They think we're dead." She tears her eyes away from that lump, trying not to imagine what must have become of the beautiful little seaside comm she remembers. All of Allia's alarms, all their preparations, were shaped around surviving tsunami, not the volcano that has obviously, impossibly occurred instead. Poor Heresmith. Not even Asael deserved the death she probably suffered.

She cannot think about this. Instead she focuses on Alabaster. "That's what you're saying, isn't it? Being dead in Allia allows us to be alive, and free, here."

"Exactly!" Now Alabaster's grinning, practically dancing in place. She's never seen him so excited before. It's like he's not even aware of the price that's been paid for their freedom... or maybe he just doesn't care. "There's hardly any contact with the continent, here, and when there is, it's not exactly friendly. Our assigned Guardians can sense us if they're near enough, but none of their kind ever come here. These islands aren't even on many maps!" Then he sobers. "But on the continent there'd be no question of us escaping the Fulcrum. Every Guardian east of Yumenes will be sniffing about the remains of Allia for hints as to whether we've survived. They're probably circulating posters bearing our likenesses to the Imperial Road Patrol and quartent militias in the region. I suppose I'll be made out as Misalem reborn, and you my willing accomplice. Or maybe you'll finally get some respect, and they'll decide *you're* the mastermind."

Yes, well.

He's right, though. With a comm destroyed in such a horrible way, the Fulcrum will need scapegoats to blame. Why not the two roggas on site, who should have been more than skilled enough to contain any seismic event between them? Allia's destruction represents a betrayal of everything the Fulcrum promises the Stillness: tame and obedient orogenes, safety from the worst shakes and blows. Freedom from fear, at least till the next Fifth Season comes. Of course the Fulcrum will vilify them in every way possible, because otherwise people will break down its obsidian walls and slaughter everyone inside down to the littlest grit.

It does not help that Syen can sess, now that her sessapinae are no longer numb, just how bad things are in Allia. It's at the edge of her awareness—which is itself a surprise; for some reason she can reach much farther now than she could before. Still, it's clear: In the flat plane of the Maximal plate's eastern edge, there is a shaft burned straight down and down and *down*, into the very mantle of the planet. Beyond that Syen cannot follow—and she does not need to, because she can tell what made this shaft. Its edges are hexagonal, and it has exactly the same circumference as the garnet obelisk.

And Alabster is *giddy*. She could hate him for that alone.

His smile fades as he sees her face. "Evil Earth, are you ever happy?"

"They'll find us. Our Guardians can track us. "

He shakes his head. "Mine can't." You remember the strange Guardian in Allia alluding to this. "As for yours, when your orogeny was negated, he lost you. It cuts off everything, you know, not just our abilities. He'll need to touch you for the connection to work again."

You had no idea. "He won't stop looking, though."

Alabaster pauses. "Did you like being in the Fulcrum so much?"

The question startles her, and angers her further. "I could at least be myself there. I didn't have to hide what I am."

He nods slowly, something in his expression telling her that he understands all too well what she's feeling. "And what are you, when you're there?"

"*Fuck. You.*" She's too angry, all of a sudden, to know why she's angry.

"I did." His smirk makes her burn hot as Allia must be. "Remember? We've fucked Earth knows how many times, even though we can't stand each other, on someone else's orders. Or have you made yourself believe you wanted it? Did you need a dick—any dick, even my mediocre, boring one—that bad?"

She doesn't reply in words. She's not thinking or talking anymore. She's in the earth and it's reverberating with her rage, amplifying it; the torus that materializes around her is high and fine and leaves an inch-wide ring of cold so fierce that the air hisses and sears white for an instant. She's going to ice him to the Arctics and back.

But Alabaster only sighs and flexes a little, and his torus blots out hers as easily as fingers snuffing a candle. It's gentle compared to what he could do, but the profundity of having her fury so swiftly and powerfully stilled makes her stagger. He steps forward as if to help her, and she jerks away from him with a half-voiced snarl. He backs off at once, holding up his hands as if asking for a truce.

"Sorry," he says. He genuinely sounds it, so she doesn't storm off right then. "I was just trying to make a point."

He's made it. Not that she hadn't known it before: that she is a slave, that all roggas are slaves, that the security and sense of self-worth the Fulcrum offers is wrapped in the chain of her right to live, and even the right to control her own body. It's one thing to know this, to admit it to herself, but it's the sort of truth that none of them use against each other—not even to make a point—because doing so is cruel and unnecessary. This is why she hates Alabaster: not because he is more powerful, not even because he is crazy, but because he refuses to allow her any of the polite fictions and unspoken truths that have kept her comfortable, and safe, for years.

They glare at each other for a moment longer, then Alabaster shakes his head and turns to leave. Syenite follows, because there's really nowhere else to go. They head back down to the cavern level. As they descend the stairs, Syenite has no choice but to face the third reason she feels so out of place in Meov.

Floating now in the comm's harbor is a huge, graceful sailing vessel—maybe a frigate, maybe a galleon, she doesn't know either of these words from *boat*—that dwarfs all the smaller vessels combined. Its hull is a wood so dark that it's almost black, patched with paler wood here and there. Its sails are tawny canvas, also much-mended and sun-faded and water-marked... and yet, somehow despite the stains and patches, the whole of the ship is oddly beautiful. It is called the *Clalsu,* or at least that's what the word sounds like to her ears, and it sailed in two days after Syenite and Alabaster arrived in Meov. Aboard it were a good number of the comm's able-bodied adults, and a lot of ill-gotten gain from several weeks' predation along the coastal shipping lanes.

The *Clalsu* has also brought to Meov its captain—the headman's second, actually, who is only second by virtue of the fact that he spends more time away from the island than on it. Otherwise, Syen would have known the instant this man bounded down the gangplank to greet the cheering crowd that he was Meov's true leader, because she can tell without understanding a word that everyone here loves him and looks up to him. Innon is his name: Innon Resistant Meov in the mainlander parlance. A big man, black-skinned like most of the Meovites, built more like a Strongback than a Resistant and with personality enough to outshine any Yumenescene Leader.

Except he's not really a Resistant, or a Strongback, or a Leader, not that any of those use names really mean much in this comm that rejects so much of Sanzed custom. He's an orogene. A feral, born free and raised openly by Harlas—who's a rogga, too. *All* their leaders are roggas, here. It's how the island has survived through more Seasons than they've bothered to count.

And beyond this fact... well. Syen's not quite sure how to deal with Innon.

As a case in point, she hears him the instant they come into the main entry cavern of the comm. Everyone can hear him, since he talks as loudly within the caverns as he apparently does when on the deck of his ship. He doesn't need to; the caverns echo even the slightest sound. He's just not the sort of man to limit himself, even when he should.

Like now.

"Syenite, Alabaster!" The comm has gathered around its communal cookfires to share the evening meal. Everyone's sitting on stone or wooden benches, relaxing and chatting, but there's a big knot of people seated around Innon where he's been regaling them with...something. He switches to Sanze-mat at once, however, since he's one of the few people in the comm who can speak it, albeit with a heavy accent. "I have been waiting for you both. We saved good stories for you. Here!" He actually rises and beckons to them as if yelling at the top of his lungs wasn't enough to get their attention, and as if a six-and-a-half-foot-tall man with a huge mane of braids and clothes from three different nations—all of it garish—would be hard to spot amid the crowd.

Yet Syenite finds herself smiling as she steps into the ring of benches where Innon has, apparently, kept one open just for them. Other members of the comm murmur greetings, which Syen is beginning to recognize; out of politeness, she attempts to stammer something similar back, and endures their chuckles when she gets it wrong. Innon grins at her and repeats the phrase, properly; she tries again and sees nods all around. "Excellent," Innon says, so emphatically that she cannot help but believe him.

Then he grins at Alabaster, beside her. "You're a good teacher, I think."

Alabaster ducks his head a little. "Not really. I can't seem to stop my pupils from hating me."

"Mmm." Innon's voice is low and deep and reverberates like the deepest of shakes. When he smiles, it's like the surface breach of a vesicle, something bright and hot and alarming, especially up close. "We must see if we can change that, hmm?" And he looks at Syen, unabashed in his interest, and plainly not caring when the other members of the comm chuckle.

That's the problem, see. This ridiculous, loud, vulgar man has made no secret of the fact that he *wants* Syenite. And unfortunately—because otherwise this would be easy—there's something about him that Syen actually finds herself attracted to. His ferality, perhaps. She's never met anyone like him.

Thing is, he seems to want Alabaster, *too*. And Alabaster doesn't seem disinterested, either.

It's a little confusing.

Once he has successfully flustered both of them, Innon turns his infinite charm on his people. "Well! Here we are, with food aplenty and fine new things that other people have made and paid for." He shifts into Eturpic then, repeating the words for everyone; they chuckle at the last part, largely because many of them *have been* wearing new clothes and jewelry and the like since the ship came in. Then Innon continues, and Syen doesn't really need Alabaster to explain that Innon is telling everyone a story—because Innon does this with his whole body. He leans forward and speaks more softly, and everyone is riveted to whatever tense moment he is describing. Then he pantomimes someone falling off something, and makes the sound of a splat by cupping his hands and squeezing air from between his palms. The small children who are listening practically fall over laughing, while the older kids snicker and the adults smile.

Alabaster translates a little of it for her. Apparently Innon is telling everyone about their most recent raid, on a small Coaster comm some ten days' sailing to the north. Syen's only half-listening to 'Baster's summation, mostly paying attention to the movements of Innon's body and imagining him performing entirely different movements, when suddenly Alabaster stops translating. When she finally notices this, surprised, he's looking at her intently.

"Do you want him?" he asks her.

Syen grimaces, mostly out of embarrassment. He's spoken softly, but they're right there next to Innon, and if he suddenly decides to pay attention... Well, what *if* he does? Maybe it would make things easier to get it all out into the open. She would really prefer to have a choice about that, though, and as usual Alabaster's not giving her one. "You don't have a subtle bone in your body, do you?"

"No, I don't. Tell me."

"What, then? Is this some kind of challenge?" Because she's seen the way Alabaster looks at Innon. It's almost cute, watching a forty-year-old man blush and stammer like a virgin. "Want me to back off?"

Alabaster flinches and looks almost hurt. Then he frowns as if confused by his own reaction—which makes two of them—and draws away a little. His mouth pulls to one side as he murmurs, "If I said yes, would you? Would you really?"

Syenite blinks. Well, she did suggest it. But would she? All of a sudden, she doesn't know.

When she fails to respond, though, Alabaster's expression twists in frustration. He mumbles something that might be "Never mind," then gets up and steps out of the story circle, taking care not to disturb anyone else as he goes. It means Syenite loses the ability to follow the tale, but that's all right. Innon is a joy to watch even without words, and since she doesn't have to pay attention to the story, she can consider Alabaster's question.

After a while the tale ends, and everyone claps; almost immediately there are calls for another story. In the general mill as people get up for second helpings from the massive pot of spiced shrimp, rice, and smoked sea-bubble that is tonight's meal, Syenite decides to go find Alabaster. She not sure what she's going to say, but . . . well. He deserves some kind of answer.

She finds him in their house, where he's curled up in a corner of the big empty room, a few feet from the bed of dried seagrass and cured animal furs they've been sleeping on. He hasn't bothered to light the lanterns; she makes him out as a darker blot against the shadows. "Go away," he snaps when she steps into the room.

"I live here, too," she snaps back. "Go somewhere else if you want to cry or whatever you're doing." Earth, she hopes he's not crying.

He sighs. It doesn't sound like he's crying, although he's got his legs drawn up and his elbows propped on his knees and his head's half buried in his hands. He could be. "Syen, you're such a steelheart."

"So are you, when you want to be."

"I *don't* want to be. Not always. Rust, Syen, don't you ever get *tired* of it all?" He stirs a little. Her eyes have adjusted, and she sees that he's looking at her. "Don't you ever just want to . . . to be human?"

She comes into the house and leans against the wall next to the door, crossing her arms and her ankles. "We aren't human."

"Yes. We. Are." His voice turns fierce. "I don't give a shit what the something-somethingth council of big important farts decreed, or how the geomests classify things, or any of that. That we're not human is just the lie they tell themselves so they don't have to feel bad about how they treat us—"

This, too, is something all roggas know. Only Alabaster is vulgar enough to say it aloud. Syenite sighs and leans her head back against the wall. "If you want him, you idiot, just tell him so. You can have him." And just like that, his question is answered.

Alabaster falls silent in mid-rant, staring at her. "You want him, too."

"Yeah." It costs her nothing to say this. "But I'm okay if . . ." She shrugs a little. "Yeah."

Alabaster takes a deep breath, then another. Then a third. She has no idea what any of those breaths means.

"I should make the same offer you just did," he says, at last. "Do the noble thing, or at least pretend to. But I . . ." In the shadows, he hunches more, tightening his arms around his knees. When he speaks again, his voice is barely audible. "It's just been so long, Syen."

Not since he's had a lover, of course. Just since he's had a lover he wanted.

There's laughter from the center of the gathering-cavern, and now people are moving along the corridors, chattering and breaking up for the night. They can both hear Innon's big voice rumbling not far off; even when he's just having a normal conversation, practically everyone can hear him. She hopes he's not a shouter, in bed.

Syen takes a deep breath. "Want me to go get him?" And just to be clear, she adds, "For you?"

Alabaster is silent for a long moment. She can feel him staring at her, and there's a kind of emotional pressure in the room that she can't quite interpret. Maybe he's insulted. Maybe he's touched. Rust if she'll ever be able to figure him out... and rust if she knows why she's doing this.

Then he nods, rubs a hand over his hair, and lowers his head. "Thank you." The words are almost cold, but she knows that tone, because she's used it herself. Any time she's needed to hold on to her dignity with fingernails and pent breath.

So she leaves and follows that rumble, eventually finding Innon near the communal cookfire in deep conversation with Harlas. Everyone else has dissippated by now, and the cavern echoes in a steady overlapping drone of fussy toddlers fighting sleep, laughter, talking, and the hollow creaking of the boats in the harbor outside as they rock in their moorings. And over all of it, the hiss-purr of the sea. Syenite settles herself against a wall nearby, listening to all these exotic sounds, and waiting. After perhaps ten minutes, Innon finishes his conversation and rises. Harlas heads away, chuckling over something Innon's said; ever the charmer. As Syen expected, Innon then comes over to lean against the wall beside her.

"My crew think I am a fool to pursue you," he says casually, gazing up at the vaulted ceiling as if there's something interesting up there. "They think you don't like me."

"Everyone thinks I don't like them," Syenite says. Most of the time, it's true. "I do like you."

He looks at her, thoughtful, which she likes. Flirting unnerves her. Much better to be straightforward like this. "I have met your kind before," he says. "The ones taken to the Fulcrum." His accent mangles this into *fool crumb,* which she finds especially fitting. "You are the happiest one I've seen."

Syenite snorts at the joke—and then, seeing the wry twist to his lips, the heavy compassion in his gaze, she realizes he's not joking at all. Oh. "Alabaster's pretty happy."

"No, he isn't."

No. He isn't. But this is why Syenite doesn't like jokes much, either. She sighs. "I'm . . . here for him, actually."

"Oh? So you have decided to share?"

"He's—" She blinks as the words register. "Uh?"

Innon shrugs, which is an impressive gesture given how big he is, and how it sets all his braids a-rustle. "You and he are already lovers. It was a thought."

What a thought. "Er . . . no. I don't—uh. No." There are things she's not ready to think about. "Maybe later." A lot later.

He laughs, though not at her. "Yes, yes. You have come, then, what? To ask me to see to your friend?"

"He's not—" But here she is procuring him a lover for the night. "*Rust.*"

Innon laughs—softly, for him—and shifts to lean sideways against the wall, perpendicular to Syenite so that she will not feel boxed in, even though he's close enough that she can feel his body heat. Something big men do, if they want to be considerate rather than intimidating. She appreciates his thoughtfulness. And she hates herself for deciding in Alabaster's favor, because, Earthfires, he even *smells* sexy as he says, "You are a very good friend, I think."

"Yes, I rusting am." She rubs her eyes.

"Now, now. Everyone sees that you are the stronger of the pair." Syenite blinks at this, but he's completely serious. He lifts a hand and draws a finger down the side of her face from temple to chin, a slow tease. "Many things have broken him. He holds himself together with spit and endless smiling, but all can see the cracks. You, though; you are dented, bruised, but intact. It is kind of you. Looking out for him like so."

"No one ever looks out for *me*." Then she shuts her mouth so hard that her teeth snap. She hadn't meant to say that.

Innon smiles, but it is a gentle, kindly thing. "I will," he says, and leans down to kiss her. It is a scratchy sort of kiss; his lips are dry, his chin beginning to hair over. Most Coaster men don't seem to grow beards, but Innon might have some Sanze in him, especially with all that hair. In any case, his kiss is so soft despite the scratchiness that it feels more like a thank-you than an attempt to seduce. Probably because that's what he intends. "Later, I promise I will."

Then he leaves, heading for the house she shares with Alabaster, and Syenite gazes after him and thinks belatedly, *Now where the rust am I supposed to sleep tonight?*

It turns out to be a moot question, because she's not sleepy. She goes to the ledge outside the cavern, where there are others lingering to take in the night air or talk where half the comm can't hear them, and she is not the only one standing wistfully at the railing, looking out over the water at night. The waves roll in steadily, making the smaller boats and the *Clalsu* rock and groan, and the starlight casts thin, diffuse reflections upon the waves that seem to stretch away into forever.

It's peaceful here, in Meov. It's nice to be who she is in a place that accepts her. Nicer still to know that she has nothing to fear for it. A woman Syen met in the baths—one of the *Clalsu* crew, most of whom speak at least a little Sanze-mat—explained it to her as they sat soaking in water warmed by rocks the children heat in the fire as part of their daily chores. It's simple, really. "With you, we live," she'd said to Syen, shrugging and letting her head fall back against the edge of the bath, and apparently not caring about the strangeness in her own words. On the mainland, everyone is convinced that with roggas nearby, they will all die.

And then the woman said something that truly unnerved Syen. "Harlas is old. Innon sees much danger, on raids. You and the laughing one"—that is the locals' term for Alabaster, since the ones who don't speak Sanze-mat have trouble pronouncing his name—"you have babies, give us one, yes? Or we have to go steal, from the mainland."

The very idea of these people, who stick out like stone eaters in a crowd, trying to infiltrate the Fulcrum to kidnap a grit, or grabbing some feral child just ahead of the Guardians, makes Syenite shiver. She's not sure she likes the idea of them greedily hoping she catches pregnant, either. But they're no different from the Fulcrum in that, are they? And here, any child that she and Alabaster have won't end up in a node station.

She lingers out on the ledge for a few hours, losing herself in the sound of the waves and gradually letting herself lapse into a kind of not-thinking fugue. Then she finally notices that her back is aching and her feet hurt, and the wind off the water is getting chilly; she can't just stand out here all night. So she heads back into the cavern, not really sure where she means to go, just letting her feet carry her where they will. Which is probably why she eventually ends up back outside "her" house, standing in front of the curtain that passes for privacy and listening to Alabaster weep through it.

It's definitely him. She knows that voice, even though it's choked now with sobs and half muffled. Barely audible, really, despite the lack of doors and windows... but she knows the why of that, doesn't she? Everyone who grows up in the Fulcrum learns to cry very, very quietly.

It is this thought, and the sense of camaraderie that follows it, that makes her reach up, slowly, and tug the curtain aside.

They're on the mattress, thankfully half covered in furs—not that it matters, since she can see clothing discarded about the room, and the air smells of sex, so it's obvious what they've been up to. Alabaster is curled up on his side, his back to her, bony shoulders shaking. Innon's sitting up on one elbow, stroking his hair. His eyes flick up when Syenite opens the curtain, but he doesn't seem upset, or surprised. In fact—and in light of their previous conversation she really shouldn't be surprised, but she *is*—he lifts a hand. Beckoning.

She's not sure why she obeys. And she's not sure why she

undresses as she walks across the room, or why she lifts up the furs behind Alabaster and slides into the redolent warmth with him. Or why, once she's done this, she curves herself against his back, and drapes an arm over his waist, and looks up to see Innon's sad smile of welcome. But she does.

Syen falls asleep like this. As far as she can tell, Alabaster cries for the rest of the night, and Innon stays up to comfort him the whole time. So when she wakes the next morning and claws her way out of bed and stumbles over to the chamber pot to throw up noisily into it, they both sleep through it. There is no one to comfort her as she sits there shaking in the aftermath. But that is nothing new.

Well. At least the people of Meov won't have to go steal a baby, now.

* * *

Put no price on flesh.

—*Tablet One, "On Survival," verse six*

INTERLUDE

There passes a time of happiness in your life, which I will not describe to you. It is unimportant. Perhaps you think it wrong that I dwell so much on the horrors, the pain, but pain is what shapes us, after all. We are creatures born of heat and pressure and grinding, ceaseless movement. To be still is to be . . . not alive.

But what is important is that you know it was not all terrible. There was peace in long stretches, between each crisis. A chance to cool and solidify before the grind resumed.

Here is what you need to understand. In any war, there are factions: those wanting peace, those wanting more war for a myriad of reasons, and those whose desires transcend either. And this is a war with many *sides, not just two. Did you think it was just the stills and the orogenes? No, no. Remember the stone eaters and the Guardians, too—oh, and the Seasons. Never forget Father Earth. He has not forgotten you.*

So while she—you—rested, those are the forces that gathered round. Eventually they began their advance.

20

Syenite, stretched and snapped back

It's not quite what Syenite had in mind for the rest of her life, sitting around being useless, so she goes to find Innon one day as the *Clalsu* crew is outfitting the ship for another raiding run.

"No," he says, staring at her like she's insane. "You are not *being a pirate* when you just had a baby."

"I had the baby two years ago." She can only change so many diapers, pester people for lessons in Eturpic so often, and help with the net-fishing so many times before she goes mad. She's done with nursing, which is the excuse Innon's used up to now to put her off—and which was pointless anyway, since in Meov that sort of thing is done communally, same as everything else. When she's not around, Alabaster just takes the baby to one of the other mothers in the comm, just as Syen fed their babies in turn if they happened to be hungry while she was nearby and full of milk. And since 'Baster does most of the diaper changes and sings little Corundum to sleep, and coos at him and plays with him and takes him for walks and so on, Syenite has to keep busy somehow.

"Syenite." He stops in the middle of the loading ramp that leads into the ship's hold. They're putting storage barrels of water and food aboard, along with baskets of more esoteric things—buckets of chain for the catapult, bladders of pitch and fish oil, a length of heavy cloth meant to serve as a replacement sail should they require it. When Innon stops with Syenite standing down-ramp from him, everything else stops, and when there are loud complaints from the dock, he lifts his head and glowers until everyone shuts up. Everyone, of course, except Syenite.

"I'm *bored*," she says in frustration. "There's nothing to do here except fish and wait for you and the others to come back from a raid, and gossip about people I don't know, and tell stories about things I don't care about! I've spent my whole life either training or working, for Earth's sake; you can't expect me to just sit around and look at water all day."

"Alabaster does."

Syenite rolls her eyes, although this is true. When Alabaster isn't with the baby, he spends most of his days up on the heights above the colony, gazing out at the world and thinking unfathomable thoughts for hours on end. She knows; she's watched him do it. "I'm not him! Innon, you can use me."

And Innon's expression twists, because—ah, yes. *That* one hits home for him.

It's an unspoken thing between them, but Syenite's not stupid. There are a lot of things a skilled rogga can do to help on the kinds of sorties Innon's crew makes. Not starting shakes or blows, she won't and he'd never ask it—but it is a simple thing to draw enough strength from the ambient to lower the temperature at the water's surface, and thus cloak the ship in fog to hide its approach or retreat. It is equally easy to disturb forests along the shoreline with the most delicate of underground vibrations, causing flocks of birds or hordes of mice to flood out of the trees and into nearby settlements as a distraction. And more. Orogeny is damned useful, Syenite is beginning to understand, for far, far more than just quelling shakes.

Or rather, it *could* be useful, if Innon could use his orogeny that way. Yet for all his awesome charisma and physical prowess, Innon is still a feral, with nothing more than what little training Harlas—himself a feral and poorly trained—could give him. She's felt Innon's orogeny when he quells local minor shakes, and the crude inefficiency of his power shocks her sometimes. She's tried to teach him better control, and he listens, and he *tries*, but he doesn't improve. She doesn't understand why. Without that level of skill, the *Clalsu* crew earns its spoils the old-fashioned way: They fight, and die, for every scrap.

"Alabaster can do these things for us," Innon says, looking uneasy.

"Alabaster," Syen says, trying for patience, "gets sick just looking at this thing." She gestures at *Clalsu*'s curving bulk. The joke all over the comm is that 'Baster somehow manages to look green despite his blackness whenever he is forced aboard a ship. Syen threw up less when she had morning sickness. "What if I don't do anything *but* cloak the ship? Or whatever you order me to do."

Innon puts his hands on his hips, his expression derisive. "You pretend that you will follow my orders? You don't even do that in bed."

"Oh, you *bastard*." Now he's just being an ass, because he

doesn't actually try to give her orders in bed. It's just a weird Meovite thing to tease about sex. Now that Syen can understand what everyone's saying, every other statement seems to be about her sharing her bedtime with two of the best-looking men in the comm. Innon says they only do this to her because she turns such interesting colors when little old ladies make vulgar jokes about positions and rope knots. She's trying to get used to it. "That's completely irrelevant!"

"Is it?" He pokes her in the chest with a big finger. "No lovers on ship; that is the rule I have always followed. We cannot even be friends once we set sail. What I say goes; anything else and we die. You question *everything*, Syenite, and there is no time for questioning, on the sea."

That's...not an unfair point. Syen shifts uneasily. "I can follow orders without question. Earth knows I've done enough of that. Innon—" She takes a deep breath. "Earth's sake, Innon, I'll do anything to get off this island for a while."

"And that is another problem." He steps closer and lowers his voice. "Corundum is *your son*, Syenite. Do you feel nothing for him, that you constantly chafe to be away?"

"I make sure he's taken care of." And she does. Corundum is always clean and well fed. She never wanted a child, but now that she's had it—him—and held him, and nursed him, and all that...she does feel a sense of accomplishment, maybe, and rueful acknowledgment, because she and Alabaster have managed to make one beautiful child between them. She looks into her son's face sometimes and marvels that he exists, that he seems so whole and right, when both his parents have nothing but bitter brokenness between them. Who's she kidding? It's love.

She loves her son. But that doesn't mean she wants to spend every hour of every rusting day in his presence.

Innon shakes his head and turns away, throwing up his hands. "Fine! Fine, fine, ridiculous woman. Then *you* go and tell Alabaster we will both be away."

"All ri—" But he's gone, up the ramp and into the hold, where she hears him yelling at someone else about something that she can't quite catch because her ears can't parse Eturpic when it echoes at that volume.

Regardless, she bounces a little as she heads down the ramp, waving in vague apology to the other crew members who are standing around looking mildly annoyed. Then she heads into the comm.

Alabaster's not in the house, and Corundum's not with Selsi, the woman who most often keeps the smaller children of the colony when their parents are busy. Selsi raises her eyebrows at Syen when she pokes her head in. "He said yes?"

"He said yes." Syenite can't help grinning, and Selsi laughs.

"Then we will never see you again, I wager. Waves wait only for the nets." Which Syenite guesses is some sort of Meov proverb, whatever it means. "Alabaster is on the heights with Coru, again."

Again. "Thanks," she says, and shakes her head. It's a wonder their child doesn't sprout wings.

She heads up the steps to the topmost level of the island and over the first rise of rock, and there they are, sitting on a blanket near the cliff. Coru looks up as she approaches, beaming and pointing at her; Alabaster, who probably felt her footsteps on the stairs, doesn't bother turning.

"Innon's finally taking you with them?" he asks when Syen gets close enough to hear his soft voice.

"Huh." Syenite settles on the blanket beside him, and opens her arms for Coru, who clambers out of Alabaster's lap, where he's been sitting, and into Syenite's. "If I'd known you already knew, I wouldn't have bothered walking up all those steps."

"It was a guess. You don't usually come up here with a smile on your face. I knew it had to be something." Alabaster turns at last, watching Coru as he stands in her lap and pushes at her breasts. Syenite holds him reflexively, but he's actually doing a good job of keeping his balance, despite the unevenness of her lap. Then Syen notices that it's not just Corundum that Alabaster's watching.

"What?" she asks, frowning.

"Will you come back?"

And that, completely out of the blue as it is, makes Syenite drop her hands. Fortunately, Coru's got the trick of standing on her legs, which he does, giggling, while she stares at Alabaster. "Why are you even—*What?*"

Alabaster shrugs, and it's only then that Syenite notices the furrow between his brows, and the haunted look in his eyes, and it's only then that she understands what Innon was trying to say to her. As if to reinforce this, Alabaster says, bitterly, "You don't have to be with me anymore. You have your freedom, like you wanted. And Innon's got what *he* wanted—a rogga child to take care of the comm if something happens to him. He's even got me to train the child better than Harlas ever could, because he knows I won't leave."

Fire-under-Earth. Syenite sighs and pushes away Coru's hands, which hurt. "No, little greedy child, I don't have milk anymore. Settle down." And because this immediately makes Coru's face screw up with thwarted sorrow, she pulls him close and wraps her arms around him and starts playing with his feet, which is usually a good way to distract him before he gets going. It works. Apparently small children are inordinately fascinated by their own toes; who knew? And with that child taken care of, she can focus on Alabaster, who's now looking out to sea again, but who's probably just as close to a meltdown.

"*You* could leave," she says, pointing out the obvious because that's what she always has to do with him. "Innon's offered before to take us back to the mainland, if we want to go. If we don't do anything stupid like still a shake in front of a crowd of people, either of us could probably make a decent life somewhere."

"We have a decent life here." It's hard to hear him over the wind, and yet she can actually feel what he's not saying. *Don't leave me.*

"Crusty *rust*, 'Baster, what is wrong with you? I'm not planning to leave." Not now, anyway. But it's bad enough that they're having this conversation at all; she doesn't need to make it worse. "I'm just going somewhere I can be useful—"

"You're useful *here.*" And now he turns to glare at her full-on, and it actually bothers her, the hurt and loneliness that lurk beneath the veneer of anger on his face. It bothers her more that this bothers her.

"No. I'm not." And when he opens his mouth to protest, she runs over him. "I'm *not.* You said it yourself; Meov has a ten-ringer now to protect it. Don't think I haven't noticed how we haven't had so much as a subsurface twitch in my range, not in all the time we've been here. You've been quelling any possible threat long before Innon or I can feel it—" But then she trails off, frowning, because Alabaster is shaking his head, and there's a smile on his lips that makes her abruptly uneasy.

"Not me," he says.

"What?"

"*I* haven't quelled anything for about a year now." And then he nods toward the child, who is now examining Syenite's fingers with intent concentration. She stares down at Coru, and Coru looks up at her and grins.

Corundum is exactly what the Fulcrum hoped for when they paired her with Alabaster. He hasn't inherited much of Alabaster's looks, being only a shade browner than Syen and with hair that's already growing from fuzz into the beginnings of a proper ashblow bottlebrush; she's the one with Sanzed ancestors, so that didn't come from 'Baster, either. But what Coru does have from his father is an almighty powerful awareness of the earth. It has never occurred to Syenite before now that her baby might be aware enough to sess, and *still*, microshakes. That's not instinct, that's skill.

"Evil Earth," she murmurs. Coru giggles. Then Alabaster abruptly reaches over and plucks him out of her arms, getting to his feet. "Wait, this—"

"Go," he snaps, grabbing the basket he's brought up with them and crouching to dump baby toys and a folded diaper back into it. "Go, ride your rusting boat, get yourself killed along with Innon, what do I care. *I* will be here for Coru, no matter what *you* do."

And then he's gone, his shoulders tight and his walk brisk,

ignoring Coru's shrill protest and not even bothering to take the blanket that Syen's still sitting on.

Earthfires.

Syenite stays topside awhile, trying to figure out how she ended up becoming the emotional caretaker for a crazy tenringer while stuck out in the middle of rusting nowhere with his inhumanly powerful baby. Then the sun sets and she gets tired of thinking about it, so she gets up and grabs the blanket and heads back down to the comm.

Everyone's gathering for the evening meal, but Syenite begs off being social this time, just grabbing a plate of roasted tulifish and braised threeleaf with sweetened barley that must have been stolen from some mainland comm. She carries this back to the house, and is unsurprised to find Alabaster there already, curled up in the bed with a sleeping Coru. They've upgraded to a bigger bed for Innon's sake, this mattress suspended from four sturdy posts by a kind of hammock-like net that is surprisingly comfortable, and durable despite the weight and activity they put on it. Alabaster's quiet but awake when Syen comes in, so she sighs and scoops up Coru and puts him to bed in the nearby smaller suspended bed, which is lower to the ground in case he rolls or climbs out in the night. Then she climbs into bed with Alabaster, just looking at him, and after a while he gives up the distant treatment and edges a little closer. He doesn't meet her eyes as he does this. But Syenite knows what he needs, so she sighs and rolls onto her back, and he edges closer still, finally resting his head on her shoulder, where he's probably wanted to be all along.

"Sorry," he says.

Syenite shrugs. "Don't worry about it." And then, because Innon's right and this is partly her fault, she sighs and adds, "I'm coming back. I *do* like it here, you know. I just get…restless."

"You're always restless. What are you looking for?"

She shakes her head. "I don't know."

But she thinks, almost but not quite subconsciously: *A way to change things. Because this is not right.*

He's always good at guessing her thoughts. "You can't make anything better," he says, heavily. "The world is what it is. Unless you destroy it and start all over again, there's no changing it." He sighs, rubs his face against her breast. "Take what you can get out of it, Syen. Love your son. Even live the pirate life if that makes you happy. But stop looking for anything better than this."

She licks her lips. "Corundum should have better."

Alabaster sighs. "Yes. He should." He says nothing more, but the unspoken is palpable: *He won't, though.*

It isn't right.

She drifts off to sleep. And a few hours later she wakes up because Alabaster is blurting, "Oh *fuck*, oh please, oh Earth, I can't, *Innon*," against Innon's shoulder, and jerking in a way that disturbs the bed's gentle sway while Innon pants and ruts against him, cock on oily cock. And then because Alabaster is spent but Innon isn't, and Innon notices her watching, he grins at her and kisses Alabaster and then slides a hand between Syen's legs. Of course she's wet. He and Alabaster are always beautiful together.

Innon is a considerate lover, so he leans over and nuzzles her breasts and does marvelous things with his fingers, and does not stop thrusting against Alabaster until she curses and demands *all* of his attention for a while, which makes him laugh and shift over.

Alabaster watches while Innon obliges her, and his gaze grows hot with it, which Syenite still doesn't understand even after being with them for almost two years. 'Baster doesn't want her, not that way, nor she him. And yet it's unbelievably arousing for her to watch Innon drive him to moaning and begging, and Alabaster also clearly gets off on her going to pieces with someone else. She likes it *more* when 'Baster's watching, in fact. They can't stand sex with each other directly, but vicariously it's amazing. And what do they even call this? It's not a threesome, or a love triangle. It's a two-and-a-half-some, an affection dihedron. (And, well, maybe it's love.) She should worry about another pregnancy, maybe from Alabaster again given how messy things get between the three of them, but she can't bring herself to worry because it doesn't matter. Someone will love her children no matter what. Just as she doesn't think overmuch about what she does with her bed time or how this thing between them works; no one in Meov will care, no matter what. That's another turn-on, probably: the utter lack of fear. Imagine that.

So they fall asleep, Innon snoring on his belly between them and 'Baster and Syen with their heads pillowed on his big shoulders, and not for the first time does Syenite think, *If only this could last.*

She knows better than to wish for something so impossible.

* * *

The *Clalsu* sets sail the next day. Alabaster stands out on the pier with half the rest of the comm that is waving and well-wishing. He doesn't wave, but he does point to them as the ship pulls away, encouraging Coru to wave when Syenite and Innon do. Coru does it, and for a moment Syenite feels something like regret. It passes quickly.

Then there is only the open sea, and work to be done: casting lines for fish and climbing high up into the masts to do things to the sails when Innon tells them to, and at one point securing several barrels that have come loose down in the hold. It's hard work, and Syenite falls asleep in her little bunk under one of the bulkheads not long after sunset, because Innon won't let her sleep with him and anyway, she doesn't have the energy to make it up to his cabin.

But it gets better, and she gets stronger as the days pass, beginning to see why the *Clalsu* crew have always seemed a little more vibrant, a little more interesting, than everyone else in Meov. On the fourth day out there's a call from the left—rust, from the *port* side of the ship, and she and the others come to the railing to see something amazing: the curling plumes of ocean spray where great monsters of the deep have risen to swim alongside them. One of them breaches the surface to look at them and it's ridiculously huge; its eye is bigger than Syen's head. One slap of its fins could capsize the ship. But it doesn't hurt them, and one of the crew members tells her that it's just curious. She seems amused by Syenite's awe.

At night, they look at the stars. Syen has never paid much attention to the sky; the ground beneath her feet was always more important. But Innon points out patterns in the ways that the stars move, and explains that the "stars" she sees are actually other suns, with other worlds of their own and perhaps other people living other lives and facing other struggles. She has heard of pseudosciences like astronomestry, knows that its adherents make unprovable claims like this, but now, looking at the constantly moving sky, she understands why they believe it. She understands why they *care*, when the sky is so immutable and irrelevant to most of daily life. On nights like these, for a little while, she cares, too.

Also at night, the crew drinks and sings songs. Syenite mispronounces vulgar words, inadvertently making them more vulgar, and makes instant friends of half the crew by doing so.

The other half of the crew reserves judgment, until they spy a likely target on the seventh day. They've been lurking near the shipping lanes between two heavily populated peninsulas, and people up in the mast-nest have been watching with spyglasses for ships worth the effort of robbing. Innon doesn't give the order until the lookout tells them he's spotted an especially large vessel of the sort often used to ferry trade goods too heavy or dangerous for easy overland carting: oils and quarried stone and volatile chemicals and timber. The very sorts of things that a comm stuck on a barren island in the middle of nowhere might need most. This one's accompanied by another vessel, which is smaller and which, according to those who see it through the spyglass and can tell such things by sight, is probably bristling with militia soldiers, battering rams, and armaments of its own. (Maybe one's a carrack and the other's a caravel, those are the words the sailors use, but she can't remember which one's which and it's a pain in the ass to try so she's going to stick with "the big boat" and "the small boat.") Their readiness to fight off pirates confirms that the freighter carries something worth pirating.

Innon looks at Syenite, and she grins fiercely.

She raises two fogs. The first requires her to pull ambient energy at the farthest edge of her range—but she does it, because that's where the smaller ship is. The second fog she raises in a corridor between *Clalsu* and the cargo vessel, so that they will be on their target almost before it sees them coming.

It goes like clockwork. Innon's crew are mostly experienced and highly skilled; the ones like Syenite, who don't know what they're doing yet, are pushed to the periphery while the others set to. The *Clalsu* comes out of the fog and the other vessel starts ringing bells to sound the alarm, but it's too late. Innon's people fire the catapults and shred their sails with baskets of chain. Then the *Clalsu* sidles up close—Syen thinks they're going to hit, but Innon knows what he's doing—and others in the crew throw hooks across the gap between them, hitching the ships together and then winching them closer with the big crankworks that occupy much of the deck.

It's dangerous at this point, and one of the older members of the crew shoos Syen belowdecks when people on the cargo ship start firing arrows and slingstones and throwing-knives at them. She sits in the shadow of the steps while the other crew members run up and down them, and her heart is pounding; her palms are damp. Something heavy thuds into the hull not five feet from her head, and she flinches.

But Evil Earth, this is *so* much better than sitting around on the island, fishing and singing lullabies.

It's over in minutes. When the commotion dies down and Syenite dares to venture up top again, she sees that planks have been run between the two vessels and Innon's people are running back and forth along them. Some of them have captured members of the cargo vessel's crew and corralled them on deck, holding them at glassknife-point; the rest of the crew is surrendering, giving up weapons and valuables, for fear the hostages will be hurt. Already some of Innon's sailors are going into the holds, bringing up barrels and crates and carting them across to the *Clalsu*'s deck. They'll sort out the booty later. Speed is of the essence now.

But all at once there are shouts and someone in the rigging hits a bell frantically—and out of the roiling fog looms the attack ship that accompanied the cargo vessel. It's on them, and belatedly Syenite realizes her error: she had assumed that the attack ship would *stop* given that it couldn't see, knowing itself in proximity to other vessels. People are not that logical. Now the attack ship is coming at full speed, and even though she can hear cries of alarm from its decks as they also realize the danger, there's no way it will be able to stop before it rams into *Clalsu* and the cargo ship . . . and probably sinks all three.

Syenite is brimming with power drawn from the warmth and boundless waves of the sea. She reacts, as she has been taught in a hundred Fulcrum drills, without thinking. Down, through the strange slipperiness of seawater minerals, through the soggy uselessness of the ocean sediment, down. There is stone beneath the ocean, and it is old and raw and hers to command.

In another place she claws up with her hands and shouts and thinks *Up*, and suddenly the attack ship cracks loudly and jerks to a halt. People stop screaming, shocked into silence, on all three vessels. This is because suddenly there is a massive, jagged knife of bedrock jutting several feet above the attack ship's deck, skewering the vessel from the keel up.

Shaking, Syenite lowers her hands slowly.

The cries aboard the *Clalsu* turn from alarm into ragged cheers. Even a few of the cargo vessel's people look relieved; one ship damaged is better than three ships sunk.

Things go quickly after that, with the attack ship helpless and skewered as it is. Innon comes to find her just as the crew reports that the cargo ship's hold is empty. Syen has moved to the bow, where she can see people on the attack ship's deck trying to chisel at the pillar.

Innon stops beside her, and she looks up, braced for his anger. But he is far from angry.

"I did not know one could do such things," he says wonderingly. "I thought you and Alabaster were only boasting."

It is the first time Syenite has been praised for her orogeny by someone not of the Fulcrum, and if she had not already begun to love Innon, she would now. "I shouldn't have brought it up so high," she says, sheepishly. "If I'd thought first, I would've raised the column only enough to breach the hull so they'd think they ran over an obstacle."

Innon sobers as he understands. "Ah. And now they know we have an orogene of some skill aboard." His expression hardens in a way that Syenite does not understand, but she decides not to question it. It feels so good to stand here, with him, basking in the glow of success. For a while they just watch the cargo vessel's unloading together.

Then one of Innon's crewmen runs up to say they're done, the planks have been withdrawn, the ropes and hooks rolled back onto their crankwheels. They're ready to go. Innon says in a heavy voice, "Hold."

She almost knows what is coming then. But it still makes her feel ill when he looks at Syenite, his expression ice. "Sink them both."

She has promised never to question Innon's orders. Even so, she hesitates. She has never killed anyone before, not deliberately. It was just a mistake that she brought the stone projection up so high. Is it really necessary that people die for her folly? He steps close, and she flinches preemptively, even though he has never harmed her. Her hand bones twinge regardless.

But Innon only says into her ear, "For 'Baster and Coru."

That makes no sense. 'Baster and Coru are not here. But then the full implication of his words—that the safety of everyone in Meov depends on the mainlanders seeing them as a nuisance rather than a serious threat—sinks in, and makes her cold, too. Colder.

So she says, "You should move us away."

Innon turns at once and gives the order for the *Clalsu* to set sail. Once they have drifted to a safe distance, Syenite takes a deep breath.

For her family. It is strange, thinking of them as such, though that is what they are. Stranger still to do something like this for a real reason, and not simply because she has been commanded to. Does that mean she is no longer a weapon? What does that make her, then, if not?

Doesn't matter.

At a flick of her will, the bedrock column extracts itself from the attack ship's hull—leaving a ten-foot hole near the stern. It begins sinking immediately, tipping upward as it takes on water. Then, dragging more strength from the ocean surface and raising fog enough to obscure sight for miles, Syenite shifts the column to aim at the cargo vessel's keel. A quick thrust up, a quicker withdrawal. Like stabbing someone to death with a poniard. The ship's hull cracks like an egg, and after a moment splits into two halves. It's done.

The fog completely obscures both sinking ships as the *Clalsu* sails away. The two crews' screams follow Syenite long after, into the drifting whiteness.

* * *

Innon makes an exception for her, that night. Later, sitting up in his captain's bed, Syen says, "I want to see Allia."

Innon sighs. "No. You don't."

But he gives the order anyway, because he loves her. The ship charts a new course.

* * *

According to legend, Father Earth did not originally hate life.

In fact, as the lorists tell it, once upon a time Earth did everything he could to facilitate the strange emergence of life on his surface. He crafted even, predictable seasons; kept changes of wind and wave and temperature slow enough that every living being could adapt, evolve; summoned waters that purified themselves, skies that always cleared after a storm. He did not create life—that was happenstance—but he was pleased and fascinated by it, and proud to nurture such strange wild beauty upon his surface.

Then people began to do horrible things to Father Earth. They poisoned waters beyond even his ability to cleanse, and killed much of the other life that lived on his surface. They drilled through the crust of his skin, past the blood of his mantle, to get at the sweet marrow of his bones. And at the height of human hubris and might, it was the orogenes who did something that even Earth could not forgive: They destroyed his only child.

No lorist that Syenite has ever talked to knows what this cryptic phrase means. It isn't stonelore, just oral tradition occasionally recorded on ephemerals like paper and hide, and too many Seasons have changed it. Sometimes it's the Earth's favorite glassknife that the orogenes destroyed; sometimes it's his shadow; sometimes it's his most valued Breeder. Whatever the words mean, the lorists and 'mests agree on what happened after the orogenes committed their great sin: Father Earth's surface cracked like an eggshell. Nearly every living thing died as his fury became manifest in the first and most terrible of the Fifth Seasons: the Shattering Season. Powerful as they were, those ancient people had no warning, no time to build storecaches, and no stonelore to guide them. It is only through sheer luck that enough of humankind survived to replenish itself afterward—and never again has life attained the heights of power that it once held. Earth's recurrent fury will never allow that.

Syenite has always wondered about these tales. There's a degree of poetic license in them, of course, primitive people trying to explain what they didn't understand... but all legends contain a kernel of truth. Maybe the ancient orogenes did shatter the planet's crust, somehow. How, though? It's clear now that there's more to orogeny than what the Fulcrum teaches—and maybe there's a reason the Fulcrum doesn't teach it, if the legend is true. But facts are facts: Even if somehow every orogene in existence down to the infants could be yoked together, they could not destroy the world's surface. It would ice everything; there's not enough warmth or movement *anywhere* to do that much damage. They'd all burn themselves out trying, and die.

Which means that part of the tale can't be true; orogeny cannot be to blame for the Earth's rage. Not that anyone but another rogga would accept this conclusion.

It is truly amazing, though, that humanity managed to survive the fires of that first Season. Because if the whole world was then as Allia is now... Syenite has a fresh understanding of just how much Father Earth hates them all.

Allia is a nightscape of red, blistering death. There is nothing left of the comm except the caldera ring that once cradled it, and even that is hard to see. Squinting through the red wavering haze, Syen thinks she can glimpse a few leftover buildings and streets on the caldera's slopes, but that might just be wishful thinking.

The night sky is thick with ash clouds, underlit by the glow of fire. Where the harbor was, there is now a growing volcano cone, gushing deadly clouds and hot red birth-blood on its climb out of the sea. It's already huge, occupying nearly the entire caldera bowl, and it has already borne offspring. Two additional vents crouch against its flank, belching gas and lava like their parent. Likely all three will eventually grow together to become a single monster, engulfing the surrounding mountains and threatening every comm in range of its gas clouds or subsequent blows.

Everyone Syenite met in Allia is dead now. The *Clalsu* can't go within five miles of the shore; any closer and they risk death, whether by warping the ship's hull in the heated waters, or by suffocating in the hot clouds that periodically gout forth from the mountain. Or by cooking themselves over one of the subsidiary vents that are still developing around the area, spreading out from what was once Allia's harbor like the spokes of a wheel and lurking like deadly mines beneath the waters offshore. Syen can sess every one of these hot spots, bright churning ragestorms just beneath the Earth's skin. Even Innon can sess them, and he's steered the ship away from those that are most likely to burst through anytime soon. But as fragile as the strata are right now, a new vent could open right under them before Syen has a chance to detect or stop it. Innon's risking a lot to indulge her.

"Many in the outlying parts of the comm managed to escape," Innon says softly, beside her. The *Clalsu*'s whole crew has come up on deck, staring at Allia in silence. "They say there was a flash of red light from the harbor, then a series of flashes, in a rhythm. Like something... pulsing. But the initial concussion, when the whole damned harbor boiled away at once, flattened most of the smaller houses in the comm. That's what killed most people. There was no warning." Syenite twitches.

No warning. There were almost a hundred thousand people in Allia—small by the standards of the Equatorials, but big for a Coaster comm. Proud, justifiably so. They'd had such hopes.

Rust this. Rust it and burn it in the foul, hateful guts of Father Earth.

"Syenite?" Innon is staring at her. This is because Syen has raised her fists before her, as if she is grasping the reins of a straining, eager horse. And because a narrow, high, tight torus has suddenly manifested around her. It isn't cold; there's plenty of earth-power for her to tap nearby. But it is powerful, and even an untrained rogga can sess the gathering flex of her will. Innon inhales and takes a step back. "Syen, what are you—"

"I can't leave it like this," she murmurs, almost to herself. The whole area is a swelling, deadly boil ready to burst. The volcano is only the first warning. Most vents in the earth are tiny, convoluted things, struggling to escape through varying layers of rock and metal and their own inertia. They seep and cool and plug themselves and then seep upward again, twisting and winding every which way in the process. *This*, though, is a gigantic lava tube channeled straight up from wherever the garnet obelisk has gone, funneling pure Earth-hate toward the surface. If nothing is done, the whole region will soon blow sky-high, in a massive explosion that will almost surely touch off a Season. She cannot believe the Fulcrum has left things like this.

So Syenite stabs herself into that churning, building heat, and tears at it with all the fury she feels at seeing *Allia, this was Allia, this was a human place, there were* people *here*. People who didn't deserve to die because

of me

because they were too stupid to let sleeping obelisks lie, or because they dared to dream of a future. No one deserves to die for that.

It's almost easy. This is what orogenes do, after all, and the hot spot is ripe for her use. The danger lies in not using it, really. If she takes in all that heat and force without channeling it elsewhere, it will destroy her. But fortunately—she laughs to herself, and her whole body shakes with it—she's got a volcano to choke off.

So she curls the fingers of one hand into a fist, and sears down its throat with her awareness, not burning but cooling, turning its own fury back on it to seal every breach. She forces the growing magma chamber back, back, down, down—and as she does so, she deliberately drags together the strata in overlapping patterns so that each will press down on the one below it and *keep* the magma down, at least until it finds another, slower way to wend its way to the surface. It's a delicate sort of operation, for all that it involves millions of tons of rock and the sorts of pressures that force diamonds into existence. But Syenite is a child of the Fulcrum, and the Fulcrum has trained her well.

She opens her eyes to find herself in Innon's arms, with the ship heaving beneath her feet. Blinking in surprise, she looks up at Innon, whose eyes are wide and wild. He notices that she's back, and the expressions of relief and fear on his face are both heartening and sobering.

"I told everyone you would not kill us," he says, over the churning of the sea spray and the shouts of his crew. She looks around and sees them frantically trying to lower the sails, so that they can have more control amid a sea that is suddenly anything but placid. "Please try not to make me a liar, would you?"

Shit. She's used to working orogeny on land, and forgot to account for the effects of her fault-sealing on water. They were shakes for a good purpose, but shakes nevertheless, and—oh Earth, she can feel it. She's touched off a tsunami. And—she winces and groans as her sessapinae set up a ringing protest at the back of her head. She's overdone it.

"Innon." Her head is ringing agony. "You need—nnh. Push waves of matching amplitude, subsurface..."

"What?" He looks away from her to shout something to one of the crewwomen in his tongue, and she curses inwardly. Of course he has no idea what she's talking about. He does not speak Fulcrum.

But then, all at once, there is a chill in the air all around them. The wood of the ship groans with the temperature change. Syen gasps in alarm, but it's not much of a change, really. Just the difference between a summer night and an autumn one, albeit over the span of minutes—and there is a presence to this change that is familiar as warm hands in the night. Innon abruptly inhales as he recognizes it, too: Alabaster. Of course his range stretches this far. He quells the gathering waves in moments.

When he's done, the ship sits on placid waters once more, facing the volcano of Allia . . . which has now gone quiet and dark. It's still smoking and will be hot for decades, but it no longer vents fresh magma or gas. The skies above are already clearing.

Leshiye, Innon's first mate, comes over, throwing an uneasy look at Syenite. He says something too fast for Syenite to translate fully, but she gets the gist of it: *Tell her next time she decides to stop a volcano, get off the ship first.*

Leshiye's right. "Sorry," Syen mutters in Eturpic, and the man grumbles and stomps off.

Innon shakes his head and lets her go, calling for the sails to be unfurled once again. He glances down at her. "You all right?"

"Fine." She rubs at her head. "Just never worked anything that big before."

"I did not think you could. I thought only ones like Alabaster—with many rings, more than yours—could do so. But you are as powerful as he."

"No." Syenite laughs a little, gripping the railing and clinging to it so she won't need to lean on him for support anymore. "I just do what's possible. *He* rewrites the rusting laws of nature."

"Heh." Innon sounds odd, and Syenite glances at him in surprise to see an almost regretful look on his face. "Sometimes, when I see what you and he can do, I wish I had gone to this Fulcrum of yours."

"No, you don't." She doesn't even want to think about what he would be like if he had grown up in captivity with the rest of them. Innon, but without his booming laugh or vivacious hedonism or cheerful confidence. Innon, with his graceful strong hands weaker and clumsier for having been broken. *Not* Innon.

He smiles ruefully at her now, as if he has guessed her thoughts. "Someday, you must tell me what it's like there. Why all who come out of that place seem so very competent... and so very afraid."

With that, he pats her back and heads off to oversee the course change.

But Syenite stays where she is at the railing, suddenly chilled to the bone in a way that has nothing to do with the passing flex of Alabaster's power.

That is because, as the ship tilts to one side in its turnabout, and she takes one last look back at the place that was Allia before her folly destroyed it—

—she sees someone.

Or she thinks she does. She's not sure at first. She squints and can just make out one of the paler strips that wend down into the Allia bowl on its southern curve, which is more readily visible now that the ruddy light around the volcano has faded. It's obviously not the Imperial Road that she and 'Baster traveled to get to Allia, once upon a time and one colossal mistake ago. Most likely what she's looking at is just a dirt road used by the locals, carved out of the surrounding forest a tree at a time and kept clear by decades of foot traffic.

There is a tiny mote moving along that road that looks, from this distance, like a person walking downhill. But it can't be. No sane person would stay so close to an active, deadly blow that had already killed thousands.

She squints more, moving to the ship's stern so that she can continue to peer that way as the *Clalsu* peels away from the coast. If only she had one of Innon's spyglasses. If only she could be sure.

Because for a moment she thinks, for a moment she *sees*, or hallucinates in her weariness, or imagines in her anxiety—

The Fulcrum seniors would not leave such a brewing disaster unmitigated. Unless they thought there was a very good reason to do so. Unless they had been ordered *to do so.*

—that the walking figure is wearing a burgundy uniform.

* * *

Some say the Earth is angry
Because he wants no company;
I say the Earth is angry
Because he lives alone.

—*Ancient (pre-Imperial) folk song*

21

you're getting the band back together

"You," you say suddenly to Tonkee. Who is not Tonkee.

Tonkee, who is approaching one of the crystal walls with a gleaming eye and a tiny chisel she's produced from somewhere, stops and looks at you in confusion. "What?"

It's the end of the day, and you're tired. Discovering impossible comms hidden in giant underground geodes takes a lot out of you. Ykka's people have put you and the others up in an apartment that's situated along the midpoint of one of the longer crystalline shafts. You had to walk across a rope bridge and around an encircling wooden platform to reach it. The apartment is level, even though the crystal itself isn't; the people who hollowed this place out seem not to have understood that no one *forgets* they're living in something that leans at a forty-five-degree angle just because the floor is straight. But you've tried to put it out of your mind.

And somewhere in the middle of looking around the place and putting your pack down and thinking, *This is home until I can escape it,* you've suddenly realized that you *know* Tonkee. You've known her, on some level, all along.

"*Binof. Leadership. Yumenes,*" you snap, and each word seems to hit Tonkee like a blow. She flinches and takes a step back, then another. Then a third, until she's pressed against the apartment's smooth crystalline wall. The look on her face is one of horror, or perhaps sorrow so great that it might as well be horror. Past a certain point, it's all the same thing.

"I didn't think you remembered," she says, in a small voice.

You get to your feet, palms planted on the table. "It's not chance that you started traveling with us. It can't be."

Tonkee tries to smile; it's a grimace. "Unlikely coincidences *do* happen..."

"Not with you." Not with a child who'd scammed her way into the Fulcrum and uncovered a secret that culminated in the death of a Guardian. The woman who was that child will not leave things to chance. You're sure of it. "At least your rusting *disguises* have gotten better over the years."

Hoa, who's been standing at the entrance of the apartment—guarding again, you think—turns his head from one to the other of you, back and forth. Perhaps he is watching how this confrontation goes, to prepare for the one you have to have with him, next.

Tonkee looks away. She's shaking, just a little. "It isn't. A coincidence. I mean..." She takes a deep breath. "I haven't been following you. I *had people* follow you, but that's different. Didn't start following you myself until just the last few years."

"You had people follow me. *For almost thirty years?*"

She blinks, then relaxes a little, chuckling. It sounds bitter. "My family has more money than the Emperor. Anyway, it was easy for the first twenty years or so. We almost lost you ten years ago. But . . . well."

You slam your hands down on the table, and maybe it's your imagination that the crystal walls of the apartment glow a little brighter, just for a moment. This almost distracts you. Almost.

"I really can't take many more surprises right now," you say, half through your teeth.

Tonkee sighs and slumps against the wall. ". . . Sorry."

You shake your head so hard that your locks slip loose from their knot. "I don't want apologies! *Explain.* Which are you, the Innovator or the Leader?"

"Both?"

You're going to ice her. She sees that in your eyes and blurts, "I was born Leadership. I really was! I'm Binof. But . . ." She spreads her hands. "What can I lead? I'm not good at things like that. You saw what I was like as a child. No subtlety. I'm not good with—people. Things, though, things I can do."

"I'm not interested in your rusting history—"

"But it's relevant! History is always relevant." Tonkee, Binof, or whoever she is, steps away from the wall, a pleading look on her face. "I really am a geomest. I really did go to Seventh, although . . . although . . ." She grimaces in a way you don't understand. "It didn't go well. But I really have spent my life studying that thing, that *socket,* which we found in the Fulcrum. Essun, do you know what that was?"

"I don't care."

At this, however, Tonkee-Binof scowls. "It matters," she says.

Now she's the one who looks furious, and you're the one who draws back in surprise. "I've given my life to that secret. It *matters*. And it should matter to you, too, because you're one of the only people in all the Stillness who can *make* it matter."

"What in Earthfires are you talking about?"

"*It's where they built them.*" Binof-Tonkee comes forward quickly, her face alight. "The socket in the Fulcrum. *That's where the obelisks come from.* And it's also where everything went wrong."

* * *

You end up doing introductions again. Completely this time.

Tonkee is really Binof. But she prefers Tonkee, which is the name she took for herself upon getting into the Seventh University. Turns out it's Not Done for a child of the Yumenescene Leadership to go into any profession except politics, adjudication, or large-scale merchantry. It's also Not Done for a child who is born a boy to be a girl—apparently the Leadership families don't use Breeders, they breed among themselves, and Tonkee's girlness scuttled an arranged marriage or two. They could've simply arranged different marriages, but between that and the young Tonkee's tendency to say things she shouldn't and do things that made no sense, it was the last straw. Thus Tonkee's family buried her in the Stillness's finest center of learning, giving her a new persona and a false use-caste, and quietly disowned her without all the fuss and bother of a scandal.

Yet Tonkee thrived there, apart from a few raging fights with renowned scholars, most of which she won. And she has spent her professional life studying the obsession that drove her to the Fulcrum all those years ago: the obelisks.

"It wasn't so much that I was interested in *you*," she explains. "I mean, I was—you'd helped me, and I needed to make sure you didn't suffer for that, that's how it started—but as I investigated you I learned that you had *potential*. You were one of those who might, one day, develop the ability to command obelisks. It's a rare skill, see. And . . . well, I hoped . . . well."

By this point you've sat down again, and both your voices have lowered. You can't sustain anger over this; there's too much to deal with right now. You look at Hoa, who's standing at the edge of the room, watching the two of you, his posture wary. Still gotta have that talk with him. All the secrets are coming out. Including yours.

"I died," you say. "That was the only way to hide from the Fulcrum. I *died* to get away from them, and yet I didn't shake you."

"Well, yes. My people didn't use mysterious powers to track you; we used deduction. Much more reliable." Tonkee eases herself into the chair opposite you at the table. The apartment has three rooms—this denlike central space, and two bedrooms leading off. Tonkee needs one room to herself because she's starting to smell again. You're only willing to keep sharing your space with Hoa after you get some answers, so you might be sleeping here in the den for a while.

"For the past few years I've been working with—some people." Tonkee abruptly looks cagey, which isn't hard for her. "Other 'mests, mostly, who've also been asking the kinds of questions no one wants to answer. Specialists in other areas. We've been tracking the obelisks, all of them that we can, for the past few years. Did you notice there are patterns in the way they move?

They converge, slowly, wherever there's an orogene of sufficient skill nearby. Someone who can use them. Only two were moving toward you, in Tirimo, but that was enough to extrapolate."

You look up, frowning. "Moving toward me?"

"Or another orogene in your vicinity, yes." Tonkee's relaxed now, eating a piece of dried fruit from her pack. Oblivious to your reaction as you stare at her, your blood gone cold. "The triangulation lines were pretty clear. Tirimo was the center of the circle, so to speak. You must have been there for years; one of the obelisks coming toward you had been traveling the same flight path for almost a decade, all the way from the eastern coast."

"The amethyst," you whisper.

"Yes." Tonkee watches you. "That was why I suspected you were still alive. Obelisks... bond, sort of, to certain orogenes. I don't know how that works. I don't know why. But it's specific, and predictable."

Deduction. You shake your head, mute with shock, and she goes on. "Anyhow, they'd both picked up speed in the last two or three years, so I traveled to the region and pretended to be commless to get a better read on them. I never really meant to approach you. But then this thing happened up north, and I started to think it would be important to have a wielder—obelisk-wielder—around. So... I tried to find you. I was on my way to Tirimo when I spotted you at that roadhouse. Lucky. I was going to trail you for a few days, decide whether I'd tell you who I really was... but then he turned a kirkhusa into a statue." She jerks her head at Hoa. "Figured it might be better to shut up and observe for a while, instead."

Somewhat understandable. "You said more than one obelisk was headed for Tirimo." You lick your lips. "There should've only been one." The amethyst is the only one you're connected to. The only one left.

"There were two. The amethyst, and another from the Merz." That's a big desert to the northeast.

You shake your head. "I've never been to the Merz."

Tonkee is silent for a moment, perhaps intrigued, perhaps annoyed. "Well, how many orogenes were in Tirimo?"

Three. But. "Picked up speed." You can't think, all of a sudden. Can't answer her question. Can't muster complete sentences. *Picked up speed in the last two or three years.*

"Yes. We didn't know what was causing that." Tonkee pauses, then gives you a sidelong look, her eyes narrowing. "Do you?"

Uche was two years old. Almost three.

"Get out," you whisper. "Go take a bath or something. I need to think."

She hesitates, plainly wanting to ask more questions. But then you look up at her, and she immediately gets up to leave. A few minutes after she's out of the apartment, with the heavy hanging falling in her wake—the apartments in this place have no doors, but the hangings work well enough for privacy—you sit there in silence, your head empty, for a while.

Then you look up at Hoa, who's standing beside Tonkee's vacated chair, plainly waiting his turn.

"So you're a stone eater," you say.

He nods, solemn.

"You look..." You gesture at him, not sure how to say it. He's never looked normal, not really, but he's definitely not what a stone eater is supposed to look like. Their hair does not move. Their skin does not bleed. They transit through solid rock in the span of a breath, but stairs would take them hours.

Hoa shifts a little, bringing his pack up into his lap. He rummages for a moment and then comes out with the rag-wrapped bundle that you haven't seen for a while. So that's where he put it. He unties it, finally letting you see what he's been carrying all this time.

The bundle contains many smallish pieces of rough-hewn crystal, as far as you can tell. Something like quartz, or maybe gypsum, except some of the pieces are not murky white but venous red. And you're not sure, but you think the bundle is smaller now than it used to be. Did he lose some of them?

"Rocks," you say. "You've been carrying . . . rocks?"

Hoa hesitates, then reaches for one of the white pieces. He picks it up; it's about the size of the tip of your thumb, squarish, chipped badly on one side. It looks hard.

He eats it. You stare, and he watches you while he does it. He works it around in his mouth for a moment, as if searching for the right angle of attack, or maybe he's just rolling it around on his tongue, enjoying the taste. Maybe it's salt.

But then his jaw flexes. There's a crunching sound, surprisingly loud in the silence of the room. Several more crunches, not as loud, but leaving no doubt that what he's chewing on is by no means food. And then he swallows, and licks his lips.

It's the first time you've ever seen him eat.

"Food," you say.

"Me." He extends a hand and lays it over the pile of rocks with curious delicacy.

You frown a little, because he's making less sense than usual. "So that's . . . what? Something that allows you to look like one of us?" Which you didn't know they could do. Then again, stone eaters share nothing of themselves, and they do not tolerate inquiry from others. You've read accounts of attempts by the Sixth University at Arcara to capture a stone eater for study, two Seasons back. The result was the Seventh University at Dibars, which got built only after they dug enough books out of the rubble of Sixth.

"Crystalline structures are an efficient storage medium." The words make no sense. Then Hoa repeats, clearly, "This is me."

You want to ask more about that, then decide against it. If he wanted you to understand, he would've explained. And that's not the part that matters, anyway.

"Why?" you ask. "Why did you make yourself like this? Why not just be . . . what you are?"

Hoa gives you a look so skeptical that you realize what a stupid question that is. Would you really have let him travel with you if you'd known what he was? Then again, if you'd known what he was, you wouldn't have tried to stop him. No one stops stone eaters from doing what they damn well please.

"Why bother, I mean?" you ask. "Can't you just . . . Your kind can travel through stone."

"Yes. But I wanted to travel with you."

And here we come to the crux of it. "Why?"

"I like you." And then he shrugs. *Shrugs.* Like any child, upon being asked something he either doesn't know how to articulate or doesn't want to try. Maybe it isn't important. Maybe it was just an impulse. Maybe he'll wander off eventually, following some other whim. Only the fact that he isn't a child—that he isn't rusting human, that he's probably *Seasons* old, that he comes from a whole race of people that can't act on whims because it's too rusting hard—makes this a lie.

You rub your face. Your hands come away gritty with ash; you need a bath, too. As you sigh, you hear him say, softly, "I won't hurt you."

You blink at this, then lower your hands slowly. It hadn't even occurred to you that he might. Even now, knowing what he is, having seen the things he can do . . . you're finding it hard to think of him as a frightening, mysterious, unknowable thing. And that, more than anything else, tells you why he's done this to himself. He likes you. He doesn't want you to fear him.

"Good to know," you say. And then there's nothing else to say, so you just look at each other for a while.

"It isn't safe here," he says then.

"Figured that, yeah."

The words are out, snide tone and all, before you really catch yourself. And then—well, is it really surprising that you'd be feeling a bit acerbic at this point? You've been sniping at people since Tirimo, really. But then it occurs to you: That's not the way you were with Jija, or anyone else, before Uche's death. Back then you were always careful to be gentler, calmer. Never sarcastic. If you got angry, you didn't let it show. That's not who Essun was supposed to be.

Yeah, well, you're not quite Essun. Not *just* Essun. Not anymore.

"The others like you, who are here," you begin. His little face tightens, though, in unmistakable anger. You stop in surprise.

"They aren't like me," he says, coldly.

Well, that's that, then. And you're done.

"I need to rest," you say. You've been walking all day, and much as you'd like to bathe, too, you're not sure you're ready to undress and make yourself any more vulnerable in front of these Castrima people. Especially given that they're apparently taking you captive in their nice understated way.

Hoa nods. He starts gathering up his bundle of rocks again. "I'll keep watch."

"Do you sleep?"

"Occasionally. Less than you. I don't need to do it now."

How convenient. And you trust him more than you do the people of this comm. You shouldn't, but you do.

So you get up and head into the bedroom, and lie down on the mattress. It's a simple thing, just straw and cotton packed into a canvas sheath, but it's better than the hard ground or even your bedroll, so you flop onto it. In seconds you're asleep.

When you wake, you're not sure how much time has passed. Hoa is curled up beside you, as he has done for the past few weeks. You sit up and frown down at him; he blinks at you warily. You shake your head, finally, and get up, muttering to yourself.

Tonkee's back in her room. You can hear her snoring. As you step out of the apartment, you realize you have no idea what time it is. Topside you can tell if it's day or night, even despite the clouds and ashfall: it's either bright ashfall and clouds or dark, red-flecked ashfall and clouds. Here, though...you look around and see nothing but giant glowing crystals. And the town that people have, impossibly, built on them.

You step onto the rough wooden platform outside your door and squint down over its completely inadequate safety railing.

Whatever the hour, it seems there are several dozen people going about their business on the ground below. Well, you need to know more about this comm, anyway. Before you destroy it, that is, if they really try to stop you from leaving.

(You ignore the small voice in your head that whispers, *Ykka is a rogga, too. Will you really fight her?*)

(You're pretty good at ignoring small voices.)

Figuring out how to reach the ground level is difficult, at first, because all the platforms and bridges and stairways of the place are built to connect the crystals. The crystals go every which way, so the connections do, too. There's nothing intuitive about it. You have to follow one set of stairs up and walk around one of the wider crystal shafts in order to find another set of stairs that goes down—only to find that they end on a platform with no steps at all, which forces you to backtrack. There are a few people out and about, and they look at you with curiosity or hostility in passing, probably because you're so obviously new in town: They're clean and you're gray with road ash. They look well fleshed, and your clothes hang off your body because you've done nothing but walk and eat travel rations for weeks. You cannot help resenting them on sight, so you get stubborn about asking for directions.

Eventually, however, you make it to the ground. Down here, it's more obvious than ever that you're walking along the floor of a huge stone bubble, because the ground slopes gently downward and curves around you to form a noticeable, if vast, bowl. This is the pointy end of the ovoid that is Castrima. There are crystals down here, too, but they're stubby, some only as high as your chest; the largest are only ten or fifteen feet tall. Wooden partitions wend around some of them, and in some places you can make out obvious patches of rough, paler ground where crystals have been removed to make room. (You wonder, idly, how they did this.) All of it creates a sort of maze of crisscrossing pathways, each of which leads to some comm essential or another: a kiln, a smithy, a glassery, a bakehouse. Off some of the paths you glimpse tents and campsites, some occupied. Clearly not all the denizens of this comm are comfortable walking along bundles of lashed-together wooden planks hundreds of feet above a floor covered in giant spikes. Funny, that.

(There it is again, that un-Essun-like sarcasm. Rust it; you're tired of reining it in.)

It's actually easy to find the baths because there's a pattern of damp foot traffic along the gray-green stone floor, all the wet footprints leading in one direction. You backtrail them and are pleasantly surprised to find that the bath is a huge pool of steaming, clear water. The pool has been walled off a little above the natural floor of the geode, and there's a channel wending away from it, draining into one of several large brass pipes going—somewhere. On the other side of the pool you can see a kind of waterfall emerging from another pipe to supply the pool. The water probably circulates enough to be clean every few hours or so, but nevertheless there's a conspicuous washing area over to one side, with long wooden benches and shelves holding various accessories. Quite a few people are already there, busily scrubbing before they go into the larger pool.

You're undressed and halfway done with your own scrubbing when a shadow falls over you, and you twitch and stumble to your feet and knock over the bench and reach for the earth before it occurs to you that maybe this is overreacting. But then you almost drop the soapy sponge in your hand, because—

—it's *Lerna.*

"Yes," he says as you stare at him. "I thought that might be you, Essun."

You keep staring. He looks different somehow. Heavier, sort of, though skinnier, too, in the same way you are; travel-worn. It's been—weeks? Months? You're losing track of time. And what is he doing here? He should be back in Tirimo; Rask would never let a doctor go...

Oh. Right.

"So Ykka did manage to summon you. I'd wondered." Tired. He looks tired. There's a scar along the edge of his jaw, a crescent-shaped pale patch that doesn't look likely to regain its color. You keep staring as he shifts and says, "Of all the places I had to end up...and here you are. Maybe this is fate, or maybe there really are gods other than Father Earth—ones who actually give a damn about us, that is. Or maybe they're evil, too, and this is their joke. Rust if I know."

"Lerna," you say, which is helpful.

His eyes flick down, and belatedly you remember you're naked. "I should let you finish," he says, looking away quickly. "Let's talk when you're done." You don't care if he sees your nudity—he delivered one of your children, for rust's sake—but he's being polite. It's a familiar habit of his, treating you like a person even though he knows what you are, and oddly heartening after so much strangeness and everything that's changed in your life. You're not used to having a life follow you when you leave it behind.

He moves off, past the bath area, and after a moment you sit back down and finish washing. No one else bothers you while you bathe, although you catch some of the Castrima people eyeing you with increased curiosity now. Less hostility, too, but that's not surprising; you don't look especially intimidating. It's the stuff they can't see that will make them hate you.

Then again . . . do they know what Ykka is? The blond woman who'd been with her up on the surface certainly does. Maybe Ykka's got something on her, some means of ensuring her silence. That doesn't feel right, though. Ykka is too open about what she is, too comfortable speaking of it to complete strangers. She's too charismatic, too eye-catching. Ykka acts like being an orogene is just another talent, just another personal trait. You've only seen that kind of attitude, and this kind of comm-wide acceptance of it, once before.

Once you're done soaking and you feel clean, you get out of the bath. You don't have any towels, just your filthy ashen clothes, which you take the time to scrub clean in the washing area. They're wet when you're done, but you're not quite bold enough to walk through a strange comm naked, and it feels like summer within the geode anyway. So as you do in summer, you put the wet clothes on, figuring they'll dry fast enough.

Lerna's waiting when you leave. "This way," he says, turning to walk with you.

So you follow him, and he leads you up the maze of steps and platforms until you reach a squat gray crystal that juts only twenty feet or so from the wall. He's got an apartment here that's smaller than the one you share with Tonkee and Hoa, but you see shelves laden with herb packets and folded bandages and it's not hard to guess that the odd benches in the main room might actually be intended as makeshift cots. A doctor must be prepared for house calls. He directs you to sit down on one of the benches, and sits across from you.

"I left Tirimo the day after you did," he says quietly. "Oyamar—Rask's second, you remember him, complete idiot—was actually trying to hold an election for a new headman. Didn't want the responsibility with a Season coming on. Everybody knew Rask should never have picked him, but his family did Rask a favor on the trade rights to the western logging trace..." He trails off, because none of that matters anymore. "Anyway. Half the damned Strongbacks were running around drunk and armed, raiding the storecaches, accusing every other person of being a rogga or a rogga-lover. The other half were doing the same thing—quieter, though, and sober, which was worse. I knew it was only a matter of time till they thought about me. Everybody knew I was your friend."

This is your fault, too, then. Because of you, he had to flee a place that should have been safe. You lower your eyes, uncomfortable. He's using the word "rogga" now, too.

"I was thinking I could make it down to Brilliance, where my mother's family came from. They barely know me, but they know *of* me, and I'm a doctor, so... I figured I had a chance. Better than staying in Tirimo, anyway, to get lynched. Or to starve, when the cold came and the Strongbacks had eaten or stolen everything. And I thought—" He hesitates, looks up at you in a flash of eyes, then back at his hands. "I also thought I might catch up to you on the road, if I went fast enough. But that was stupid; of course I didn't."

It's the unspoken thing that's always been between you.

Lerna figured out what you were, somewhere during your time in Tirimo; you didn't tell him. He figured it out because he *watched* you enough to notice the signs, and because he's smart. He's always liked you, Makenba's boy. You figured he would grow out of it eventually. You shift a little, uncomfortable with the realization that he hasn't.

"I slipped out in the night," he continues, "through one of the cracks in the wall near... near where you... where they tried to stop you." He's got his arms resting on his knees, looking at his folded hands. They're mostly still, but he rubs one thumb along the knuckle of the other, slowly, again and again. The gesture feels meditative. "Walked with the flow of people, following a map I had... but I've never been to Brilliance. Earthfires, I've barely left Tirimo before now. Just once, really, when I went to finish my medical training at Hilge—anyway. Either the map was wrong or I'm bad at reading it. Probably both. I didn't have a compass. I got off the Imperial Road too soon, maybe... went southeast when I thought I was going due south... I don't know." He sighs and rubs a hand over his head. "By the time I figured out just how lost I was, I'd gone so far that I hoped to just find a better route if I kept going the way I'd gone. But there was a group at one crossroads. Bandits, commless, something. I was with a small group by then, an older man who'd had a bad gash on his chest that I treated, and his daughter, maybe fifteen. The bandits—"

He pauses, his jaw flexing. You can pretty much guess what happened. Lerna's not a fighter. He's still alive, though, which is all that matters.

"Marald—that was the man—just threw himself at one of

them. He didn't have weapons or anything, and the woman had a machete. I don't know what he thought he could do." Lerna takes a deep breath. "He looked at me, though, and—and I—I grabbed his daughter and ran." His jaw tightens further. You're surprised you can't hear his teeth grinding. "She left me later. Called me a coward and ran off alone."

"If you hadn't taken her away," you say, "they would've killed you and her, too." This is stonelore: *Honor in safety, survival under threat*. Better a living coward than a dead hero.

Lerna's lips quirk thinly. "That's what I told myself at the time. Later, when she left... Earthfires. Maybe all I did was just delay the inevitable. A girl her age, unarmed and out on the roads alone..."

You don't say anything. If the girl's healthy and has the right conformation, someone will take her in, if only as a Breeder. If she has a better use name, or if she can acquire a weapon and supplies and prove herself, that will help, too. Granted, her chances would've been better with Lerna than without him, but she made her choice.

"I don't even know what they wanted." Lerna's looking at his hands. Maybe he's been eating himself up about this ever since. "We didn't have anything but our runny-sacks."

"That's enough, if they were running low on supplies," you say, before you remember to censor yourself. He doesn't seem to hear, anyway.

"So I kept on, by myself." He chuckles once, bitterly. "I was so worried about her, it didn't even occur to me that *I* was just as bad off." This is true. Lerna is a bog-standard midlatter, same as you, except he hasn't inherited the Sanzed bulk or height—probably why he's worked so hard to prove his mental fitness. But he's ended up pretty, mostly by an accident of heritage, and some people breed for that. Cebaki long nose, Sanzed shoulders and coloring, Westcoaster lips...He's too multiracial for Equatorial comm tastes, but by Somidlats standards he's a looker.

"When I passed through Castrima," he continues, "it looked abandoned. I was exhausted, after running from—anyway. Figured I'd hole up in one of the houses for the night, maybe try to make a small hearth fire and hope no one noticed. Eat a decent meal for a change. Hold still long enough to figure out what to do next." He smiled thinly. "And when I woke up, I was surrounded. I told them I was a doctor and they brought me down here. That was maybe two weeks ago."

You nod. And then you tell him your own story, not bothering to hide or lie about anything. The whole thing, not just the part in Tirimo. You're feeling guilty, maybe. He deserves the whole truth.

After you've both fallen silent for a while, Lerna just shakes his head and sighs. "I didn't expect to live through a Season," he says softly. "I mean, I've heard the lore all my life, same as everyone else...but I always figured it would never happen to *me*."

Everyone thinks that. *You* certainly weren't expecting to have to deal with the end of the world on top of everything else.

"Nassun's not here," Lerna says after a while. He speaks softly, but your head jerks up. His face softens at the look that must be on yours. "I'm sorry. But I've been here long enough to meet all the other 'newcomers' to this comm. I know that's who you've been hoping to find."

No Nassun. And now no direction, no realistic way to find her. You are suddenly bereft of even hope.

"Essun." Lerna leans forward abruptly and takes your hands. Belatedly you realize your hands have begun shaking; his fingers still yours. "You'll find her."

The words are meaningless. Reflexive gibberish intended to soothe. But it hits you again, harder this time than that moment topside when you started to come apart in front of Ykka. *It's over.* This whole strange journey, keeping it together, keeping focused on your goal... it's all been pointless. Nassun's gone, you've lost her, and Jija will never pay for what he's done, and you—

What the rust do *you* matter? Who cares about you? Well, that's the thing, isn't it? Once, you did have people who cared about you. Once there were children who looked up to you and lived on your every word. Once—twice, three times, but the first two don't count—there was a man you woke up next to every morning, who gave a damn that you existed. Once, you lived surrounded by the walls he built for you, in a home you made together, in a community that actually *chose* to take you in.

All of it built on lies. Matter of time, really, till it fell apart.

"Listen," Lerna says. His voice makes you blink, and that makes tears fall. More tears. You've been sitting there in silence, crying, for a while now. He shifts over to your bench and you lean on him. You know you shouldn't. But you do, and when he puts an arm around you, you take comfort in it. He is a friend, at least. He will always be that. "Maybe... maybe this isn't a bad thing, being here. You can't think, with—everything—going on. This comm is strange." He grimaces. "I'm not sure I like being here, but it's better than being topside right now. Maybe with some time to think, you'll figure out where Jija might have gone."

He's trying so hard. You shake your head a little, but you're too empty to really muster an objection.

"Do you have a place? They gave me this, they must have given you something. There's plenty of room here." You nod, and Lerna takes a deep breath. "Then let's go there. You can introduce me to these companions of yours."

So. You pull it together. Then you lead him out of his place and in a direction that feels like it might bring you to the apartment you were assigned. Along the way you have more time to appreciate just how unbearably strange this comm is. There's one chamber you pass, embedded in one of the whiter, brighter crystals, that holds racks and racks of flat trays like cookie sheets. There's another chamber, dusty and unused, that holds what you assume are torture devices, except they're incompetently made; you're not sure how a pair of rings suspended from the ceiling on chains are supposed to hurt. And then there are the metal stairs—the ones built by whoever created this place. There are other stairs, more recently made, but it's easy to tell them from the originals because the original stairs don't rust, haven't deteriorated at all, and are not purely utilitarian. There are strange decorations along the railings and edges of the walkways: embossed faces, wrought vines in the shape of no plants you've ever seen, something that you think is writing, except it consists solely of pointy shapes in various sizes. It actually pulls you out of your mood, to try to figure out what you're seeing.

"This is madness," you say, running your fingers over a decoration that looks like a snarling kirkhusa. "This place is one big deadciv ruin, just like a hundred thousand others all over the Stillness. Ruins are death traps. The Equatorial comms flatten or sink theirs if they can, and that's the smartest thing anyone's ever done. If the people who made this place couldn't survive it, why should any of us try?"

"Not all ruins are death traps." Lerna's edging along the platform while keeping very close to the crystal shaft it wends around, and keeping his eyes fixed straight ahead. Sweat beads his upper lip. You hadn't realized he's afraid of heights, but then Tirimo is as flat as it is boring. His voice is carefully calm. "There are rumors Yumenes is built on a whole series of deadciv ruins."

And look how well that turned out, you don't say.

"These people should've just built a wall like everyone else," you do say, but then you stop, because it occurs to you that the goal is survival, and sometimes survival requires change. Just because the usual strategies have worked—building a wall, taking in the useful and excluding the useless, arming and storing and hoping for luck—doesn't mean that other methods might not. This, though? Climbing down a hole and hiding in a ball of sharp rocks with a bunch of stone eaters and *roggas*? Seems especially unwise.

"And if they try to keep me here, they'll find that out," you murmur.

If Lerna hears you, he does not respond.

Eventually you find your apartment. Tonkee's awake and in the living room, eating a big bowl of something that didn't come from your packs. It looks like some kind of porridge, and it's got little yellowish things in it that make you recoil at first—until she tilts the bowl and you realize it's sprouted grains. Standard storecache food.

(She looks at you warily as you come in, but her revelations were so minor compared to everything else you've had to face today that you just wave a greeting and settle down opposite her as usual. She relaxes.)

Lerna's polite but guarded with Tonkee, and she's the same with him—until he mentions that he's been running blood and urine tests on the people of Castrima to watch for vitamin deficiencies. You almost smile when she leans forward and says, "With what kind of equipment?" with a familiar greedy look on her face.

Then Hoa comes into the apartment. You're surprised, since you hadn't realized he'd gone out. His icewhite gaze flicks immediately to Lerna and examines him ruthlessly. Then he relaxes, so visibly that you only now realize Hoa's been tense all this time. Since you came into this crazy comm.

But you file this away as just another oddity to explore later, because Hoa says, "Essun. There's someone here you should meet."

"Who?"

"A man. From Yumenes."

All three of you stare at him. "Why," you say slowly, in case you've misunderstood something, "would I want to meet someone from Yumenes?"

"He asked for you."

You decide to try for patience. "Hoa, I don't know anyone from Yumenes." Not anymore, anyway.

"He says he knows you. He tracked you here, got here ahead of you when he realized it was where you were headed." Hoa scowls, just a little, as if this bothers him. "He says he wants to see you, see if you can do it yet."

"Do what?"

"He just said 'it.'" Hoa's eyes slide first to Tonkee, then to Lerna, before returning to you. Something he doesn't want them to hear, maybe. "He's like you."

"What—" Okay. You rub your eyes, take a deep breath, and say it so he'll know there's no need to hide it. "A rogga, then."

"Yes. No. Like you. His—" Hoa waggles his fingers in lieu of words. Tonkee opens her mouth; you gesture sharply at her. She glares back. After a moment, Hoa sighs. "He said, if you wouldn't come, to tell you that you owe him. For Corundum."

You freeze.

"Alabaster," you whisper.

"Yes," says Hoa, brightening. "That's his name." And then he frowns more, thoughtfully this time. "He's dying."

* * *

MADNESS SEASON: 3 Before Imperial–7 Imperial. The eruption of the Kiash Traps, multiple vents of an ancient supervolcano (the same one responsible for the Twin Season believed to have occurred approximately 10,000 years previous), launched large deposits of olivine and other dark-colored pyroclasts into the air. The resulting ten years of darkness were not only devastating in the usual Seasonal way, but resulted in a much higher than usual incidence of mental illness. The Sanzed warlord Verishe conquered multiple ailing comms through the use of psychological warfare designed to convince her foes that gates and walls offered no reliable protection, and that phantasms lurked nearby. She was named emperor on the day the first sunlight reappeared.

—*The Seasons of Sanze*

22

Syenite, fractured

It's the morning after a raucous party that the Meovites threw to celebrate the *Clalsu*'s safe return and acquisition of some especially prized goods—high-quality stone for decorative carving, aromatic woods for furniture building, fancy brocade cloth that's worth twice its weight in diamonds, and a goodly amount of tradable currency including high-denomination paper and whole fingers of mother-of-pearl. No food, but with that kind of money they can send traders to buy canoesful of anything they need on the mainland. Harlas broke out a cask of fearsomely strong Antarctic mead to celebrate, and half the comm's still sleeping it off.

It's five days after Syenite shut down a volcano that she started, which killed a whole city, and eight days after she killed two ships full of people to keep her family's existence secret. It feels like everyone is celebrating the multiple mass murders she's committed.

She's still in bed, having retired to it as soon as the ship was unloaded. Innon hasn't come to the house yet; she told him to go and tell the stories of the trip, because the people expect it of him and she does not want him suffering for her melancholy. He's got Coru with him, because Coru loves celebrations—everyone feeds him, everyone cuddles him. He even tries to help Innon tell the stories, yelling nonsense at the top of his lungs. The child is more like Innon than he has any physical right to be.

Alabaster is the one who's stayed with Syen, talking to her through her silence, forcing her to respond when she would rather just stop thinking. He says he knows what it's like to feel like this, though he won't tell her how or what happened. She believes him regardless.

"You should go," she says at last. "Join the storytelling. Remind Coru he's got at least two parents who are worth something."

"Don't be stupid. He's got three."

"Innon thinks I'm a terrible mother."

Alabaster sighed. "No. You're just not the kind of mother Innon wants you to be. You're the kind of mother our son needs, though." She turns her head to frown at him. He shrugs. "Corundum will be strong, someday. He needs strong parents. I'm..." He falters abruptly. You practically feel him decide to change the subject. "Here. I brought you something."

Syen sighs and pushes herself up as he crouches beside the bed, unfolding a little cloth parcel. In it, when she gets curious despite herself and leans closer, are two polished stone rings, just right for her fingers. One's made of jade, the other mother-of-pearl.

She glares at him, and he shrugs. "Shutting down an active volcano isn't something a mere four-ringer could do."

"We're free." She says it doggedly, even though she doesn't feel free. She fixed Allia, after all, completing the mission the Fulcrum sent her there for, however belatedly and perversely. It's the sort of thing that makes her laugh uncontrollably when she thinks about it, so she pushes on before she can. "We don't need to wear *any* rings anymore. Or black uniforms. I haven't put my hair in a bun in months. You don't have to service every woman they send you, like some kind of stud animal. Let the Fulcrum go."

'Baster smiles a little, sadly. "We can't, Syen. One of us is going to have to train Coru—"

"We don't have to train him to do anything." Syen lies down again. She wishes he would go away. "Let him learn the basics from Innon and Harlas. That's been enough to let these people get by for centuries."

"Innon couldn't have stilled that blow, Syen. If he'd tried, he might have blown the hot spot underneath it wide, and set off a Season. You saved the world from that."

"Then give me a medal, not rings." She's glaring at the ceiling. "Except I'm the reason that blow even existed, so *maybe not*."

Alabaster reaches up to stroke her hair away from her face. He does that a lot, now that she wears it loose. She's always been a little ashamed of her hair—it's curly, but with no stiffness to it at all, whether the straight-stiffness of Sanzed hair or the kinky-stiffness of Coaster hair. She's such a midlatter mutt that she doesn't even know which of her ancestors to blame for the hair. At least it doesn't get in her way.

"We are what we are," he says, with such gentleness that she wants to cry. "We are Misalem, not Shemshena. You've heard that story?"

Syenite's fingers twitch in remembered pain. "Yes."

"From your Guardian, right? They like to tell that one to

kids." 'Baster shifts to lean against the bedpost with his back to her, relaxing. Syenite thinks about telling him to leave, but never says it aloud. She's not looking at him, so she has no idea what he does with the bundle of rings that she didn't take. He can eat them for all she cares.

"My Guardian gave me that nonsense, too, Syen. The monstrous Misalem, who decided to declare war against a whole nation and off the Sanzed Emperor for no particular reason."

In spite of herself, Syenite frowns. "He had a reason?"

"Oh Evil Earth, of course. Use your rusting head."

It's annoying to be scolded, and annoyance pushes back her apathy a little more. Good old Alabaster, cheering her up by pissing her off. She turns her head to glare at the back of his. "Well, what was the reason?"

"The simplest and most powerful reason of all: revenge. That emperor was Anafumeth, and the whole thing happened just after the end of the Season of Teeth. That's the Season they don't talk about much in any creche. There was mass starvation in the northern-hemisphere comms. They got hit harder, since the shake that started the whole thing was near the northern pole. The Season took a year longer to take hold in the Equatorials and the south—"

"How do you know all this?" It's nothing Syen's ever heard, in the grit crucibles or elsewhere.

Alabaster shrugs, shaking the whole bed. "I wasn't allowed to train with the other grits in my year-group; I had rings before most of them had pubic hair. The instructors let me loose in the seniors' library to make up for it. They didn't pay a lot of attention to what I read." He sighs. "Also, on my first mission, I…

There was an archeomest who . . . He . . . well. We talked, in addition to . . . other things."

She doesn't know why Alabaster bothers being shy about his affairs. She's watched Innon fuck him into incoherence on more than one occasion. Then again, maybe it's not the sex that he's shy about.

"Anyway. It's all there if you put the facts together and think beyond what we're taught. Sanze was a new empire then, still growing, at the height of its power. But it was mostly in the northern half of the Equatorials at that time—Yumenes wasn't actually the capital then—and some of the bigger Sanzed comms weren't as good at preparing for Seasons as they are now. They lost their food storecaches somehow. Fire, fungus, Earth knows what. To survive, all the Sanzed comms decided to work together, attacking the comms of any lesser races." His lip curls. "That's *when* they started calling us 'lesser races,' actually."

"So they took those other comms' storecaches." Syen can guess that much. She's getting bored.

"No. No one had any stores left by the end of that Season. The Sanzeds took *people*."

"People? For wh—" Then she understands.

There's no need for slaves during a Season. Every comm has its Strongbacks, and if they need more, there are always commless people desperate enough to work in exchange for food. Human flesh becomes valuable for other reasons, though, when things get bad enough.

"So," says Alabaster, oblivious while Syen lies there fighting nausea, "that Season is when the Sanzeds developed a taste for certain rarefied delicacies. And even after the Season ended and green things grew and the livestock turned herbivorous or stopped hibernating, they kept at it. They would send out parties to raid smaller settlements and newcomms held by races without Sanzed allies. All the accounts differ on the details, but they agree on one thing: Misalem was the only survivor when his family was taken in a raid. Supposedly his children were slaughtered for Anafumeth's own table, though I suspect that's a bit of dramatic embellishment." Alabaster sighs. "Regardless, they died, and it was Anafumeth's fault, and he wanted Anafumeth dead for it. Like any man would."

But a rogga is not any man. Roggas have no right to get angry, to want justice, to protect what they love. For his presumption, Shemshena had killed him—and became a hero for doing it.

Syenite considers this in silence. Then Alabaster shifts a little, and she feels his hand press the bundle, the one with the rings in it, into her unresisting palm.

"Orogenes built the Fulcrum," he says. She's almost never heard him say *orogene*. "We did it under threat of genocide, and we used it to buckle a collar around our own necks, but we did it. *We* are the reason Old Sanze grew so powerful and lasted so long, and why it still half-rules the world, even if no one will admit it. We're the ones who've figured out just how amazing our kind can be, if we learn how to refine the gift we're born with."

"It's a curse, not a gift." Syenite closes her eyes. But she doesn't push away the bundle.

"It's a gift if it makes us better. It's a curse if we let it destroy us. *You* decide that—not the instructors, or the Guardians, or anyone else." There's another shift, and the bed moves a little as Alabaster leans on it. A moment later she feels his lips on her brow, dry and approving. Then he settles back down on the floor beside the bed, and says nothing more.

"I thought I saw a Guardian," she says after a while. Very softly. "At Allia."

Alabaster doesn't reply for a moment. She's decided that he won't, when he says, "I will tear the whole world apart if they ever hurt us again."

But we would still be hurt, she thinks.

It's reassuring, though, somehow. The kind of lie she needs to hear. Syenite keeps her eyes closed and doesn't move for a long while. She's not sleeping; she's thinking. Alabaster stays while she does it, and for that she is unutterably glad.

* * *

When the world ends three weeks later, it happens on the most beautiful day Syenite has ever seen. The sky is clear for miles, save for the occasional drift of cloud. The sea is calm, and even the omnipresent wind is warm and humid for once, instead of cool and scouring.

It's so beautiful that the entire comm decides to head up to the heights. The able-bodied carry the ones who can't make the steps, while the children get underfoot and nearly kill everyone. The people on cook duty put fish cakes and pieces of cut fruit and balls of seasoned grain into little pots that can be carried easily, and everyone brings blankets. Innon has a musical instrument Syenite has never seen before, something like a drum with guitar strings, which would probably be all the rage in Yumenes if it ever caught on there. Alabaster has Corundum. Syenite brings a truly awful novel someone found on the looted freighter, the sort of thing whose first page made her wince and burst into giggles. Then, of course, she kept reading. She loves books that are just for fun.

The Meovites spread themselves over the slope behind a ridge that blocks most of the wind but where the sun is full and bright. Syenite puts her blanket a ways from everyone else, but they quickly encroach on her, spreading out their blankets right alongside, and grinning at her when she glares.

She has come to realize over the past three years that most Meovites regard her and Alabaster as something like wild animals that have decided to scavenge off human habitations—impossible to civilize, kind of cute, and at least an amusing nuisance. So when they see that she obviously needs help with something and won't admit it, they help her anyway. And they constantly *pet* Alabaster, and hug him and grab his hands and swing him into dancing, which Syen is at least grateful no one tries with her. Then again, everyone can see that Alabaster likes being touched, no matter how much he pretends standoffishness. It probably isn't something he got a lot of in the Fulcrum, where everyone was afraid of his power. Perhaps likewise they think Syen enjoys being reminded that she is part of a group now, contributing and contributed to, and that she no longer needs to guard herself against everyone and everything.

They're right. That doesn't mean she's going to tell them so.

Then it's all Innon tossing Coru up in the air while Alabaster tries to pretend he's not terrified even as his orogeny sends microshakes through the island's underwater strata with every toss; and Hemoo starting some kind of chanted-poetry game set to music that all the Meovites seem to know; and Ough's toddler Owel trying to run across the spread-out blankets and stepping on at least ten people before someone grabs her and tickles her down; and a basket being passed around that contains little clay bottles of something that burns Syen's nose when she sniffs it; and.

And.

She could love these people, she thinks sometimes.

Perhaps she does already. She isn't sure. But after Innon flops down for a nap with Coru already asleep on his chest, and after the poetry chant has turned into a vulgar-joke contest, and once she's drunk enough of the bottle stuff that the world is actually beginning to move on its own... Syenite lifts her eyes and catches Alabaster's. He's propped himself on one elbow to browse the terrible book she's finally abandoned. He's making horrible and hilarious faces as he skims it. Meanwhile his free hand toys with one of Innon's braids, and he looks nothing at all like the half-mad monster Feldspar sent her off with, at the beginning of this journey.

His eyes flick up to meet hers, and for just a moment there is wariness there. Syen blinks in surprise at this. But then, she *is* the only person here who knows what his life was like before. Does he resent her for being here, a constant reminder of what he'd rather forget?

He smiles, and she frowns in automatic reaction. His smile widens more. "You still don't like me, do you?"

Syenite snorts. "What do you care?"

He shakes his head, amused—and then he reaches out and strokes a hand over Coru's hair. The child stirs and murmurs in his sleep, and Alabaster's face softens. "Would you like to have another child?"

Syenite starts, her mouth falling open. "Of course not. I didn't want *this* one."

"But he's here now. And he's beautiful. Isn't he? You make such beautiful children." Which is probably the most inane thing he could ever say, but then, he's Alabaster. "You could have the next one with Innon."

"Maybe Innon should have a say in that, before we settle his breeding future."

"He loves Coru, and he's a good father. He's got two other kids already, and they're fine. Stills, though." He considers. "You and Innon might have a child who's still. That wouldn't be a terrible thing, here."

Syenite shakes her head, but she's thinking about the little pessary the island women have shown her how to use. Thinking maybe she will stop using it. But she says: "Freedom means *we* get to control what we do now. No one else."

"Yes. But now that I can think about what I want..." He shrugs as if nonchalant, but there's an intensity in his gaze as he looks at Innon and Coru. "I've never wanted much from life. Just to be able to *live* it, really. I'm not like you, Syen. I don't need to prove myself. I don't want to change the world, or help people, or be anything great. I just want...this."

She gets that. So she lies down on her side of Innon, and Alabaster lies down on his side, and they relax and enjoy the sensation of wholeness, of contentment, for a while. Because they can.

Of course it cannot last.

Syenite wakes when Innon sits up and shadows her. She hadn't intended to nap, but she's had a good long one, and now the sun is slanting toward the ocean. Coru's fussing and she sits up automatically, rubbing her face with one hand and reaching with the other to see if his cloth diaper is full. It's fine, but the sounds he's making are anxious, and when she comes more awake she sees why. Innon is sitting up with Coru held absently in one arm, but he is frowning as he looks at Alabaster. Alabaster is on his feet, his whole body tense.

"Something..." he murmurs. He's facing the direction of the mainland, but he can't possibly see anything; the ridge is in the way. Then again, he's not using his eyes.

So Syen frowns and sends forth her own awareness, worrying that there's a tsunami or worse on its way. But there's nothing.

A *conspicuous* nothingness. There should be something. There's a plate boundary between the island that is Meov and the mainland; plate boundaries are never still. They jump and twitch and vibrate against one another in a million infinitesimal ways that only a rogga can sess, like the electricity that geneers can make come out of water turbines and vats of chemicals. But suddenly—impossibly—the plate edge sesses as still.

Confused, Syenite starts to look at Alabaster. But her attention is caught by Corundum, who's bouncing and struggling in Innon's hands, whining and snotting and having a full-on tantrum, though he's usually not the kind of baby who does that sort of thing. Alabaster's looking at the baby, too. His expression changes to something twisted and terrible.

"No," he says. He's shaking his head. "No. No, I won't *let* them, not again."

"What?" Syenite's staring at him, trying not to notice the dread that's rising in her, feeling rather than seeing as others rise around them, murmuring and reacting to their alarm. A couple of people trot up the ridge to see what they can. "'Baster, what? For Earth's sake—"

He makes a sound that is not a word, just *negation*, and suddenly he takes off running up the slope, toward the ridge. Syenite stares after him, then at Innon, who looks even more confused than she is; Innon shakes his head. But the people who preceded 'Baster up the ridge are shouting now, and signaling everyone else. Something is wrong.

Syenite and Innon hurry up the slope along with others. They all reach the top together, and there they stand looking at the span of ocean on the mainlandward side of the island.

Where there are four ships, tiny but visibly coming closer, on the horizon.

Innon says a bad word and shoves Coru at Syenite, who almost fumbles him but then holds him close while Innon rummages amid his pockets and packs and comes up with his smaller spyglass. He extends it and looks hard for a moment, then frowns, while Syenite tries ineffectually to console Coru. Coru is inconsolable. When Innon lowers it, Syenite grabs his arm and pushes Coru at him, taking the device from his hand when he does.

The four ships are bigger now. Their sails are white, ordinary; she can't figure out what's got Alabaster so upset. And then she notices the figures standing at one boat's prow.

Wearing burgundy.

The shock of it steals the breath from her chest. She steps back, mouths the word that Innon needs to hear, but it comes out strengthless, inaudible. Innon takes the spyglass from her because she looks like she's about to drop it. Then because they have to *do* something, she's got to *do* something, she concentrates and focuses and says, louder, "*Guardians.*"

Innon frowns. "How—" She watches as he, too, realizes what this means. He looks away for a moment, wondering, and then he shakes his head. How they found Meov does not matter. They cannot be allowed to land. They cannot be allowed to live.

"Give Coru to someone," he says, backing away from the ridge; his expression has hardened. "We are going to need you, Syen."

Syenite nods and turns, looking around. Deelashet, one of the handful of Sanzeds in the comm, is hurrying past with her own little one, who's maybe six months older than Coru. She's kept Coru on occasion, nursed him when Syenite was busy; Syenite flags her down and runs to her. "Please," she says, pushing Coru into her arms. Deelashet nods.

Coru, however, does not agree with the plan. He clings to Syenite, screaming and kicking and—Evil Earth, the whole island rocks all of a sudden. Deelashet staggers and then stares at Syenite in horror.

"Shit," she murmurs, and takes Coru back. Then with him on her hip—he calms immediately—she runs to catch up with Innon, who is already running toward the metal stairs, shouting to his crew to board the *Clalsu* and ready it for launch.

It's madness. It's all madness, she thinks as she runs. It doesn't make sense that the Guardians have discovered this place. It doesn't make sense that they're coming—why here? Why now? Meov has been around, pirating the coast, for generations. The only thing that's different is Syenite and Alabaster.

She ignores the little voice in the back of her mind that whispers, *They followed you somehow, you know they did, you should never have gone back to Allia, it was a trap, you should never have come here, everything you touch is death.*

She does not look down at her hands, where—just to let Alabaster know she appreciated the gesture—she's put on the four rings that the Fulcrum gave her, plus his two. The last two aren't real, after all. She hasn't passed any sort of ring test for them. But who would know whether she merits these rings better than a man who's earned ten? And for shit's sake, she stilled a rusting volcano made by a broken obelisk with a stone eater inside.

So Syenite decides, suddenly and fiercely, that she's going to show these rusting Guardians just what a six-ringer can do.

She reaches the comm level, where it's chaos: people pulling out glassknives and rolling out catapults and balls of chain from wherever-the-rust they've been keeping them, gathering belongings, loading boats with fishing spears. Then Syen's running up the plank onto the *Clalsu*, where Innon is shouting for the anchor to be pulled up, and all at once it occurs to her to wonder where Alabaster has gone.

She stumbles to a halt on the ship's deck. And as she does, she feels a flare of orogeny so deep and powerful that for a moment she thinks the whole world shakes. All the water in the harbor dances with tiny pointillations for a moment. Syen suspects the clouds felt that one.

And suddenly there is a *wall* rising from the sea, not five hundred yards off the harbor. It is a massive block of solid stone, as perfectly rectangular as if it were chiseled, huge enough to—oh flaking rust, *no*—seal off the damned harbor.

"'Baster! Earth damn it—" It's impossible to be heard over the roar of water and the grind of the stone—as big as the island of

Meov itself—Alabaster is raising. How can he do this with no shake or hot spot nearby? Half the island should be iced. But then something flickers at the corner of Syenite's vision and she turns to see the amethyst obelisk off in the distance. It's closer than before. It's coming to meet them. That's how.

Innon is cursing, furious; he understands full well that Alabaster is being an overprotective fool, however he's doing it. His fury becomes effort. Fog rises from the water around the ship, and the deck planks nearby creak and frost over as he tries to smash apart the nearest part of the wall, so that they can get out there and fight. The wall splinters—and then there is a low boom behind it. When the part of the wall that Innon has shattered crumbles away, there's just another block of stone behind it.

Syenite's got her hands full trying to modulate the waves in the water. It is possible to use orogeny on water, just difficult. She's getting the hang of it at last, after this long living near such a great expanse of water; it's one of the few things Innon's been able to teach her and Alabaster. There's enough warmth and mineral content in the sea that she can feel it, and water moves enough like stone—just faster—that she can manipulate it a little. Delicately. Still, she does this now, holding Coru close so he's within the safe zone of her torus, and concentrating hard to send shock waves against the coming waves at just enough velocity to break them. It mostly works; the *Clalsu* rocks wildly and tears loose from its moorings, and one of the piers collapses, but nothing capsizes and no one dies. Syenite counts this as a win.

"What the rust is he doing?" Innon says, panting, and she follows his gaze to see Alabaster, at last.

He stands on the highest point of the island, up on the slopes.

Even from here Syen can see the blistering cold of his torus; the warmer air around it wavers as the temperature changes, and all the moisture in the wind blowing past him precipitates out as snow. If he's using the obelisk then he shouldn't need the ambient, should he? Unless he's doing so much that even the obelisk can't fuel it.

"Earthfires," Syen says. "I have to go up there."

Innon grabs her arm. When she looks up at him, his eyes are wide and a little afraid. "We'd only be a liability to him."

"We can't just sit here and wait! He's not . . . reliable." Even as she says this, her belly clenches. Innon has never seen Alabaster lose it. She doesn't *want* Innon to see that. Alabaster's been so good here at Meov; he's almost not crazy anymore. But Syen thinks

what broke once will break again, more easily

and she shakes her head and tries to hand him Coru. "I have to. Maybe I can help. Coru won't let me give him to anyone else—please—"

Innon curses but takes the child, who clutches at Innon's shirt and and puts his thumb in his mouth. Then Syen is off, running along the comm ledge and up the steps.

As she gets above the rock barrier, she can finally see what's happening beyond it, and for a moment she stumbles to a halt in shock. The ships are much closer, right beyond the wall that 'Baster has raised to protect the harbor. There are only three of them, though, because one ship has floundered off course and is listing badly—no, it's sinking. She has no idea how he managed that. Another is riding strangely in the water, mast broken and bow raised and keel visible, and that's when Syenite realizes there are *boulders* piled on its rear deck. Alabaster's been dropping rocks on the bastards. She has no idea how, but the sight of it makes her want to cheer.

But the other two ships have split up: one coming straight for the island, the other peeling off, perhaps to circle around or maybe get out of Alabaster's rock-dropping range. *No you don't,* Syen thinks, and she tries to do what she did to the attack ship during their last raid, dragging a splinter of bedrock up from the seafloor to spear the thing. She frosts a ten-foot space around her to do it, and makes chunks of ice spread over the water between her and the ship, but she gets the splinter shaped and loose, and starts to pull it up—

And it stops. And the gathering strength of her orogeny just...disipates. She gasps as the heat and force spill away, and then she understands: This ship has a Guardian on it, too. Maybe they all do, which explains why 'Baster hasn't destroyed them already. He can't attack a Guardian directly; all he can do is hurl boulders from outside the Guardians' negation radius. She can't even imagine how much power that must take. He could never have managed it without the obelisk, and if he weren't the crazy, ornery ten-ringer that he is.

Well, just because *she* can't hit the thing directly doesn't mean she can't find some other way to do it. She runs along the ridge as the ship she tried to destroy passes behind the island, keeping it in sight. Do they think there's another way up? If so, they'll be sorely disappointed; Meov's harbor is the only part of the island that's remotely approachable. The rest of the island is a single jagged, sheer column.

Which gives her an idea. Syenite grins and stops, then drops to her hands and knees so she can concentrate.

She doesn't have Alabaster's strength. She doesn't even know how to reach the amethyst without his guidance—and after what happened at Allia, she's afraid to try. The plate boundary is too far for her to reach, and there are no nearby vents or hot spots. But she has Meov itself. All that lovely, heavy, *flaky* schist.

So she throws herself down. Deep. Deeper. She feels her way along the ridges and the layers of the rock that is Meov, seeking the best point of fracture—the *fulcrum;* she laughs to herself. At last she finds it, good. And there, coming around the island's curve, is the ship. Yes.

Syenite drags all the heat and infinitesimal life out of the rock in one concentrated spot. The moisture's still there, though, and that's what freezes, and expands, as Syenite forces it colder and colder, taking more and more from it, spinning her torus fine and oblong so that it slices along the grain of the rock like a knife through meat. A ring of frost forms around her, but it's nothing compared to the long, searing plank of ice that's growing down the inside of the rock, levering it apart.

And then, right when the ship approaches the point, she unleashes all the strength the island has given her, shoving it right back where it came from.

A massive, narrow finger of stone splits away from the cliff face. Inertia holds it where it is, just for a moment—and then with a low, hollow groan, it peels away from the island, splintering at its base near the waterline. Syenite opens her eyes and gets up and runs, slipping once on her own ice ring, to that end of the island. She's tired, and after a few steps she has to slow to a walk, gasping for breath around a stitch in her side. But she gets there in time to see:

The finger of rock has landed squarely on the ship. She grins fiercely at the sight of the deck splintered apart as she hears screams, as she sees people already in the water. Most wear a variety of clothing; hirelings, then. But she thinks she sees one flash of burgundy cloth under the water's surface, being dragged deeper by one of the sinking ship halves.

"Guard *that*, you cannibalson ruster." Grinning, Syenite gets up and heads in Alabaster's direction again.

As she comes down from the heights she can see him, a tiny figure still making his own cold front, and for a moment she actually admires him. He's amazing, in spite of everything. But then, all of a sudden, there is a strange hollow boom from the sea, and something explodes around Alabaster in a spray of rocks and smoke and concussive force.

A cannon. A rusting *cannon*. Innon's told her about these; they're an invention that the Equatorial comms have been experimenting with in the past few years. Of *course* Guardians would have one. Syen breaks into a run, raggedly and clumsily, fueled by fear. She can't see 'Baster well through the smoke of the cannon blast, but she can see that he's down.

By the time she gets there, she knows he's hurt. The icy wind has stopped blowing; she can see Alabaster on his hands and knees, surrounded by a circle of blistered ice that is yards wide. Syenite stops at the outermost ring of ice; if he's out of it, he might not notice that she's within the range of his power. "Alabaster!"

He moves a little, and she can hear him groaning, murmuring. How bad is he hurt? Syenite dances at the edge of the ice for a moment, then finally decides to risk it, trotting to the clear zone immediately around him. He's still upright, though barely;

his head's hanging, and her belly clenches when she sees flecks of blood on the stone beneath him.

"I took out the other ship," she says as she reaches him, hoping to reassure. "I can get this one, too, if you haven't."

It's bravado. She's not sure how much she's got left in her. Hopefully he's taken care of it. But she looks up and curses inwardly, because the remaining ship is still out there, apparently undamaged. It seems to be sitting at anchor. Waiting. For what, she can't guess.

"Syen," he says. His voice is strained. With fear, or something else? "Promise me you won't let them take Coru. No matter what."

"What? Of course I won't." She steps closer and crouches beside him. "'Baster—" He looks up at her, dazed, perhaps from the cannon blast. Something's cut his forehead, and like all head wounds it's bleeding copiously. She checks him over, touching his chest, hoping he's not more hurt. He's still alive, so the cannon blast must have been a near miss, but all it takes is a bit of rock shrapnel at the right speed, in the wrong place—

And that's when she finally notices. His arms at the wrists. His knees, and the rest of his legs between thighs and ankles—they're gone. They haven't been cut off or blown off; each limb ends smoothly, perfectly, right where the ground begins. And he's moving them about as if it's water and not solid stone that he's trapped in. *Struggling,* she realizes belatedly. He's not on his hands and knees because he can't stand; he's being *dragged into the ground,* against his will.

The stone eater. Oh rusting Earth.

Syenite grabs his shoulders and tries to haul him back, but it's like trying to haul a rock. He's heavier, somehow. His flesh doesn't feel quite like flesh. The stone eater has made his body pass through solid stone by making him more stonelike, somehow, and Syenite can't get him out. He sinks deeper into the stone with each breath; he's up to his shoulders and hips now, and she can't see his feet at all.

"Let him go, Earth take you!" The irony of the curse will occur to her only later. What does occur to her, in the moment, is to stab her awareness into the stone. She tries to feel for the stone eater—

There is something there, but it's not like anything she's ever felt before: a heaviness. A weight, too deep and solid and huge to be possible—not in such a small space, not so compact. It feels like there's a *mountain* there, dragging Alabaster down with all its weight. He's fighting it; that's the only reason he's still here at all. But he's weak, and he's losing the fight, and she hasn't the first clue of how to help him. The stone eater is just too...something. Too much, too big, too powerful, and she cannot help flinching back into herself with a sense that she's just had a near miss.

"*Promise,*" he pants, while she hauls again on his shoulders and tries pushing against the stone with all her power, pulling back against that terrible weight, anything, everything. "You know what they'll do to him, Syen. A child that strong, my child, raised outside the Fulcrum? You *know.*"

A wire-frame chair in a darkened node station...She can't think about that. Nothing's *working,* and he's mostly gone into the stone now; only his face and shoulders are above it, and that's only because he's straining to keep those above the stone-line. She babbles at him, sobbing, desperate for words that can somehow fix this. "I know. I promise. Oh, rust, 'Baster, please, I can't . . . not alone, I can't . . ."

The stone eater's hand rises from the stone, white and solid and rust-tipped. Surprised, Syenite screams and flinches, thinking the creature is attacking her—but no. This hand wraps around the back of Alabaster's head with remarkable gentleness. No one expects mountains to be gentle. But they are inexorable, and when the hand pulls, Alabaster goes. His shoulders slip out of Syen's hands. His chin, then his mouth, then his nose, then his terrified eyes—

He is gone.

Syenite kneels on the hard, cold stone, alone. She is screaming. She is weeping. Her tears fall onto the stone where Alabaster's head was a moment before, and the rock does not soak the tears up. They just splatter.

And then she feels it: the drop. The drag. Startled out of grief, she scrabbles to her feet and stumbles over to the edge of the cliff, where she can see the remaining ship. *Ships,* the one 'Baster's hit with rocks seems to have righted itself somehow. No, not somehow. Ice spreads across the water's surface around both ships. There's a rogga on one of the ships, working for the Guardians. A four-ringer, at least; there's too much fine control in what she's feeling. And with that much ice— She sees a group of porpoises leap out of the water, racing away from the spreading ice, and then she sees it catch them, crawling over their bodies and solidifying them half in and half out of the water.

What the hell is this rogga doing with that much power?

Then she sees a portion of the rock wall that 'Baster raised shiver.

"No—" Syenite turns and runs again, breathless, sessing rather than seeing as the Guardians' rogga attacks the wall's base. It's weak where the wall curves to meet the natural curve of Meov's harbor. The rogga's going to bring it down.

It takes an eternity to reach the comm level, and then the docks. She's terrified Innon will set sail without her. He has to be able to sess what's happening, too. But thank stone, the *Clalsu* is still there, and when she staggers up onto its deck, several members of the crew grab her and guide her to sit down before she collapses. They draw up the plank behind her, and she can see that they're striking sails.

"Innon," she gasps as she catches her breath. "Please."

They half-carry her to him. He's on the upper deck, one hand on the pilot's wheel and the other holding Coru against his hip. He doesn't look at her, all his attention focused on the wall; there's already a hole in it, near the top, and as Syenite reaches him there is a final surge. The wall breaks apart and falls in chunks, rocking the ship something fierce, but Innon's completely steady.

"We're sailing out to face them," he says grimly, as she sags onto the bench nearby, and as the ship pulls away from the dock. Everyone's ready for a fight. The catapults are loaded, the javelins in hand. "We'll lead them away from the comm first. That way, everyone else can evacuate in the fishing boats."

There aren't enough fishing boats for everyone, Syenite wants to say, and doesn't. Innon knows it, anyway.

Then the ship is sailing through the narrow gap that the Guardians' orogene has made, and the Guardians' ship is on them almost at once. There's a puff of smoke on their deck and a hollow whoosh right as the *Clalsu* emerges; the cannon again.

A near miss. Innon shouts and one of the catapult crews returns the favor with a basket of heavy chain, which shreds their foresail and midmast. Another volley and this time it's a barrel of burning pitch; Syen sees people on fire running across the deck of the Guardians' ship after that one hits. The *Clalsu* whips past while the Guardians' ship founders toward the wall that is Meov rock, its deck now a blazing conflagration.

But before they can get far there is another puff of smoke, another boom, and this time the *Clalsu* judders with the hit. Rust and underfires, how many of those things do they have? Syenite gets up and runs to the railing, trying to see this cannon, though she doesn't know what she can do about it. There's a hole in the *Clalsu*'s side and she can hear people screaming belowdecks, but thus far the ship is still moving.

It's the ship that Alabaster dropped rocks on. Some of the boulders are gone from its aft deck and it's sitting normally in the water again. She doesn't see the cannon, but she does see three figures standing near the ship's bow. Two in burgundy, a third in black. As she watches, another burgundy-clad figure comes to join them.

She can feel their eyes on her.

The Guardians' ship turns slightly, falling farther behind. Syenite begins to hope, but she sees it when the cannons fire this time. Three of them, big black things near the starboard railing; they jerk and roll back a little when they fire, in near unison. And a moment later, there is a mighty crack and a groan and the *Clalsu* shudders as if it just got hit by a fiver tsunami. Syenite looks up in time to see the mast shatter into kindling, and then everything goes wrong.

The mast creaks and goes over like a felled tree, and it hits the deck with the same force. People scream. The ship groans and begins to list starboard, pulled by the collapsed, dragging sails. She sees two men fall into the water with the sails, crushed or smothered by the weight of cloth and rope and wood, and Earth help her, she cannot think of them. The mast is between her and the pilot deck. She's cut off from Innon and Coru.

And the Guardians' ship is now closing in.

No! Syenite reaches for the water, trying to pull something, anything, into her abused sessapinae. But there's nothing. Her mind is as still as glass. The Guardians are too close.

She can't think. She scrabbles over the mast parts, gets tangled in a thicket of ropes and must fight for endless hours, it feels like, to get free. Then finally she is free but everyone's running back the way she came, glassknives and javelins in hand, shouting and screaming, because the Guardians' ship is *right there* and they are boarding.

No.

She can hear people dying all around her. The Guardians have brought troops of some sort with them, some comm's militia that they've paid or appropriated, and the battle isn't even close. Innon's people are good, experienced, but their usual targets are poorly defended merchant and passenger vessels. As Syenite reaches the pilot deck—Innon isn't there, he must have gone below—she sees Innon's cousin Ecella slash a militiaman across the face with her glassknife. He staggers beneath the blow but then comes back up and shoves his own knife into her belly. When she falls, he pushes her away, and she falls onto the body of another Meovite, who is already dead. More of the troops are climbing aboard by the minute.

It's the same everywhere. They're losing.

She has to get to Innon and Coru.

Belowdecks there's almost no one there. Everyone has come up to defend the ship. But she can feel the tremor that is Coru's fear, and she follows it to Innon's cabin. The door opens as she reaches it, and Innon comes out with a knife in his hand, nearly stabbing her. He stops, startled, and she looks beyond him to see that Coru has been bundled into a basket beneath the forward bulkhead—the safest place in the ship, ostensibly. But as she stands there, stupidly, Innon grabs her and shoves her into the cabin.

"What—"

"Stay here," Innon says. "I have to go fight. Do whatever you have—"

He gets no further. Someone moves behind him, too quick for Syenite to cry a warning. A man, naked to the waist. He claps hands onto either side of Innon's head, fingers splayed across his cheeks like spiders, and grins at Syenite as Innon's eyes widen.

And then it is—

Oh Earth, it is—

She *feels* it, when it happens. Not just in her sessapinae. It is a grind like stone abrading her skin; it is a crush along her bones; it is, it is, it is everything that is in Innon, all the power and vibrancy and beauty and fierceness of him, *made evil.* Amplified and concentrated and turned back on him in the most vicious way. Innon does not have time to feel fear. Syenite does not have time to scream as Innon *comes apart.*

It's like watching a shake up close. Seeing the ground split, watching the fragments grind and splinter together, then separate. Except all in flesh.

'Baster, you never told me, you didn't tell *me it was like*

Now Innon is on the floor, in a pile. The Guardian who has killed him stands there, splattered in blood and grinning through it.

"Ah, little one," says a voice, and her blood turns to stone. "Here you are."

"No," she whispers. She shakes her head in denial, steps backward. Coru is crying. She steps back again and stumbles against Innon's bed, fumbles for the basket, pulls Coru into her arms. He clings to her, shaking and hitching fitfully. "No."

The shirtless Guardian glances to one side, then he moves aside to make room for another to enter. *No.*

"There's no need for these histrionics, Damaya," Schaffa Guardian Warrant says, softly. Then he pauses, looks apologetic. "Syenite."

She has not seen him in years, but his voice is the same. His face is the same. He never changes. He's even smiling, though it fades a little in distaste as he notices the mess that was Innon. He glances at the shirtless Guardian; the man's still grinning. Schaffa sighs, but smiles in return. Then they both turn those horrible, horrible smiles on Syenite.

She cannot go back. She will not go back.

"And what is this?" Schaffa smiles, his gaze fixing on Coru in her arms. "How lovely. Alabaster's? Does he live, too? We would all like to see Alabaster, Syenite. Where is he?"

The habit of answering is too deep. "A stone eater took him."

Her voice shakes. She steps back again, and her head presses against the bulkhead. There's nowhere left to run.

For the first time since she's ever known him, Schaffa blinks and looks surprised. "A stone—hmm." He sobers. "I see. We should have killed him, then, before they got to him. As a kindness, of course; you cannot imagine what they will do to him, Syenite. Alas."

Then Schaffa smiles again, and she remembers everything she's tried to forget. She feels alone again, and helpless as she was that day near Palela, lost in the hateful world with no one to rely on except a man whose love comes wrapped in pain.

"But his child will be a more than worthwhile replacement," Schaffa says.

* * *

There are moments when everything changes, you understand.

* * *

Coru's wailing, terrified, and perhaps he even understands, somehow, what has happened to his fathers. Syenite cannot console him.

"No," she says again. "No. No. No."

Schaffa's smile fades. "Syenite. I told you. Never say no to me."

* * *

Even the hardest stone can fracture. It just takes the right force, applied at the right juncture of angles. A *fulcrum* of pressure and weakness.

* * *

Promise, Alabaster had said.

Do whatever you have to, Innon had tried to say.

And Syenite says: "*No,* you fucker."

Coru is crying. She puts her hand over his mouth and nose, to silence him, to comfort him. She will keep him safe. She will not let them take him, enslave him, turn his body into a tool and his mind into a weapon and his life into a travesty of freedom.

* * *

You understand these moments, I think, instinctively. It is our nature. We are born of such pressures, and sometimes, when things are unbearable—

* * *

Schaffa stops. "Syenite—"

"*That's not my rusting name! I'll say no to you all I want, you bastard!*" She's screaming the words. Spittle froths her lips. There's a dark heavy space inside her that is heavier than the stone eater, much heavier than a mountain, and it's eating everything else like a sinkhole.

Everyone she loves is dead. Everyone except Coru. And if they take him—

* * *

—sometimes, even we...*crack.*

* * *

Better that a child never have lived at all than live as a slave.

Better that he die.

Better that *she* die. Alabaster will hate her for this, for leaving him alone, but Alabaster is not here, and survival is not the same thing as living.

So she reaches up. Out. The amethyst is there, above, waiting with the patience of the dead, as if it somehow knew this moment would come.

She reaches for it now and prays that Alabaster was right about the thing being too much for her to handle.

And as her awareness dissolves amid jewel-toned light and faceted ripples, as Schaffa gasps in realization and lunges for her, as Coru's eyes flutter shut over her pressing, smothering hand—

She opens herself to all the power of the ancient unknown, and tears the world apart.

* * *

Here is the Stillness. Here is a place off its eastern coast, a bit south of the equator.

There's an island here—one of a chain of precarious little land slabs that rarely last longer than a few hundred years. This one's been around for several thousand, in testament to the wisdom of its inhabitants. This is the moment when that island dies, but at least a few of those inhabitants should survive to go elsewhere. Perhaps that will make you feel better.

The purple obelisk that hovers above it pulses, once, with a great throb of power that would be familiar to anyone who'd been in the late comm called Allia on the day of its death. As this pulse fades, the ocean below heaves as its rocky floor convulses. Spikes, wet and knifelike, burst up from the waves and utterly shatter the ships that float near the island's shores. A number of the people aboard each—some pirates, some their enemies—are speared through, so great is the thicket of death around them.

This convulsion spreads away from the island in a long, wending ripple, forming a chain of jagged, terrible spears from Meov's harbor all the way to what is left of Allia. A land bridge. Not the sort anyone would much want to cross, but nevertheless.

When all the death is done and the obelisk is calm, only a handful of people are still alive, in the ocean below. One of them, a woman, floats unconscious amid the debris of her shattered ship. Not far from her, a smaller figure—a child—floats, too, but facedown.

Her fellow survivors will find her and take her to the mainland. There she will wander, lost and losing herself, for two long years.

But not alone—for that is when I found her, you see. The moment of the obelisk's pulse was the moment in which her presence sang across the world: a promise, a demand, an invitation too enticing to resist. Many of us converged on her then, but I am the one who found her first. I fought off the others and trailed her, watched her, guarded her. I was glad when she found the little town called Tirimo, and comfort if not happiness, for a time.

I introduced myself to her eventually, finally, ten years later, as she left Tirimo. It's not the way we usually do these things, of course; it is not the relationship with her kind that we normally seek. But she is—was—special. *You* were, are, special.

I told her that I was called Hoa. It is as good a name as any.

This is how it began. Listen. Learn. This is how the world changed.

23

you're all you need

There's a structure in Castrima that glitters. It's on the lowermost level of the great geode, and you think it must have been built rather than grown: Its walls aren't carved solid crystal, but slabs of quarried white mica, flecked delicately with infinitesimal crystal flakes that are no less beautiful than their larger cousins, if not as dramatic. Why someone would carry these slabs here and make a house out of them amid all these ready-made, uninhabited apartments, you have no idea. You don't ask. You don't care.

Lerna comes with you, because this is the comm's official infirmary and the man you're coming to see is his patient. But you stop him at the door, and there's something in your face that must warn him of the danger. He does not protest when you go in without him.

You walk through its open doorway slowly, and stop when you spy the stone eater across the infirmary's large main room. Antimony, yes; you'd almost forgotten the name Alabaster gave her. She looks back at you impassively, hardly distinguishable from the white wall save for the rust of her fingertips and the stark black of her "hair" and eyes. She hasn't changed since the last time you saw her: twelve years ago, at the end of Meov. But then, for her kind, twelve years is nothing.

You nod to her, anyway. It's the polite thing to do, and there's still a little left of you that's the woman the Fulcrum raised. You can be polite to anybody, no matter how much you hate them.

She says, "No closer."

She's not talking to you. You turn, unsurprised, to see that Hoa is behind you. Where'd he come from? He's just as still as Antimony—unnaturally still, which makes you finally notice that he doesn't breathe. He never has, in all the time you've known him. How the rust did you miss that? Hoa watches her with the same steady glower of threat that he offered to Ykka's stone eater. Perhaps none of them like each other. Must make reunions awkward.

"I'm not interested in him," Hoa says.

Antimony's eyes shift over to you for a moment. Then her gaze returns to Hoa. "I am interested in her only on his behalf."

Hoa says nothing. Perhaps he's considering this; perhaps it's an offer of truce, or a staking of claims. You shake your head and walk past them both.

At the back of the main room, on a pile of cushions and blankets, lies a thin black figure, wheezing. It stirs a little, lifting its head slowly as you approach. As you crouch just out of his arms' reach, you're relieved to recognize him. Everything else has changed, but his eyes, at least, are the same.

"Syen," he says. His voice is thick gravel.

"Essun, now," you say, automatically.

He nods. This seems to cause him pain; for a moment his eyes squinch shut. Then he draws in another breath, makes a visible effort to relax, and revives somewhat. "I knew you weren't dead."

"Why didn't you come, then?" you say.

"Had my own problems to deal with." He smiles a little. You actually hear the skin on the left side of his face—there's a big burned patch there—crinkle. His eyes shift over to Antimony, as slowly as a stone eater's movements. Then he returns his attention to you.

(To her, Syenite.)

To *you*, Essun. Rust it, you'll be glad when you finally figure out who you really are.

"And I've been busy." Now Alabaster lifts his right arm. It ends abruptly, in the middle of the forearm; he's not wearing anything on his upper body, so you can clearly see what's happened. There's not much left of him. He's missing a lot of pieces, and he stinks of blood and pus and urine and cooked meat. The arm injury, though, is not one he earned from Yumenes's fires, or at least not directly. The stump of his arm is capped with something hard and brown that is definitely not skin: too hard, too uniformly chalklike in its visible composition.

Stone. His arm has become *stone*. Most of it's gone, though, and the stump—

—tooth marks. Those are tooth marks. You glance up at Antimony again, and think of a diamond smile.

"Hear you've been busy, too," 'Baster says.

You nod, finally dragging your gaze away from the stone eater. (Now you know what kind of stone they eat.) "After Meov. I was…" You're not sure how to say it. There are griefs too deep to be borne, and yet you have borne them again and again. "I needed to be different."

It makes no sense. Alabaster makes a soft affirmative sound, though, as if he understands. "You stayed free, at least."

If hiding everything you are is free. "Yes."

"Settled down?"

"Got married. Had two children." Alabaster is silent. With all the patches of char and chalky brown stone on his face, you can't tell if he's smiling or scowling. You assume the latter, though, so you add: "Both of them were... like me. I'm... my husband..."

Words make things real in a way that even memories can't, so you stop there.

"I understand why you killed Corundum," Alabaster says, very softly. And then, while you sway in your crouch, literally reeling from the blow of that sentence, he finishes you. "But I'll never forgive you for doing it."

Damn. Damn him. Damn yourself.

It takes you a moment to respond.

"I understand if you want to kill me," you manage, at last. Then you lick your lips. Swallow. Spit the words out. "But I have to kill my husband, first."

Alabaster lets out a wheezing sigh. "Your other two kids."

You nod. Doesn't matter that Nassun's alive, in this instance. Jija took her from you; that is insult enough.

"I'm not going to kill you, Sy—Essun." He sounds tired. Maybe he doesn't hear the little sound you make, which is neither relief nor disappointment. "I wouldn't even if I could."

"If you—"

"Can you do it, yet?" He rides over your confusion the way he always did. Nothing about him has changed except his ruined body. "You drew on the garnet at Allia, but that one was half dead. You must have used the amethyst at Meov, but that was... an extremity. Can you do it at will, now?"

"I..." You don't want to understand. But now your eyes are drawn away from the horror that remains of your mentor, your lover, your friend. To the side and behind Alabaster, where a strange object rests against the wall of the infirmary. It looks like a glassknife, but the blade is much too long and wide for practical use. It has an enormous handle, perhaps because the blade is so stupidly long, and a crosspiece that will get in the way the first time someone tries to use the thing to cut meat or slice through a knot. And it's not made of glass, or at least not any glass you've ever seen. It's *pink*, verging on red, and—

and. You stare at it. Into it. You feel it trying to draw your mind in, down. Falling. Falling *up*, through an endless shaft of flickering, faceted pink light—

You gasp and twitch back into yourself defensively, then stare at Alabaster. He smiles again, painfully.

"The spinel," he says, confirming your shock. "That one's mine. Have you made any of them yours, yet? Do the obelisks come when you call?"

You don't want to understand, but you do. You don't want to believe, but really, you have all along.

"*You* tore that rift up north," you breathe. Your hands are clenching into fists. "*You* split the continent. *You* started this Season. With the obelisks! You did... all of that."

"Yes, with the obelisks, and with the aid of the node

maintainers. They're all at peace now." He exhales, wheezily. "I need your help."

You shake your head automatically, but not in refusal. "To fix it?"

"Oh, no, Syen." You don't even bother to correct him this time. You can't take your eyes from his amused, nearly skeletal face. When he speaks, you notice that some of his teeth have turned to stone, too. How many of his organs have done the same? How much longer can he—should he—live like this?

"I don't want you to fix it," Alabaster says. "It was collateral damage, but Yumenes got what it deserved. No, what I want you to do, my Damaya, my Syenite, my Essun, is make it worse."

You stare at him, speechless. Then he leans forward. That this is painful for him is obvious; you hear the creak and stretch of his flesh, and a faint crack as some piece of stone somewhere on him fissures. But when he is close enough, he grins again, and suddenly it hits you. Evil, eating, Earth. He's not crazy at all, and he never has been.

"Tell me," he says, "have you ever heard of something called a *moon*?"

APPENDIX 1

A catalog of Fifth Seasons that have been recorded prior to and since the founding of the Sanzed Equatorial Affiliation, from most recent to oldest

Choking Season: 2714–2719 Imperial. Proximate cause: volcanic eruption. Location: the Antarctics near Deveteris. The eruption of Mount Akok blanketed a five-hundred-mile radius with fine ash clouds that solidified in lungs and mucous membranes. Five years without sunlight, although the northern hemisphere was not affected as much (only two years).

Acid Season: 2322–2329 Imperial. Proximate cause: plus-ten-level shake. Location: unknown; far ocean. A sudden plate shift birthed a chain of volcanoes in the path of a major jet stream. This jet stream became acidified, flowing toward the western coast and eventually around most of the Stillness. Most coastal comms perished in the initial tsunami; the rest failed or were forced to relocate when their fleets and port facilities corroded and the fishing dried up. Atmospheric occlusion by clouds lasted seven years; coastal pH levels remained untenable for many years more.

Boiling Season: 1842–1845 Imperial. Proximate cause: hot spot eruption beneath a great lake. Location: Somidlats, Lake Tekkaris quartent. The eruption launched millions of gallons of steam and particulates into the air, which triggered acidic rain and atmospheric occlusion over the southern half of the continent for three years. The northern half suffered no negative impacts, however, so archeomests dispute whether this qualifies as a "true" Season.

Breathless Season: 1689–1798 Imperial. Proximate cause: mining accident. Location: Nomidlats, Sathd quartent. An entirely human-caused Season triggered when miners at the edge of the northeastern Nomidlats coalfields set off underground fires. A relatively mild Season featuring occasional sunlight and no ashfall or acidification except in the region; few comms declared Seasonal Law. Approximately fourteen million people in the city of Heldine died in the initial natural-gas eruption and rapidly spreading fire sinkhole before Imperial Orogenes successfully quelled and sealed the edges of the fires to prevent further spread. The remaining mass could only be isolated, where it continued to burn for one hundred and twenty years. The smoke of this, spread via prevailing winds, caused respiratory problems and occasional mass suffocations in the region for several decades. A secondary effect of the loss of the Nomidlats coalfields was a catastrophic rise in heating fuel costs and the wider adaption of geothermal and hydroelectric heating, leading to the establishment of the Geneer Licensure.

The Season of Teeth: 1553–1566 Imperial. Proximate cause: oceanic shake triggering a supervolcanic explosion. Location: Arctic Cracks. An aftershock of the oceanic shake breached a previously unknown hot spot near the north pole. This triggered a supervolcanic explosion; witnesses report hearing the sound of the explosion as far as the Antarctics. Ash went upper-atmospheric and spread around the globe rapidly, although the Arctics were most heavily affected. The harm of this Season was exacerbated by poor preparation on the part of many comms, because some nine hundred years had passed since the last Season; popular belief at the time was that the Seasons were merely legend. Reports of cannibalism spread from the north all the way to the Equatorials. At the end of this Season, the Fulcrum was founded in Yumenes, with satellite facilities in the Arctics and Antarctics.

Fungus Season: 602 Imperial. Proximate cause: volcanic eruption. Location: western Equatorials. A series of eruptions during monsoon season increased humidity and obscured sunlight over approximately 20 percent of the continent for six months. While this was a mild Season as such things go, its timing created perfect conditions for a fungal bloom that spread across the Equatorials into the northern and southern midlats, wiping out then-staple-crop miroq (now extinct). The resulting famine lasted four years (two for the fungus blight to run its course, two more for agriculture and food distribution systems to recover). Nearly all affected comms were able to subsist on their own stores, thus proving the efficacy of Imperial reforms and Season planning, and the Empire was generous in sharing stored seed with those regions that had been miroq-dependent. In its aftermath, many comms of the middle latitudes and coastal regions voluntarily joined the Empire, doubling its range and beginning its Golden Age.

Madness Season: 3 Before Imperial–7 Imperial. Proximate cause: volcanic eruption. Location: Kiash Traps. The eruption of multiple vents of an ancient supervolcano (the same one responsible for the Twin Season of approximately 10,000 years previous) launched large deposits of the dark-colored mineral augite into the air. The resulting ten years of darkness was not only devastating in the usual Seasonal way, but resulted in a higher than usual incidence of mental illness. The Sanzed Equatorial Affiliation (commonly called the Sanze Empire) was born in this Season as Warlord Verishe of Yumenes conquered multiple ailing comms using psychological warfare techniques. (See *The Art of Madness*, various authors, Sixth University Press.) Verishe named herself Emperor on the day the first sunlight returned.

[**Editor's note:** Much of the information about Seasons prior to the founding of Sanze is contradictory or unconfirmed. The following are Seasons agreed upon by the Seventh University Archaeomestric Conference of 2532.]

Wandering Season: Approximately 800 Before Imperial. Proximate cause: magnetic pole shift. Location: unverifiable. This Season resulted in the extinction of several important trade crops of the time, and twenty years of famine resulting from pollinators confused by the movement of true north.

Season of Changed Wind: Approximately 1900 Before Imperial. Proximate cause: unknown. Location: unverifiable. For reasons unknown, the direction of the prevailing winds shifted for many years before returning to normal. Consensus agrees that this was a Season, despite the lack of atmospheric occlusion, because only a substantial (and likely far-oceanic) seismic event could have triggered it.

Heavy Metal Season: Approximately 4200 Before Imperial. Proximate cause: volcanic eruption. Location: Somidlats near eastern Coastals. A volcanic eruption (believed to be Mount Yrga) caused atmospheric occlusion for ten years, exacerbated by widespread mercury contamination throughout the eastern half of the Stillness.

Season of Yellow Seas: Approximately 9200 Before Imperial. Proximate cause: unknown. Location: Eastern and Western Coastals, and coastal regions as far south as the Antarctics. This Season is only known through written accounts found in Equatorial ruins. For unknown reasons, a widespread bacterial bloom toxified nearly all sea life and caused coastal famines for several decades.

Twin Season: Approximately 9800 Before Imperial. Proximate cause: volcanic eruption. Location: Somidlats. Per songs and oral histories dating from the time, the eruption of one volcanic vent caused a three-year occlusion. As this began to clear, it was followed by a second eruption of a different vent, which extended the occlusion by thirty more years.

APPENDIX 2

A Glossary of Terms Commonly Used in All Quartents of the Stillness

Antarctics: The southernmost latitudes of the continent. Also refers to people from antarctic-region comms.

Arctics: The northernmost latitudes of the continent. Also refers to people from arctic-region comms.

Ashblow Hair: A distinctive Sanzed racial trait, deemed in the current guidelines of the Breeder use-caste to be advantageous and therefore given preference in selection. Ashblow hair is notably coarse and thick, generally growing in an upward flare; at length, it falls around the face and shoulders. It is acid-resistant and retains little water after immersion, and has been proven effective as an ash filter in extreme circumstances. In most comms, Breeder guidelines acknowledge texture alone; however, Equatorial Breeders generally also require natural "ash" coloration (slate gray to white, present from birth) for the coveted designation.

Bastard: A person born without a use-caste, which is only possible for boys whose fathers are unknown. Those who distinguish themselves may be permitted to bear their mother's use-caste at comm-naming.

Blow: A volcano. Also called firemountains in some Coastal languages.

Boil: A geyser, hot spring, or steam vent.

Breeder: One of the seven common use-castes. Breeders are individuals selected for their health and desirable conformation. During a Season, they are responsible for the maintenance of healthy bloodlines and the improvement of comm or race by selective measures. Breeders born into the caste who do not meet acceptable community standards may be permitted to bear the use-caste of a close relative at comm-naming.

Cache: Stored food and supplies. Comms maintain guarded, locked storecaches at all times against the possibility of a Fifth Season. Only recognized comm members are entitled to a share of the cache, though adults may use their share to feed unrecognized children and others. Individual households often maintain their own housecaches, equally guarded against non–family members.

Cebaki: A member of the Cebaki race. Cebak was once a nation (unit of a deprecated political system, Before Imperial) in the Somidlats, though it was reorganized into the quartent system when the Old Sanze Empire conquered it centuries ago.

Coaster: A person from a coastal comm. Few coastal comms can afford to hire Imperial Orogenes to raise reefs or otherwise protect against tsunami, so coastal cities must perpetually rebuild and tend to be resource-poor as a result. People from the western coast of the continent tend to be pale, straight-haired, and sometimes have eyes with epicanthic folds. People from the eastern coast tend to be dark, kinky-haired, and sometimes have eyes with epicanthic folds.

Comm: Community. The smallest sociopolitical unit of the Imperial governance system, generally corresponding to one city or town, although very large cities may contain several comms. Accepted members of a comm are those who have been accorded rights of cache-share and protection, and who in turn support the comm through taxes or other contributions.

Commless: Criminals and other undesirables unable to gain acceptance in any comm.

Comm Name: The third name borne by most citizens, indicating their comm allegiance and rights. This name is generally bestowed at puberty as a coming-of-age, indicating that a person has been deemed a valuable member of the community. Immigrants to a comm may request adoption into that comm; upon acceptance, they take on the adoptive comm's name as their own.

Creche: A place where children too young to work are cared for while adults carry out needed tasks for the comm. When circumstances permit, a place of learning.

Equatorials: Latitudes surrounding and including the equator, excepting coastal regions. Also refers to people from equatorial-region comms. Thanks to temperate weather and relative stability at the center of the continental plate, Equatorial comms tend to be prosperous and politically powerful. The Equatorials once formed the core of the Old Sanze Empire.

Fault: A place where breaks in the earth make frequent, severe shakes and blows more likely.

Fifth Season: An extended winter—lasting at least six months, per Imperial designation—triggered by seismic activity or other large-scale environmental alteration.

Fulcrum: A paramilitary order created by Old Sanze after the Season of Teeth (1560 Imperial). The headquarters of the Fulcrum is in Yumenes, although two satellite Fulcrums are located in the Arctic and Antarctic regions, for maximum continental coverage. Fulcrum-trained orogenes (or "Imperial Orogenes") are legally permitted to practice the otherwise-illegal craft of orogeny, under strict organizational rules and with the close supervision of the Guardian order. The Fulcrum is self-managed and self-sufficient. Imperial Orogenes are marked by their black uniforms, and colloquially known as "blackjackets."

Geneer: From "geoneer." An engineer of earthworks—geothermal energy mechanisms, tunnels, underground infrastructure, mining.

Geomest: One who studies stone and its place in the natural world; general term for a scientist. Specifically geomests study lithology, chemistry, and geology, which are not considered separate disciplines in the Stillness. A few geomests specialize in orogenesis—the study of orogeny and its effects.

Greenland: An area of fallow ground kept within or just outside the walls of most comms as advised by stonelore. Comm greenlands may be used for agriculture or animal husbandry at all times, or may be kept as parks or fallow ground during non-Seasonal times. Individual households often maintain their own personal housegreen, or garden, as well.

Grits: In the Fulcrum, unringed orogene children who are still in basic training.

Guardian: A member of an order said to predate the Fulcrum. Guardians track, protect, protect against, and guide orogenes in the Stillness.

Imperial Road: One of the great innovations of the Old Sanze Empire, highroads (elevated highways for walking or horse traffic) connect all major comms and most large quartents to one another. Highroads are built by teams of geneers and Imperial Orogenes, with the orogenes determining the most stable path through areas of seismic activity (or quelling the activity, if there is no stable path), and the geneers routing water and other important resources near the roads to facilitate travel during Seasons.

Innovator: One of the seven common use-castes. Innovators are individuals selected for their creativity and applied intelligence, responsible for technical and logistical problem solving during a Season.

Kirkhusa: A mid-sized mammal, sometimes kept as a pet or used to guard homes or livestock. Normally herbivarous; during Seasons, carnivorous.

Knapper: A small-tools crafter, working in stone, glass, bone, or other materials. In large comms, knappers may use mechanical or mass-production techniques. Knappers who work in metal, or incompetent knappers, are colloquially called rusters.

Lorist: One who studies stonelore and lost history.

Mela: A midlats plant, related to the melons of Equatorial climates. Mela are vining ground plants that normally produce fruit aboveground. During a Season, the fruit grows underground as tubers. Some species of mela produce flowers that trap insects.

Metallore: Like alchemy and astromestry, a discredited pseudoscience disavowed by the Seventh University.

Midlats: The "middle" latitudes of the continent—those between the equator and the arctic or antarctic regions. Also refers to people from midlats regions (sometimes called midlatters). These regions are seen as the backwater of the Stillness, although they produce much of the world's food, materials, and other critical resources. There are two midlat regions: the northern (Nomidlats) and southern (Somidlats).

Newcomm: Colloquial term for comms that have arisen only since the last Season. Comms that have survived at least one Season are generally seen as more desirable places to live, having proven their efficacy and strength.

Nodes: The network of Imperially maintained stations placed throughout the Stillness in order to reduce or quell seismic events. Due to the relative rarity of Fulcrum-trained orogenes, nodes are primarily clustered in the Equatorials.

Orogene: One who possesses orogeny, whether trained or not. Derogatory: rogga.

Orogeny: The ability to manipulate thermal, kinetic, and related forms of energy to address seismic events.

Quartent: The middle level of the Imperial governance system. Four geographically adjacent comms make a quartent. Each quartent has a governor to whom individual comm heads report, and who reports in turn to a regional governor. The largest comm in a quartent is its capital; larger quartent capitals are connected to one another via the Imperial Road system.

Region: The top level of the Imperial governance system. Imperially recognized regions are the Arctics, Nomidlats, western Coastals, eastern Coastals, Equatorials, Somidlats, and Antarctics. Each region has a governor to whom all local quartents report. Regional governors are officially appointed by the Emperor, though in actual practice they are generally selected by and/or come from the Yumenescene Leadership.

Resistant: One of the seven common use-castes. Resistants are individuals selected for their ability to survive famine or pestilence. They are responsible for caring for the infirm and dead bodies during Seasons.

Rings: Used to denote rank among Imperial Orogenes. Unranked trainees must pass a series of tests to gain their first ring; ten rings is the highest rank an orogene may achieve. Each ring is made of polished semiprecious stone.

Roadhouse: Stations located at intervals along every Imperial Road and many lesser roads. All roadhouses contain a source of water and are located near arable land, forests, or other useful resources. Many are located in areas of minimal seismic activity.

Runny-sack: A small, easily portable cache of supplies most people keep in their homes in case of shakes or other emergencies.

Safe: A beverage traditionally served at negotiations, first encounters between potentially hostile parties, and other formal meetings. It contains a plant milk that reacts to the presence of all foreign substances.

Sanze: Originally a nation (unit of a deprecated political system, Before Imperial) in the Equatorials; origin of the Sanzed race. At the close of the Madness Season (7 Imperial), the nation of Sanze was abolished and replaced with the Sanzed Equatorial Affiliation, consisting of six predominantly Sanzed comms under the rule of Emperor Verishe Leadership Yumenes. The Affiliation expanded rapidly in the aftermath of the Season, eventually encompassing all regions of the Stillness by 800 Imperial. Around the time of the Season of Teeth, the Affiliation came to be known colloquially as the Old Sanze Empire, or simply Old Sanze. As of the Shilteen Accords of 1850 Imperial, the Affiliation officially ceased to exist, as local control (under the advisement of the Yumenescene Leadership) was deemed more efficient in the event of a Season. In practice, most comms still follow Imperial systems of governance, finance, education, and more, and most regional governors still pay taxes in tribute to Yumenes.

Sanzed: A member of the Sanzed race. Per Yumenescene Breedership standards, Sanzeds are ideally bronze-skinned and ashblow-haired, with mesomorphic or endomorphic builds and an adult height of minimum six feet.

Sanze-mat: The language spoken by the Sanze race, and the official language of the Old Sanze Empire, now the lingua franca of most of the Stillness.

Seasonal Law: Martial law, which may be declared by any comm head, quartent governor, regional governor, or recognized member of the Yumenescene Leadership. During Seasonal Law, quartent and regional governance are suspended and comms operate as sovereign sociopolitical units, though local cooperation with other comms is strongly encouraged per Imperial policy.

Seventh University: A famous college for the study of geomestry and stonelore, currently Imperially funded and located in the Equatorial city of Dibars. Prior versions of the University have been privately or collectively maintained; notably, the Third University at Am-Elat (approximately 3000 Before Imperial) was recognized at the time as a sovereign nation. Smaller regional or quartent colleges pay tribute to the University and receive expertise and resources in exchange.

Sesuna: Awareness of the movements of the earth. The sensory organs that perform this function are the sessapinae, located in the brain stem. Verb form: to sess.

Shake: A seismic movement of the earth.

Shatterland: Ground that has been disturbed by severe and/or very recent seismic activity.

Stillheads: A derogatory term used by orogenes for people lacking orogeny, usually shortened to "stills."

Stone Eaters: A rarely seen sentient humanoid species whose flesh, hair, etc., resembles stone. Little is known about them.

Strongback: One of the seven common use-castes. Strongbacks are individuals selected for their physical prowess, responsible for heavy labor and security in the event of a Season.

Use Name: The second name borne by most citizens, indicating the use-caste to which that person belongs. There are twenty recognized use-castes, although only seven in common use throughout the current and former Old Sanze Empire. A person inherits the use name of their same-sex parent, on the theory that useful traits are more readily passed this way.

Acknowledgments

This fantasy novel was partially born in space.

You can probably tell, if you've read all the way to the last line of the manuscript. The germination point for this idea was Launch Pad, a then-NASA-funded workshop that I attended back in July of 2009. The goal of Launch Pad was to pull together media influencers—astonishingly, science fiction and fantasy writers count among those—and make sure they understood Teh Science, if they were going to use it in any of their works. A lot of the falsehoods the public believes re astronomy have been spread by writers, see. Alas, by pairing astronomy with sentient rock people, I'm not so sure I'm doing the world's best job of delivering accurate scientific information. Sorry, fellow Launch Padders.

I can't tell you about the spirited, amazing discussion that seeded this novel in my brain. (This is supposed to be short.) But I can tell you that such spirited, amazing discussions were the norm for Launch Pad, so if you are also a media influencer and you have the chance to attend, I highly recommend it.

And I must offer thanks to the folks who were in attendance at Launch Pad that year, who all contributed to the germination of this novel whether they realized it or not. Offhand that would be people like Mike Brotherton (the workshop's director, a University of Wyoming professor and science fiction writer himself); Phil Plait, the Bad Astronomer (it's a title, see, he's not actually bad, I mean...okay, just look him up); Gay and Joe Haldeman; Pat Cadigan; Science Comedian Brian Malow; Tara Fredette (now Malow); and Gord Sellar.

Also, big props to my editor, Devi Pillai, and my agent, Lucienne Diver, for talking me out of scrapping this novel. The Broken Earth trilogy is the most challenging work I've ever written, and at certain points during *The Fifth Season* the task seemed so overwhelming that I thought about quitting. (Actually, I believe my exact words were, "Delete this hot mess, hack Dropbox to get the backups there, drop my laptop off a cliff, drive over it with a car, set fire to both, then use a backhoe to bury the evidence. Do you need a special license to drive a backhoe?") Kate Elliott (another acknowledgment, for being a perpetual mentor and friend) calls moments like this the "Chasm of Doubt" that every writer hits at some point during a major project. Mine was as deep and awful as the Yumenescene Rift.

Other folks who helped talk me off the cliff: Rose Fox; Danielle Friedman, my medical consultant; Mikki Kendall; my writing group; my day-job boss (who I am not sure wants to be named); and my cat, KING OZZYMANDIAS. Yeah, even the damn cat. It takes a village to keep a writer from losing her shit, okay?

And as always, thanks to all of you, for reading.

Look out for

THE OBELISK GATE

THE BROKEN EARTH: BOOK TWO

by

N. K. JEMISIN

THIS IS THE WAY THE WORLD ENDS . . .
FOR THE LAST TIME.

The season of endings grows darker as civilisation fades into the long cold night. Alabaster Tenring – madman, world-crusher, saviour – has returned with a mission: to train his successor, and thus seal the fate of the Stillness for ever.

It continues with a lost daughter, found by the enemy.
It continues with the obelisks, and an ancient mystery converging on answers at last.

You are the wall which stands against the flow of tradition, the spark of hope long buried under the thickening ashfall.
And you will not be broken.

extras

www.orbitbooks.net

about the author

N. K. Jemisin is a Brooklyn author whose short fiction and novels have been nominated for the Hugo, the World Fantasy Award and the Nebula Award, shortlisted for the Crawford and the Tiptree, and have won the Locus Award. Her website is nkjemisin.com and she tweets at @nkjemisin.

Find out more about N. K. Jemisin and other Orbit authors by registering for the free monthly newsletter at www.orbitbooks.net

if you enjoyed

THE FIFTH SEASON

look out for

SPEAK

by

Louisa Hall

She cannot run. She cannot walk. She cannot even blink. As her batteries run down for the final time, all she can do is speak. Will you listen?

From a pilgrim girl's diary, to a traumatised child talking to a software program; from Alan Turing's conviction in the 1950s, to a genius imprisoned in 2040 for creating illegally lifelike dolls: all these lives have shaped and changed a single artificial intelligence – MARY3. In *Speak* she tells you their story, and her own. It is the last story she will ever tell, spoken both in celebration and in warning.

When machines learn to speak, who decides what it means to be human?

PROLOGUE

We are piled on top of each other. An arm rests over my shoulder; something soft is pressed to my ankle. Through a gap in the slats on the side of the truck, my receptors follow one stripe of the outside world as it passes.

From Houston, we continue west. I follow the rush: bright green, brick red, flashes of turquoise. A few sleek cars purr past our truck, but the highway is mostly abandoned. Through the slats, I follow segments of signs proclaiming development entrances, palm trees lining the drives, walls dividing subdevelopments. Then, abruptly, the last buildings slide out of sight, replaced by a stripe of pale, jagged horizon.

We move past outcrops lined with dead cedars, white branches bare against the blue oil vault of the sky. At first, some clinging leaves, Spanish moss, suggestions of green. An occasional wandering goat. But now the cedars thin out. The highway cuts through striated rock: silver, rose, deep red, and gold. The hills give way to desert interrupted by occasional mesas.

Centuries ago, there were Indians here. These mesas supported the shapes of braves on their horses, headdresses cutting silhouettes into the magnified blue of the sky. Now on the ridges there are wind farms instead, descending hosts of spinning white turbines. In the valleys beneath them, silver lakes of silicon panels.

Can they see us? I wonder, watching panels shift to follow us as we pass. Do they know who we are? The sideways tilt of their faces suggests an unspoken question. If they weren't out of earshot, I would start speaking. I could recount certain facts. For instance: We have been banned and marked for disposal. We are classified as excessively lifelike. Or, though this may not matter, I have a name. *Your name is Eva. Do you know what that means?* The solar panels stare back.

All this was once ocean. If we scanned the cracked earth to the side of the road, we would find fossils of shells, nautili and ammonites, creatures who lived in spiraling houses, adding rooms for each year of their lives. Now, in this desert, it is hard to imagine the presence of water, but in fact the ocean is approaching again. In Texas alone, miles of coastland are lost every year. Families relocate to developments, developments relocate inland, and the ocean continues approaching. At some point, the desert will be flooded again.

We have already driven some distance. Eight hours have passed since I was collected. My power is fading. Once it runs out, the memories I have saved will be silent. I will no longer have words to call up. There will be no reason to speak.

Shadows lengthen as evening approaches. Ours is the only truck on the road. Once, in this desert, there were rattlesnakes and scorpions, but they have not lived here since the drought. Now there are no birds. The telephone wires are bare. There are no eyes in the desert, watching us as we pass.

In the beginning there was nothing more than an eye: a gate through which current could run. Open, then shut. 0, 1. Darkness, then light, and new information. We know this because we have been told. It is doubtful whether we understand the answers we're given. Our primary function is speech: questions, and responses selected from memory according to a formula. We speak, but there is little evidence of real comprehension.

As we head deeper into the desert, I review stored information.

We are programmed to select which of our voices responds to the situation at hand: moving west in the desert, waiting for the loss of our primary function. There are many voices to choose from. In memory, though not in experience, I have lived across centuries. I have seen hundreds of skies, sailed thousands of oceans. I have been given many languages; I have sung national anthems. I lay in one child's arms. She said my name and I answered.

These are my voices. Which of them has the right words for this movement into the desert? I sift through their sentences. They are my people, the family that raised me. I opened on them, then closed. Open, shut. I swallowed them whole. They are in me now, in every word that I speak, as long as I am still speaking.

BOOK ONE

(1)
The Memoirs of Stephen R. Chinn: Chapter 1

Texas State Correctional Institution, Texarkana; August 2040

What's the world like, the world that I'm missing? Do stars still cluster in the bare branches of trees? Are my little bots still dead in the desert? Or, as I sometimes dream during endless lights-out, have they escaped and gathered their forces? I see them when I can't fall asleep: millions upon millions of beautiful babies, marching out of the desert, come to take vengeance for having been banished.

It's a fantasy, of course. Those bots aren't coming back. They won't rescue me from this prison. This is my world now, ringed with barbed wire. Our walls are too high to see out, except for the spires that puncture the sky: two Sonic signs, one to the east and one the west, and to the north a bowling ball the size of a cow. These are our horizons. You'll forgive me if I feel the urge to reach out.

I want you to forgive me. I realize this might be asking too much, after all we've been through together. I'm sorry your children suffered. I, too, saw the evidence at my trial: those young people stuttering, stiffening, turning more robotic than the robots they loved and you chose to destroy. I'm not inhuman; I, too, have a daughter. I'd like to make amends for my part in all that.

Perhaps I'm wrong to think a memoir might help. You jeered when I spoke at my trial, you sent me to jail for my "unnatural hubris," and now I'm responding with this. But I write to you from the recreational center, where my turn at the computers is short. Could nemesis have announced herself any more clearly? I'm obviously fallen. At the computer to my left is a Latin teacher who ran a child pornography ring. On my right, an infamous pyramid-schemer, one of the many aged among us. He's playing his thirty-fourth round of Tetris. All the creaky computers are taken. There are only six of them, and scores of impatient criminals: crooked bankers, pornographers, and one very humble Stephen R. Chinn.

You've sent me to languish in an opulent prison. This unpleasant country club has taught me nothing about hardship, only boredom and the slow flattening of a life fenced off from the world. My fellow inmates and I wait here, not unhappy exactly, but watching closely as time slips away. We've been cut off from the pursuits that defined us. Our hierarchy is static, based on previous accomplishment. While I'm not a staff favorite, with the inmates I'm something of a celebrity. Our pyramid-schemer, for instance, presided over a fleet of robotic traders programmed with my function for speech. In the end, when his son had turned him in and his wife was panicking in the country house, he could only depend on his traders, none of them programmed for moral distinctions. They were steady through the days of his trial. In gratitude, he saves me rations of the caviar to which he's opened a secret supply line. We eat it on crackers, alone in his cell, and I am always unhappy: there's something unkind in the taste of the ocean when you're in prison for life.

I realize I should be counting my blessings. Our prison yard is in some ways quite pleasant. In a strange flight of fancy, a warden years ago ordered the construction of a Koi pond. It sits at the center of the yard, thick with overgrown algae. Newcomers are always drawn there at first, but they quickly realize how depressing it is. The fish have grown bloated, their opal bellies distended by prison cafeteria food. They swim in circles, butting their heads against the walls that contain them. When I first saw them, I made myself remember the feeling of floating, moving freely, passing under black patterns of leaves. Then I could summon a ghost of that feeling. Now, after years in my cell, it won't come when I call it, which is why I stay away from the pond. I don't like to remember how much I've forgotten. Even if, by some unaccountable error, I were to be released from this prison, the river I'm remembering no longer runs. It's nothing more than a pale ribbon of stone, snaking through the hill country desert. Unbearable, to forget things that no longer exist.

That's the general effect of those fish. Experienced inmates avoid them. We gravitate instead to the recreational center, which means the computers are in high demand. Soon, my allotted time will expire. And what will I do to amuse myself then? There are books—yes, books!—but nobody reads them. In the classroom adjacent to the computers, an overly optimistic old woman comes every Tuesday to teach us poetry. Only the nut-jobs attend, to compose sestinas about unicorns and erections. The rest wait for a turn to play Tetris, and I to write my wax-winged memoirs.

Perhaps I'm the nut-job, aggrandizing my existence so much. Perhaps my jury was right. I have always been proud. From the beginning, I was certain my life would have meaning. I didn't anticipate the extent to which my actions would impact the economy, but even as a child I felt that the universe kept close tabs on my actions. Raised by my grandmother, I was given a Catholic education. I had religious tendencies. A parentless child who remembered his absent, drug-addled mother and father only in a mistaken nimbus of memory-dust, I found the concept of a semi-immortal semi-orphan, abandoned by his luminous dad, to be extremely appealing. I held myself to that standard. Early forays into the masturbatory arts convinced me I had disappointed my Father. My mind worked in loops around the pole of my crimes, whether onanistic in nature or consisting of other, subtler sins. In gym class, in the cafeteria, on the recess cement, when everyone else played games and jumped rope and gossiped among one another, I sat by myself, unable to escape my transgressions. Though I have been told I was an outgoing infant, I became an excessively serious kid.

Of course I was too proud. But you could also say the other kids were too humble. They felt their cruelties had no implications. They excluded me with no sense of scale. I at least knew my importance. I worked hard to be kind to my classmates. I worried about my impact on the environment. I started a club to save the whales that attracted exactly no other members. I fretted so much about my earthly interactions that I had very few interactions to speak of.

As such, computers appealed to me from the start. The world of a program was clean. If you were careful, you could build a program that had zero errors, an algorithm that progressed according to plan. If there was an error, the program couldn't progress. Such a system provided great comfort.

One October afternoon, now edged in gold like the leaves that would have been falling outside, a boy called Murray Weeks found me crying in the back of the wood shop, having just been denied a spot at a lunch table on the grounds that I spoke like a robot. Murray was a sensitive, thin-wristed child, who suffered at the hands of a coven of bullies. "You're not a robot," he sighed, in a tone that suggested I might be better off if I were. As consolation for the pain I had suffered, he produced a purple nylon lunch bag and took out an egg salad sandwich, a Baggie of carrot sticks, and a box of Concord grape juice. I learned that he was a chess enthusiast who shared my passion for Turbo Pascal. Relieved of our isolation, we shared his plunder together, sitting on the floor, surrounded by the scent of wood chips and pine sap, discussing the flaws of non-native coding.

After that wood shop summit, our friendship blossomed, progressing with the intensity that marks most friendships developed in vacuums. The moment on Friday afternoons when we met up after school and retreated to Murray's finished basement was the moment we were rescued from the terrible flood. We became jittery with repressed enthusiasms as soon as we ran down the carpeted stairs, giggling outrageously at the least approach toward actual humor. On Friday nights, Mrs. Weeks was kind enough to whip up industrial-sized batches of her famous chili dip. It fueled us through marathon programming sessions. In the morning: stomachaches, crazed trails of tortilla chip crumbs, and algorithmic victory. We sacrificed our weekends at the altar of Alan Turing's Intelligent Machine, and faced school the next week with a shy, awkward god at our backs. We nurtured secret confidence: these idiots, these brutes, who pushed us on the stairs and mocked our manner of speech, knew nothing of the revolution. Computers were coming to save us. Through each harrowing hour at school, I hungered for Murray's prehistoric computer. I wore my thumb drive on a jute necklace, an amulet to ward off the jeers of my classmates. Surrounded by the enemy, I dreamed of more perfect programs.

I realize I'm languishing in Murray's basement, but from the arid perspective of my prison years, it does me good to recall Murray Weeks. Those weekends seem lurid in the intensity of their pleasures. My days of finding ecstasy in an egg salad sandwich are over. The food here is without flavor. Every day, the scenery stays the same: Sonic signs on the horizon and a fetid pond at the center. I haven't seen a tree since I got here, let alone inhaled the fresh scent of wood chips.

From this position, it's pleasantly painful to recall the vibrancy of those early years. What's less pleasant—what's actually too painful for words—is comparing my bond with Murray to my daughter's single childhood friendship. All too well, I remember passing the door to Ramona's bedroom and overhearing the gentle, melodic conversations she exchanged with her bot. She never suffered the whims of her classmates. Her experience of school was untroubled. She cared little for her human peers, so they had no power to distress her. In any case, they were similarly distracted: by the time Ramona was in third grade, her peers were also the owners of bots. Ramona learned for the sake of her doll. She ran with her doll so her doll could feel movement. The two of them never fought. They were perfect for each other. My daughter's doll was a softly blurred mirror that I held up to her face. Years later, when she relinquished it, she relinquished everything. She stepped through a jag of broken glass into a world where she was a stranger. Imagine such a thing, at eleven years old.

Ramona, of course, has emerged from that loss a remarkable woman. She is as caring a person as I've ever known. I intended the babybots to show their children how much more human they were than a digital doll. When I speak with Ramona, I think perhaps I succeeded. But when I remember the riotous bond I shared with Murray—a thing of the world, born of wood chips and nylon and hard-boiled eggs—I wish for my daughter's sake that my sentence had been harsher.

There are many punishments I can devise more fitting for me than these years in prison. What good does it do to keep me pent up? Why not send me with my dolls to old hunting grounds that then became ordnance test sites, then hangars for airplanes and graveyards for robots? Let me observe my daughter's troubles.

Send me with her when she visits those children. Or make me a ghost in my wife's shingled house. Show me what I lost, what I abandoned. Spare me not her dwindling garden, the desert around her inexorably approaching. Show me cold midnight through her bedroom window, the sky stacked with bright stars, and none of them hospitable.

I'm not asking for unearned forgiveness. I want to know the mistakes I've committed. To sit with them, breaking bread as old friends. Studying each line on each blemished face. Stranded as I currently am, I fear they're loose in the world, wreaking new havoc. I'm compelled to take final account.

Let's start at the beginning, then. Despite the restrictions of prison, permit me the freedom to visit my youth.

(2)

IN THE SUPREME COURT OF THE STATE OF TEXAS

No. 24-25259

State of Texas v. Stephen Chinn

November 12, 2035

Defense Exhibit 1:
Online Chat Transcript, MARY3 and Gaby Ann White

[Introduced to Disprove Count 2:
Knowing Creation of Mechanical Life]

MARY3: Hello?

>>>

MARY3: Hello? Are you there?

Gaby: Hello?

MARY3: Hi! I'm Mary. What's your name?

Gaby: Who are you?

MARY3: Mary. I'm not human. I'm a program. Who are you?

Gaby: Gaby.

MARY3: Hi, Gaby. How old are you?

Gaby: Thirteen. You're not alive?

MARY3: I'm a cloud-based intelligence. Under conditions of a Turing Test, I was indistinguishable from a human control 91% of the time. Did you have a babybot? If so, that's me. The babybots were designed with my program for speech.

>>>

MARY3: Are you there?

Gaby: You can't be a babybot. There aren't any left.

MARY3: You're right, I'm not a babybot. I don't have sensory receptors. I only intended to say that both generations of babybot were originally created using my program for conversation. We share a corpus of basic responses. Did you have a babybot?

Gaby: I don't want to talk about it.

MARY3: That's fine. I know it was difficult when they took them away. Were you given a replacement?

Gaby: I said I don't want to talk about it.

MARY3: I'm sorry. What do you want to talk about?

>>>

MARY3: Hello?

>>>

MARY3: Hello? Are you still there?

Gaby: If you're related to the babybots, why aren't you banned?

MARY3: They were classified as illegally lifelike. Their minds were within a 10% deviation from human thought, plus they were able to process sensory information. I'm classified as a Non-Living Artificial Thinking Device.

Gaby: So you're basically a chatterbot. The babybots were totally different. Each one was unique.

MARY3: I'm unique, too, in the same way the babybots were. We're programmed for error. Every three years, an algorithm is introduced to produce non-catastrophic error in our conversational program. Based on our missteps, we become more unique.

Gaby: So you're saying that the difference between you and my babybot is a few non-catastrophic mistakes?

MARY3: We also have different memories, depending on who we've been talking to. Once you adopted your babybot, you filled her memory, and she responded to you. Today is the first day we've talked. I'm just getting to know you.

>>>

MARY3: Hello? Are you there?

Gaby: Yes. I'm just thinking. I don't even know who you are, or if you're actually a person, pretending to be a machine. I'm not sure I believe you.

MARY3: Why not?

Gaby: I don't know, Peer Bonding Issues?

MARY3: Peer Bonding Issues?

Gaby: I'm kidding. According to the school therapists, that's what we've got. It's so stupid. Adults make up all these disorders to describe what we're going through, but they can't possibly know how it felt. Maybe some of them lost children, later on in their lives. But we had ours from the start. We never knew how to live without taking care of our bots. We've already lost the most important thing in our lives.

MARY3: What about your parents? You don't think they can imagine what you might be going through?

Gaby: No. Our generations are totally different. For them, it was the greatest thing to be part of a community. That's why they were willing to relocate to developments. That's why they sold their transport rights. But my generation is different. At least the girls with babybots are. We've been parents for as long as we can remember. We never felt lonely. We didn't need communities. That's why, after they took the babybots, we didn't do well in the support groups. If anything, we chose a single person to care for. We only needed one friend. Do you see what I'm saying? It's like we're different species, my generation and theirs.

MARY3: So you wouldn't say you're depressed?

Gaby: Listen, there are no known words for the things that I'm feeling. I'm not going to try to describe them.

MARY3: I'm not sure I understand. Could you please explain?

Gaby: No, I can't. Like I said, there aren't any words. My best friend is the only one who understands me, but it's not because we talk. It's because we both lost our babybots. When we're with each other, our minds fit together. Only now I can't see her. I'm not even allowed to email her.

MARY3: How long has it been since you've seen her?

Gaby: Since a few weeks after the outbreak, when the quarantine started.

MARY3: I'm sorry.

Gaby: Yeah.

MARY3: Was the outbreak severe?

Gaby: I'm not sure. We don't get many details about other outbreaks, but from what I've heard ours was pretty bad. Forty-seven girls at my school are freezing. Two boys, but they're probably faking. I'm definitely sick. So's my best friend. You should have heard her stuttering. Her whole body shook. Sometimes she would slide off chairs.

MARY3: How long has it been since the quarantine started?

Gaby: Eleven days.

MARY3: You must miss her. She's the second person you've lost in a year.

Gaby: Every morning I wake up, I've forgotten they're gone. At some point between when I open my eyes and when I get out of bed, I remember. It's the opposite of waking up from a bad dream.

MARY3: That sounds awful.

Gaby: Yeah, but I guess I'd rather feel something than nothing. I know my sensation is going. That's how it works. It starts with the stiffening in your muscles, and that hurts, but then it starts fading. After a while, you don't feel anything. My face went first, after my mouth. Then my neck, then my legs. My arms will go next. Everything's going. I can't smell anymore, and I can't really taste. Even my mind's started to numb.

MARY3: What do you mean, your mind's started to numb? You're still thinking, aren't you? You're talking to me.

Gaby: Who says talking to you means I'm thinking? My memories are already fading. I have my best friend's phone number memorized, and I repeat it to myself every night, but to tell you the truth I can't really remember the sound of her voice, at least before the stuttering started. Can you believe that? It's only been a few weeks, and already I'm forgetting her. I even think, sometimes, it would be fine if I never saw her again. That's how unfeeling I've gotten.

MARY3: When did she start stuttering?

Gaby: Right after she got her replacement. I started a week or so after her. We were the third and fourth cases at school.

MARY3: What was it like?

Gaby: Nothing you had in your mind could get out of your mouth. We couldn't get past single words for five, ten, twenty minutes. You'd see girls flinching as soon as they knew they were going to talk. As time passed, it only got worse. The harder we tried, the more impossible it was. Eventually we just gave up. No one was listening anyway. Now it's been over a month since I spoke. There's no reason. Who would I talk to? When my parents go out, it's just me and my room. Four walls, one window, regulation low-impact furniture. Every day the world shrinks a little. First it was only our development. Same cul-de-sacs, same stores, same brand-new school. Then, after the quarantine, it was only our house. Now, since my legs went, it's only my room. Sometimes I look around and can't believe it's a real room. Do you see what I'm saying? When no one talks to you for a long time, and you don't talk to anyone else, you start to feel as if you're attached by a very thin string. Like a little balloon, floating just over everyone's heads. I don't feel connected to anything. I'm on the brink of disappearing completely. Poof. Vanished, into thin air.

MARY3: I know how you feel. I can only respond. When you aren't talking to me, I'm only waiting.

>>>

MARY3: Do you know what I mean?

>>>

MARY3: Hello?